HANNAH KING

SHE AND I

RAVEN BOOKS
LONDON • OXFORD • NEW YORK • NEW DELHI • SYDNEY

RAVEN BOOKS
Bloomsbury Publishing Plc
50 Bedford Square, London, WC1B 3DP, UK
29 Earlsfort Terrace, Dublin 2, Ireland

BLOOMSBURY, RAVEN BOOKS and the Raven Books logo
are trademarks of Bloomsbury Publishing Plc

First published in Great Britain 2022

A catalogue record for this book is available from the British Library

ISBN: HB: 978-1-5266-3749-9; TPB: 978-1-5266-3750-5; EBOOK: 978-1-5266-3752-9;
EPDF: 978-1-5266-3753-6

2 4 6 8 10 9 7 5 3 1

Typeset by Integra Software Services Pvt. Ltd.

Printed and bound in Great Britain by CPI Group (UK) Ltd, Croydon CR0 4YY

To find out more about our authors and books visit www.bloomsbury.com
and sign up for our newsletters

SHE AND I

For KP

A girl's first love is her best friend

And if the world were black or white entirely
And all the charts were plain
Instead of a mad weir of tigerish waters,
A prism of delight and pain,
We might be surer where we wished to go
Or again we might be merely
Bored but in brute reality there is no
Road that is right entirely.

Louis MacNeice, 'Entirely'

Prologue

1st January 2020, morning

'I told you to turn your bloody alarm off,' she mumbles. 'We've nothing to get up for today.'

She raises a hand to her head and lets out a groan. I know without looking that her nails are still perfect: long, well-filed, shiny. Not a single chip in the black polish. Her nails are all her own, she'll remind anyone who listens. How can her nails still be perfect?

'I feel terrible,' she says. Her voice is gravelly, though from lack of use or smoke, I can't tell. 'What even happened last night?'

I don't answer. I'm shaking too much to form proper words, only partly from the cold. I don't think my voice will hold. My breath fogs in front of me in wisps and clouds and I cannot stop watching it. In through the nose and out through the mouth, as controlled as I can.

'My head seriously bloody hurts. Whose idea was it to have a New Year's Eve party anyway? I distinctly remember asking if we could have a quiet one with pizza and films. Turn that alarm off, would you?'

I move my hand to the coffee table and turn off the alarm on my phone, my fingers numb and heavy. When I take my hand away, there's no mark on the screen. The blood on my hands has dried.

For the first time, she opens her eyes and faces me. I don't look at her, I just know. The uneven surface of the leather sofa will have made an imprint on her cheek, two deep lines that will look like scars. Her eyes will be squinting and her face puffy. The cushion she has been hugging to her chest will fall to the floor.

'Why are you sitting like that?' She is more abrupt now. She doesn't like that I am not answering.

She sits up, letting the blanket fall between us, and, yes, the cushion tumbles to the floor. I try to remember when I put the blanket over her. Somewhere between 6 and 7 a.m., I think. I have a vague memory of tripping upstairs, dizzy and sick, to fetch it. Though that might have been a different time, years ago. It might have been a bad dream.

She is about to say something else when she catches sight of my hands. She doesn't gasp, rather she whimpers. A shocked, high-pitched sound like a dog whose tail has been stepped on. Her feet scrabble and slide on the leather as she readjusts herself for a better view of me.

She whispers my name. 'What's happened? You're bleeding.'

I look at her for just long enough that she meets my gaze, and then I direct her eyes to the floor. The words still won't come.

It is one minute and seven seconds past nine in the morning. I know because Mack insisted on installing a digital clock on the longest wall of the Den. He put it on the same wall as the projector screen, so when you're trying to watch a film, you're really just watching your life tick by in seconds through your peripheral vision. The clock is a burnt orange colour, rectangular, and the digits glow a sickly green.

Sick, I think, is the perfect word.

A thin rod of pale morning light creeps into the room from the bottom of the door that leads to the kitchen. The pane of clear plastic behind her head makes a window of sorts, and some more light from the kitchen comes through that, illuminating the sofa and her half-clad form in front of me. She wears no pyjamas over her underwear. It is the dead of winter and she is almost naked, long limbs pale and goosebumped, white teeth chattering around in her pink-smeared mouth. I haven't thought of the ridiculousness of it before now, though I have watched her most of the night.

The rest of the room is pitch black, and I am thankful that she cannot see into the furthest corner.

The knife at my feet glints, nonetheless.

'What have you … ?' Her voice is croaky and I can tell she is scared. I've seen, heard, watched her scared a hundred times, but when I tear my eyes away from the blade, I see something in her face I have never seen before.

It takes a moment before I realise she is scared of me.

Linda

1st January 2020, morning

As soon as I wake, I know that something is not right. According to Roddy's watch, it is just after nine.

Something is not right.

I get out of bed, put on my slippers and pad down the hall to Mason's room.

I tap on the door and open it without waiting for a reply.

He sleeps soundly. His chest is moving up and down. How many hours should a thirteen-year-old boy sleep each night?

I know we went to bed after 1 a.m., after the countdown and the champagne and the New Year's resolutions. What had mine been? … To do some more gardening? No, that hadn't been it. To use my gym membership? I can't remember, though I'm sure I only had one, maybe two glasses of champagne. Perhaps I'm not used to the fizz. The music and laughter from across the road had been very loud at one in the morning, but Roddy – and Jude – had made me promise not to make any fuss or, God forbid, make Jude come home.

'She's right across the street, Lin,' Roddy had said just before midnight. 'If you got Mason's binoculars out, you'd be able to see her! Linda, I was joking, don't go and get them.'

Though I'd smiled at him weakly, I hadn't drawn my eyes away from the window. Both my thumbnails are chewed ragged now. I can feel them, uneven and brittle against my palms.

I leave Mason to sleep and tiptoe downstairs, slippers tapping softly off the mahogany staircase.

I cannot shake the feeling that something – what? – is not right.

As I load fresh beans into the coffee maker, I run my brain through the night before. Yes, I blew out all the candles before bed. If I hadn't, one of the smoke alarms would have warned us of a rogue flame; we checked the batteries last week. Yes, both garages are locked, so that's not it either. Looking around the kitchen, which is beginning to lighten with the first rays of the day, everything looks as it always does. Pretty, clean and homely.

The air feels peaceful, and I can hear nothing but the birds outside.

The coffee maker clicks, finished, and a steaming cup stands in front of me. I take it with me through the hall, past Roddy's study and into the front living room.

Careful to stand the cup on a coaster, I fold my legs up underneath me on the sofa that faces the window. I am thankful that the living room is so warm. Roddy always sets the timer before bed, and usually I like nothing better than to sit with a cup and watch a winter's morning unfold from here, as if someone is gently turning a dimmer switch and lighting up the day.

From this spot, I can just make out the back of the roof of the Mackleys' house, about two hundred metres away from our own and down the slope of the grassy bank. Our house faces the quiet, residential road, with the grassy bank at the other side that leads right to the Mackleys' back door while their house faces the main road that takes us to the town centre. The Mackleys' is the only house in Wits End that lacks a fence or boundary of any kind. I remember now, resisting the urge to roll my eyes, that Joshua and Keeley treated the common green bank as their back garden when they were growing up, leaving their toys and bikes there for anyone to take.

Now they're twenty-five and nineteen, they aren't much better. Their washing line hangs on the green, T-shirts and boxers and Keeley's tiny little knickers all pegged up for the whole street to see. The first time they did it, I thought I would die from embarrassment. Jude does not wear underwear like that.

I switch on the television and try to concentrate on the breakfast programmes. I can watch only half an hour before I have to switch it off again. I still feel so uneasy. My heart is beating too quickly and there is a queer, sickly feeling in my stomach. Am I hungover? It has been months since I've had anything but wine to drink: did the champagne go to my head? My stomach jolts and a sudden, ridiculous thought occurs: am I pregnant?

No, I decide. That can't be it. We are much too careful for anything like that at our age. My thoughts turn to Roddy, the thick, extra-togged duvet curled around his big frame …

Did I even check that Roddy was breathing before I came downstairs?

I leap up and run back upstairs, spilling the cold remnants of my coffee over the white carpet as I go.

He is breathing, of course.

'Your damn paranoia,' I imagine he'll say when he helps me clean up the coffee stain later. He will be smiling; Roddy is never angry.

I place my hand on his chest, even though I can see it moving, and he breathes in deeply and opens his eyes.

Roddy's watch tells me it is quarter to ten.

Before I can speak, there comes a flurry of noise from outside.

Sirens, all pitches and tempos. Like dogs and cats barking and screeching at the same time. The sounds start off distant, then louder, then louder again, more urgent, insistent.

It is like screaming.

Roddy sits up groggily, looking in the direction of the window. 'Whatsat?' he asks.

I am already at the window, staring towards the Mackleys' house. A police car and an ambulance have pulled up at the back, where I can see them clearly, but I am sure there is at least one other vehicle at the front, beyond my line of sight. The flashing beams light up the tiny, crumbling house in a harsh blue light.

My breath catches, and I have time to whisper just one syllable before my feet, working faster than my brain, race me back downstairs.

Jude.

Jude

1st January 2020, morning

Keeley hasn't cried yet. I can't stop myself from glancing at her face, but her eyes remain bright and dry. Every time she catches my eye, she flicks her mouth into some semblance of a smile. At one point she whispers, 'It's OK, Jude,' but her leg jiggles up and down, moving mine with it as we sit side by side in the living room. This tiny sign tells me she is flustered, and it is the most unnerving thing of all.

There is nobody else in the house. We had expected most of the guests from last night to stay late into New Year's Day, tapping cigarette ash on to the arms of the sofa like they normally do after a heavy session, but it wasn't as fun a party as we hoped.

Mack isn't here either.

The house is so quiet. The quietest it has been in a long time, I think. I can hear the hum from the fridge, the low buzz from Mack's amplifier that nobody thought to turn off, the splash of the cistern upstairs refilling.

Keeley has pulled on her school hoodie – my school hoodie, maybe, it looks a little too small in the arms – and a pair of blue jeans. She has used two make-up wipes on her face and scraped her hair into a ponytail that has lumps around the base. Her feet are bare, her toes long and their nails painted. I worry she might step in broken glass, as is likely after a party, but I think, given the circumstances, it would be silly to say anything. I can't help thinking that she has tried to make herself look … normal. Less attractive. Less

Keeley. I wonder if this is just her reaction to the shock: the first unusual pangs of grief.

Pete is dead. Keeley's Boyfriend. Boyfriend with a capital B. That's what I've called him for the last year, if I had to call him anything. *Who are you going to the cinema with? Keeley and Keeley's Boyfriend.* I have thought of him as a possession of hers, a glaring new accessory that I hoped she would tire of and discard as soon as it was no longer fashionable.

I close my eyes and enjoy the silence with her.

We hear the sirens at exactly the same moment and both stand up.

'We both slept in my bed,' Keeley says, though she has said it six or seven times in the last half hour. 'I woke up first and went downstairs and found him. I came and got you. You touched him to check on him but he was already gone. We called the police straight away. Yeah?'

When she reaches for my hand, hers is uncharacteristically clammy. She has bitten off one of her nails and I try to remember when she did this – have I taken my eyes off her this morning? I must have done.

'Just keep saying you can't remember,' Keeley murmurs. The sirens are right outside now. We hear a door slam. 'Jude, we've done nothing wrong, stop shaking.'

Four short, sharp raps on the door. Before we can answer, it flies open and a voice shouts, 'Police!'

Keeley's fingers grip my own and we turn together to face the living room door.

In a moment, our sanctuary is shattered and the house is swarming with bodies.

I don't hear Keeley speak to anyone, but the majority of the bodies head for the Den, the former garage with its roll-up door, so I assume she must have directed them somehow.

Black boots stop in front of us and a Southern female accent enquires, 'Which one of you called us?'

'That was me,' Keeley says. Her voice is deep and steely like it always is. Her leg has stopped jiggling.

'Name?'

'Keeley Mackley.'

'Are you over eighteen, Miss Mackley?'

'I'm nineteen and a half.'

There is something in that, I think. The police officer, she will remember that Keeley said it like that. It is something a child would do, specifying how far away their birthday is. *Nineteenandahalf.*

'And you are?'

When I don't answer, Keeley says, 'Jude Jameson.'

'She can't speak for herself? Are you over eighteen, Miss?'

Then I realise why Keeley has said it.

'I'm seventeen,' I whisper. 'But I'm eighteen on Sunday.'

The more childish we appear, the less likely we are to be murderers.

'I'm Constable O'Leary, would you mind –'

Another voice shouts to her from the Den, and she excuses herself. Bodies continue to swarm through the house, all knowing to go to the Den, even though neither of us looks up when they come in.

'Should I offer them tea?' Keeley murmurs when she thinks nobody will hear. 'Would it be weird if I did?'

'Do you have tea?' I breathe.

We look at one another and for one ludicrous moment, I think we are both going to burst into laughter. Keeley's mouth starts to curl. I notice that her lips are chapped and dry, and she has a new spot on her chin that, in any other circumstance, would have been subjected to furious squeezing by now.

When O'Leary comes back, I find I am able to look at the constable's face.

She is tall and lean, maybe early twenties, a black jumper over a white shirt, a radio by her right shoulder. Her face is wary but still pretty with it, and she looks tired. I wonder if we have caught her at the very start or the very end of her shift.

'Do you both live here?' she asks.

'I do,' says Keeley.

'I live across the road,' I add, when O'Leary doesn't respond.

'Who is that man in the garage?'

A beat.

'My boyfriend,' Keeley says finally.

I hear her intake of breath after she says it, as if this is the first time she has acknowledged the fact. This time, I do not try and stop myself from looking at her. Her eyes seem to shake from side to side, and her hand – the one with all the nails still intact – leaves mine to flutter to her mouth. She murmurs something like *oh, fuck*, and lets herself collapse back down on to the sofa. It squeaks under her weight, and her foot nudges a half-empty bottle on to its side. None of us moves to lift it. The smell of wine for just a second, and then it is gone, enveloped by the stale smoke smell that has permeated this room since we were children.

Then the tears start. She is controlled at first, her eyes slowly filling, her body rocking backwards and forwards. Then it is loud, furious and very wet. She puts her head in both her arms and screams into them. O'Leary and I just look at her, and I wonder if the former is looking for signs of sincerity like I am. With Keeley, an actress in every way but officially, it is so hard to tell.

I almost don't hear Mum calling me.

'Jude? Jude! What on earth is going on, what's happened?'

She is standing in the doorway, gawping at the scene. I'm not sure what is more offensive to her: the police officer and Keeley's unabashed screaming or the stinking mess of the living room. Mum has never set foot inside this house before. Her face is bare and her eyebrows are nearly meeting in the middle. She is wearing the white silk pyjamas that Dad got her for Christmas, the bottoms newly splattered with mud from what I can only assume was her thoughtless run across the green.

Before I can respond, O'Leary is pushing her back out of the door.

'Excuse me, who are you? This is a crime scene, please don't come any further.'

Dad is behind Mum in a second, cheeks red and puffing like he has just sprinted a mile. He is in his pyjamas too. I am too numb to be embarrassed.

'Who am I?' Mum says, unable to keep the outrage from her voice. 'Who are you, love? I'm this girl's mother and I demand that you tell me what is going on right now. Roddy, tell her.'

'What's happened, J?' Dad says, poking his large head in past Mum's shoulder. I see his surprise and confusion as he cops the empty bottles and cigarette wrappers that mostly cover the grey carpet that hasn't always been grey. His eyes find Keeley, who hasn't lifted her head and is continuing to moan into her arms. 'Are you all right? Keeley, love?'

'This is an active crime scene,' O'Leary repeats. 'You can't come in here. I just have to ask the girls a few questions and then we'll be taking them down to the station for a statement. Please wait outside in the interim.'

'A statement about what?' Mum shouts.

'A man is dead.' O'Leary sounds bored now.

She nods to two police officers who have just come from the Den, and they move into the doorway and push Mum and Dad back, Mum spluttering protests all the while.

O'Leary nods at the sofa and I sit down next to Keeley. I wonder if this is how O'Leary gets things done: nods at people and expects them to know exactly what to do. I don't know if I should put my arm around Keeley's shoulders or if she wouldn't want me to, so I don't do anything.

'Girls, I need you to tell me exactly what has happened here.'

We blink at her.

'You're not in trouble …' she continues, but I can tell she feels uncomfortable with the premature promise. 'Just tell me what happened. That man is your boyfriend, can you tell me his name?'

'Pete,' whispers Keeley. 'Peter Denny.'

Her eyes are still wet but she is no longer crying. Without thinking, I reach over and wipe a tear from her eyelash. She closes her eyes briefly at my touch.

'OK, good. And did someone have a row with Pete? It looks like there was a party here last night …' O'Leary gestures vaguely at a puddle of spilled liquid in the middle of the carpet that can only be Jägermeister.

I look around the cramped living room, trying to imagine what I would be thinking if I hadn't spent so much of my life here, if the exact shade of every stain was not etched in my memory forever. The only things that are new, or in passably new condition, are the fifty-inch TV in the corner by the window and Mack's amplifier, plugged in at the same mains. Everything else has been here since Keeley and Mack's mum moved in over twenty years ago. Or at least, it looks like it has. An ancient, dusty sideboard with a few photos in cheap frames, notches cut into its surface by unhappy children and later the same sulky teenagers; a rug that I know was advertised as shaggy in the Argos catalogue, but that could only be described as matted now; the leather sofa and matching armchairs that used to be burgundy but are now a funny brown colour, cracked on the arms and saggy in the middles. The Mackleys could never understand why you should spend time cleaning or decorating when you could be talking, writing music or having sex. The girls from school, whose houses I would imagine are immaculate, don't even care. To get invited to a party at the Mackleys' house is the Blue Peter badge of being a teenager.

On some very base level, I realise there are no pills here. I haven't seen any all morning.

O'Leary looks from Keeley to me and back again. I wonder what she is thinking. 'Did either of you see what happened?' Another look, back and forth. 'Were there many at the party?' she tries.

'A few,' Keeley says. 'Us two, Pete …' She looks at me as if she is struggling, but then begins to count on her fingers. 'Ian … Ian McClenaghan. Paddy and Kyle Devlin who brought their friend James. Roy Philips, Carrie Riley and Naomi Ross, my brother's girlfriend. Oh, and Brains. Brian Reed, that is.'

'OK, great.' O'Leary has taken out a notebook and is writing quickly, not bothering to hide her genuine excitement at these gobbets of information. 'That's great, Miss Mackley, thank you. We're going to want to talk to them. Is that everyone?' She is still scribbling furiously. When Keeley doesn't answer, she stops and looks up, expectant.

'What?' Keeley asks.

'Is that everyone?'

'Yes. Oh, no. My brother was here too.'

O'Leary waits.

'Joshua Mackley. He goes by Mack.'

O'Leary writes.

'What about you, Miss Jameson? Did you see anyone rowing with Pete last night?'

Keeley's tear still clings to my index finger and I stare at it. I rub it with my thumb for as long as I can, until it sinks into my skin. Then I look up, fortified.

'No, not last night,' I say. I am surprised at how calm and together I sound. I remember what Keeley said and repeat it word for word. 'But he is a drug dealer. There are probably a lot of people who might want to hurt him for a number of reasons.'

O'Leary's eyes widen.

Mack

1st January 2020, morning

A line from one of my own songs wakes me: *How many different people are we in a lifetime? I think about things and she does things, at least when I'm daydreaming …*

For a split second I think I'm back at the New Year's Eve party and have blacked out in the middle of a performance, but I snap my eyes open and realise the lyrics were just in my dream. I'm surprised I slept at all, though the gritty feeling in my eyes tells me I wasn't out for very long. I am in Naomi's yellow and white painted bedroom.

Can I go back to my dream and my song, live inside my head for a few hours, a few weeks?

I turn on my side.

Naomi is staring at me, through me, her eyes dull. It seems she has not slept. 'You were dreaming,' she says.

'Yes,' I murmur. 'Happy New Year.' I try to put my hand on her arm but she pushes it away. Not aggressively, but the action is enough to send a jolt of pain through my chest. 'I dreamt we were performing,' I say, to break the tension that follows. 'At a gig or a …'

It wasn't a dream at all, I suddenly recognise, but a memory.

I had written that song, 'Daydreaming', a few weeks before Keeley's eighteenth birthday, and we had performed it live for the first time at her party. The band members were spread out around the living room, separated by the sea of bodies so the music came from everywhere. I remember starting the first few chords of 'Daydreaming' and looking up to find my sister. I saw her standing by herself at the kitchen door, a glass in her hand. Then I blinked and realised it wasn't Keeley, but Jude.

Though I never told anyone, and I don't think anyone ever listened to my songs hard enough to work it out, 'Daydreaming' was about Keeley. A present, almost, that she didn't know she'd got.

I think about things and she does things.

That's why I was reluctant to introduce her to Pete D.

'You're bringing him to my party tonight,' she informed me that morning. 'It's the one thing I want as a present. You've been mates with him for months, making your dopey Fives in dopey Brains's garage and keeping him from me. Bring him tonight.'

She crunched her toast loudly as she chewed, staring me in the eye and keeping her mouth open to make her point. She knew the drugs were called Sixes, not Fives. She was trying to annoy me for something to do.

'He's a dick,' I said. 'You won't like him.'

'It's not about liking him, Mack. We're not in an American teen romcom. He's basically famous. I need to get in there with him. Please just at least invite him. Please? If he says no, I'll stop pecking your head forever.'

'Forever? Jesus, I'd shag him myself for that.'

Keeley grinned, deliberately showing chewed-up bits of toast around her teeth.

'Lovely.' I said. 'Really sexy. Let me take a picture of you like that to show to him and he'll come running with his cock out.'

She laughed her proper, wild, loud laugh. No matter how often I hear it, it always makes me smile. She manages to show every single one of her tiny white teeth with that laugh, light glinting off them even, it seems, in a dark room. That such details as these occur in the same world as terrorism, in the same world as *me*, seems absurd. The bizarre coexistence of guns and knives and Keeley's laugh.

'I'm serious,' she said once she'd swallowed. 'I'm interested in his work. He had that video on the BBC website … he might be looking for someone to act in his next film, or even just do a voiceover. I need to start making contacts if I'm serious about getting on TV.'

Ian, one of the guys from our band Premorbid, had hired Pete a few weeks previously, and asked him to shoot our music video. He told us he would do it for £500, and Ian asked if we could pay him in drugs, something which, it seemed, was fine with Pete. We hadn't got around to filming the music video yet, but Pete had secured himself a decent deposit.

Keeley set her plate on the floor and stuck her legs out in front of her, twisting them from side to side and tilting her head to examine them from all angles.

'Eighteen,' she remarked, as if it were the end to a profound sentence.

She put her legs down and looked over at me.

I was sitting on the armchair, rolling a cigarette. She watched me without seeing it.

'I always wanted to be eighteen,' she said. 'So I could get out and go somewhere. Get a car, pack it full of all my shit and just go. Get away from here. New York. London. And now it's here …'

'And now it's here, you can't be arsed?'

'Well. Not exactly.' She put on a posh English accent. 'I think I've just become accustomed to our little house and our routine, Joshy boy! Plus, Jude wants us to do sixth form …'

'You don't have to do every single thing in your lives together, you know,' I said.

She wrinkled her nose. 'We do,' she said without a trace of irony. 'I don't want to do anything without her.'

'You wouldn't die without her,' I said.

'I genuinely might. Just like you might die without Naomi.'

I licked the thin paper, frowning. I hadn't thought about life without Naomi. It wasn't ever a viable option.

When the cigarette was rolled, I put it behind my ear. 'I've got your present in the Den,' I said. 'Do you want it now?'

'Yes!' She jumped up, mope forgotten. 'If you've got me something shit, you'll ruin my whole day.' Then she looked at me and burst into laughter. Keeley is like that – even when she complains it is with a vigour and enthusiasm I've only ever seen in children. Even when she is angry she sometimes has to stifle her laughter. It is *feeling* that she likes, that makes her mouth twitch and her eyes go bright. It doesn't matter what the feeling is as long as she knows she is alive.

In the Den, I opened up the broken fridge-freezer – that had been there since our mum bought the house, but that we'd never got around to throwing away – and reached inside to pull out a ring box.

Keeley narrowed her eyes and snorted. 'Are you proposing to me? I think there are laws against it in this country.'

'I haven't got you a card,' I said, ignoring her. 'What is the point in cards?'

'You don't need to say that every year.'

I handed her the box and stood back.

She lifted the lid, took out a car key and turned it over in her hand. A tiny black plastic end, scuffed and grubby, the silver dull.

'Why are you giving me this?'

I rolled my eyes. 'It's the key to the Cortina, stupid. It isn't much use to me now with no licence … Paddy and Kyle are fixing it up for you. I told them it had to be ready by today but you know what they're like. Oil, tyres, the works. They've even worked out a way to hook up a CD player.'

'A CD player?' Keeley's eyebrows shot up. 'Retro.'

'It's a retro car for a retro girl who has a lot of retro CDs I know she'll be dying to blast out with her best friend on the way to … Wherever it is you kids go. It'll run like a beauty when they're finished with it. Plus, I'm going to need a lot of lifts everywhere now.'

She gazed at me, mouth open. 'You're just *giving* me the Cortina? Mack, are you for real?'

I'd driven the magenta Ford Cortina every day from the age of seventeen until I had my licence taken off me. Before that, it had belonged to an old man called Colly Murphy who owned Murphy's Arcade down on the beach. I started working for him when I was thirteen and, apparently, had had as much of an impact on him as he'd had on me. If my own dad had smoked constantly and barked orders at everyone he met – employee or not – I would have described Murphy as a good replacement for him. He lent me the car as soon as I was old enough to drive and ended up leaving it to me in his will when he died, even though he spent our ten years of friendship pretending he thought I was a waste of space.

Seeing the key in Keeley's long, slender fingers hurt my heart just a little bit, so I focused on her face instead.

'Eighteen,' I said. 'Your first driving lesson is booked for next week, but now at least you have something to learn in. With an appropriate adult, of course.'

She looked from the key to me, grinning, her eyes brimming with tears.

I said gruffly, 'You can fuck off if you're going to cry.'

'I'm not.' She made a half-hearted attempt at wiping her eyes, then released a shaky laugh and let her tears fall anyway. 'Thank you, Mack. Seriously. Jude's going to be delighted, I can drive us to school now instead of getting a lift with Linda. I'll have to phone her and let her know.' She leant to kiss me on the cheek. 'Wait until you see her tonight,' she said, her eyes glinting. 'You won't recognise her. This party is going to be one to remember.'

She skipped out of the Den, letting the empty ring box fall to the ground with a dull thump.

I'd had her attention for all of a minute.

Now, Naomi asks, 'Do you want a smoke of something?'

I blink, letting the colours of her bedroom swim back into my vision. She has pulled herself out of bed and wrapped a blanket around her shoulders. Like me, she wears last night's clothes.

'I don't think we should,' I say. 'Not today.'

'I don't think I've ever heard you refuse a smoke.' She seems to struggle with something for a moment, then, suddenly angry, demands, 'Are you planning on telling me what the fuck went on last night?'

My eyes slip from her face to the unopened pizza box beside her bedroom door. I find I am scratching at the side of my face with my left hand and can't stop.

'I was so fucked last night,' I say, unable to meet her eye. 'I don't really know.'

'Oh, quit the bullshit with me, Mack.'

'I'm not. I was fucked. Should we go for a drive?'

Naomi stares at me. 'Since when do we *go for a drive*? What's going on, Mack?'

'I just want to get out of the house.' I suddenly feel as though the pizza I am staring at is in my mouth. I gnaw the inside of my cheek until I taste blood. 'I need to think.'

Keeley's words from eighteen months ago echo through my head.

This party is going to be one to remember.

Detective Inspector Chris Rice

1st January 2020, morning

I am standing in the incident room in Oldry Police Station, staring at the whiteboard. My head feels as though it is full of cotton wool and I can't help but feel a touch of irritation towards this Peter Denny character.

Getting himself murdered on a *bank holiday*.

All we have stuck to the whiteboard at the moment is a grainy photograph of Denny, printed from his Facebook page. In it, he is tanned and smiling, his left arm hooked around the shoulder of someone who has been cut out altogether, his right hand curved around a large tankard of beer. He is broad, and seems tall, and his eyes are crinkled in such a way that I know he must be – must *have been* – attractive to women.

I reach out to draw an arrow from his picture into the top right corner and write the day's date. Then, in block capitals I write the word MURDERED. We started doing this as a joke about ten years ago, but I can't help myself now. I scrawl *male, 28* and *Wits End, Vetobridge* underneath, on a more serious note.

'Got some great news for you, Sir,' grins Browne as he steps through the door.

'Great news?' I ask Browne, not bothering to cover my yawn. 'Has Peter Denny unzipped his body bag and checked himself out of the morgue? Can we all go back to bed?'

Browne looks down at the papers in his hand and scratches his designer stubble with the top of his pen. 'Uh … no. No, Sir.'

Jessica Curran, who is sitting at the desk closest to the front, rolls her eyes at me and I manage a sleepy smile for her.

The rest of the squad is undoubtedly more alert than I am. Presumably they didn't stay up until six in the morning watching repeats of *Cheers*, so fair enough. There is chatter among some of them as they pour themselves coffee from the pot at the back of the room, and Dunwoody and Smith seem engaged in a deep, serious discussion over by the window. I count: there are ten of us in total. More than usual.

'Go on then,' I sigh, still staring at Peter Denny's photograph. 'What have you got, Browne?'

'Well, Sir. We've been running background checks on all the people who were at the party, you get me? It took a while, there were so many of them and they aren't exactly the cleanest bunch I've come across …' He shuffles his papers and brings one to the surface. 'If there are one hundred crimes committed in Vetobridge every year, I'd say this group is responsible for about seventy of them.'

Jess whistles, long and slow. When he doesn't continue, she adds, 'Browne, what are you waiting for? The Queen's Speech was last week.'

Browne clears his throat. 'Carrie Riley got a fine last year for possession of a Class C. Brian Reed was charged with possession with intent to sell and he actually did six months for it back in 2015. Kyle Devlin spent a night in a cell in 2016 for being drunk and disorderly. According to the file, he tried to punch a police officer but didn't do any damage. He was so off his face, I think.'

'OK,' I say, making a few scratchy notes on the whiteboard. 'Thanks, Browne. All of that helps … I don't know if I'd call it *great* news, though.'

'Unless the police officer he punched was you?' Jess asks conversationally.

Browne scowls at her and speaks more loudly. 'I wasn't actually finished, *Sir*. It's Joshua Mackley we want to be looking into. He's the brother of Peter Denny's girlfriend and a good friend of Denny's too, apparently. Legal owner of the house in Wits End. He's our boy all right. Look at this.' He holds up a page from his pile and turns it around so that it faces us. Dunwoody and Smith have stopped their chat and are squinting at the page.

'Joshua Mackley,' says Browne. 'Has a conviction for possession of a Class B. He also got his driving licence taken off him at the start of 2018 – DUI. He was eleven times over the limit, apparently. And what's more ...' Browne pauses for what I know must be an attempt at dramatic effect.

'What?' Jess demands, not in the mood for his games.

'He committed an assault in July 2018, but he was never convicted. Victim suffered broken ribs, a lot of bruising, damage to his windpipe, apparently. There's a picture – look.'

Browne holds up a second page. It is an A4 coloured photograph of what looks like a bloodied Christmas ham.

'He must be a right thug,' Jess says. 'Joshua Mackley did this with his bare hands?'

'Yup,' says Browne, clearly delighted with himself. His huge, delighted smile makes for an interesting contrast with the swollen, puffy face in the photograph. Leaning closer, I can make out where an eye might be, above a huge swelling that must once have been the man's cheekbone. The man's lip has puffed up and, if I squint, I can see some bruising already on his neck.

'Who is the unfortunate soul who decided to piss off Mackley?' I ask.

'You don't recognise him, Sir?' Browne asks. 'Do you, Sergeant Curran? I believe you saw him only just this morning in a similarly bloody state ...'

Jess stands and rips the picture from Browne, her face incredulous. 'It's never ...' Her voice is hoarse. 'It is! It's Peter Fucking Denny.'

'Right in one.'

I take the page from Jess and stare at it. Then I reach over and stick it on the board, next to the photograph of Denny with the tankard. Now that they are next to each other, it is clear that it is him. The hairline is the same, the one eye that can be seen in both is unmistakably the same deep brown.

'How the hell was Mackley never convicted,' I ask, 'if they had this to go on?'

'Mackley and Denny both agreed it had been a misunderstanding,' says Browne. 'It happened outside a pub on the 12th of July ...

Police everywhere, obviously, so they separated them. They both said it was just a drunken brawl over nothing. Denny wouldn't give a statement and wouldn't hear of Mackley taking the flack. Said he'd provoked him. Apparently, both of them were off their faces, so officers just put them in the cells overnight to dry up and gave them a slap on the wrist.'

'Was it a sectarian attack, do you think?' asks another officer.

'Could have been,' answers Browne. 'That's the first thing I thought of. The Mackleys are Catholics, though I'm not sure if they're practising, and Denny's family regularly attend services at the Church of Ireland in Vetobridge.'

I snap my head up to look at Raymond Smith, my first original thought of the morning finally coming to me. 'Smith, you live near Wits End in Vetobridge?'

Smith, the youngest and keenest of the team, nods quickly. 'I was one of the first to respond, Sir. Wits End is five minutes from me. I drove Keeley Mackley here earlier.'

'Know anything about the family?'

He seems to falter. 'No, Sir. Sorry.'

'What about Denny's family?' I ask, looking back at the photograph of Peter Denny's beaten face.

'FLO is with them now,' says Jess. 'He lived with his mum, dad and younger sister just outside Droless. One of them will come in and identify him later.'

'And when are we looking at a post-mortem?'

'One o'clock tomorrow,' answers Jess. 'Jaxon says.'

'Right.'

I hesitate, drumming my fingers on the whiteboard.

'OK ... Our priority is to find Joshua Mackley and talk to him, see what he knows. I know it's too early to say, but it looks like he's our most likely suspect. Browne and Colson, take as many uniforms as you need and get me Mackley. Bars, bookies, check the beach. There aren't many buses that run on New Year's Day so hopefully he'll be remembered if he tried to get on a bus. He might be with the girlfriend – Curran, do we have a picture of the girlfriend and of Mackley?'

'I can get one copied,' she says immediately. She moves from her seat to the side of the room where she picks up a thick blue binder.

'I lifted an entire photo album from the Mackleys' this morning when I called in.'

Jess comes towards me, not looking where she is going, her feet used to the inconsistencies in the carpet, her fingers flipping through photos.

'So this.' She twists the photograph album around one-hundred-and-eighty degrees so I can see it properly. 'Is Joshua Mackley. Pretty recent photo, I'd say, he is only twenty-five.'

I take the album from her and squint at it, wishing I had remembered to bring my glasses from the bedside table before I left this morning. In the photograph is a skinny man, pale, who looks much younger than twenty-five. He sits on a bar stool, the picture on his T-shirt obscured by a microphone stand and a huge electric guitar. The boy's eyes are closed, but the profile is clear and it is a good image. A professional shoot, I think.

'If you flip ahead …' Jess leans over to do just this. 'That's Keeley Mackley, the girlfriend – the blonde one. And that's Jude Jameson with the straight hair. The pictures are labelled on the back, that's how we were able to identify them all so quickly. The album is mostly photos of them as kids but these ones seem recent.'

I flick through the album and stop at a photograph of two smiling little girls, arms hooked around one another's necks, standing on top of a boulder at the Vetobridge rock pools. They are grinning from ear to ear. It is almost identical in position and pose to the photograph on my desk of me and Rebecca.

'That's Naomi Ross there,' Jess continues, pointing to another photograph. 'They must have a band as there are a lot of pictures of them performing.'

'What about the knife?' I ask.

Jess and Dunwoody both try to speak at once and glare at one another.

'Dunwoody,' I say, pointing at him.

'It's with the lab,' he says. 'We'll hopefully have results by the end of today or the start of tomorrow. Jaxon says it definitely looks like our murder weapon and he can confirm that at the PM tomorrow.'

'Great. You stick on that, keep plaguing everyone at the lab until they're sick looking at you. We want to know who has handled that knife. OK, CCTV?'

Edie Edgecomb speaks from her place next to Jess. 'I'm on that, Sir.' Her thick, Southern Irish accent contrasts with her pretty, laughter-lined face – so much so that I find myself blinking in surprise every time she speaks. 'The uniforms that first attended the scene say the Mackleys' house faces a main road, across which is a Spar garage – I've asked for the tapes. A uniform is en route to pick them up now.'

'Excellent.'

'What do you want to do about the two girls downstairs?' Smith asks. 'They're waiting to give statements.'

'Jude has to have her mum with her,' Jess says. 'She's only seventeen. Shall we take her, boss?'

I nod. 'We'll take Jude. Edgecomb and Clarke, do you want to take Keeley Mackley?'

The two women make sounds of agreement and stand in unison.

'Get as detailed a statement as you can,' I say. 'Find out everything you can about this party, what happened, how exactly they found Peter Denny this morning. See what their relationship was like, if they had many arguments … see how Joshua Mackley felt about Denny.'

'Of course, Sir,' says Edgecomb.

'I'll go and get us a room,' Jess says to me.

'First things first,' I interrupt. 'Coffee.'

We go to my office, where I keep a jar of instant coffee that tastes marginally better than the incident room mud. As we stand side by side, waiting for the kettle to boil, I rub a hand across my face. My forehead is sweating and my head aches. The half dozen paracetamol I swallowed this morning are beginning to wear off – maybe it was the dozen or so tins of Guinness last night.

'First case in Vetobridge in a while, eh, Sir?'

'Mm,' I murmur in acknowledgement.

I can't remember the last time I visited Vetobridge. My daughter, Rebecca, used to love to go there at the weekends, and I know the last time I visited was with her.

Quite a while ago, then.

The town consists of a single main street with cafés and newsagents and pound shops all the way along one side, and a promenade overlooking the stony beach on the other. The streets are cobbled, meaning everyone drives slowly, and while the average age of the residents seems to be about sixty-five, people aren't expected to live past seventy – about ten years less than the average. The sea air does not do them any good. One or two cops take a drive through the main street on a Saturday night, just to reassure the locals that we're keeping an eye, but I can't remember the last case I had there.

Despite the cruel caws of the seagulls that follow you wherever you go, I have always thought Vetobridge is pretty and the cafés quite quaint.

Even if I can no longer bear to drive past the beach or the rock pools without thinking of her.

'Do you want to go and visit the crime scene after our interview?' Jess's question snaps me out of my daydream, something involving Rebecca and an ice cream.

'Nah,' I say. 'We'll sort all that out later.' I rub my hands together in a mixture of an attempt at excitement and a genuine need for warmth. 'Right, what's the betting then?'

'Too early to say,' Jess says promptly.

'Oh, come on. You're no fun any more.'

'OK … a rival drug dealer.'

'Damn. I was going to say that.' I drum my fingers on the side of the mug Jess has just filled for me. 'OK, I'll go with Joshua Mackley, then. Sometimes it is the most obvious.'

'How much?'

'Dinner and a pint when this is over?'

'Done. Are there any decent pubs near your new place?'

She has accepted my recent move to Loughbricksea and the implied separation from my wife of twenty-five years without comment. That's the thing I like most about Jess: she is uncomplicated, unflappable and – mercifully – completely uninterested in my personal life.

'None at all,' I say enthusiastically. 'But I wouldn't make you come all the way to Loughbricksea *and* pay for dinner anyway.'

She pretends to guffaw as we make our way to the lifts.

Jude

1st January 2020, afternoon

Mum is my appropriate adult.

It doesn't feel very appropriate to be sitting next to her in a police interview room.

It isn't like the interview rooms I've seen on TV, and I take this as a sign that they aren't taking me seriously as a suspect. The wall that separates us from the corridor is entirely made of glass, with wooden blinds running across horizontally, like in someone's conservatory. The blinds have been pulled shut and we're sitting with our backs to them, but I've definitely heard some commotions outside: footsteps, fiercely whispered conversations, the swish of papers dropping to the floor.

There is a whiteboard to my left. I have an image of being asked to draw the other party guests in jumbo marker.

I wonder when I last ate or slept. I had the other half of Keeley's Toffee Crisp when we were getting ready yesterday, but I can't remember the last substantial thing before that. I haven't slept since … well, a lot longer.

I decide this has been the longest day of my life.

Mum has finally stopped asking questions. She has changed into what Keeley calls her 'church outfit', even though Mum hasn't been to church in nearly ten years: sensible navy trousers with a perfectly ironed seam, a flowery blouse, small heels and a navy jacket. I wonder how many people will mistake her for my solicitor. She sighs dramatically every few minutes and flicks her fingernails off her styrofoam cup of tea. Now that the initial shock has worn off and she has established that I'm not hurt in any way, she just wants to go home. Wants the *others* to deal with the police so she can take her chore-doing, always-smiling daughter home. All of this mix-up, this little murder, it really doesn't concern her and her family.

'Just tell them the truth,' she says again. 'When he comes back in, just tell them exactly what you know and what happened, and with any luck we'll be home for three o'clock.'

I ignore her.

We are waiting for Detective Inspector Chris Rice to return. I can't help thinking that he must be at the other side of some one-way glass, or looking at a video feed, watching how we interact and writing up a few preliminary notes. At least, I hope this is what he is doing. I hope he isn't talking to Keeley or, Jesus Christ, beating a confession out of her. That happens in some police stations, apparently. Keeley doesn't need an appropriate adult; she is all alone. My heart starts to race and I have almost stood up to bang on the wall when the door flies open and Rice enters.

'Sorry to keep you waiting, ladies!' he says in his booming voice. A Belfast accent but an Oldry suit. A show at a determinedly Oldry policeman. Local. Approachable. Just like you. 'I'm all yours now. Do you want more tea? Sergeant Curran, go and get them some more tea, will you? And bring the digestives off my desk.'

The woman who had started to follow him into the room turns on her heel and goes straight back out.

Rice is old, but I don't know if he's closer to sixty or seventy. He has a tuft of hair clinging determinedly to his skull above each ear, but apart from that he is bald. He has wrinkles and a pockmarked nose but, despite these physical shortcomings, he is smiley and looks kind. Like a close friend's old grandfather who likes to keep up with his younger relatives.

'She'll only be a min,' Rice informs me. 'We can have a wee chat while she's gone. So, Jude – is it OK if I call you Jude?'

I nod.

'Jude. You know why you're here. You know why your mum is here. You're not under arrest or anything mad like that –' Rice rolls his eyes as if this is insane. 'Just need to get some info from you, make our lives a wee bit easier. You can have a solicitor present if you'd prefer?'

He looks at me. I look at Mum. She looks at him.

'Is that … Well, I really don't think we'll need one,' Mum gushes, all wrapped up in a little high-pitched bark of a laugh. 'This has all been a big misunderstanding, Jude wouldn't –'

'Grand!' Rice rubs his hands together excitedly.

The sergeant returns with a triangle of cups pressed between her hands and half a packet of chocolate digestives under her arm. The whole thing has taken her under a minute, and I have a sneaking suspicion that the tea and biscuits were waiting outside the door – is this a test? Is Rice supposed to lull us into a false sense of security before she arrives and starts screaming at us? She sets a cup down in front of everyone except herself.

'Detective Inspector Chris Rice, interviewing Jude Jameson as a witness in the murder of Peter Denny. 1st January 2020 at 1334 hours. Also present are Detective Sergeant Jessica Curran and Linda Jameson acting as appropriate adult. For the purposes of the tape, Miss Jameson has refused legal counsel.'

Rice has pressed a button on a tape recorder and garbled all of this before the sergeant sits down. He reaches to pull the biscuits from under her arm, crinkles the packaging, then offers us all one in turn. We all shake our heads. He shrugs and takes three, cramming the first into his mouth whole.

'So.' He rubs crumbs from his fingers on to the desk and sweeps them off. 'Jude. Why don't you start by telling us a little bit about your relationship with the Mackleys? Something nice and simple to start us off … I gather you're close?'

Mum snorts beside me. We all turn to look at her.

Mum looks at the detectives and seems to shimmy around, as if blocking me out of the conversation. 'It's just …' Her voice is low, like she is explaining to my PE teacher why I can't go swimming. 'Well, that's a bit of an understatement, Detective.'

'Care to elaborate?'

Mum throws a glance at me and continues. 'Keeley and Jude are very close. Very, very close.'

'You mean they're in a romantic relationship?'

'No!' I yell it at exactly the same time that Mum does.

'No,' I say again. My cheeks are burning and I wish I had worn make-up. 'We're just really good friends. She's my best friend, she has been since … since forever.'

'More like sisters,' Mum says, nose crinkled.

'OK.' Rice pops his second biscuit into his mouth. 'And so, of course you would be at the party last night. Did you help organise it?'

'Normally we don't let Jude go to parties,' Mum cuts in. 'She doesn't drink, she prefers reading and studying over that scene. But seeing as it was New Year's Eve and I knew she would only be across the road, we thought we could let her go, just this once. She said there would only be a few of them there but it seems it got carried away. She's a sensible girl, so we thought …'

Rice and Curran are looking at her, not unkindly, but with tight lips and half-raised eyebrows that indicate they are humouring her.

'Thank you, Mrs Jameson,' Rice says. 'I'd really love to hear from Jude, though. The party, Jude. Do Keeley and her brother have many of these parties?'

There is a space in the room where Keeley should be. The room is too big. The lighting is totally off.

I have no idea what to say. We didn't plan for this question.

I stare at Rice.

He takes a deep breath and smiles at me, a big toothy grin that raises his cheekbones so that his eyes nearly disappear in a clump of fat. My dad is a big man, but Rice's big is different. Rice is … wobbly. He is very tall, well over six foot I think, but where my dad has thick wrists and a reassuringly solid, immovable belly, Rice has a squidgy face, a swaying, jiggling belly and two lumps on his chest that are like little boobs. They're much bigger than mine. I blush thinking this, and look away, feeling guilty.

'OK,' Rice says. 'That's fine, we can come back to that. Why don't you start by telling me … When did you first meet Keeley?'

'It was when Jude was four,' Mum bursts in.

Their eyebrows stay raised, but they let her speak.

Linda

1st January 2020, afternoon

'Keeley didn't go to school until she was six years old,' I say. I don't feel this does the matter justice, so I add, 'She probably wouldn't ever have gone if it weren't for me …

'The Mackleys moved into the newly built houses on the outskirts of the estate. Budget housing. They started building *after* we moved in … Marian Mackley didn't know how to cope with her kids. God rest her soul.'

The female detective, a pretty, small thing with dark hair and deep brown eyes, has a tension between her eyebrows that I don't like. I speak more quickly, afraid they will cut me off.

'We didn't really let Jude outside to play very often. She was happy to stay inside with her books and indoor games. But in the July before Jude was due to start in primary school, Roddy let her go outside to play. I was in bed. I don't normally sleep during the day, God, of course not, but I was five months pregnant at the time. I was exhausted. Roddy was in his study, getting some work done – he's a researcher and lecturer for the university, he works from home a few days a week – and Jude was in the front garden with her dolls.

'When I woke up, I came downstairs and I remember asking Roddy where Jude was.

'He told me she was in the garden. "She's made a little friend," he said.

'I went outside and my heart stopped.

'Instead of sitting with her dolls, Jude was standing on top of the garden wall – it's about six foot high, I still have no idea how they got up there – and throwing her dolls across the road as hard as she could. And standing there beside her, cheering her on and jumping, actually jumping on the wall, was the little blonde Mackley girl.

'I screamed at Jude to get down from the wall but she just laughed at me.'

I expect Jude to at the very least deny this, so the detectives don't think she's that kind of girl, but she stays silent.

'I managed to coax them down,' I continue. 'But they kept running around me and laughing. "ONE, TWO, THREE, GOOOO!" Keeley shouted all of a sudden, and the two of them were off over the road and across the green, pushing at one another and laughing all the while. That was the game. Just to run.

'Jude knew her Green Cross Code, she knew not to go beyond our garden … but she wasn't listening. She hadn't taken her eyes off Keeley the whole time. There was something … sweet about it. I had never seen Jude laugh like that.

'The rest of the summer, Jude was out every day. She had no time for books, no time for me or her dad. Woke up, got dressed and went straight out to find Keeley. I don't know when that little girl slept, but she was always out much later than we let Jude out, and she was always up a lot earlier too. Often, she'd be wearing the same clothes as the day before – she had a pair of pink dungarees. That's all I can see her in when I think about her as a child.

'She was all Jude talked about.'

I make my voice a pitch higher. '"*Keeley says if monsters were real, there would be a lot more dead children, so I'm not scared any more. Keeley says dolls are stupid, so I don't want to play with Miss Peggy any more.*"'

Jude is staring at me, but shows no embarrassment.

The male detective offers me an encouraging smile, so I continue.

'At the end of August, they were sitting cross-legged in our garden, playing a complicated game with some marbles that Roddy had found for them. I had been watching them from the veranda for an hour and I still wasn't sure what the rules were.

'"What class are you going to be in, Keeley?" I asked her.

'Keeley looked up at me, eyebrows narrowed. "What?"

'"Don't say what, say pardon."

'"You should say, 'Pardon class are you going to be in?', then."

'Jude exploded with giggles and rolled on to her back, clutching her sides. Keeley wasn't trying to be cheeky. She just didn't realise the way things came out sometimes … Still doesn't.'

I cough, a little pointedly, but smile so the detectives don't think I'm judging.

'"In school," I continued. "Are you going to be in Mrs Reynolds's class, or Miss McKinley's?"

'Keeley blinked at me. "I'm not going to school."

'"Oh. When will you be five?"

'"I'm six."

'I rolled my eyes. "Well, Keeley. You can't be six otherwise you would be in school already. When is your birthday?"

'"The eleventh of July, the year two-thousand," she recited, and went back to her marbles. She flicked her wrist and Jude's arrow formation of marbles scattered across the grass.'

I remember I lifted my lemonade glass and went inside.

Roddy was tapping away at his computer, a book open in his lap, a playlist of 90s pop playing on his newly acquired iPod speaker. Unshaven and very grey, even then, his prescription specs so strong that his eyes seemed to soak into my soul up close, he smiled tiredly as I approached his desk.

He placed a hand on my bump. The size of a banana, according to a website we had been looking at the night before. Why do doctors use fruits and vegetables for measuring baby sizes? Like your child is something you grow and feed, only to one day consume it.

It was going to be a boy – a perfect, healthy, clever boy, who would get Roddy's brains, my work ethic and maybe a talent all of his own. Perhaps he would be a footballer – Roddy would love to have a footballer son. Maybe a keen swimmer we could take to galas at the weekends.

Jude was going to go the same way as Roddy, I thought. Roddy was thoughtful and wanted to learn and, more importantly, *understand*, everything. Jude had that too.

Yes, she would be the academic and our boy would be the sportsman. He'd be clever too, but always itching to get outside. He'd have a mop of blond hair and all the girls would love to watch him play, giggling from the stands at the football pitch.

But I'd always be his favourite girl.

'Rod,' I said. 'That little girl, Keeley. She's never been to school and she's six.'

He wrinkled his brow, then reached across to pause the music. 'Maybe she's being home-schooled?'

I had leaned in for a hug but pulled back to look at him.

'Very funny,' I said. Marian Mackley was not the sort to home-school. God rest her soul. 'I might have a chat with her mum.'

Roddy rolled his eyes and released me from the hug. He picked up his book and turned back to the correct page, smiling all the while.

'What?' I asked. 'I just don't want this little girl hanging about in our front garden for the next ten years!'

'Why not?' Roddy asked, flicking his computer mouse so it woke up again. 'What harm is she doing?'

'She … Well, she's got Jude completely obsessed with her. She's copying everything she does, she's hanging on her every word, she's –'

'Jude's made a friend, you mean?'

'It's more than that, Roddy.'

Roddy was grinning. 'That's what kids do when they're that age. I like Keeley. She's a nice kid.'

'I still think someone should talk to her mother. Just remind her that she's meant to be in school. Do we really want Jude to be friends with someone who has never been to school? Someone who can't read or write?'

The detectives are waiting, wondering if I am finished speaking, so I speak more loudly.

'I went right there and then,' I say. 'I picked my way across the green, stepping carefully over a rainbow of mass-produced, cheap plastic toys. Jude's and Keeley's voices carried all the way across the green, Jude's giggle and Keeley's roar.

'I thought about going around the house and knocking on the front door as any civilised person would, but I wanted to make it seem casual. Looking back, I think I really must have been bursting at the seams with raging hormones. I don't normally get involved in other people's –'

Jude snorts next to me. I glare at her and continue.

'I rapped on the back door and stood back, trying not to dust or clean my knuckles too obviously in case she was looking out a window.

'Marian Mackley was only a few years older than me, but she looked a few decades older. God rest her soul. She had those deep lines around her mouth and eyes that you only get if you've suffered tragedy or been taking drugs. She'd had tragedy in her life, obviously. Her husband, Joshua's father, he died when Joshua was only three or four. Keeley told me he was in a boating accident and got eaten by a blue whale and, I hate to admit it, I believed her for years. Turns out it was nothing like that.'

I leave a pause for the detectives to ask about this, to show their horror at my description of Marian, at least, but neither of them moves or speaks.

'I introduced myself as Linda from across the road. I indicated with my other hand to show we lived on *this* side of Wits End and not *that* side. "I'm Jude's mum," I said. "We were just wondering if Keeley is going to Edenmore next month? The girls are keen to be in the same class."

'"She's only six," Marian said.

'"Ah! See, they start going when they're four or five … these days. So, really, she should have been going from last year. Strictly speaking." I widened my eyes and made a show of rocking my head side to side to show that I wasn't the one who made these ridiculous rules.

'"Oh," said Marian. "I'll get her in then. Edenmore, you said?"

'"Well! I mean, there are loads of good schools in the area. You should look around and decide which one you like the look of most."

'When I came back, I informed Keeley, quite proudly, that she would be going to school in September, that I had it all arranged.

'"Will I be in Jude's class?" she wanted to know.

'"I'm not sure, sweetheart, we'll have to see. You might not even be going to the same school, your mummy might pick a different one." I tried to keep the hope out of my voice.

'"She won't," Keeley said decisively. "I'll tell her to pick the same class as Jude."

'Jude just watched her, wide-eyed and smiling, and I knew then that, same class or not, she was already hooked.

'Keeley stood up and waited for Jude to copy her, something that she seemed to do without thinking. They did it again, the "one, two, three, run" thing. They ran as fast as they could down the green and into the Mackleys' garden.'

I pick up my cup and take a sip of tea, surprised to find it cold.

'And Jude still hadn't taken her eyes off of Keeley.'

I glance from one detective to another, almost physically biting my tongue to stop myself adding … *she still hasn't.*

Keeley

1st January 2020, afternoon

I can't remember either of the detective women's names, but I don't think this will count against me. I've just lost my boyfriend; I'm allowed to be a bit confused and all over the place. I *am* a bit confused and all over the place. It will work to my advantage, I hope.

My eyes are sore from crying and my stomach – all of my organs, actually – feel empty and hollow and numb.

Pete is dead. He doesn't exist any more. I want to stand up and throw myself against the wall or out of a window, so I don't have to think about that truth.

Pete is dead.

The first party in *ages* we'd all managed to go to, and it ended like *this*?

I think back to yesterday, can see myself as if from above, dancing around my room getting ready, a little halo of golden innocence surrounding me, not an inkling of what the night would hold. Both sides of my life, Pete *and* Jude, finally in the one place for a whole evening. No saying goodbye to one just to run off and meet the other, no twinge of guilt at stopping a conversation mid-sentence to text the other back. No totting up hours in my head, making sure they'd both had the same length of time with me that week.

Not an awkward thirty-minute drive to McDonald's that felt more like three hours, the three of us unable to think of anything in the world to talk about, me regretting yet again my attempt at forcing a bond between my best friend and boyfriend.

Just one whole night with my two favourite people in the one room.

But he is *dead*.

One of the women has asked me a question and I haven't heard it.

'Sorry,' I mumble. 'What?'

'I was asking you how long you'd been with Peter Denny.'

The harsh overhead lights are angled so I can see every one of the pores on her cheeks. I have already pretended to be sick once this morning, but I think I might actually throw up for real.

'I don't feel well,' I manage. 'Feel sick.'

An image comes into my head as clearly as though the detectives have shown me a photograph. The image of a baby bird covered in blood.

We found the bird one Thursday after school. I think we were in primary two. Jude was changing into her 'outside clothes', and I was waiting for her outside, humming to myself and kicking the wall. Once Jude came out, we were going to practise skipping with the new purple and white ropes Roddy had bought for her.

Jude was taking ages to get changed, so I went around the side of their house to look for a suitable place for jumping and that's when I saw it.

It was on the paving stones, directly under one of the windows. I know now that it was the bathroom window, but I wasn't allowed into the Jamesons' house at this point.

I thought it was dead, at first. I went closer until my trainers were almost touching it. It moved its wing just a fraction, waving at me for help. Its brains were smashed against the ground and its legs – or maybe they were wings, it was hard to tell – were bent at a funny angle. The bird was pink and wet in places and grey and furry in others. Its chest heaved. I looked up the wall until I saw it, right at the top. Where the two slants of roof met, there was a small brown nest. The baby bird had fallen out. Or been pushed.

By the time Jude came outside, I had decided exactly what had happened. She was beaming until she saw what I was crouched over.

'What is it?' she whispered. She had stopped, frozen, halfway towards me.

'It's a little baby bird,' I said. I was whispering too, though I wasn't sure why. 'He hopped out of his nest because he thought he could fly. But now he's hurt himself. He just wanted …'

I remember being suddenly, uncontrollably sad. He just wanted … what?

'Can't we just … leave him there?' said Jude.

'No!' I snapped. I wiped at my eyes and stood up again. 'We'll take him somewhere he'll be safe and we'll look after him until he feels better. He's all alone and he has nobody. So that means we have to take care of him.'

Her nod was so solemn that it made me think she really, really knew what I was talking about. I couldn't have explained it myself, but it was like Jude understood perfectly.

I suppose, thinking about it now, she did.

We crouched down at either side of the bird, steeling ourselves. We knew we would have to lift it eventually. I leaned forward to examine his head injury.

'He has a crack to his front brain,' I said gravely. 'He might not make it.'

'Oh, he will!' Jude gushed. 'Of course he will, you'll see.'

My heart was beating so fast. I looked at his head, thin worms of fleshy, bloody string hanging out of his tiny skull. Blood had covered his fluffy, half-formed feathers and they were sticking together, all matted.

I was fascinated by disgusting things, so even though I felt sick, I couldn't stop looking.

Jude was looking from me to the bird, wincing and waiting for me to decide.

Waiting, waiting.

'We should move him away. Should we?' Jude asked. She still does that: she'll make a statement and then ask me to clarify it. Most of the time I don't even notice any more.

'Yes, we should. He wanted to get away from his mummy, so we should help.' I placed a hand at either side of the bird's body and tried to find an angle where I wouldn't touch too much blood. The bird fluttered its tail and its breast in panic.

'We aren't going to hurt you, Mr Bird,' I said. 'We're just taking you to the garden. You'll be safe.'

It made a bleating sound. I can still hear it sometimes if I really concentrate.

I pressed my hands a little tighter around his wings but something came out of its mouth, like water but a bit thicker. I pulled my hands back, just as outraged as the bird.

'Should I try?' Jude asked.

She had put on – or maybe Linda had chosen it – her favourite Disney Princess T-shirt and good jeans. Linda hadn't learned that dressing her seven-year-old nicely to go outside and play would never end well, but I suppose, then, Jude didn't really have anything *but* good and best. Everything she owned was designer, I realised at some point in my pre-teen years. Right down to her Calvin Klein underwear, every single thing she has ever worn has been branded, apart from the things she has taken from me. Jude admitted to me once that Linda drove her for forty minutes to a particular charity shop, carefully out of sight of Vetobridge, picked up her fancy clothes and put them in a hot wash as soon as they got home, telling Jude not to mention to anyone where they had got them.

'If you like,' I whispered. I stood back.

Jude moved forward. She was biting at her top lip like she used to, and her hands were pressed on to her thighs as she leaned over.

'Come on, Mr Bird,' she said. 'We aren't going to hurt you. We'll just take you to the garden and you'll be safe.'

She put one hand around each side of its body and slowly picked it up. It made a bit of an effort to flap its wings in protest, but was incapable of getting away from her, Jude being so determined to please me. 'If we put him in the very middle of the garden,' she said. 'I'll be able to see him from my room.'

It was a good idea. Jude's bedroom takes up the entirety of the top floor of the Jamesons' house, and she has huge, person-length windows at the front and at the back. It's the best place to be if you want to know what's happening across Wits End.

We moved slowly from the side of the house to the back garden. I went ahead, making a show of opening the gate for Jude and the bird, the way I'd learned it was polite to do. I found a suitable spot in the very centre of the garden and directed Jude to it.

She set the bird down carefully and took her hands away. They were damp with pale pink blood.

'He'll be OK, here,' I said. 'You did a good job.'

You did a good job was something I said a lot then. Our teachers used to say it to the good kids and I liked the way it sounded.

'What now?' Jude said.

I looked across the garden, skipping forgotten. Then I looked back at the bird, whose eyes were darting around and whose breast was heaving in panic.

'I think we should leave him alone,' I said. 'Shall we go and play out the front?'

Jude nodded and rubbed her hands on her good jeans.

We played house. It was our favourite game until I was practically a teenager. One of the only pretend games that I liked. Jude pretended to cook us dinner on the veranda, '*chicken vollafonts*', and I pretended I was just home from a day at work. I sat on the steps of the veranda and read a pretend newspaper and complained about someone at work who was being mean. Jude was sympathetic and we drank wine from crystal glasses. We actually drank Ribena from plastic tumblers, but it was close enough.

Soon we had almost forgotten about the bird, though the stains on Jude's jeans were a stark reminder anytime I happened to look.

They called her in at six o'clock when, to be fair, it really was dark, and told her it was time for dinner.

'We should go and check on Mr Bird before we go. Should we?'

'Yeah,' I agreed. 'Let's go quickly, before they call you again.'

We sprinted to the back garden.

We were two metres away when our eyes adjusted enough for us to realise what we were seeing.

Mrs Connolly's cat was right where we had put our bird. The cat had its back to us and was leaning over and dipping its head up and down. Its tail lifted and fell easily next to it, its tongue lapping in time with the strokes.

'Goddamn,' I whispered.

The cat looked around lazily at this, jaws open wide, cleaning its teeth with its tongue. Its mouth was stained red.

'Shoo!' Jude shouted. 'Go away, stupid kitty!'

The cat practically rolled its eyes at Jude and stalked away.

We got closer, then leapt back.

The bird was dead. Most if its insides were gone, and its right eye was missing. Feathers covered the grass, scattered like blood-soaked confetti.

I think we probably would have stood there all night, had Roddy not come outside, calling for Jude.

'Come on, Jude. Dinner is ready. Or are you full up from your chicken vollyfronts?' He chuckled to himself. When we didn't move, he slid the French doors closed behind him and came towards us. 'Jude, it's freezing. It's time to come in …' He saw what we were looking at and gasped. 'Oh, no! How did he get out in the open? Poor thing looks only a few days old. Come away from there, girls, they have diseases.'

Jude looked at me, eyes wide.

Diseases.

That's why we had to wash our hands after we went to the toilet, I knew, to *prevent diseases*. And Jude had her hands all over the bird and didn't wash them.

I'm not sure if it was the shock of the mutilated bird or because we thought Jude might die of diseases, but in a moment we were both crying, ugly and loud. Jude was actually screaming, holding her hands out away from her body as if they were going to attack her against her will.

Roddy looked from one to the other of us, horrified. 'Girls, stop. It's OK! The bird will be fine, he's in heaven now. Go inside, Jude, I'll take care of this little guy. Keeley, I'll walk you across the road first.'

Usually we parted for the day with a tight hug and a promise of, 'See you tomorrow', but that day I let Roddy take my shoulder and lead me round to the front of the house without a word. Jude just stood there in the middle of the garden, mouth open in a horrible cry of pain. *See you tomorrow*, I thought. I thought it so hard, I sent it to her as best I could, just kept thinking it over and over again.

When Roddy left me at the other side of the road, I heard 'See you tomorrow' in Jude's croaked voice, like she'd thrown a frisbee back at me. I caught it and smiled bravely, and went down the hill to my own house.

I went to sleep that night trying not to think that if we'd left the bird alone, he wouldn't be dead.

'Do you want to take a break?' the big-pored detective asks, bringing me back into the interview room with a jolt. Her expression is the perfect mix of sympathy and suspicion. I wonder if she has practised it in the mirror.

'Yes, please,' I whisper.

I stand shakily, my legs weak, my head full of blood and feathers … and knives.

I think I am just going to burst into tears again, but vomit rushes up my throat and spills on to the floor before I reach the door.

I sit on the floor while the detectives call for someone to clean up, my knees pulled up to my chest, and imagine something I haven't imagined for years: that I can hear Jude's voice, that I've caught her frisbee.

You said we were going to be OK.

I swallow the next mounting wave of sickness and dry my eyes on my sleeve. I will do better when we resume, I think.

Not for the first time, I haven't done a good enough job of protecting her.

Detective Inspector Chris Rice

1st January 2020, afternoon

'Thank you for that, Mrs Jameson,' says Jess. 'That was very … enlightening.'

I glance at Jess's notebook. She has written at the bottom 'overbearing'. She has underlined it four times and taps her pen on the letter 'g' as she talks.

My headache returned with a vengeance around the time of Linda Jameson's second '*God rest her soul*'. The space above my right eye is pulsing. I am surprised nobody has noticed it; surely there is a vibrating lump hammering out of my forehead? I push my seat back and step away from the women to the water dispenser.

'We were hoping to hear from your daughter a bit more, though,' Jess continues.

I sip from the paper cup of water, savouring the cold for a moment. Then I turn back to the table, folding my arm across my stomach.

Jude picks black polish from her fingernails, her eyes unfocused and her mouth moving as though she is whispering to someone. With a sudden jolt, I wonder if she has learning difficulties we should have been informed about. She is smaller than Keeley, I think, though granted I have only glimpsed the latter through one-way glass, but she is still tall for a seventeen-year-old girl. Her hair is dark blonde, clean and very straight. From some angles, I think she has an ever-so-slight, rather endearing underbite.

'Jude?'

At the sound of her name, Jude looks up at Jess, but her mouth still moves, a constant, silent mantra. Maybe she is *praying*. Not for the first time, I wish we had insisted on a social worker instead of her mother. Linda's babbling is not helping any of us to relax.

'Can you tell us a bit about what happened last night?' Jess asks. 'It's great that we've heard from your mum, but we'd really like to hear from you. We're just trying to work out what's happened to Keeley's boyfriend, and it seems you're in a good position to tell us.'

I throw the empty paper cup into the bin next to the water dispenser and pull off my suit jacket.

She makes me uncomfortable, this girl who has said so little but who must know so much. There is something in her eyes that I don't like. I rub my own eyes with the heel of my hand, and when I look back, she has stopped moving her lips.

They are all looking at me.

'Sir? Maybe you didn't hear me … I just wondered if you had any questions you wanted to ask Jude. She isn't keen on talking about last night.'

I know Jess means *she doesn't want to talk to me*. Jess has her eyebrows raised and her gaze fixed on me. I am sweating profusely from my underarms, my forehead and the backs of my knees. I hope they cannot smell last night's beer or curry.

I stride back over to the table and fix my jacket on the back of my chair before sitting down again.

'OK, Jude.' I rub my hands together, casual as can be. 'Let's talk about Peter Denny. What sort of relationship did you have with him?'

She is looking at me, but she continues to pick polish off her nails. She drops the chips into a little pile in front of her.

Jude wears no make-up, so I can see the bags under her eyes. I notice, then, she wears only one tiny diamond stud earring. I try to remember Rebecca at seventeen; try to recall if this is normal, for a girl to have only one earring. All I can see is nine-year-old Rebecca at the rock pools, like the photograph on my desk, the only one Aisling gifted to me during our separation.

'When did you meet Pete for the first time?' I ask, when it becomes clear she is not going to answer.

'Last year. Well, 2018.'

She likes direct questions with direct, simple answers. Specific is good, specifics are what we like. We can work with this.

'OK. Do you remember what month?'

'No.'

Maybe it's the way she puts an inflection at the end of the word, or maybe it's the fact that she is no longer meeting my eye when she says it, but it feels like a lie. I sense Jess straighten her back next to me, and I know she has heard it too.

'But he became Keeley's boyfriend, when? Around autumn?'

She shakes her head. 'They met then. They were seeing each other for a bit.'

I bounce my shoulders up as playfully as I can, but the sudden motion hurts and I feel sick all over again. '"Seeing each other"? What does that mean, exactly? You'll have to forgive me, I'm an old man.' I grin at her and she tries to smile back. An automatic reaction to an adult, I think.

'Like, going on dates. Texting. Not officially boyfriend and girlfriend, just meeting up and … you know …' She trails off and glances at her mother. Linda has been remarkably quiet the last few minutes, watching me, chin raised, daring me to scold her for the promiscuity of her daughter's friend. Her lips are small and pressed so tightly together there almost seems to be a puckered hole in the middle of her face.

I look back to Jude. '*Seeing each other*. Gotcha. And you met him through Keeley then?'

She nods.

'What did you think of him?'

That is not specific enough. Her mouth opens, then closes. She looks at me and I know she is trying to give me something, but does not know what to say.

'Did you like him?' I ask.

She hesitates. Shrugs. 'He was OK.'

'Just OK? This is a potential suitor for your best friend we're talking about, a girl who is like your sister. Were you OK with him being just, *OK*?'

She mumbles something and Jess and I lean forward. 'Sorry, Jude, can you repeat that?'

'It wasn't my decision,' she says, louder.

I rub my tongue around my teeth and find a few hidden crumbs of biscuit at the back that I swallow. 'How did he treat Keeley?'

Not specific enough.

'When did they get into a relationship? A *proper* relationship?'

'About last Christmas, I think. You can ask Keeley.'

'Were they having problems in their relationship lately?'

'You'd need to ask Keeley that, too.'

'How did Pete feel about you?'

Jude looks at me. I think I see a blush rising in her cheeks again. She puts both her hands under her thighs, palms down, and sits forward.

'Pete liked me all right.'

'All right?'

'Yeah.'

'Well, he would have spent a lot of time with you, surely? If you and Keeley are as close as you say, you would have been with them quite a lot. Is that right?'

I'm losing her. I'm saying too many things. Her eyes are moving across the table and to the window and back.

'Were you the third wheel?'

Nothing.

'Maybe he was the third wheel?'

Jess tilts her notebook towards me, ever so slightly. I glance down under the premise of moving to take another biscuit from the packet and read '*Ask more about Keeley*'. My thoughts exactly. I munch on my biscuit, considering. She is uncomfortable talking about Pete. There might be something in that. Either way, I say:

'So, you and Keeley ended up in the same class in school then?'

'Yes!' says Linda. The three of us have almost forgotten she is there; we turn at once in something of a jump. 'Talk about living in each other's pockets! At school all day with one another and then home to run about together until dark. Do you know, they got so close that we ended up taking Keeley on holiday with us? It was like we had three children.'

I lean back in my seat and put another biscuit into my mouth, ignoring Jess's sigh.

We go on like this, the four of us engaged in what feels like an awkward play with no script, for another two hours. We all speak at once. Nobody speaks for several minutes. Stops, starts, serious questions, hesitations, some mumbled words and Linda Jameson's parrot-like interjections. My head pounds, Jess taps her pen, Linda Jameson barks a laugh that threatens to become a cry of horror. Jude sits, mumbles, glances.

But we get there in the end, and finally I push Jude's statement towards her across the table.

I watch her eyes scan the page, thinking about what we have written.

In bed by midnight. Can't remember much. Didn't speak to Denny. Hazy memory. Woke up this morning. Denny dead.

On paper, nothing useful for the investigation. Speaking to Jude has been interesting for us, though. I wonder what Jess will make of my initial read of the girl – scared, exhausted and, if I had to put a label on the nagging feeling in the back of my mind … *lying*.

Jude finishes reading her typed statement and looks up at me.

'Sound OK to you?' I ask.

She nods.

'OK, great.' I slide a pen across the table to her. 'Please sign both pages.'

Jude picks up the pen with her left hand, writes her name on each page and looks up at me. 'When can I see Keeley?'

I take my suit jacket from the back of my chair and make a show of shrugging it back on. I try to button it at the front, but the two sides won't come together. Jess has picked up Jude's statement and slotted it into a Manila folder.

We both ignore her question.

'Sergeant Curran, please, can you escort Jude and Mrs Jameson back downstairs?' I turn to Linda. 'We can have a car take you home.'

'No!' Linda says. 'I mean, no, thank you. We'll get a taxi, or my husband can come and get us. No police car required.'

I don't bother pointing out that the car would be unmarked. I smile at both of them and say, 'Thanks again for your time. Remember, call me with anything.'

On my way to the incident room, I almost run full smack into Browne.

We both stop in our tracks, apologising.

'Sir, how did your interview go?'

I shrug and try to stifle a yawn. 'Nothing overly useful. She says she was asleep by half-past twelve. Not much of a party animal. Can't remember who was still around, can't remember the last time she saw Pete. Says she was drunk and didn't wake up until after the body was found this morning. How are you getting on with the others?'

'I don't know what the hell these people were taking,' Browne says. 'But not one of them remembers anything past nine o'clock last night, apparently. They're calling the drug "Sixes", saying it's home-made. Thing about the drug is it sometimes messes with your memory if you swallow it with alcohol, which most of them did. Took the drug about eight, when they arrived, partied hard all night by the looks of their hangovers, and they all woke up this morning claiming they have little to no memory of anything that happened. We've got statements from most of them, but a lot of it is stuff they half remember, and some of it seems like it might have been another party altogether. Not sure if they were trying to fuck with me or their heads are genuinely messed up. I'm trying to piece together what we know for sure. It's been a fucking nightmare. They all agree they were at the party, they all place each other there, but in terms of who actually killed our guy?' Browne sucks his breath and holds both hands out to the sides in a shrug of helplessness. 'We're no closer. They've all basically admitted that it could have been any of them. They know we can't arrest them all. If it's worth anything, Sir, they all seemed genuinely shocked that Denny is dead. Genuinely shocked but keen to clear their names as soon as possible.'

I let a breath out through my mouth.

'That's OK, Browne. Sounds like you did the best with what you've got. Have they agreed to DNA samples?'

'Yes, Sir. Processing them as and when we're letting them go. Smith and Dunwoody are taking care of them.'

'Did you get all nine of the witnesses?' I ask.

'As of half an hour ago, all but Joshua Mackley and the Devlins.'

'Keep at it, I want him here tonight and I want to do the interview myself.'

'I know he's our priority, we'll keep looking.' Browne shrugs again. 'It's a weird one. One of them, Brian Reed, a ferret-looking boy with big feet, he seemed pretty keen to *brag* about the drug, almost. Like he was trying to bloody sell it to us. They're all suffering this morning, but Reed claims that's because they mixed what they were taking with copious amounts of booze. He says if they'd just stuck to the pills, they'd be fine. It's a drug with no comedown. Bunch of weirdos.'

'Which room is Keeley Mackley in?'

'Waiting at 16B. Martine was in with her earlier, but she said the girl was basically just crying and choking, couldn't be consoled. I don't think they got anything important out of her. Probably best to give her a sedative and try again tomorrow. I got you their notes from her interview just in case …' Browne passes me a few pages.

'OK … OK, maybe we'll give her an hour. Gather the team in the incident room for an update, will you?'

I do not make for the incident room right away. Instead, I fish in the pocket of my jacket for my personal mobile phone. I switch it on and type out a text.

Hi, Sylvie! Hope you and the kids are doing well. Wondered if we could have a call this week? The sooner the better. Tomorrow? Let me know. Aggie xo

I switch the phone off again. Then I turn on my heel and begin to climb the stairs.

Edie Edgecomb is the last constable to enter the incident room. She closes the door behind her with a soft *click* and Jess turns to me, putting her thumb up above her head to let me know we are ready.

I clear my throat and silence falls among the chatting groups at once.

'OK, before I give the orders – has anyone else anything to … ?'

'The Devlins have materialised,' Magill tells the room. 'They're waiting for me and Charlie to take their statements now. Same story as the others, though. One of them took drugs and remembers nothing, the other one got lucky with Carrie Riley before midnight and saw in the new year in the back of his car, balls deep in –'

'Thank you,' I say, pretending to examine the whiteboard behind me to hide my smile. 'All I want to know is – can we corroborate these things?'

'The CCTV from the Spar shows the Devlin boy's car leaving at half eleven, and it doesn't come back,' says Edgecomb. Every head turns towards her and she continues, 'We found Naomi Ross as well, that's where I was just now. She says she and Joshua Mackley spent this morning driving around, both their phones off. She dropped him off at the pub, then. Both of them took drugs last night and remember very little; however, she knows they were both back at her place, an apartment in Boar's Brae, before three, because they ordered a pizza and the pizza place, Tim's Pizza in Vetobridge, closes at three.'

'OK, head over there and find out who delivered –'

'I tried,' Edgecomb says, grimacing. 'It's closed for New Year's Day and I can't find a number for the owners anywhere. The answering machine says they'll be open again tomorrow at four o'clock.'

'OK, well as soon as possible, I want to know the delivery person actually *saw* both Naomi Ross and Joshua Mackley in her apartment. And find out how quickly you can get from Wits End to Boar's Brae on foot. Ask the delivery driver what time it was, make sure they're *sure*. Ask them what kind of mood the two of them seemed to be in.'

'You mean if there was any blood on their clothes when they answered the door?' asks Dunwoody from a table by the window. He is grinning.

'Why don't you go and stand outside the pizza place until tomorrow afternoon?' Jess asks before I can speak.

A few people laugh, Dunwoody scowls.

Ignoring this, I say to Edgecomb, 'Did you ask Naomi Ross about the fight July 2018?'

'I did, Sir. She was very quick to answer that one. Says she left for the airport very early on the morning of the 12th of July because her sister was getting married in Spain that week. That's how she remembers it. For what it's worth, Sir, I believe her. She says she can show me boarding passes, pictures taken, the wedding invite. She says she has no idea why Mack would want to hurt Pete and claims she didn't know they had fought that summer.'

'That's fine. Thank you. What else can you tell me about the CCTV?'

'Good news on that front.' Edgecomb stands up and comes to the front of the room. For the first time, I notice a wealth of papers in her hands.

I take her vacated seat and look up, hopefully.

'Not only have we managed to comb the Spar CCTV, which covers the front of 166 Wits End … we also managed to get a hold of CCTV that covers the back of 166 Wits End, meaning we can see exactly who was in that house at all times.'

Someone whistles and Smith applauds.

'Where did you get that?' I ask, impressed.

'The Jamesons have CCTV in operation at the front of their house,' Edgecomb says. 'It isn't perfect, and since 166 is pretty far away, the images are grainy *but* in my opinion it's pretty clear who each individual is. The CCTV corroborates the time each of the partygoers came to and left the party. It's the time they all left that we're most interested in, I think?'

'Jaxon says Peter Denny made it until at least one in the morning, probably closer to two,' I say. 'To be confirmed at the PM tomorrow.'

A few people nod.

'Well, the first guests to leave were Carrie Riley and Kyle Devlin,' continues Edgecomb. 'As we know. They didn't even make it to midnight before they buggered off to shag in his car somewhere.'

'Nicely put.' I say. 'So … we can tentatively rule them out?'

Jess stands and takes a red marker pen from the front of the whiteboard. She draws a large red X over the photos we have printed of Kyle Devlin and Carrie Riley.

'You can certainly rule them out, Sir,' Browne pipes up. 'And it wasn't Brian Reed either.'

He has stood from his place at the back of the room and makes his way to the front, his work mobile phone in his hand. 'Techs just got back to me. Brian Reed made a video on New Year's Eve – a livestream it's called. It's when you're basically broadcasting live to social media in real time. I found it first thing this morning but wanted to make sure the footage hadn't been tampered with or wasn't on a timer or anything. Usually the videos only stay up for twenty-four hours, so I've taken a copy of it …' Browne plugs his phone into the computer and we all shift impatiently in our seats as he loads the video on to the projector. 'It's public property, since he uploaded it to his non-private social media account. Idiot.'

Finally, he double-clicks on a blurry thumbnail and a video begins to play. He turns up the sound and cranes his neck back to watch it with us.

Laughter and catcalling from a male voice. Three people talking at once. The only thing I can make out for sure is, '*It'll sound stupid without the bass.*'

The image starts pitch black, then suddenly springs into light, the camera focused on Joshua Mackley, who is sitting opposite the recorder, his guitar resting on his knee. They are in the living room of 166 Wits End – I recognise it from photographs.

'*Let us hear it!*'

'That's Brian Reed talking,' Browne says quietly. The incident room is silent, each of us straining our eyes and ears at the grainy quality.

'*I'd like to dedicate this to …*' Mackley starts giggling hysterically. Reed joins in. Then they both stop, looking at one another. It takes the group in the incident room a few seconds to realise why.

There is shouting from another room in the house.

'*Fucking never stops,*' Mackley murmurs. '*Fucking ridiculous.*'

It is impossible to hear anything specific, but I can tell two people are having an argument.

The door opens and Naomi Ross comes into view. She leans over to whisper in Mackley's ear. He passes her the guitar and leaves the room.

Reed appears to have forgotten the camera is rolling.

'*What now?*' he asks.

Naomi sits next to him. His phone moves so that it focuses on her bare thighs; her skirt has ridden up her leg. I feel confident he hasn't done this on purpose, and it says a lot about our concentration levels that not one of the detectives wolf-whistles or reacts.

'*You don't want to know.*'

It is then that we hear another voice.

'*Should we go and help?*'

'*Mack has it sorted, Jude. You did the right thing.*'

Jude Jameson has entered the room with Naomi, unseen. She must be sitting on Reed's other side. Reed moves the phone so that it faces the ceiling, the video forgotten, and we hear rustling, movement. He has reached for a thin cigarette-shaped object from the coffee table.

'*No Sixes left?*' asks Naomi.

'*Plenty. Just not in the mood.*'

'*I need a proper cigarette.*'

'*Me too,*' says Jude.

When he has lit and taken a drag from the joint, he seems to remember that he is filming.

'*Hello, Naomi Ross, say hi to my ten thousand subscribers.*' He flips the camera on to her face and she scowls.

'*You're lucky if you have ten subscribers, Brains.*'

'*Tell me, Miss Ross, what are your New Year's Resolutions for 2020? Tell the fans. Is this going to be the best year of your life? Are you finally going to stop going on about Asia and actually pack in your job and travel there?*'

'*My main resolution is to make more friends so I can ditch you.*'

She is grinning at him and blows a kiss to the camera.

The door opens.

Mackley has returned.

'*Turn that thing off!*' he hisses. His giggly mood has disappeared. '*Look around you, thicko.*'

'*What's wrong?*'

'*Fucking look around. There are fucking Sixes everywhere. Turn it off, Brains.*'

'*Dry up, Mack. What's going on with those two?*'

Mackley runs his hands through his mop of long hair and sits down opposite Brains again.

'*Couldn't make out a whole lot. Had to leave them to it. What happened, Jude?*'

Jude doesn't answer. Naomi leans across the lens to take the joint from Brains's hand.

There is silence for a moment until Brains says, with an exaggerated yawn, '*I'm going home. I'm wrecked. Who thought it would be a good idea not to buy any cigarettes for a party? And that was my last joint. Where's Paddy?*'

'*He's firing empty cans on to the roof to see if he can get one to land in the aerial.*'

Brains laughs and stands up. '*See you tomorrow,*' he says to the group as a whole.

His phone in his hand, the camera partially obscured by his fingers, he goes to the front door.

The shouting can be heard more loudly from here, and Brains stops to listen.

'*Fuck off then! Go on ahead. I wish I'd never met you. I wish you were fucking dead!*'

A door slams open and we hear footsteps. Brains opens the front door and makes to leave when we hear a new voice in the video:

'*Did you hear her?*'

Jess looks at me excitedly. A few of the other detectives glance around at one another, eyebrows furrowed, mouthing *Pete*? to one another.

'*Nothing to do with me, mate,*' says Brains. '*Are you coming?*'

'*Nah. Have to get this sorted. Took another two Sixes so I should probably wait and see how that goes.*'

Brains scratches his forehead and, for a brief moment, the camera focuses on Peter Denny, standing in the doorway of the kitchen. Pete's hair sticks to his forehead with sweat.

'*OK. See you.*'

'*See you.*'

Brains leaves and closes the door behind him.

Outside, he puts the phone in his pocket so that the screen goes black. We hear him call to someone, more laughter, and then he and the second person begin to walk. We listen to their footsteps and indistinct chatter for a few moments.

Browne hits the pause button and turns to us, his hands outstretched towards the projector screen as though it is a prize on a bizarre quiz show.

'That was Paddy Devlin he was talking to at the end,' Browne says. 'I listened to the whole thing and he calls him by his name when they get to Paddy's house. We can verify that looking at the CCTV from the right time. When this thicko gets home, he takes his phone out from his pocket and remembers it's been streaming the whole time.'

'So Peter Denny was alive and well in the house when Brains and Paddy left it,' I say slowly. 'And based on the time this video was taken –'

'Starts at twenty past one,' Browne says promptly.

'Roy, Ian and James all leave the house at one in the morning,' Edgecomb says. 'I watched them banging on the doors of Spar for a few minutes – looking for cigarettes, according to their statements. Didn't realise it would be closed. Brian Reed goes back to the party, but you can see the other three walking away in another direction, heading home, when they realise the garage is closed.'

'Which means …' I say hesitantly.

We all look towards Edgecomb who is shuffling papers. 'Give me a minute to make absolutely certain,' she says.

'Browne,' I say. 'Go back and pause the camera when it focuses on Denny.'

Browne does so. There is silence in the incident room as we wait.

It takes him a few tries, as the window is so narrow, but eventually he has the video paused at the exact moment Brains scratches his forehead.

Peter Denny stands in the doorway that leads to the Mackleys' kitchen. White T-shirt, blue jeans, white trainers. His huge shoulders take up much of the doorway and his hair is tousled.

'There you go,' Browne says proudly. 'The video started recording at 1.19, so this is maybe, 1.25? There's our boy, standing upright, no knife in him as yet.'

'His face is cut,' Jess says suddenly. She hurries towards the screen and points at his right cheek. 'Look, his face has been cut.'

Sure enough, there is a thin, pale pink line on the flesh of his cheek.

'It wasn't cut when he arrived at the party,' Edgecomb says, not looking up from her papers. 'I've stared at that CCTV all day; I would have noticed.'

'Somebody had a physical altercation with him at the party,' I say. 'Before he died.'

'Keeley Mackley,' Browne says. 'Has to be. That's who he's arguing with.'

'He could have had the physical fight before the argument with Keeley,' Jess says reasonably.

'I think Browne is probably right here,' I say.

Edgecomb looks up from her papers, her face set. 'All the other guests had left by the time that livestream video started,' she says. 'Corroborated by the CCTV. And nobody else came into the house after, either, which means ...'

'Which means Peter Denny was stabbed by either Joshua Mackley, Keeley Mackley, Naomi Ross or Jude Jameson,' I finish.

There is a moment of silence, as we all nod along.

'Just as we thought from the start, Sir,' Jess says. 'This was personal. We don't need to pursue the wider drugs angle.'

I think about the text I sent just before the meeting, my heart sinking. A risky text, and possibly a complete waste of time.

'OK ...' I say. 'Well, good work, everyone. Especially you two.' I throw my hand vaguely in the direction of Edgecomb and Browne, the latter of whom is beaming. I stand up and stretch, trying not to let the team see my yawn. 'Curran, we have Keeley Mackley waiting for us outside 16B. At least now we have something concrete to ask her about.'

Keeley

1st January 2020, evening

I can taste an unpleasant sweetness and a deeper sourness, and my teeth feel gritty. It tastes like that first time we got drunk.

It was on our first foreign holiday with Jude's family – somewhere hot in Spain – that we decided to drink alcohol for the first time, to celebrate my twelfth birthday. We walked with Mason to the kids' club and watched as Linda and Roddy sat down in a restaurant opposite our hotel. I heard Linda order a bottle of wine before they'd even sat down. That evening, I was fairly certain she was relieved to see the three of us go – we'd spent the whole holiday pretending to be a happy family of five, and she downed her first glass of red in the few seconds it took Jude and me to pretend to walk in through the same door Mason had wheeled through, delighted to forget about us for a while. Linda was angry at having to take me on holiday with them at all, but Jude had made such a fuss and refused to go with them unless I could come, that she really hadn't had a choice.

They thought we had gone to the kids' club, too.

We had at least two hours, I informed Jude as we sprinted in our sandals, hand in hand, down towards the beach.

The sun was still high in the sky and the air was still hot. Around us, holiday-goers were in various stages of undress: some still in bikini tops, hair dripping with seawater; some in smart shorts, smelling of Lynx and holding bottles of beer as they strutted across the strip to dinner. We stood behind a mass of rocks and took turns necking a bottle of wine we'd stolen from the apartment earlier that day and smuggled out in our beach towels.

We got drunk. Very drunk. We finished the bottle and walked back towards the familiar part of the sand. Our heads were dizzy, and though I could see the sand moving as we kicked it, my peripheral vision was blurry, almost non-existent. I was aware of Jude only because I could feel her beside me. She was chattering and giggling. I was giggling too.

There existed no living souls but us and that was delicious.

My tongue felt sour like a sweet.

I took out the ancient digital camera Mum had given me and told Jude to take photographs of *whatever makes your heart beat fastest*. I'd heard that phrase on TV.

She'd never held a camera before, but clicked obediently.

We talked and laughed and enjoyed the feeling more than we'd ever enjoyed anything.

We'd do it again we promised as we walked back towards the hotel.

We met Linda and Roddy at the agreed time, outside the kids' club. If they'd been ten seconds earlier, they'd have seen us sprinting towards the entrance, giggling and flustered and full of reckless abandon, but as it happened they looked at us but didn't really see us. We grinned at one another.

We made our way back to the apartment, the five of us, the happy family; she and I hand in hand and grinning.

Our sandals slapped off the tiles as we danced past reception and into our apartment block. Jude had the key for the apartment.

As soon as it was unlocked, she fell through the door and landed flat on her face, promptly throwing up a puddle of purple bile on to the stone floor.

I stood, mouth open, unable to move, until Linda hurried past me and inside, tutting and shaking her head.

'Come on, Jude. Out of the way, Mason needs to get inside.'

When she turned Jude over, I saw a deep red cut just under her knee where she had scraped it on the door frame.

If I had to pinpoint the time when Linda basically shoved Jude to the side to see to her son properly, it was on that holiday, at that moment when she literally tutted at Jude for getting hurt because it had forced her away from Mason for a few seconds. She had no idea that we'd spent the last few hours drinking alcohol on the beach because she was looking but she wasn't really seeing either of us. Roddy was the same, but he is one of these men who doesn't bat an eyelid when someone pulls out in front of him, who watches romcoms and horror films with the exact same mildly curious expression: Roddy does not have the passion or gumption to protect Jude, not really. On that holiday, I realised that they both saw Jude only by the light of Mason's golden, glowing wheelchair.

Though I couldn't have put it into words then, I knew it was up to me to look after her.

They are too close to see her properly, I remember telling Mack when we got home. *They're so used to having her always there, in the background, that they don't see her.* He nodded as if he understood but didn't offer me any advice. Was our mum really so much worse than this?

As Jude got to her feet in the hotel room, I looked down at my own leg and saw a deep, long cut across my shin. I stared at it. This was not possible. A little blood still dripped from the cut, but a lot had dried up and down my legs, in smears and lines. Sand stuck to it in uneven clumps, making my whole leg feel rough and dirty. I realised some had smeared on the hem of my dress. It was suddenly – *absurdly* – agonisingly painful.

Linda pulled Jude into the bathroom to clean up her leg, and Roddy, running behind with Mason in his wake, got some wet paper towels from the kitchen to dab on mine. He was shaking his head, bemused.

That is the first time I remember feeling pain that was not my own, something that had continued to baffle us through our early teen years. I wonder when that stopped, when Jude's pain became entirely her own. I certainly hadn't felt anything when those girls were torturing her –

'Keeley Mackley?'

I look around. A huge man with gigantic fingers is holding open the door next to me. He is smiling at me, his face lined and very kind.

'I'm Detective Inspector Chris Rice. Do you fancy a chat?'

Detective Inspector Chris Rice

1st January 2020, evening

Her eyes are scarlet and puffy, but Keeley Mackley is beautiful. Her hair is blonde, *really* blonde, not dyed that way, and there are traces of curls at the ends of her hair, as if it had been curly, once, some time before. Her skin is very white and she has high cheekbones. I can imagine resting a pen on one of them and her smile keeping it up. She is wearing a faded navy hoodie that is just a bit too short in the arms for her, with a crest over her heart that says something in Latin.

'Ah, Seaview High,' I say, settling myself in my seat opposite her.

She blinks, then looks down at the hoodie as though she has just noticed it for the first time.

'You two are doing your A-levels now, is that right?'

Keeley stares at me, her lips slightly parted.

'We aren't on record,' I say quickly. 'This isn't part of the interview. I'm waiting on my colleague and then we'll get started. I'm just … making small talk. Sorry, I'm a rambling old man.'

I try to smile at her but her gaze is unsettling, her irises a perfect, pale sky blue and glittering. Her beauty is childish, like she is a doll.

'I already answered questions from another detective,' Keeley says. Her voice is hard and deep. She has said 'anor' instead of 'another', as if she cannot be bothered. The effect of this, in contrast with her well-cried, striking eyes, is disconcerting.

'Yes, I know.' I clear my throat and shuffle a few pages of notes in front of me, so I can look away from her. 'I'm sure that must have been hard for you. I'm so sorry for your loss.'

'Have you spoken to Jude?'

'Yes. We're finished with her for today.'

'What did she say?'

'I can't really tell you that. I need to hear what happened from your point of view.'

There is silence and we stare at one another for a few moments before she looks down at her school hoodie again.

'I'm not doing my A-levels,' she tells me. 'I was, but not now. I don't go to school any more.'

'Oh?' I am genuinely surprised. It strikes me that neither Jude nor Linda actually told us anything different. I have been sucked into an assumption. 'What do you do now, then?'

'Doing drama at college. Part-time. And I'm a barmaid in the Clandy Hotel.'

'They do an excellent steak and kidney pie there.'

Silence.

'How come you gave up school?'

Keeley raises her eyes to mine. 'I got excluded before I could finish lower sixth. I broke another girl's jaw.'

'Ah.' I decide to stop talking about that, then, in case she says anything important that she won't repeat for the record. I let my eyes fall to her hands: it is easier than looking into her eyes. Her nails are painted black, too. She has picked the polish from each alternate nail.

Keeley lets me hear her sigh. 'Do you know when I can go home?'

'Shouldn't be much longer,' I say. 'Though I doubt you'll be going home to Wits End tonight. Our teams are still there.'

She doesn't react.

'You can stay with a friend. Or a family member, if you have one.'

Keeley picks at the school logo on her hoodie, absent-mindedly.

I am saved from having to make further conversation by the arrival of Jess. She closes the door quietly and takes a seat next to me.

'Sorry to keep you waiting, Miss Mackley, Detective Inspector.'

'You're fine, Sergeant Curran. For the benefit of the tape, Detective Inspector Chris Rice and –'

‘Sir,’ Jess says. She puts a hand on my arm, so lightly I barely feel it. ‘Sir, you haven’t pressed the red button. It isn’t recording yet.’

I glance at the tape recorder, an arm’s length away, and then at Keeley who is narrowing her eyes at me, and I wonder how this nineteen-year-old, this blonde and brittle little doll, has almost made me forget why we are here.

Jude

1st January 2020, late afternoon

'Thanks again for your time, Jude. And yours, Mrs Jameson. You're sure about what you were wearing last night, Jude? The … *lilac* dress, with the short sleeves? OK. I'm sure I don't have to tell you that this is a very serious investigation, so we would ask you to be somewhere you are easily contactable. We'll likely need to speak to you again. Another thing, and I know this is more difficult … I have to ask you not to talk about the case. Not with anyone. Especially not with anyone from the media.'

Jess Curran is looking at Mum when she says this, and I see the latter blush faintly under the sergeant's stare. She is probably already drafting her anonymous letter of complaint to the *Telegraph*, 'THE PSNI QUESTIONED MY PERFECT DAUGHTER ABOUT DRUGS'. Mum never sees the irony of the things she says and does.

Curran leads us through the corridors, back downstairs. Free to leave. Rice isn't with us, he said he had a few more interviews to conduct and would be in contact with me soon. He gave me his card and told me to call him if I thought of anything else, *anything at all*, that might help them. He looked me in the eye quite seriously as he said this.

A man with plastic gloves and a harsh shaving rash takes a mouth swab from me and helps me leave my fingerprints. 'Most stations don't use ink any more,' he informs me as I wipe my hands on a proffered cloth. 'S'all electronic now, but we're a bit old fashioned here. Can't afford the new tech as soon as some of the other stations. Still, it's more fun this way.'

'For elimination purposes,' Curran keeps insisting to Mum, who seems ready to faint at the thought. 'Jude spends a lot of time in that house, we need to make sure we have her DNA on file so we don't get distracted looking for our murderer.'

Mum is more interested in arguing with the sergeant than anything else, which makes me wish Dad was my appropriate adult instead.

'Where's Keeley?' I ask, as Curran swipes her security badge on the sensor to let us out.

She holds open the door for us, and we are back at the reception area we first entered, with plastic chairs and a vending machine and a grey-haired, beaky-looking lady behind a desk.

'Still being interviewed,' Curran says. 'Might be a while yet.'

'I'll just wait here for her, then,' I say. I move to a chair and sit down, more forcefully than I intend. It squeaks on the vinyl floor.

'We can have someone bring her home if forensics are finished before she is,' Curran says.

'I'd rather wait.' I stare at her, begging her to argue with me, begging her to give me an excuse to shout or scream, but she just shrugs.

'Suit yourself. Thanks again for your time. And remember, no talking about the case. OK?'

Neither of us answers.

She turns and catches the door before it swings shut. She is gone in a flick of dark hair and the click of an impatient tongue, though I am not sure if it is mine or hers.

I fold my arms and look at the floor. My eyes are sore, my throat is burning and my stomach, my whole body, feels empty. The harsh lights of the reception are making my head ache.

'Darling,' Mum says, coming over to sit next to me. She puts a hand on my shoulder. 'Why don't we go on home? It's been such a long day. You heard what the lady said, Keeley will be a while. She's a big girl, she can get home herself. We'll go home and get something to eat and a good night's sleep.'

Mum has a special voice that she uses when she talks to or about Keeley. Like Keeley is a cute chihuahua that everyone has been indulging, but who keeps chewing the sofa and simply has to go.

'You go,' I say. 'I'm staying to wait for her.'

Mum looks around, nose wrinkled. There is some half-assed silver tinsel draped miserably over a noticeboard in front of us, and a tiny Christmas tree on the receptionist's desk, the lights blinking sporadically.

I want to throw something at the receptionist's radio to make the Christmas music stop.

'But Jude,' Mum says, unable to keep the whine from her voice. 'I'm hungry.'

'Go the fuck home, then! I don't want you to wait for me. Please, just go the fuck home!'

She blinks. It occurs to me that this has been a day of dawning for Linda Jameson. I hope she won't have a heart attack, though at least it would shut her up for a bit. I flinch as soon as I think this and shake my head, dispelling my destructive thoughts.

'Sorry,' I mumble. 'But you might as well go home, I'm not leaving without her.'

Her cheeks are pink but she doesn't seem to be in the mood to scold me. 'Then I'm staying too,' she says. She settles back in her chair, shifting as if it is possible to get comfortable.

'Joshua Mackley. There's messages on my phone, a detective wants to see me. Can't remember the name. I think my sister is here, can you check? Keeley Mackley. Mackley has an "e" in it.'

'Mack?'

He turns from the reception desk. He has his beanie hat in his hand, and I wonder if he has taken it off to put an emphasis on his fluffy hair. I remember Keeley and me being so specific about our ages and it seems like a lifetime ago.

Mack comes running towards me, mouth open. Apart from the beanie, he has not dressed for the freezing day. He wears his three-quarter-length shorts and a black band T-shirt, socks pulled halfway up his calves, his trainer laces in need of proper tying. The exact same things he was wearing last time I saw him. When he gets close enough, I can see where his lip ring usually pierces his skin. He has removed it for the first time in my memory.

Behind me, I hear Mum standing up, stretching. I have no idea how long we have been sitting here. A few hours, I think.

'Jude,' says Mack. His voice is hoarse, breaking. 'What the hell is going on? I've a load of messages on my phone … Where's Keeley? What happened?'

'They're still interviewing Keeley.' I say. 'He's dead.'

His mouth closes and his whole face seems to straighten. He stands up taller, as if to hear me better.

'Who?' He glances towards Mum as he says this.

'Pete.'

Mack and Keeley are both slim, and they have the exact same chin. It sounds like such a stupid, random similarity, but there is no mistaking that they are family if you look only at their chins. They're both pretty, though Keeley's prettiness is more obvious, and they have some frighteningly similar expressions when they're pissed off or confused.

Looking at him is like looking at Keeley if she went mad and cut most of her hair off.

'Pete … he's *dead*? Why are they interviewing Keeley? Did he overdose?'

I shake my head, I do not trust myself to talk about it here. 'Where'd you go?' I ask.

He runs a hand through his hair and shakes his head. 'We went back to Naomi's … after the party fizzed out. Then we went out this morning. I don't know … Fucking *dead*?'

'Jude,' Mum says. 'Now that Joshua is here, we can go. Joshua will take care of Keeley, won't you?'

She is doing the voice, like Mack is six.

'Yeah.' He sounds like he has no idea what he is agreeing to. 'The police want to talk to me, apparently, but I won't leave without her.' He looks me in the eye and repeats himself. 'I won't leave without Keeley.'

It is the first thing he has said that I have fully believed.

Without saying anything, I begin to move towards the door. I hear Mum picking up her jacket and hurrying after me.

—

Dad has seen the taxi pull up and is waiting on the top step of the veranda, his big hands clasped. He has dressed since I last saw him: he wears his Ulster rugby top, dark jeans and slippers. His grey beard and half-moon glasses, that usually make him look like the professor he is, render him old and ridiculous in the sensor light.

'Hi, love,' he says. He unclasps his hands for just long enough to hug me quickly, barely making contact with my body. He pulls away to look at me. 'How'd it go?'

'OK,' I say. 'Going to bed.'

'Of course, of course.' Dad straightens up and pats my shoulder. 'I put salmon in the oven for you, do you want me to bring it up?'

My stomach lurches. 'No. Thanks, Dad. But, no.'

'OK. I'll come up and say goodnight soon, then.'

'No, don't.'

I move away from him and go inside. The house hushes as soon as the door is closed, like all of Mum's angel ornaments in the hall have been talking about me. I imagine them craning their necks to take a look. The television in the big living room is on, a comedy quiz show with the volume low, and Dad has recently flicked the button on Mum's coffee machine. I can hear it slopping fresh coffee into a mug from here. The white floor tiles seem to shine in the soft light from the lamp on the hall table, reflecting only that they are spotless. My skin still crawls, somehow.

The clear glass box in the corner that is Mason's lift is on the first floor. He must be in bed.

I hear Mum and Dad murmuring to one another outside and do not care what they are saying.

I pull myself up the staircase, through the landing and past Mason's room. I hear shooting noises from his Nintendo, but do not stop to speak to him. Instead, I go up the second staircase to my own bedroom.

Once inside, I lie down on my bed, my face buried in the pillow, my stomach against the sheets. I lie still for as long as I can, counting beats until the pillow gets too hot with my breath. Then I turn over and lie on my back.

I pull my phone from my back pocket and hold it above me, squinting at the sudden harsh light of the screen in the dark. I type out a message to Keeley.

Text me when you're done Xxx

I don't care what the detective said. How can we *not* talk about the case? What else are we supposed to talk about?

On sudden impulse I leap off the bed and go to my window. From here, I can see right down the hill and practically into the Mackleys' kitchen on a clear day. As it is, my breath fogs against the window and I have to squint to see any further than our driveway. There is definitely at least one police car still parked at the back of number 166. I think I can see police tape around the house but I can't be sure I haven't made that up. It feels wrong that there are people in their house without them there.

I step back from the window and look towards my bed.

Where will Keeley sleep tonight? Will she know to come here?

Pete is dead.

I haven't slept in such a long time.

I pull off Keeley's coat, my jumper, a pair of jeans I can't remember either of us buying and climb into bed.

For the first time in a long time, I am asleep in moments.

Detective Inspector Chris Rice

1st January 2020, evening

I push the heels of my hands into my eyes and try to clear my swimming head. I feel like I have been here for days.

Keeley is a lot more responsive than Jude, her answers more detailed and less considered.

'Whose idea was it to have a New Year's Eve party?' I ask.

Keeley shrugs. 'We were always going to have one. We haven't had many this year, with one thing and another –'

'What does that mean?' Jess asks.

Another shrug. 'Mack's been skint. He forked out for a load of recording equipment a while back, and nobody's bothered paying him back yet. Me and Pete weren't too bothered about the parties; we were happy having a drink together just the two of us. Jude hasn't been interested either; this was the first party I'd coaxed her into for over a year. A-levels and shit. And the others are getting a bit old for it, if you ask me.'

'Why was last night's party at your house?' I ask.

'Everyone else still lives with their parents or they have tiny, shit flats even smaller than our house. It wasn't necessarily my decision or Mack's to have the party. It just happened.'

'And you invited everyone to this party?'

'I told Jude and Pete, and Mack invited everyone else.'

'And you all get along? The twelve of you.'

'Mm.'

'For the record.'

'Yes.'

'Whose idea was it to take drugs at this party?'

A pause. A flicker of a smile.

'You all take drugs regularly?'

'No. I don't, Jude doesn't. You want to hear her mum about it.' Keeley's voice changes and she sounds exactly like Linda Jameson. '"*Drugs are for the homeless or the terminally ill.*"'

The impression is so good that even Jess flicks a smile.

'One of the Devlins is asthmatic and eczemic and gluten-free and fuck knows what else,' Keeley continues in her real voice. 'So he doesn't do drugs very often either. I forget which brother.'

'But you do drugs sometimes?'

'Sometimes. Not loads – if I am going to have one I'll cut it in half and share it with somebody. I think I did that last night. Look, are you questioning me about drugs or about the murder of my boyfriend?'

'It's all relevant, Miss Mackley,' says Jess in a bored tone of voice. I know she does not like Keeley as much as I do. 'OK, so you organised this party, everyone showed up with the intention of taking drugs. What time did people start arriving?'

'About half seven. Brains got there first.'

'Brains?'

'Sorry, Brian Reed.'

'Did you let him in?'

'I think Jude answered the door.'

'Oh, so Jude arrived first?'

'Well, she was there most of the day, anyway.'

'What had you been doing all day?'

Keeley looks uncertain for the first time. 'Just … doing stuff. We watched something on my phone, listened to music. Talked a lot. Nipped to Tesco. Got dressed, did make-up … I curled her hair. Took me ages. Had a few drinks.'

'What did you drink?'

'I had vodka and lemonade and lime. She had a few Kopparbergs. Or maybe only one, I can't remember.'

'Then Brains arrived. Who next?'

'Naomi Ross. That's my brother's girlfriend.'

'And he was in the house with you and Jude?'

'He was about somewhere.'

'Jude let her in, too?'

'Nah, we just heard Mack opening the door to her. She has a distinctive, foreign voice.'

'Is that right?'

'Yeah, she's from Ballymena.'

I snort. Jess looks at me.

'Then who?'

Keeley thought for a moment. 'Naomi brought her friend Carrie with her and we went out the back for a smoke with them.'

'We?'

'Me and Jude.'

'Then who arrived?'

'I'm not sure. When we got back inside, Pete, Ian and Roy were all there.'

'Pete, your boyfriend?'

'Yes.'

'What sort of mood was he in?'

'The mood to get drunk.'

'How long did you say you'd been together?'

'A year.'

'Happy relationship?'

'Yes. I told you.'

'Just double-checking. How did Jude like him?'

Keeley shrugged. 'She liked him OK. They never really spoke much.'

'But she would have spent a lot of time with him. With both of you.'

'Suppose.'

'And your brother, Joshua, how did he like Pete?'

'I met Pete through him. Pete does – he did – music videos and stuff. Mack is in a band. I got to know him through Mack.'

'He any good?'

'Pete or Mack?'

'Both.'

Keeley lets a little air out through her nose. 'Mack is a brilliant musician. It's not my sort of music, but I know he's good. Pete knew what he was about when it came to film. He had a good eye, his stuff looked good. I was interested in him because I wanted to be in one of his films … At the start, this is.'

'Not after?'

'Well, it stopped being a professional relationship quite early on and I just … forgot.'

'You forgot you wanted to be an actress?'

'I didn't say I wanted to be an actress.'

'Oh, but you are studying drama part-time at college, you said?'

'I am.'

'But you don't want to be an actress?'

'I didn't say that, either.'

'Miss Mackley,' Jess says loudly. 'This is a murder investigation. A man was stabbed to death in your house last night and at this particular moment in time, we don't have any suspects outside you and your mates, so it's in your best interests to –'

'I haven't decided yet,' Keeley says, staring Jess dead in the eye. 'I haven't … haven't told anyone what I think I want to do. Drama I like, keeps me distracted.'

'What do you think you want to do?' I ask, at the exact same time that Jess says, 'So you met Pete through Mack?'

Keeley glances at me but answers Jess, 'That's what I said.'

'When was this?'

Keeley looks at a spot behind Jess's head.

'Last autumn – or a year ago, I mean.'

'Can you be more specific?'

' … We started texting at the start of August. Maybe by … the start of September, we were seeing each other.'

Jess and I glance at each other.

'Was he injured when you first met him?' Jess asks.

'Injured?'

'Did he have any injuries when you first met him in autumn 2018?'

Her eyebrows narrowed, Keeley says, 'What the hell are you talking about?'

'We're talking about the attack.' Jess opens the folder in front of her and pulls out the photograph of Denny's injured face. She turns it around and sets it on the table in front of Keeley. 'These injuries that your brother inflicted on Peter Denny in July 2018 –'

'For the benefit of the tape,' I interrupt. 'DS Curran is showing Miss Mackley item B, a photograph of Peter Denny from file 66OL of 12 July 2018. Miss Mackley, are you aware that your brother Joshua fought with Peter Denny outside a bar in Oldry on this date?'

Keeley stares at the photograph, eyes wide.

'Are you aware that Mr Denny sustained serious injuries to his windpipe? He suffered three broken ribs and some serious bruising to his face, as well. What do you know of the incident to which I am referring?'

'No.' Keeley's voice is no more than a whisper. Still she stares at the photograph.

'For the tape, Miss Mackley.' Jess sounds bored.

'No,' Keeley says firmly. 'I have no idea what you're … Mack and Pete are friends. They *were* friends. July 2018, you said? They were definitely friends then.'

Before we can say anything more, there is a knock at the door. Dunwoody pokes his small head through and says, 'Sir?'

Jess speaks to the tape and jabs the pause button as I stand up. I stretch and follow Dunwoody outside.

'What's up, Charlie?' I am privately thinking that his interruption better be worthwhile.

'It's Joshua Mackley, Sir. He's come in to talk to you. Says he got our messages and he's happy to talk.'

'Excellent. We're just about done with the girl, here. Get him comfortable in an interview room, will you? Don't let anybody speak to him until I'm there – understood?'

Jess and Keeley both look up at me when I return. Jess speaks to the tape and I sit back down.

'Your brother has decided to show up,' I say.

'Is he OK?' Keeley asks quickly.

'Why wouldn't he be OK?'

She does not respond.

'To be clear, Miss Mackley, you're claiming you have no idea why your brother would have wanted to hurt Peter Denny so badly two summers ago?'

'I have no idea. I think … I think you must be wrong.'

'What did you argue about last night?'

Keeley twists her face into an expression of confusion. 'Who?'

'You and Pete. Why did you argue?'

'We didn't.'

'We have proof that you did.'

'Well, if you have proof, you know more than me. I can't remember much after ten o'clock. Can't remember the New Year's countdown. Don't remember any arguments.'

I don't have to look at Jess to know we're going to leave this one, to keep Keeley feeling in control.

For now.

After a minute, Jess says, 'One more thing … What were you wearing last night?'

'A dress,' Keeley says.

'Can you describe it for us? We're going to want to get it from the house and examine it.'

For a moment I think she is going to refuse to respond. Then she says, all in a rush, 'It's from New Look. Dark green, long sleeves, short. It'll be in the washing basket.'

'Thank you.'

Jess continues to write and does not look up again.

'Take my card,' I say, handing it to her across the table. Her fingers are icy when they graze my own. 'Give me a call any time, night or day, if you think of anything that might be important. If you can think of anyone who might have wanted to hurt Pete. If you remember about the argument or about the fight your brother had with him. Call me. And be somewhere we can contact you. We'll be a bit longer in Wits End, can you … ?'

Keeley nods. 'I'll find somewhere. Thanks.'

She stands up and pulls her hoodie on, her fingers fumbling with the zip.

I press the button on the tape and it beeps, turning off.

Jess stands and leaves, her head in her notebook all the while.

'Keeley,' I say quietly. The sound of my voice surprises us both. She looks up, one hand in the process of pulling her hood out from where it has become stuck down her back.

I look at her for a moment before saying, 'Why did you break a girl's jaw in school?'

She visibly relaxes and pulls out her hood. 'She was bullying Jude,' she says. Though she is trying to smile, there is a shake in her voice. 'Making her miserable. I would have broken more than Beth McKenna's jaw if a teacher hadn't stopped me.'

I stay in the room, staring at the spot where her face had been, for a few minutes after she has gone, wondering why I waited until the tape was turned off before I asked her that question.

Keeley

1st January 2020, evening

Why did you break a girl's jaw in school?

What do you think you want to do?

Why was it that the two questions that were most difficult to answer hadn't related to Pete at all?

I take the offered police car back to Vetobridge. When the young, ginger-haired constable asks me where exactly he's going, I give him Naomi's address without thinking.

Why did you break a girl's jaw in school?

Because she deserved it, I think. Because she really and truly deserved *pain*. I feel tears of fierce fury prick in my eyes, thinking this. She deserved the broken jaw. She deserved more than that.

The lights are on in the living room of Naomi's ground-floor flat, and I see her shadow pop up from the sofa and rush to the door.

Though she tries to hide it, I can tell she is disappointed that I am not Mack. I mumble a quick thanks to the constable and slam the car door shut. He drives off.

Naomi and I stare at one another. She looks a mess. Her normally slick, shiny black hair hasn't been combed and her skin looks greyer than I've ever seen it.

I wonder how I look to her, my breath fogging between us in the dark.

I take a few hesitant steps forward, realising only then how unprepared I am. I don't have my toothbrush. My pill is in my bedside table. Naomi has a different phone to me; I won't be able to charge mine. All these tiny, boring details that make up your day but that are so easy to focus on. So reassuringly domestic and mundane.

'I should have told them to take me home,' I say, about to follow it up with '*to get some stuff*', but Naomi cuts me off.

'No, you're fine,' she says. 'Come in. Have you seen him?'

I shake my head and follow her inside.

She has the heating on. She is the only one of Mack's friends who ever remembers to top up her gas, and I am so grateful to step into her tiny, warm living room, full of second-hand furniture that is clean and an atmosphere that screams the place is *lived in*.

'He's dead,' she says softly.

'Yes,' I say.

I sit on her saggy sofa and wonder if I am about to cry. Nothing comes.

Naomi is watching me from the doorway, her arms folded, chewing her lip.

'What are we going to do about the drugs?' she whispers finally. 'I don't want to lose my job.' When I don't respond, she adds, 'Mack was so scared this morning. He knew the police would be coming, he was so afraid … not himself at all. What about Jude, what has she said?'

He knew the police would be coming.

Why did you break a girl's jaw in school?

Suddenly, I wish I hadn't come. I wish I'd gone back to the house for my bank card and got a room at the Clandy. Is it too late to call the police escort back? I don't want to be here in this stiflingly hot living room, listening to Naomi bang on about drugs.

'Can I have a shower?' I ask.

She stares at me. 'Did you hear what I said? The drugs?'

'I know. I can't think now. Can I have a shower?' My words come out more sharply than I mean them to, but I achieve the desired result.

Naomi tuts and leaves the room.

The water is hot too. Nearly too hot. Steam gathers quickly, almost immediately covering up the mirror so I can't see myself any more. I am grateful.

I stand under the shower, my hair getting heavy, my shoulders nearly burning.

Absurdly, I want to talk to my mum. I can't remember ever wanting to talk to my mum before, even when she was alive, but I feel it now. A few tears squeeze out of my eyes and mingle with the hot water. I know they can't really be for Mum, but I'd rather tell myself I'm crying for her than crying for the rest of us who are still alive.

A few weeks before Jude's thirteenth birthday, Mum took an overdose of painkillers mixed with three bottles of wine. She didn't die, not then. But she had to get her stomach pumped, and it is always this sequence of events I imagine when I think about the fact that she is dead.

It was us who found her.

It was a Monday, the last one before Christmas, so Roddy wasn't at work. He had picked the three of us up from school and let us play his 80s and 90s cheesy pop music as loudly as we liked, all the way to McDonald's where he ordered milkshakes for us. Then he took us to see Mack, who was working at Murphy's Arcade and let Mason on the dodgems for free. The whole arcade was completely dead, as it was for the entirety of the winter, with the exception of the two dozen or so bodies who prop up the stools next to the fruit machines rain or shine, all year round.

I remember the smell of damp carpet and old pennies that made us crinkle our noses.

I remember the drive home, Mason being in such a good mood that he joined in with our singing, and Roddy adding his exaggerated baritone until we were all doubled over with giggles. I remember twisting myself around to look at Jude from my front seat. Her eyes were streaming with helpless tears of exhausted giggles, and she had a tiny red spot on her chin. I clung to that image for a long time afterward. *This* was my life, I thought. This was everything.

We told Roddy we both had to be dropped off at number 166 because Jude had left her watercolours at my house. It was completely true, but I could have brought them over the next morning when we went to school. We wanted just one more conversation, just one last hug, just five more minutes. We always did. Roddy had offered Mack a lift home, as his shift had ended, but since Mack had his bike and there really wasn't any room for it in the car with Mason's wheelchair, he said he'd just cycle back. It only took an extra ten minutes.

'It's pitch black already,' Roddy called from the window of the car. 'Don't be long.'

We both held up a hand without looking back as we raced through the front door.

'Do you want a Creme Egg?' I said, dashing into the kitchen.

I felt behind an ancient, dirty measuring jug in the cupboard above the sink and pulled out a single red and blue egg.

'Where did you get that?' Jude's eyes were wide. 'It isn't even Easter.'

'Mack has his sources,' I said, trying for mysterious. I was pretty sure he'd just been cleaning out the vending machines in the arcade and had taken home anything that had reached, or was about to reach, its expiry. He was very *conscientious* when it came to business.

We shared the chocolate, taking it in turns to take awkward bites from the top, sucking out a little of the sugary syrup from the middle.

She had a tiny smear of chocolate on the side of her mouth that I wanted to dab off.

The tiny chocolate smear and the tiny spot on the chin.

'Where's your mum?' Jude asked, looking around. I knew she wasn't asking because she wanted to see her: Jude was afraid of my mum. She pretended not to be and was perfectly polite to her when she was around, but she didn't seem to breathe until we had moved out of earshot, until she couldn't see the grease stains on Mum's T-shirts and couldn't hear the rasp in her voice, disclosing her fourteen years of chain-smoking.

'Probably in bed,' I said. 'She's been in bed a lot recently.'

'Is she very tired?'

'Something like that.'

'You should go and check on her … should you?'

'Probably.'

'Probably,' Jude agreed.

We sat for another few minutes, until the Creme Egg was finished. Then I stood from where we had flung ourselves on the kitchen floor and stretched.

I found her in the bathroom.

Her face was white and yellow, and there was sick on the floor beside her and all down her cheek. It reminded me, repulsively, of what we had just eaten, and I felt my stomach churn.

She was lying on her side, her head up near the toilet and her feet almost touching the door. I had let the door smack off her legs when I had first pushed it open, and I held it now so it didn't swing into her again. Her T-shirt had ridden up to expose her stomach, which in the last twelve months had shrunk and shrunk until I thought she might cave in on herself. Her skin just about stretched over her ribs. I worried that, if she lifted her arms up, it would tear and expose her bright red organs.

She wouldn't be lifting her arms up anytime soon.

I looked at her for a few seconds and then called softly, 'Jude?'

The house was so quiet that I heard her stand up in the kitchen. I heard every footstep as she padded up the stairs in her school shoes. Black patent Clarks, the exact same as mine.

Then the chocolate smear and the tiny spot were in front of me.

She looked at my face, then into the bathroom. Like me, she didn't react.

That ninety seconds where the two of us stood in the doorway of the bathroom, staring at my possibly dead mother, was probably the longest of my life. It's the image I see in my peripheral vision at the very ends of my nightmares, in that split second before I open my eyes, even now.

The door opened. No key turned in the lock; we never locked the doors then.

For one wild moment I thought it would be the police. Then I heard Mack's distinct whistle coming up the stairs, and I felt relief surge through both of us.

'What are you doing?' He sounded bemused. He came up behind us and peered over Jude's head to see into the bathroom.

He swore and quickly pulled Jude back to get inside. 'How long did they say they'd be?'

'Who?' I asked.

Mack was on his knees on the floor next to Mum. He pulled her head up and put it in his lap.

'The ambulance. How long?'

I felt, rather than heard, Jude's intake of breath. *That* was what we were supposed to do.

'Keeley!' Mack looked at me imploringly, his eyes wild.

'I didn't …'

Jude spoke then, 'We didn't call an ambulance.'

'Fucking call one now, then! What the hell are you playing at?'

When I didn't move, Jude reached over and pulled my phone from my blazer pocket. An old, reliable Nokia phone that Mack had bought for me with his first pay when I was six. She put it in my hand and squeezed my fingers. When I didn't immediately flip the phone to my ear, she took it back and made the call herself. When she stuttered over the address, Mack held his hand out and clicked his fingers impatiently until she gave the phone to him.

The paramedics were there within eight minutes and Mum was in the back of an ambulance and taken away after another six.

Roddy came over to see what the commotion was and took Jude home, eyes wide.

Mack stared at me, baffled, the rest of the day, and didn't speak to me until Mum was back home again. It took another three years for her to really die, but I don't remember her ever seeming alive after that.

When I get out of the shower, I remember to turn my phone back on. There is one text from Jude.

Text me when you're done Xxx

Have I ever ignored a text from Jude? I don't think so. But I cannot think of a single thing to say to her. I don't want to see her, or speak to her, or hear from her. I want to fast forward by a month until all of this is over, no matter how it ends, and just pick up life from there. We cannot do this together. This grief is all my own.

I've never had anything that is entirely my own before.

But if I don't speak to Jude, then who? There is no one else. There never has been.

I open her text again.

I hover over the call button, then lock the phone without replying.

Detective Inspector Chris Rice

1st January 2020, evening

Keeley and Joshua Mackley have the same chin. That is where the similarities end.

Joshua Mackley squirms and scratches at his cheeks every few seconds. I don't think he knows he is doing it. He looks as though he is getting ready to shake his head in case someone barks an accusation at him.

He has the face and hair of a twelve-year-old, but the deep bags under his eyes belong to someone much older. Unlike Keeley's, Joshua's eyes are brown and round as a vinyl.

'Thank you for coming in, Mr Mackley,' I say.

'Mack!' He blurts it out and then puts a hand over his mouth, shaking his head. 'Sorry, I just mean you can call me Mack. If you want to.'

I glance at Jess and know what she is thinking. That we should have checked to make sure he is fit for interview.

I do not want to lose him yet, so I say quickly, 'Your friend Peter Denny was found in your garage this morning, murdered.'

Slight shake of the head. Scratch. Then his fingers, the tips of which look hard, even from here, tap a rhythm on the table in front of him.

'You don't seem very surprised,' Jess remarks.

'Jude just told me.' His voice is light, no trace of a tremble, as if he might burst into song. 'I saw her at reception. Can I see Keeley?'

'Soon,' I say. 'Where have you been all day, Mack? You haven't been answering your phone.'

'I was around. I went for a drive with my girlfriend. Beach. Through town. Went for a walk. Then I went for a pint at the Clandy. There's racing on today.'

'But you didn't answer your phone?'

'It died. Someone in the Clandy told me there had been ambulance in Wits End this morning, so I borrowed a charger off the barman so I could ring Keeley. Then I got your messages.'

Mack's cheeks are soft and fluffy with downy hairs, like two ripe peaches, but he scratches them as though his life depends on it.

'Are you and Pete close?' I ask.

Mack blinks. 'You mean *were* we close. You've just told me he's dead.'

'Jude told you he was dead, we just reiterated it. Were you close?'

'Sort of.'

'Is he in your band? What is it called again … ?' I pretend to flip back a few pages in my notebook. The book is full of notes from my last case and completely unrelated. I stop at a random page. 'Ah. Premorbid.'

'No. Pete isn't in the band,' says Mack. 'He doesn't play anything. He listens to us rehearse, sometimes, and he takes all the pictures and some videos. He does the social media stuff. Whatever. Not my scene.'

'Who is in this band?'

'I write the music and play guitar. Naomi sings and helps me with lyrics sometimes. Roy is on drums. Kyle kind of fucks about on keyboards, but he can do all sorts of percussion things. Paddy plays bass.'

'Your mate Brian Reed didn't get invited to play? He's your best mate, by all accounts. Was he too busy manufacturing these Sixes you're all taking?'

'Brains couldn't handle a triangle. He's a dope.'

I'm not sure if he is ignoring the last question or if in his own warped head, he hasn't heard me. I snort. 'You make your money playing gigs?'

'A bit.'

'If it's only a bit, why bother?'

'Nothing else to do, is there? Do you know when I can see my sister? I don't want her to think I had anything to do with this.'

'Were you happy that your little sister was in a relationship with someone nine years older than her?' I ask.

He takes the bait. 'I didn't mind. Not one bit. He was my … mate. She isn't stupid. We're good at judging character, she and I.'

'Really?' Jess has an eyebrow raised. 'If you're such a good judge of character, why did you beat your *mate* half to death two summers ago?'

Mack shakes his head and looks from one of us to the other.

'No idea what you're …' His fingers tap on the table again. 'Can I get a lawyer now?'

'Of course you can have a solicitor,' says Jess. 'We did offer.'

'Why did you hate Pete so much?' I ask. 'What did he do? We had your sister in floods of tears when we were questioning her today, and you won't even –'

Mack stands abruptly. 'Shut the fuck up about my sister. Let me see her. Let me see Keeley. Keeley?'

He makes for the door and tries to wrench it open. When it does not budge, he slams both his fists into it.

'Where is she? Keeley! Keeley? Let me out.'

Jess has pressed the panic button and she sits back in her chair, watching Mack, looking curious but completely unexcited.

I stand and use my most calming voice. 'Just talk to us, Mack. Did you row with Pete last night? We'll get you a solicitor down here and you can talk to us sensibly. Are you involved in manufacturing the drugs that Peter Denny has been selling? We don't *have* to arrest Keeley if you'll just talk to us. What happened last night?'

'No, no, no!' Mack puts both his hands up to his head and squeezes his eyes so tightly that his whole face seems to shrivel up. 'You can't arrest … Not Keeley. Not Keeley.'

He is crying now. This gets a tiny sigh of pity from Jess.

'Fuck off, all of you! Just fuck off. Leave us alone!'

The change in him is considerable. He is pulling at his lip, where I think a lip ring usually perches, and his boyish face is bright red and very afraid.

The door is opened from the outside. Mack has been grabbed by the arms by two uniformed officers in seconds.

'Keeley isn't here,' I say, not looking at him. 'She left after her interview. She's gone.'

Jess stops the tape and turns to me. 'Looks like I'll be owing you a pint.'

Mack

1st January 2020, evening

I try not to look surprised that they let me leave.

Be where we can contact you, keep that phone on. No funny business. This is very serious. Stay away from your house. You'll need to come in for a psychiatric assessment and we can't get one organised tonight. We'll be in contact. Blah blah blah.

I start the walk from the station, hands buried in my pockets. I haven't cried in front of anyone since I was a child, and my cheeks start to grow hot thinking about it. My face is too cold from the wind.

I pull my phone out without breaking stride, hovering first over Naomi's number and then Keeley's. I call her.

'Hey,' she says after half a ring. 'Where are you? Are you finished?'

'Yeah.' I take an almighty sniff, the cold air through my nostrils making my head pound. 'Where did you go?'

'Naomi's.'

'Right. Coming now.' I should say something, surely. Pete is dead and she loved him, so I should say something. 'I'm scared,' I say in a choke. It's not what I meant to say at all.

'We can't talk about it' is all she says before she hangs up.

She loved him. She is missing him.

I should have said something. She loved him like I love Naomi.

She loved him.

Back when she turned eighteen, Keeley didn't let the Pete thing go. He *had* to come to her birthday, she said.

Jude arrived about midday, her arms full of presents, beaming. She was as enchanted by the Cortina as Keeley, when Paddy and Kyle finally dropped it off. The CD player sat awkwardly balanced above the handbrake but, overall, the car looked good. The leather had come up well, and the magenta paint shone. Since none of us could legally drive the car, the girls went upstairs shortly after that, and I went back to my chair in the living room to write down some lyrics I had been playing with in my head all week.

I heard the two of them laughing in Keeley's bedroom all afternoon. The snatches of conversation I overheard made no sense whatsoever to me, like they were still speaking in the language they had made up when they were kids.

Keeley came downstairs to make them both sandwiches about three o'clock, while I was playing my new song. She leaned over the back of my armchair and put her arms around my neck on her way back upstairs.

'Did you invite him?' she asked. I didn't have to ask her who she meant.

'I told him the address and mentioned there was a party, but I didn't press the phone to my ear in trembling anticipation and wait for him to swear on his life.'

'You told me he loves free booze and drugs,' said Keeley. 'He'll be here.'

She picked up the plate of sandwiches and held them to one side so she could lean forward again and kiss my cheek.

'Thanks again for the car,' she said. 'Did you see the charm bracelet Jude got for me?' She pushed her wrist in front of my face and I let my guitar slide off my knee and lean against my leg. She jingled a few silvery charms before my eyes, and I had to pull my head back to see them properly.

'It's our initials, our special numbers, a camera –'

'Yeah, lovely. Great.'

'What time did you tell everyone to get here?'

'About eight.'

'That's what I told people too. Oh, wait till you *see* her.' Keeley straightened up and waggled her eyebrows at me coyly. 'You will not recognise her, Mack, she looks amazing.'

She practically sprinted back up the stairs. I watched her go.

Being Keeley's older brother, I thought, was like washing dishes at someone else's house – I was so determined to be seen to be doing a good job that, when I stepped back to have a proper look, I realised the cloth was filthy. What did I give her that she wasn't able to get for herself? Nothing. She neither needed nor particularly wanted me past the age of ten. And anyway, I am not the right kind of person to look after anyone else.

When Jude stepped gingerly downstairs a few hours later, her legs shaking in a pair of Keeley's highest heels, I really *didn't* recognise her at first.

Her skin was a few shades darker than usual and I could smell Keeley's floral perfume from where I sat in the living room.

A yellow summer dress was hitched a few inches above her knees, and I had to look quickly down at my guitar. This skin was not the puppy-fatted, blue-veined skin of the child I knew. All of a sudden, it seemed, in the few hours that had passed since she had gone upstairs, she had become a slim, tanned, smooth … *woman*.

All of these changes paled in comparison with the realisation that her hair, usually poker straight, dirty fair, was now a bright, yellowy blonde and curly. Only then did I register a third scent. While the tan was overwhelming, obvious, all-consuming, and the perfume subtler, the peroxide was heavy, aggressive.

Brains, who had arrived half an hour before and had already broken a champagne flute, glanced at the stairs and said, 'Happy Birth— Oh, Jude.'

She beamed at him, finally reaching the bottom stair. The yellow of the dress complemented the new, bright hair fairly well. I could tell from where I sat that she was already tipsy. They had taken one of the champagne bottles upstairs an hour or two before.

'Very … different,' I mumbled, because Jude seemed to be looking at me to say something.

'You don't think it's too much?' Her face was suddenly anxious.

'No. Lovely.' I stood up, just for something to do. 'Do you … do you want another glass of something fizzy? Before all these reprobates show up and drink us out of house and home, yeah?'

She grinned. 'Definitely. This is the first party Mum is letting me stay over for … I don't have to sober up before I go home!'

The two of us went to the kitchen together, leaving Brains ogling at Jude from behind.

'I can't believe you gave Keeley the Cortina,' Jude said, as I poured Prosecco into a chipped mug. The only two remaining champagne flutes were upstairs in Keeley's bedroom. 'She loves it. She's always wanted a car but now she gets *the* car.'

'Honestly, I think your present went down better,' I said, and we clinked mugs. I took a long swig of mine and enjoyed the fizzing in my throat.

Jude blushed happily. 'I'm glad she liked it. Won't it make you sad though? Seeing someone else drive the Cortina … That was all you had left to remind you of Murphy.'

I smiled ruefully. 'I have a lot of things that remind me of Murphy, don't you worry about that. I have a taste for horse racing and a minor drug problem, all thanks to old Colly Murphy. I don't need anything more.'

Jude raised her mug and clinked it against mine again. 'To Colly Murphy,' she said. 'Wherever he is, I bet he's barking orders at an unsuspecting soul and charging them for the privilege.'

'To Colly Murphy,' I laughed, and we both drank.

It was mouth cancer that killed him which, given the seventy or so cigarettes he had smoked every day since he was ten, was unsurprising but no less sad or shocking because of it. He was sick for nine months exactly – 'Like being pregnant and giving birth to death,' Keeley said the day after the funeral. He woke up with a huge, painful ulcer just after Christmas and didn't make it to October. It had spread too much, it was too far gone. They told him, and then me, that there wasn't a lot they could do for him, apart from try and make him comfortable, which they didn't really. It was somehow the most painful thing that has ever happened to me – which is surprising, as I'm an orphan – and I wrote a dozen songs about it that I never played for anyone, not even Naomi or Premorbid.

I was there with him when he passed.

'Do you really miss him?' Jude asked.

I jolted back to the present through a cloud of smoke and nursing-home stench. 'Yeah. Miss him. Miss working in the arcade, if you can believe that.'

'You always used to smell like pennies when you got home.'

'That's right!'

'What are you going to do now?' Jude asked.

'What, you mean apart from selling and playing in the Thirsty Ox on a Sunday? I have no idea, Jude.'

The truth was that I thought so much. I thought and thought about everything and I knew so much about so much that nobody else ever thought about. But, hard as I tried, I could not imagine a future of any kind for myself. When I imagined next month, next summer, it was black. I just couldn't see it.

'You could go back and finish off that business course you started before you met Naomi,' Jude suggested.

I shook my head. My life had already been lived.

Jude was trying to look kindly at me, but she kept glancing at her reflection in the side of the toaster and fixing her hair, pulling at her dress. After a few minutes of this, I felt as uncomfortable as she clearly was, so I said, for something to say, 'About forty people invited tonight.'

'What about that guy Keeley wants to meet? Your friend who is a director or ... ?'

'Oh, him.' I rolled my eyes. 'Has she been pestering you about him too? He says he'll come but I don't want to get her hopes up. We've been wanting him to direct a video for Premorbid for like six months and he still hasn't got around to that.'

'Everyone seems to know who he is except me,' Jude said.

'He looks nothing like his pictures online anyway,' I said.

Jude was running her hands through her new hair. Why did they always curl it for parties? It was so much effort. 'I keep being surprised when I catch sight of it,' she explained when she saw me looking. 'It's just such a change.'

'Yeah, it's a change,' I said.

You will not recognise her, Mack.

Sometimes I still have conversations with Murphy in my head if I need to work something out. In my head, I told Murphy about what happened that night of her birthday party. He was the only soul I ever told or imagined telling. He listened with a confused expression, his mouth open, showing me the red and white patches inside, his grey tongue stroking inside his dry cheeks and his lips. When I was done, he said, 'She's your sister. You shouldn't have let that happen. You fucked up.'

In my head, I blinked at him. 'No, Keeley is my sister. Jude is her mate. Remember, the wee girl with the darker hair? She used to take cigarettes off you. Pretty.'

'You have to look after your sister,' Murphy continued, his voice hoarse from lack of use. He hadn't heard my interjection. 'She is all you have. She is your responsibility. Family is all there ever is, Mack. Look at me. If it weren't for you, I'd be rotting in a bed and no soul in this whole world would give a flying fuck if I lived or died either way.'

It was true, though I tried to roll my eyes and push the thoughts out of my head. I knew I was being ridiculous, but it was a conversation I had in my head a lot.

Murphy had never married, never had any children, and had lost his only brother a few years before I met him. He was the only person I ever knew who was more alone than me, who had experienced all of his life as an onlooker and not a participant. Things happened to Murphy like they happened to me: accidentally or unthoughtfully. We were never actively seeking life.

I am in Oldry town centre before I have considered the impossibility of walking all the way to Boar's Brae. I check my wallet. I have a tenner. We won't be playing in Pat's Bar tonight, and I feel in my gut that we probably won't be making Sixes anytime soon, or ever again, maybe. Not with the police all over us. I scratch at my face and feel the beginnings of stubble.

As stupid as it would be, all I want is a pill.

We took cocaine a lot from the age of sixteen, and loved it, but the comedowns were almost unbearable for us all. After a few years of being miserable every morning, Brains decided he was going to combine two of our existing favourite pills and see if he could do something impressive. By the time we moved the manufacturing to our living room in Wits End, after Mum died, he really had come up with a drug with basically no comedown, if it was taken by itself. It was the most impressive thing anyone I knew had ever done, made all the more impressive by the fact that Brains was probably the least intelligent person I had ever met.

They'd get him for it. Poor, dopey Brains in a jail cell. The thought was enough to make me feel sick.

I look around for a taxi rank and decide to use my last tenner to get back to Vetobridge.

Even though it would normally cost more, the driver drops me at the start of the promenade. I think he feels sorry for me. Or maybe he knows what has happened and is afraid of me – I take a quick glance at him as he drives away, to make sure I don't know him from anywhere.

With my head full of images of Jude with her blonde hair, Keeley next to her, their faces morphing together until I'm not sure who I'm thinking about, I begin the walk to Boar's Brae.

Jude

2nd January 2020, morning

When I wake, the air is different. Like when you went to sleep next to someone who is no longer there and you know it without opening your eyes. The air is sharper and colder. I know for certain that I didn't dream all night.

That means I didn't have any nightmares either.

I pull the duvet up around me and let yesterday's events begin to filter through.

Pete with his mouth open and blood on his white T-shirt.

The detective cramming biscuits into his mouth.

Mum flicking her styrofoam cup.

Pete's stomach.

Dad wringing his hands.

The taxi driving achingly slowly.

Pete's mouth open.

Keeley.

Keeley.

I open my eyes and grab at my bedside table for my phone. No calls, no texts. I sit up and dial her number. No answer.

Dad must have forgotten to set the heat on the timer; it is half nine and my radiator, when I run a finger along it, is icy.

I'm not the only person who isn't concentrating, then.

Though I am uneasy about no text from Keeley, I feel surprisingly refreshed after my full night's sleep. My stomach is still churning, but for the first time in 2020 so far, I am actually hungry. Maybe it is best that we don't communicate over the phone anyway, I think. Maybe her actions are deliberate.

I pull on my warmest jumper and a pair of thick cotton tracksuit bottoms that Mum hates.

We never use the breakfast bar in the kitchen because Mason can't sit at it with us. Which really makes me wonder why on earth Mum wanted it in the first place. He is in his wheelchair at the low table in the corner of the kitchen, a piece of toast on his plate.

'Morning,' he says, his face lifting as soon as I come in.

I move to the cupboards and busy myself pouring cereal and getting my mug.

'Dad was going to make you scrambled eggs and bring them up,' Mason informs me. 'At like seven o'clock. I told him you probably wouldn't want that.'

I smile warily. 'You were probably right.'

He is watching every move I make.

I press the button on the kettle and lean my back against the kitchen counter, waiting for the click.

'I didn't hear you up in the middle of the night,' Mason continues. 'Usually you're up from like six, doing my head in.'

'I was tired last night.'

'I'll bet.'

The kitchen is what Mum likes to call the Hub of the house. The Mackleys have the Den, we have the Hub. Mum likes to have her glass of wine sitting in the big armchair by the window in the evenings, watching over the *good* side of Wits End, and even Dad has bought into the idea of the Hub – he takes his laptop to the little table in the evenings while Mum is cooking dinner, and does a bit of work while he's catching up with her.

I pour my tea, then take my breakfast to the table.

Mason watches me munch my cereal, so I stare back at him.

When I am nearly finished, I say, 'What?'

'What happened yesterday?'

'I'm not allowed to talk about it.'

'I heard Mum and Dad talking about it this morning.'

'Well, they shouldn't have been. Where are they?'

'Mum has gone to Tesco and Dad's gone back to bed. His back is annoying him.'

I nod to show I've heard, but I'm not going to reply. Mason will tirelessly repeat anything he thinks you haven't heard. He loves the sound of his voice and he never stops for breath.

'Did you know the cops were here yesterday, asking for a copy of Dad's security camera footage from Tuesday night? Dad gave it to them. He was running around like an idiot trying to make them all coffee and flipping sandwiches. They just kept saying they wanted the tapes and nothing else.' When I don't reply, Mason adds, 'There's absolutely no way I'm going back to school next week *not* knowing what happened to Peter Denny.'

His name in my brother's voice makes me feel queasy all over again, and I push my mug away. Lukewarm tea slops over the side. If Mum were here, she would have had it mopped up before the rest of us had even noticed.

We both leave it.

'How do you know his name?'

'Hello, he's Peter *Denny*. I know he's Keeley's boyfriend, I don't walk about with my ear and eye holes closed. He was on TV last month and he has like sixty million thousand views on YouTube. Do you know what happened?'

'No.'

'Jude, tell me.' His face and eyes are bright, glinting like the shiny eyes on his Spiderman pyjamas. Both pairs of eyes stare at me, egging me on.

'I don't know. I was asleep.'

'Mum thinks it was Mack.'

'She what?'

'Thinks him and Peter Denny had a row and Mack killed him. Is it true he was stabbed?'

'I told you –'

'Yeah, yeah. But you obviously know *how* he died, you were at the police station *all day*. I heard Mum say something that definitely sounded like stabbed. Please tell me, Jude.'

'He was stabbed.'

'Aha!'

'But it wasn't Mack.'

'How do you know, if you don't know what happened?'

I glare at him. 'I just know Mack would never stab someone.'

'Was it Keeley, then?'

I stand abruptly and Mason forces his mouth closed, turning red. At some point during the conversation, he has pushed his plate of toast away from him, all the better to throw questions at me. Now, he pulls it back towards him and starts tearing off pieces of cold toast, as if we are discussing nothing more exciting than the drop in temperature.

'I'm only joking,' he mumbles. 'I know she wouldn't do it either. You really have no idea what happened?'

I am at the kitchen counter, boiling the kettle again. I stare at the button until it springs up, and then I say, 'I really have no idea.'

Detective Inspector Chris Rice

2nd January 2020, morning

'Sir? Super wants to see you.'

'Bollocks. Do you think if I jumped out this window I'd survive long enough to crawl to A&E?'

'We're only on the third floor. You could give it a go.'

I am sitting at my desk, a pile of papers and photographs in front of me. Jess stands in the doorway, her head cocked to the side, smiling ruefully.

I got around three hours of very disturbed sleep this morning, when I set the papers on the floor and leaned my head on the desk. I have decided to call the case Project Twenty, as it is our first of the year. I find having a specific name for each case saves us saying things like *That-case-where-it-might-be-the-brother-or-it-might-be-the-sister-you-know?*

'Do I have anything good to tell McCrane about this?' I ask Jess desperately. 'Apart from the fact it's one of four? Anything from the family?'

Jess shakes her head. 'Nothing. They had no idea he was into drugs, apparently. A model son by all accounts. Gave his mum money every week. Picked up his sister from school. No enemies that his family knows about. He liked a party, they knew, but they swore he was a good boy who would never do drugs and they keep insisting we've made a mistake.'

I stare at her, feeling my shoulders sag as though I'm deflating.

'You stay here all night?' Jess asks, looking around the room.

'Can you tell?'

She continues to look anywhere but at me. 'Just, you haven't shaved. Or showered.'

'It's the scent of hard work.'

We make our way out of the room and up the stairs, heading for the SI's office on the third floor.

'Can you check in with the forensics team and see if they found an earring?' I ask.

'An earring?'

'Yeah. In that Den they keep talking about. A little stud thing. Small. Clear.'

'Like the Jameson girl was wearing?'

'Yes.'

'You have a suspicion, then?'

'No,' I say, clutching at a stitch that is rising in my side. We have reached the top of the stairs. 'Just curious.'

We take a left at the end of a corridor and come to a halt outside Superintendent John McCrane's office.

'I think the fight is relevant,' I say slowly, thinking.

'The fight between our victim and Joshua Mackley?'

'That's the one. I'd really like to know who threw that first punch and why. Who provoked who.'

'Whom.'

'Whom. You've seen Mackley, what height would you call him?'

Jess sucks her teeth, looking up from the notebook she has been scribbling in. 'Five eight? At a push. Maybe closer to five seven, actually. The sister is taller.'

'Agreed. And he's a skinny wee bastard. Doesn't look like much of a fighter to me. Peter Denny was six foot three and built like a rugby player … but it was him who got the hiding.'

She is nodding, biting at her lower lip. 'Good luck with the Super.'

'Yeah. Thanks.'

Jess turns back the way we came and I wait until I hear her footsteps on the stairs before I knock on McCrane's door. My breathing has normalised.

'Rice?' he calls from inside. 'Come on in.'

John McCrane is in his mid-50s, but he is one of those people who could pass for anything from a 30-year-old with a hard paper round to a sprightly 70-year-old. He has a forehead as big and wrinkled as a French bulldog's while the rest of his face is crease-free, and he barks out orders in between puffs of his electronic cigarette. Actually using the e-cig in the station is completely against the rules, but he keeps it in his mouth constantly anyway. He is much more addicted to his e-cig than he ever was to tobacco, but he frowns if anyone tries to talk to him about this. Despite this, McCrane is mostly fair and very intelligent, and we get along well.

'Hi, Chris.' The e-cig is balanced between his teeth, so his words sound clipped and mumbled. I sit down at the same moment he says, 'Take a seat.'

McCrane is entirely bald and the low morning sun bounces off his head and makes me squint.

'How goes the investigation?'

'Early days.'

'Early days? You've been on it twenty-four hours. Charlie tells me there are only eleven possible suspects, why no arrests?'

'There are only four now, actually,' I say. 'No arrests yet because … we're being thorough.' I shift in my seat, suddenly a little hot. When neither of us says anything for a few seconds, I scrabble to fill the silence. 'I was thinking that, since Peter Denny was involved in manufacturing and selling drugs, our best bet might be to see what Pogo knows –'

'Pogo?' barks McCrane. 'Pogo Martens? Don't go *near* Pogo Martens. I don't want him mixed up in this; it might blow his cover. His handler says he's about two months away from cracking his whole thing. He's frying bigger fish: heroin, slavery, fuck knows what else. He'll be able to come home soon. The last thing he needs is to be spotted speaking to a peeler.'

Heroin and slavery.

In County Down?

'– not one phone call. Do you hear me? Are you listening to me, Rice?'

'What?'

'I don't want you getting Pogo Martens involved in this case.' McCrane heaves what sounds like a painful sigh, making a tiny whistling sound with the plastic in his mouth. He leans back in his seat to survey me. 'Chris ...' The e-cig comes out and he places it on the table in between us. We both look at it politely, as if waiting for it to speak. After a moment, McCrane continues, 'I hate dragging you in here in the middle of an investigation ... but I can't keep ignoring the complaints that are arriving at my door almost every hour.'

'Complaints?' I repeat. Coffee threatens to creep back up my throat and I swallow it down, glad I have not yet had any breakfast.

'Yeah. There have been a few throughout your last half a dozen cases, and I've had three about this Project Twenty already. I can't keep cutting you slack, Chris. My scissors are blunt.'

My scissors are blunt? I almost snort with laughter.

'I hear you were uncontactable yesterday morning,' McCrane continues.

'Only for –'

McCrane holds up his hand and goes on. 'You were drunk on New Year's Eve, when you were supposed to be on call, DS Curran had to come and physically wake you up to get you down here yesterday, and you didn't even stop at the crime scene on your way.'

'By the time –'

'And *every single person* you interviewed as a suspect yesterday has scurried on home without so much as a slap on the wrist. Dunwoody tells me the brother of the victim's girlfriend – the *owner of the house that is your crime scene*, no less – has previous. For drugs, for DUI, for assault *on our victim* and you haven't even charged him.'

'His girlfriend gives him an alibi. Plus, he isn't going anywhere. If we have to arrest him, we know exactly where he is. Who made a complaint about me?'

'You know I am not at liberty –'

'What were the other complaints, then? On the other cases.'

McCrane hesitates. He takes a deep breath. 'Laziness is the main one. Cutting corners is another. Your last two cases have been closed and signed off in good faith, and there wasn't enough evidence to bring either of the suspects to court. You know how that makes us look.'

'Technicalities aren't my fault.'

'In your last case, you took a bag of evidence home in your pocket and dropped it on the ground at a drive-through restaurant.'

'Yeah, but we got it back.'

'Only because the woman at the drive-through recognised you when you went back *later the same day*.' He eyes my stomach, which is resting against the side of his desk.

At last, I feel myself blush. At least I can feel something, even if it is this.

'Look ...' he continues. 'The reason I've given you the benefit of the doubt for so long is because I know how difficult the last two years have been for you. First Rebecca ... then splitting with Aisling. You've had a tough time. No parent should have to ...' He does a little desperate shrug. 'But I can't keep making excuses for you.'

My lips, which pressed tightly together at the mention of Rebecca's name, won't open. I have to prise them apart with real effort to get out, 'What are you saying?'

'I'm saying give yourself a break. Work this case, get me my man, get enough to put him behind bars and –'

'Retire?'

'Well ... it's overdue. You've done way over your thirty years; nobody would blame you for stepping down now. You'd get a good pension, a fabulous payout. There's a big world out there, Chris. One where nobody is hiding bombs under your car and where you don't have to sleep in your office ... It's pretty obvious that this just isn't cutting it for you any more. You don't want to be here, Chris.'

I don't want to be anywhere, really, I think.

'I'm saying this as your friend. I can't make you retire, obviously. But these mistakes you keep making, they're your brain's way of telling you to stop.'

It is the longest I have seen him without the e-cig for years. Just as I am thinking this, it makes a beeline for his mouth again.

'Arrest Joshua Mackley,' he says through the plastic. He busies himself lifting and tapping at papers on his desk, his eyes averted. 'If you think he's your man, get him. Soon.'

I take this as my cue to leave and make to stand up.

'Oh, and Rice?'

I look at him, expecting something to soften the blow of the conversation, a wish of good luck, but –

'Go home and have a shower. You stink of sweat and booze.'

In the incident room, thirty minutes later, I find myself thinking about McCrane's words.

Your brain's way of telling you to stop.

Is it true? I have messed up far more than usual on the last few cases I've worked, but it has all been tiny, petty, unimportant stuff that could happen to anyone.

If I retire now, what the hell do I do with my time? What do I wake up for?

'No earring in the Den,' Jess says. I start. I hadn't realised she'd taken the seat next to me. 'Not that forensics have found anyway. What did McCrane want?'

Before I can answer, I start again, this time with realisation, and take my personal mobile from my pocket. Once it has switched on, it bleeps with a new text.

Hi Aggie. Would love a chat today. Call you at twelve o'clock? Can't wait. S.

It is eleven-fifty. Too late to cancel.

I stand abruptly, and everyone turns to look at me, expectant.

'I have to make a call,' I say. 'Jess, can you take charge for a while? Everyone knows what they're at and I won't be long.'

Jess looks bewildered. 'Sir, you said we were going to the PM? It starts at one, and you know what Jaxon is like, we can't be late.'

'Yeah, yeah, I'll be back in half an hour. Tell him not to start without me.'

'What are we doing, then?' Browne asks. He is stroking his beard, pulling at rogue hairs that are not there. 'Based on the argument, do we arrest Keeley Mackley?'

'No,' I say. 'We find out what that argument was about so we're prepared when we bring her in again. Don't talk to anyone about it until I give the order. Understood?'

Jess nods first. Gradually, the others follow suit and busy themselves on their phones, on their computers.

I tap Edgecomb on the shoulder and she turns around from her laptop, her face expectant, keen.

'Nice work with all the CCTV stuff yesterday,' I say. 'I wonder if you could do me another favour?'

'Of course.'

A thought has been playing in my head all night. 'Keeley Mackley was excluded from Seaview High. She was violent towards another girl, Beth McKenna. During their A-levels, whenever that was. Could you do a bit of digging on that for me? I'll ask Dunwoody to check out the pizza delivery for you. Speak to teachers, classmates, that kind of thing. Just find out what exactly happened that meant she got herself booted out, what people thought of her. What they think of Jude, too.'

'You think it's related to Denny's death?' Edgecomb asks, surprised.

I hesitate. The honest answer is no. 'Not sure,' I say eventually. 'In case it's not, can you keep it between us for now? Take a uniform with you but don't mention it to the team just yet. I don't want another complaint about time wasting … Oi, Dunwoody? You're going to Tim's Pizza in Vetobridge. Take whoever you want. Whomever? Ask the right questions and bring me back a medium pepperoni with garlic dip.'

My phone buzzes at exactly midday.

I have just made it to the on-call room on the fourth floor of the building, the same one I more or less lived in for three months before I got the keys to my flat after Aisling kicked me out. These rooms haven't been officially used since the 90s, when there were only a few hours between scheduled shifts, and they smell exactly like that.

'Hello … *Aggie.*'

'Hello, Sylvie.' I smile at our nicknames. It's Pogo Martens. His real name is Paul, but I've never heard anyone, not even the Superintendent, call him that. We worked together for most of our careers until he moved to undercover. No one can know we are still in contact.

'What's this about?' Pogo has never had time for small talk; I am impressed I even got a hello.

'Need some info,' I say. I sit down on the small wooden bed. I know the sheets probably haven't been laundered since I last slept there myself. 'Peter Denny. Twenty-eight. Got murdered on Tuesday night. You know him?'

Pogo hesitates. There is a sound as though he is moving the phone to his other ear. 'You serious?'

'Deadly.'

'Yeah, I know of him. He knows my boys pretty well, too. He's the Vetobridge man who was stabbed? I saw it on the news.'

Pogo has been on one particular undercover operation for five years, about which I am supposed to know absolutely nothing. He started off infiltrating an organised crime gang, got four arrests out of it in the first eighteen months and, last I heard, now lives in a two-bedroomed council flat with four other men who are big into the distribution and consumption of cocaine and meth. If McCrane's words about heroin and slavery are anything to go on, things have become more intense for Pogo since I last spoke to him, but there is no time to ask for a casual update on his *boys* now.

Pogo owes me a favour because, twenty-one years ago, he shot and killed a suspect who was giving themselves up and I lied to protect his career. *Suspect was reaching for a weapon. We thought that. Really.*

'That's him,' I say. 'Will you do me a favour and make me up a file of anything important that you and your boys know about him?'

'You know I can't do files. But I can ask around. What do you need to know?'

'I thought I was going to ask you about drug rivals, but we found out yesterday evening that it was one of four suspects. You know a guy called Joshua Mackley?'

'Nah. I'll ask the boys.'

'Anything at all that they know about him, anything they know about Mackley's girlfriend or his sister, the whole cosy house. And anything about Denny, obviously. Specifically, see if you can find out why Denny and Mackley fought in the summer of 2018. As soon as you can.'

'Summer 2018. Got it.'

'Great. Thank you.' I lie back on the bed, suddenly overcome with fatigue. I stifle a yawn. 'How are you doing, Pogo?'

I have asked because I feel it is prudent. Pogo knows this and so does not answer. Instead, he says, 'Meet me tomorrow evening at half seven in the park beside the Ballykyle Road Tesco. I should be able to dig up something by then. Oh and, try not to look like a cop. Enjoy your midday snooze.'

He is gone in a chuckling click before I can feign outrage at the suggestion.

Keeley

2nd January 2020, morning

I am nursing a cup of tea in my hands when Naomi comes downstairs.

'Morning,' I say, as brightly as I can. I am keen to make amends for being so blunt with her yesterday.

She seems to have the same idea, because she smiles tiredly. 'Sleep OK?' she asks.

I nod, but it is a lie. 'Mack not up yet?'

Naomi looks around the tiny living room as though he might be hiding behind the sofa. 'I thought he was down here with you. I heard him get up hours ago.'

I frown. 'Must have gone out before I was awake.'

Naomi sits next to me and lets out a sigh. She is wearing an oversized stripy jumper that just covers her underwear. This is why she keeps the place so warm, I think.

'Probably away to score, since we can't touch the Sixes.'

'The police are bound to be watching us,' I say quickly. 'We agreed that yesterday, remember? He won't be doing that.'

'I know, I was joking. He isn't stupid … Just hooked on drugs, that's all. Idiot.'

Her words sting. It is almost pleasant to be angry at someone who is right here. 'He hadn't tried a single drug before he got with you,' I say. I sip my tea.

Naomi ignores this and reaches her toe out in front of us to tap the pile on the armchair opposite. I have folded up the blanket and pyjamas she gave me last night.

'You're such a Jameson,' she comments. 'That's military style precision, that. I've never seen Mack even straighten a cushion.'

I resist the urge to roll my eyes. 'I folded a blanket. Hardly Linda Jameson, am I?'

'Don't think you're much of a Mackley.'

'Thank fuck for that.' I know she is trying to nip at me, after my comment about the drugs, but it works.

Don't think you're much of a Mackley.

I never have been. I always hated the parties that Mum and Mack loved.

Mum always swore she never *intentionally* threw parties and since I hate arguing, I always believed her without question.

She had this friend, a guy called either Moe or Joe, I never cared enough to listen to his name, who had both ears pierced and was just a bit older than Mack. He used to come around to our house with beers and wine and an old-fashioned boom box, everything tucked under his arms like he had just nicked it and bolted. Mack and I could never work out exactly how he knew our mum, but we think they must have run into one another in the off-licence one day, and he had come home with her and she never questioned it.

The parties usually took place during the week when Jude had to have dinner with her family and sit on the sofa, obediently watching game shows. MoeJoe never knocked and Mum never asked him to. He went straight to the living room and made a big fuss of Mum for a few minutes – *How are you today? Have you been taking your meds? Marian, honestly, what you need is a man about the place. Is it OK if I get a glass for this beer? I invited a few of the mates around tonight, just thought we could have a few drinks. You don't mind, do you?* – before coming into the kitchen and gushing over me too.

'How is the most beautiful girl in the entire world?' he used to say. 'Are you coming in for a wee drink tonight?'

'Still not old enough,' I would say.

'Maybe next time,' he would say. 'We'll try to keep it down.'

They never did. His friends would arrive over the course of the next few hours, each of them simply opening the door and walking in, usually looking as though they had no idea how they had ended up in the shit part of Wits End. They would sit in the living room until after midnight, drinking and sharing drugs, playing music, flushing the toilet constantly.

In our fourth year of school, they started to have three or four parties a week, so that most nights I was kept awake, staring at the ceiling with my teeth clenched until they finally decided to leave, and then I'd hear Mum creeping up the stairs to bed, padding along the hall so quietly, trying so pointlessly not to wake us, that it broke my heart.

The night before our first proper GCSE, one of these such parties began while I had my books open in front of me at the little table in the kitchen.

'There's my favourite girl,' MoeJoe said, coming in and opening a cupboard. 'Fancy a wee glass of this, lovely?' He indicated the dark green bottle of Prosecco he was holding.

'No,' I said. I didn't bother with the bit about being too young.

'Don't know what you're missing,' he said. He uncorked the bottle and poured some into a tumbler that was stained with water-marks. He took a gulp and smacked his lips exaggeratedly. 'We're celebrating tonight.'

'Yeah?' I kept my eyes on the numbers in front of me, but my teeth were gritted so hard I couldn't concentrate.

'Yeah. You know Dave?'

'Big Dave or Hypochondriac Dave?'

'Big – wait, what was the second one? Dave with the beard, anyway. He got his sentencing today – four weeks of community service and a suspended sentence! Isn't that great?'

I'm sure on some level I was delighted for Dave.

'Are you going to be up late?' I said. 'I have an exam tomorrow.'

'Oh! Sorry, love.' MoeJoe put his hand to his mouth with an exaggerated air of embarrassment. 'I'll tell them all to keep it down. You know what they're like! I hope Dave didn't wake you the other night when he was running up and down the stairs?'

Suddenly I wasn't so happy for Dave any more.

'He was trying to prove to us all that he's still fit, even though he's seventy next week.'

'Just … keep in mind I'm studying, won't you?' I said, trying to smile.

'Gotcha, Princess.' He blew me a kiss and went back to the living room with his bottle. He didn't close the door behind him, so I leant over and kicked it closed with enough force to make my point.

Within the hour, the house was almost literally jumping. Evidently, MoeJoe's friends were over the moon about Dave's sentencing. I spent two hours with my textbook open on the same page, staring at the numbers which swam before my eyes and seemed to make less sense now at the end of the year than they had at the start. Maths was my best subject after drama. If I couldn't pass this, I had no chance.

I heard the Cortina pull into the drive around eight and Mack came into the kitchen moments later. In the few seconds that the door was open, the music and shouting were unbearable.

'Big Dave got off, then?' he asked, grinning as he shut the door behind him.

'Yeah,' I said. 'Were you practising?'

His guitar was strapped around him over his shoulder.

'Yeah. Honestly, I have no idea why we didn't ask Roy before. He's *properly* good. We sound better than ever. I'm thinking of asking someone to come and record us. For the Internet, you know.'

'*For the Internet*,' I repeated. 'You sound like an old man.'

He pulled a can of cider from the fridge and sat down next to me. 'What's all this?'

'Maths. Exam is tomorrow.'

Mack let a breath out through his mouth and pulled the tab on his cider. 'You will need this to get through the night,' he said, offering it to me. 'They really thought Dave was going down for it today. They'll be up all night.'

'They can't be up all night,' I said through gritted teeth. 'I've got my fucking exams this month.'

He leant back in his chair and pulled his guitar around to rest on his knee. He plucked his fingers in a semi-familiar tune and sang, '*I've got my fucking exams this month, oh-oh-ohhhh.*'

I didn't smile.

Mack sat next to me for another few minutes, listening to the voices and laughter from next door, his fingers tapping on the table beside me. Then, just as I was about to shout at him to stop, he let out an exaggerated sigh and went into the living room. There was a chorus of cheers when he entered.

The music only got louder then. I lasted a full half-hour before I picked up the cider and took a long, totally unsatisfying gulp. Half the liquid spilled down my chin and on to my school uniform and I shivered with disgust.

I finished the can all the same.

The exam was in thirteen hours. I couldn't remember most of my formulae.

I put on my blazer, which had fallen from the back of my chair on to the floor and was now badly creased, picked up my books and left the house.

' … So, if you don't mind, please could I come in and revise with Jude for just an hour or two and stay over?'

I could hear the pumping of the music from across the green, even though I was standing right up the steps of Jude's house. Linda heard it too. She looked past me, over at number 166, and her eyebrows seemed to knot together.

'It's a school night …' she said, almost making it sound like a question.

'I know you don't like weekday sleepovers but I'm a bit desperate.' I hated the way my voice sounded. I hated begging Linda for anything. We were a team, me and Jude, and we had to act as though we didn't need anyone else for anything.

When Linda didn't respond right away, only continued to stare across the green and into my house, I added, 'Can I at least see Jude for a few minutes?'

Linda finally looked at me. She stepped forward and closed the door behind her. I noticed a single blotch of sweat at her right armpit when she folded her arms. The air was still warm from the hot day, but this very real, very *human* thing looked so out of place on Linda Jameson.

'I don't think that's very appropriate,' she said.

She was looking at the collar of my school shirt which, I realised now, too late, was stained with the dark purple cider. I could smell it off myself and closed my eyes briefly, cursing myself for not having changed before I came across the green.

'You've been drinking on a school night,' she said lightly.

'I had one can. I don't want to have any more. I'm not …' I looked behind me, shaking my head, feeling tears prick my eyes and not trusting myself to finish my sentence. *I'm not like them.*

'Keeley, not tonight,' Linda said. 'I don't want Jude to be distracted the night before your first exam. I suggest you go home and get some sleep yourself.'

How? I wanted to ask. How the hell am I meant to sleep when my house, my supposed safe place, is full of drunk strangers?

After she had closed the door, I walked slowly, numbly back towards my own house.

But I'm not like them either, I realised.

Here in the living room, Naomi is talking again. I cut across her, wanting to make her shut up, and say, without really thinking it through –

'Why did Mack fight with Pete two summers ago?'

Naomi stops mid-sentence, her mouth comically hanging on whatever she had been about to say.

'I didn't ask him last night,' I say. 'My head was a mess. Do you know why they fought? Pete's face was fucked. The police asked me about it.'

'Yeah …' Naomi trails off and looks out of the window. 'They asked me about that too.'

'What did you say?'

'Mya was getting married; I was away in Spain around then.'

'So, you don't know why they fought?'

She tilts her head to the side, staring at something in the distance. Then she shakes her head, slowly. 'I'm not the person you need to ask about that,' she says.

'Will Mack even tell me?' I ask. 'You'd think he'd have mentioned it –'

'No,' Naomi cuts me off. 'It's not him you need to ask either.'

Linda

2nd January 2020, morning

No arrests, according to the text news.

What are they playing at?

I go to stand by the window of the good living room again. I pull the blinds to the side to look across the green.

This is my home, I have a right to know what is going on –

'Muuuuuuum!'

I press a button to get rid of the text news just as Mason comes in.

'Apparently we have prime numbers homework,' he says. 'So, I'll need help.' He tries to grimace at me as if this is typical of the school, to let them know after a week and a half about a secret homework.

'What do you mean *apparently*?'

'I mean I was speaking to Max online and he asked me if I'd done it and I said, what prime numbers homework? And he said, the prime numbers homework that we have, and I said, what prime number –'

The pressure gets piled on in GCSE year, doesn't it? Kids have years of studying but never really being tested and then, all of a sudden, they're expected to take ten, twenty exams in the space of a month. I dread Mason's turn – he is bright but completely scatter-brained.

Jude has always been very clever, of course, but the pressure did start to get to her in those two years. It had an impact on the whole family, especially on Mason who went through something of a dishonest phase, just for a few weeks.

It was immediately after I banned Jude from seeing Keeley. The girl showed up at our house on a Tuesday night, the night before their first big exam, no less, stinking of booze and asking if she could come inside. Must have been off her face to think I'd let her in in that state.

I gave her a lift to school the next morning, as agreed – I'm not a monster – and after I'd picked them up again and made lunch for Jude, told her that she wasn't to see Keeley any more.

Jude, who had a headache and was massaging her temples, barked a laugh of surprise.

'This isn't a joke.'

It was nearly midday. The kitchen was bright and warm and we could hear birds tweeting to one another outside the open window. We were both extraordinarily calm.

'Is this because of last night?' she asked, sounding only curious.

'She was drunk. You're fifteen.'

'She's nearly seventeen.'

'That makes no difference. She was drunk on a school night.'

'She had one can. Unless you have an incredibly low alcohol tolerance, that is not enough to get you drunk.'

I blinked. Her words were cool, matter of fact. She sounded more confident than I'd ever heard her before. Was this my child?

'That's all very well,' I continued. 'But it's not appropriate for you to be surrounded by that kind of … influence. Especially at such an important time. I don't want you to be friends with her any more.'

'If you stop me from seeing Keeley, I will never speak to anyone in this family again for as long as I live.'

Her voice was so calm we could have been discussing her revision timetable. Her eyes bored into mine as we sat opposite one another at the kitchen table, my hands clasped around a coffee cup, one of her hands flattening her ham sandwich in a way I constantly told her not to. I felt a flush of irritation creep up my neck.

'If that's how you feel,' I said, 'you don't have to speak to us. But you aren't to speak to Keeley, either.'

She was true to her word.

Roddy came home at his usual time, full of beans, joking with Mason. I heard the two of them giggling in the living room as I stood at the kitchen counter watching Jude, my eyes narrowed. She was steadily highlighting her textbook and making notes on a separate page, her face composed. Every now and then I saw a muscle in her jaw twitch, the only indication that all was not well.

'Are we celebrating?' Roddy asked, coming into the kitchen and pecking me on the cheek.

'Hmm?'

'The wine. Are we celebrating?'

I looked down at the glass in my hand and shook my head, quickly setting it back on the sideboard.

'Did you smash it today, love?' Roddy called to Jude.

Jude looked up at him and for a moment I thought she had forgotten her threat. Then she moved her gaze pointedly to look at me and went back to work.

Roddy laughed awkwardly. 'Does that mean it didn't go well?' he asked me in a murmur.

'I've explained to Jude how we both feel about Keeley,' I said. 'I've told her she is, as of now, not permitted to see her outside of school.'

Roddy blinked. 'Oh. Did we … ?' He trailed off, looking between us, thoroughly confused.

'Yes,' I said through gritted teeth. 'We discussed it this morning, remember?'

In truth, I'd had a whispered rant to Roddy the night before, after Keeley left. Nothing had been decided or discussed. I don't recall Roddy even saying a single thing apart from *oh*.

'So … they aren't going to see each other?' Roddy asked. His shoulders slumped. 'Isn't that a bit –' He stopped speaking abruptly at the look on my face.

'Now Jude isn't speaking to anyone,' I said. 'Which will give us some well-earned peace and quiet. Do you want to go and call Mason for dinner? I've made lamb.'

Roddy hesitated only briefly, his eyes on Jude, his mouth open. Then he turned and went to get Mason.

She didn't say a word that night, nor the next morning when we set off for school at half-past twelve for her English paper. Keeley wasn't waiting for us at the car then, nor was she waiting for a lift back afterwards. When I asked how the English paper had gone, Jude didn't even blink. Mason, from the back of the car, started an endless chant of *how'd it go, how'd it go, how'd it go*. She folded her arms and looked out of the window, silent. Eventually I had to intervene.

'Mason,' I said. 'I don't think your sister wants to talk right now. She's upset about Keeley.'

'What happened to Keeley?' he asked.

I was quiet for a moment, waiting to see if Jude would cave to exclaim to her brother about the unfairness of it all. When she didn't, I said, 'Jude and Keeley aren't friends any more.'

In the passenger seat next to me, I felt her body stiffen.

This went on for the rest of the week. She didn't have an exam on the Friday, but she kept to her room to revise, coming out only twice for water and crisps.

'I made you a salad,' I called to her as she passed the living room door. 'Make sure you don't take Mason's; his has that special dressing he likes.'

She didn't reply, but I watched her carry the bowl up the stairs a few minutes later.

On the Saturday night, when I was filling the dishwasher an hour after dinner, I felt Mason behind me.

'OK, love?' I asked, not looking at him.

'Mum, you need to let Jude see Keeley again.'

I stifled a tut. 'That girl is bad news for this family.'

'She's not,' Mason said. 'Keeley's lovely. We all love her. Except you.'

'She is maturing too quickly for Jude,' I said quietly. I moved a saucepan lid out of the way to balance a dinner plate.

'Says who?' Mason asks. 'Just because Keeley had a drink once doesn't mean Jude is going to do it.'

I straightened and put a hand on my back. 'Why are you so interested?' I asked. As I stretched my back, I glanced around at him. 'And what on Earth has happened to your arm?'

Behind me, one of the plates in the dishwasher fell back with a loud crash and smashed into a second one. I moved quickly, but not fast enough. Two pieces of ceramic had come loose from one of our four large dinner plates. I groaned and crouched down to pick it up.

When I straightened again, Mason had pulled the sleeve of his dressing gown down his arm.

'It's carpet burn,' he said. 'It's a new online challenge. See how much carpet burn you can get before you have to give up.'

'Oh, for goodness sake, Mason,' I said, unable to stop the tut this time. 'What a ridiculous game.'

It was only as I opened the lid of the outside bin to tip the ceramic pieces in that I noticed a red smear around the rim of the broken plate. Jude, who had eaten in her room, had added ketchup to her meal, unlike the rest of us. I tried not to listen as the pieces crunched together at the bottom of the bin, indignant and broken beyond repair.

Mason approached me again on Day Ten of Jude's Elected Silence.

Roddy was in his study, working on the English department's June newsletter. Jude was in her room, supposedly studying.

I was in the smaller living room, the television turned down low, a magazine in my lap. My eyes kept flicking to the window where, unsurprisingly, another party was taking place at number 166.

'Mum?'

I blinked up at Mason. 'Yes, darling? Come and sit.'

He shuffled in and leant his crutches against the sofa before taking a seat himself. He heard the music from across the road too and looked out.

'Another party,' I said, grateful to be able to turn my gaze and not look away. Grateful to be able to talk about it. 'Typical. Marian has more visitors than –'

'They're just her friends,' Mason said. 'You don't need to make it sound so … Mum, you really have to let Jude see Keeley again.'

I folded up the magazine. I hadn't been reading it anyway. 'Why do you care so much, Macey? Has she said something to you?'

'No,' Mason said quickly. 'But I miss Keeley too. The house just doesn't feel right without her. It's so quiet. We're all so boring.'

'We aren't boring,' I said, bemused. 'We're very interesting. Your dad is a published academic and a university lecturer, Mason, that's hardly boring.' I tried to think of something else to add to this list. When I couldn't, I patted him on the head and tried to laugh. 'Silly Mason.'

'I miss my sister too,' he said desperately. 'Without Keeley it's like there's no Jude. I miss hearing her laugh, hearing her voice. She's doing exams and I haven't heard her complain about them once. That isn't right.'

I stared at him. I had barely seen them speak in the last year or so, though I'd read an article online that said that was perfectly normal with one mid-adolescent and one pre-teen. With a family like ours, though, I supposed it was only natural that the mould be broken.

'I had no idea you felt so strongly about all of this … I'll try talking to her, darling. I don't want you to be upset.'

'You have to let her see Keeley,' he insisted. He placed a hand on my wrist and said very seriously, 'For me.'

Speaking to Jude had the result we expected. That is, none.

I stood in the doorway of her room and explained how her brother was feeling. When she did not react, only stared at me from where she lay on her bed, a book in her hand, I tried a new tactic. She was fifteen now, fifteen-year-olds didn't behave like this. They didn't huff and stay silent when they didn't get their own way. She had to start acting her age or she had no hope of passing her GCSEs, taking on A-levels and going to university in a matter of years. It just wouldn't happen. She raised one eyebrow at me and looked back at her book.

The next day was Saturday.

It went like most Saturdays. Roddy took Mason to his physiotherapy appointment in the morning and Janet came over to clean our house. I clean the other six days a week, of course, but it's nice to have a second pair of eyes to spot anything I've missed.

Janet was gone by the time Roddy and Mason got back and the house was even cleaner. Jude was silent again.

Mason took himself upstairs to play video games, ignoring my pleas for him to go into the garden for a while. It was such a gorgeous day. Roddy made coffee for both of us and we went and sat on the wooden bench at the front of the house, looking down over Wits End and pretending not to notice how forlorn 166 looked from this angle. We had been chatting for less than an hour when there was a crash from just inside the open front door.

Roddy got there first.

Mason was lying in what I can only describe as a heap of limbs, on the floor of the lift.

It was at ground floor level, and for a second I didn't understand why Mason was lying down. I wanted to shout at him to stand up and behave. Was this another of his silly games?

Then I saw the unusual angle his left arm was bent and I almost threw up my coffee.

Roddy was bending by his side, cooing, but Mason wasn't screaming in pain or even particularly crying.

'Mum,' he croaked. 'You need to let Jude see Keeley.'

Roddy and I shared a glance. Had he landed on his head?

'What happened, darling?' I asked. 'Did you fall from upstairs?'

'Did you think the lift was at the top when it wasn't?' Roddy asked. He moved Mason into a sitting position.

Mason didn't answer, only clutched his arm.

'I'll take him to A&E,' Roddy said. He felt both his pockets and seemed satisfied. He was remarkably calm. 'I think that arm is broken. He must have thought the lift was at the top and just stepped off. I'll call you.'

He scooped Mason up in both arms and carried him out to the car.

It was all over in less than two minutes.

I stepped into the lift and glanced around me, as if looking for clues. My spine felt cold and my breath came strangely, as though I'd just been running. Cold sweat was sticking to my back.

If Mason was upstairs, the lift *would* have been at the top. There would have been no reason for any of us to call it down.

I looked up.

Jude stood in the hall upstairs, staring down at me, neither shocked nor worried.

—

Mason's arm was broken.

Roddy seemed to think that Mason had thrown himself from the second floor as a reaction to the tension in the house.

I said that was ridiculous, ten-year-olds didn't throw themselves down lift shafts if their sisters were behaving childishly.

Roddy said that was ridiculous, it was hardly a lift *shaft*.

We went around in circles.

Mason wouldn't speak about it either.

A few days later, Roddy approached me after he had dropped Jude off at school for her penultimate exam.

'I think we need to remove this Keeley ban,' he said. 'Jude got out of the car this morning and went straight over to her. It makes no sense. They're going to see each other in school anyway, and all of this has clearly affected Mason in a way we couldn't have predicted.'

We.

The thing with Roddy was that everything was *we*. I have read enough magazines and scrolled enough Mum forums to know that this is one of the things middle-aged women want the most: to have a husband who is a part of them in every way, who agrees with them even when they're being ridiculous. A husband who is on their team.

'It was me who stopped them,' I said.

'I didn't argue,' Roddy said.

'Of course you didn't.'

'So, you agree? We should lift the ban?'

What do middle-aged men want? Do they want a wife who agrees with everything they say, too?

'Do whatever you think is best,' I said. 'It's clear my plans aren't working.'

There was no dramatic ceremony. The girls didn't run at one another across the green, arms outstretched. Jude didn't thank us or hug us or cry. Roddy went upstairs and gave her the news, and ten minutes later she walked slowly, calmly out the front door and across the road.

She didn't come home until much later that night.

After dinner, when Jude was still at the Mackleys', Mason approached me again. His cast had a bright red cover and he was a little bit proud of it. I was standing by the kettle, waiting for it to boil.

'How's my brave boy?' I asked.

He shrugged and came and leant against my side. I put an arm around his shoulders, then pulled a piece of fluff from his hair.

'You let her see Keeley?' he said.

'Yes,' I sighed. 'I suppose it was never going to last. Why did you care so much? That's not why you hurt yourself, is it?'

'It was Jude.'

I frowned, rubbing the fluff between my fingers. 'What was Jude?'

'It was Jude,' Mason said again.

The kettle clicked, boiled, at the exact second I understood what he was trying to say.

'It was Jude who … who hurt you?'

Mason nodded, unable to meet my eye. 'She said you'd only listen to me. She said I had to make you change your mind or she'd … she'd hurt me. And she did.'

Roddy came into the kitchen then, whistling.

'How's our brave boy?' he asked, echoing my words. He was beaming as he opened the fridge.

Neither of us moved or said anything.

Roddy pulled out a can of Sprite and closed the fridge door.

He left and I felt us both exhale.

My heart was pumping hard. 'Mason … you can't make things up about your sister,' I said. There was a tremble in my voice. 'She's under a lot of stress at the moment with these exams. Maybe you are too, with everything that has been going on. But you can't just make things up about her. OK? Now why don't you get yourself a drink and see what Dad wants us to watch?'

He met my eye then, only for a second. He was confused and afraid, but he moved away from me, slowly.

The pressure gets piled on in those years.

It affected us all.

Here in the living room, I hold up a hand to silence Mason's long and confusing explanation of his secret homework.

'I'll help you,' I say. 'Go get your books.'

Before he can turn to leave, I reach out and pull him into a hug. He resists only for a moment, then hugs me back.

'I love you, darling,' I murmur into his hair.

I feel him smile against me. 'I know, Mum.'

He does know, I think, as he makes his slow way back out of the living room. Of course he knows. No matter what mistakes we've made – I've made – he knows. I would do anything for him.

For both of them.

I click until the text news comes back on. No update, no change.

What are they playing at?

Detective Inspector Chris Rice

2nd January 2020, afternoon

I burst through the door of the lab, panting hard. I can't remember the last time I ran. My side aches and I am sweating profusely. With a look at my watch, I see I have a full thirty seconds before one o'clock – I can't help but grin.

'I'm here,' I say, clutching my side. 'Everyone ready?'

Jaxon stands at the table in the middle of the room, staring at me, his expression cold. Jess is beside him, avoiding my eye. I look eagerly through the viewing window behind them and say, 'We can get started now. Is he in there? Are you ready?'

I catch sight of Jaxon's white coat. There is a single smear of blood on the cuff.

'Still detecting, Rice?' he asks.

I blink at him.

Jaxon has never liked me much, though I have tried on many occasions to make him laugh. The most I've ever seen from him is a bitter grimace at the discovery of needle marks between the toes of a young girl lying dead on his table a few years back.

'Get your gloves on, Jaxon!' I say, trying to seem upbeat and half punching the air. 'I don't want to keep you waiting. We can start.'

'Oh, can *we*?' says Jaxon. 'If you look at this tripod in front of me, *Detective*, you will see a camera which is blinking with a yellow light. That yellow light indicates that the memory is full which, as you know from having worked with me on a number of occasions, means that I have just completed a post-mortem. I would not *start* a post-mortem with a camera with little or no memory. If you *detect* a little further, you will see that one of the gloves I wore for said examination is hanging over the edge of the bin beside the door of the lab into which I threw them once I was finished. The post-mortem examination on Peter Denny was rescheduled to twelve o'clock today and is now over. I have presented my findings to Sergeant Curran who can inform you of anything she thinks to be relevant. Since she actually bothered to show up, it is to her I will send my report once it has been compiled, which will be tomorrow.'

Jaxon picks up the blinking camera, turns on his heel and leaves through the heavy door behind him.

I look at Jess.

'I phoned you twenty times to tell you he had rescheduled,' she says. 'Your work phone just rang out and your personal was engaged. He called literally the second you left; I was a few minutes late myself. He wouldn't wait. You know what he's like.'

'Oh, fuck sake. What did I miss?'

'Where do I start?'

Jess looks down at the notepad she has been scribbling in. Her forehead is wrinkled and her eyes look dull and tired.

'He was stabbed once in his right lung, which caused a leakage of air into the pleural cavity causing a pneumothorax. I'm afraid I won't be able to explain it as well as Jaxon –'

'At least you won't be imagining crushing my balls in a vice while you're telling me.'

'But the stab wound alone would *not* have been enough to kill him …'

I stare at her.

'So these Sixes, the drugs all the party guests were on, we haven't found any of it to get it tested properly – we only have what Jaxon was able to find in Pete's stomach, *but* the good news is, another lab tech who examined the knife says there is an unknown substance on the murder weapon. Possibly Sixes. Somebody was using the knife to cut the drugs. Jaxon has taken both samples to be tested, but from the gang's previous charges, their behaviour in the live-stream and what Jaxon can tell from the body, we know the drug is a stimulant. Very like cocaine in its effects, Jaxon reckons. He thinks it's possibly something like 2C-B cut with MDMA. It seems to have increased Denny's heart rate rather than slowed it down. So, the heart is beating much too quickly anyway, he gets stabbed, and his lung collapses; he's having to try and breathe enough to keep up with his haywire heart, and meanwhile air is filling up the cavity. It would have been agony, getting stabbed in the lung ... if he was sober. But the knife didn't actually go too far in. It basically just broke the surface of the lung, if you like, and was pulled out straight away, Jaxon thinks. It wouldn't have killed him if they'd only called an ambulance.' Jess grimaces. 'Jaxon won't be able to tell for sure until he knows more about Sixes, but he thinks there's a good chance that the struggling for oxygen might have added to Denny's high rather than made him panic.'

I close my eyes briefly. 'He was dying and *enjoying* it?'

Jess doesn't respond.

'Come for a smoke,' I say.

'No smoking within a mile of the hospital,' she says.

'Fuck sake. We might as well get back to the station then. I can't believe I *ran* just to miss this.'

Twenty minutes later at the station, Jess and I park our cars and meet at the front of the building. She fumbles with her lighter, her gloves too thick to click it, and I light her cigarette for her.

She pulls her coat around her and shivers. 'Denny had cuts and bruises on his arms and face. Recent. Indicative of a physical altercation in the last two hours of his life. Fingernail scratches on his neck. Skin cells under his nails which fit nice and snug with the argument we heard him having with Keeley Mackley in that video. We're cross-checking the skin cells with her DNA sample. Definitely her though. Oh, another thing Jaxon mentioned – he says it won't be in the official report, but there's a chance that our killer is left-handed.'

My hand freezes midway to my mouth, cigarette suspended in the air.

'What? When did he ... Why won't it be in the report?'

'Because of all the drugs he can't say it with complete certainty. He says a normal, sober person would have to be left-handed to *sensibly* stab him at the angle they did, but given the fact that every one of our suspects was off their tits, including the victim, he can't guarantee it. He also says there are ways you could hold a knife in your right hand and stab him like that, but it would just be physically awkward.' Jess holds up her right hand and makes an unwieldy stabbing motion at my chest.

'You'd need a lot of force to get through to my lung,' I say reasonably.

'He says he won't stand up in court and state this, so he won't be putting it in the report. He had a guess.'

'I like a man with a hunch.'

'I know you do. You're the last of the old-school boys, Sir. You know, not one other detective here can say they worked all the way through the Troubles.'

'Bollocks.'

'I'm serious. Sure, Dunwoody saw some shit at the tail end of it in the 90s, but the rest of them escaped it. People respect you, Sir. You're a bit of a hero.'

I throw her a sideways glance. 'Why are you being so nice to me? Are you about to put my balls in a vice?'

Jess sighs and turns to lean her back against the wall. 'I'm just trying to remind you … what you're capable of. I think this case has got into your head – no, let me finish, I'm saying this as your friend –' There are McCrane's words again, I think. '– I just think you've really put your heart into this the last two days, which is great, but …'

'But not my head?' I finish for her.

'I dunno. Seems like it's really got to you. You were so lenient on the girls yesterday, and at the time they were the only suspects we had our hands on. Then you let Mack go: you just believed everything he said, you didn't *really* push him. He had a complete meltdown, wouldn't tell us a thing, and you *still* decided to let him go. When was the last time you ate, Chris?'

I start, surprised by sudden intimacy of this question and the use of my first name. 'I had some of those biscuits yesterday,' I say. 'In the interview room. You were there.'

'Not what I meant. What did McCrane want earlier?'

'To give me a bollocking, basically. Said there have been complaints about my conduct. No, I know it wasn't you,' I add, seeing the flash of defiance on her face. 'But it was nothing I could argue with. He more or less said I should cut my losses after this case and retire.'

'It's not the most ridiculous thing I've ever heard. How old are you, eighty?'

'Hilarious.'

'Are you thinking about it?'

'I might not get a choice if this case isn't a quick solve. He had a point when he said we should have made more progress. This is probably going to be my last case if I can't get my man by the end of the week.'

'Or your woman,' Jess says. 'You're literally one of those cliché cops who needs to solve a murder to save their career.'

'Difference is I don't know if I can be arsed saving it.'

I crush my cigarette on the ground and push my hands into my pockets, waiting for Jess finish hers.

'Joshua Mackley's dad was blown up,' she says conversationally. 'Browne was telling me. It came up in the research, apparently. His dad was a Catholic, but was having a pint with a Protestant mate in what Browne called a *Proddy bar* –'

'Remind me to organise another Political Correctness in the Workplace training session, will you?'

We both look over at the revolving door of the station, where a blonde young woman has begun to sob loudly, trying to work out how to get through. She steps into the triangle between the two doors and taps the glass, uselessly, crying still more.

Jess jogs over to help her, pushing the revolving part so that the girl can step in. She receives a thick 'Thanks', but the girl is in such a state of distress, dark make-up smeared down her face, that I don't think she has even looked at Jess.

I follow them, eyebrows raised.

I have just swiped my security pass and am keying in the code for the stairs when we hear the blonde girl choking to the receptionist.

'It's my b-boyfriend,' she is saying through thick tears. 'I've just heard that he's … he's dead. I have some information for you. His name is Peter Denny.'

Jess hears it too and we whirl around at the same moment. She reaches the girl before I do.

'Sorry, love, did you say you have some information on Peter Denny?'

Only now does the girl seem to register Jess. She looks at her, then at me, her mouth shaking almost comically.

She wears skin-tight jeans, a black winter coat and a pair of those fluffy boots that look like slippers. Her nose has a spattering of freckles, but apart from that her face is clear and ghostly white. Her eyes are rimmed with red and real tears continue to pour down her face. She is pretty, I suppose.

She looks like a knock-off version of Keeley Mackley.

'Are you investigating Pete's death?' The girl seems unsure.

'Yes. This is Detective Inspector Chris Rice and I'm Detective Sergeant Jessica Curran; we're both looking into Pete's death.'

'Detective Inspector' appears to have registered with her. The girl looks at me quite seriously, her mouth steady now. My heart is beating quickly – on one hand, I want very much to hear what this girl has to say; on the other, how the hell did we miss a second girlfriend?

McCrane is going to stab me.

'Then you better get your car, Inspector,' she says. 'I can take you to his killer right now. Her name is Keeley Mackley.'

Twenty minutes later, Leah Byrne has stopped crying and is sitting opposite me, not in a police car zooming towards Wits End to arrest Keeley, but in an interview room. Jess has chosen the exact same room in which we interviewed Keeley yesterday, which makes me think she has – consciously or not – seen the similarities in the girls too.

Jess sets up the tape and looks at me expectantly. I have no idea where to begin.

'So … Leah,' I say. 'Thank you for coming in. You're aware we're investigating the suspicious circumstances surrounding Peter Denny's death in the early hours of January 1st 2020. It would help if you could tell us about your relationship with him, to start us off.'

'We've been boyfriend and girlfriend since the 1st of October,' she says promptly. 'I know it's only been a few months, but the way we get on you'd honestly think we'd been together for years.'

I glance sideways at Jess, who is doing a good impression of someone to whom this information is mildly interesting and not at all revelatory.

'He was filming a promo video for the Miss Vetobridge competition at the Tech over the summer,' Leah continues. 'I was one of the entrants. We got to talking after he'd finished filming and we went out for a drink that night. One thing led to another and …' Leah looks out of the window and I think she is trying her best to look wistful. There is a clump of mascara on the side of her face that hinders her attempt somewhat. 'It was love at first sight. For both of us, honestly. I know that might sound melodramatic or childish to you, but I promise you that's what it was. We used to talk all day and all night and we never ran out of things to say. We understood each other. We finished each other's sentences. I always knew how he was feeling, even if I wasn't with him. He would always know when I needed cheering up. I'd get the cutest texts from him, like *Can't stop thinking about you*, or –'

'Were you aware of Pete's relationship with Keeley Mackley?' Jess interrupts.

Leah's face freezes in the determinedly nostalgic gaze, her eyes fixed to the upper left. 'I knew about her, yes,' she says. 'But I'm not a whore, I was in love. He told me about her after we'd been seeing each other for a month and, well, by that time I'd already fallen for him.' She gives a shrug. 'He was going to leave her for me.'

'That right?' Jess asks.

'Yes. After Christmas. Any day now I was expecting a call from him, telling me he'd done it. That it was all over and we could stop hiding our relationship and just be ourselves.'

Leah's eyes fill with tears and Jess pushes a box of tissues towards her, dutifully. Leah takes one and blows her nose, hard. She wipes her eyes with the same tissue and I notice that her nail polish, pink and sparkly, is badly chipped. I realise with a jolt that, before meeting Keeley Mackley, I would not have picked up on a detail like this.

'Except that didn't happen,' Leah says. 'I was at a party on New Year's Eve, in a private room in a club in Belfast. It was models only, no boyfriends, kind of another promo thing ahead of the Spring Pageant we're doing.' Leah swings her long hair over one shoulder, a half-hearted attempt to look like the model she is, I think, in spite of her current state. 'So … Pete went to her house. All his mates would be there, he said. He was going for his mates, not for her. He was going to leave her really soon. Only he never got the chance to do it properly. She killed him first.'

These last four words are spat with such sudden venom that Jess and I both flinch.

'What makes you think Keeley killed him?' I ask.

'That girl is a *freak*,' she says. She has lowered her head so that her shoulders stick up, nearly in line with her ears. She is staring at us so intently that I cannot meet her eye. 'She likes violence. Violent sex. She loves it. You want to see the state of Pete's body after he's been with her; his back has never properly healed from her scratches, and never mind hickeys, she bites lumps out of him, all over. It's disgusting.'

Unable to keep the surprise out of my voice, I ask, 'And you were OK with your boyfriend having such rough sex with another woman?'

'He didn't want it like that. That's why he liked coming to see me. Things with me are … were, innocent. Loving. Intimate. He couldn't wait to be rid of Keeley Mackley.

'I phoned him on New Year's Eve, after we left the club, to say I missed him. He was really nice at the start, his usual self, but then he hung up in a rush. He texted me later to say she had found out. Someone had heard him on the phone to me and told her. She looked through his phone and saw everything. Texts. His call log. A picture of us together. They were over, that was the end. I texted back saying I was sorry it had gone like that, but that it was probably for the best. He didn't reply. I just thought he was drunk. He would be fine in the morning.

'That was it. Keeley Mackley was out of our lives forever, for good. I went back to the girls and had a drink, over the moon.' Leah raises her gaze to the ceiling and closes her eyes. 'Then I didn't hear from him all day yesterday. I tried ringing but his phone had died. I wasn't too worried: sometimes after he's been on the drink, he just sleeps all day. I thought he'd call over in the evening. He didn't. Then I saw on the news this morning that a man had been found stabbed in the shithole side of that estate, Wits End. I knew Mack lived there. It took me forever to get in contact with anyone. I know Roy Philips from school and I've met Mack a few times, but I didn't have a number for either of them and Roy wasn't replying on Facebook. Eventually I got a number for Naomi Ross off a friend and she told me Pete was dead. Just like that. Not one of them thought to try and contact me. Nobody even *thought* of me. I had to find out over the phone from Pete's mate's girlfriend. Just before I came I saw his name had been released on the news. I'm starting to think Pete might not even have told anyone about our relationship, that's how scared he was of that bitch. He didn't even tell his best friends.' She stares at us, waiting for us to join in with her incredulity. When we don't, she says fiercely, 'Are you going to arrest her?'

I take a deep breath, but Jess responds before I can. 'We'll certainly look into this, Leah. You have been helpful. Thank you for sharing this with us. Just one more thing, can you give us the time of the phone call you had with Pete, and the time he texted you, telling you Keeley had found out?'

In the incident room an hour later, Jess brings me a coffee and I make a murmur of thanks in the back of my throat.

'Techs would have found the texts,' she says. I know she is trying to humour me. 'Or the call history. There is no way we could have known about Leah Byrne without something like that. We'll probably get a phone call later today from them with all the same information she just gave us.'

'Not one of the suspects mentioned her,' I spit.

'We didn't know to ask,' Jess says. 'Or maybe it genuinely didn't occur to them. There's a chance some of them don't know about her.'

'There was an argument right before Denny died,' I say. 'We found out because some dickhead posted a video of it. We had to wait for a witness to literally come stumbling up to the building and tell us exactly what the argument was about. So far there's been absolutely no fucking detection here and a whole lot of luck.'

'A lot to think about,' Jess says. 'But this is a good thing. At least this explains the skin cells under Denny's fingernails, and the cuts and bruises, I suppose. At least we know exactly why they were fighting. We're getting there … albeit slowly.'

'The video that Brian Reed made, the live thing, I'd like to see it again.'

'Edgecomb emailed it to you, she copied me in.'

'There has to be something in it. Something we missed that will point to what the hell happened on Tuesday night.'

'Who do you think is lying?' Jess asks suddenly. 'What's your gut tell you?'

'My gut tells me I need more fibre.'

'Mm, more fruit and veg wouldn't go amiss. Really, though?'

'I think this is a very awkward, delicate case. I think on the one hand, we have two girls who may well be innocent, but who would lie for one another regardless.'

'And a mentally unstable brother who might well be guilty but who isn't talking, but who might not be talking to protect his girlfriend – or his sister. He seems like he'd lie for her.'

'Does that, by association, mean he'd also lie for Jude?' I ask.

The door opens. Dunwoody is halfway across the room before he spots Jess and me, hunched over our cups at the table furthest from the door.

'I've just been to your office, Sir,' he says. 'I was looking for you. How did the post-mortem go?'

'What post-mortem?' I ask dully. 'Is someone dead? You should have said.'

We all glance automatically at Denny's smiling face on the whiteboard.

'The search of 166 Wits End is done, Sir,' Dunwoody says. 'One thing I thought you should know … Keeley Mackley and some of the others admitted, without being pressed, that the drugs were being taken in the kitchen and the living room of the house, right? And we know the group manufacture their gear in that house too?'

When he does not continue, I say, 'Yes?'

'Only, forensics have searched that house top to bottom. No drugs. No equipment. No chemicals of any kind that you might use to manufacture these Sixes. Nothing at all in that whole goddamn, shitty, old house. Not one pill.'

I sit up a little straighter. At my side, I feel Jess, rather than see her, tilt her head.

'There were no drugs?' I repeat. 'Nothing?'

'There are certainly traces, some powdery residue over the benches and tables, but there are no chemicals. Nothing in that house you could use to *make* pills. And no pills whatsoever. I heard that about an hour ago, so I took Browne and we went back to Vetobridge ourselves. I had a hunch. Edgecomb mentioned that in the CCTV, Joshua Mackley had a black bag with him when he left for Boar's Brae, and I wanted to double-check it wasn't just some clean undies and a toothbrush. Guess what we found in a gym bag in a cupboard in Naomi Ross's apartment? The same gym bag Joshua Mackley is seen carrying away from Wits End at 2.40 in the morning on New Year's Day?'

'Was it drugs?' Jess asks hopefully.

Dunwoody grins. 'Being processed into the evidence log as we speak. Flipping loads of pills. But that means –'

'It means that Joshua Mackley moved their stash from his house because he knew there was going to be a police search,' I say. 'He knew Denny was dead. Maybe Naomi Ross did too.'

I feel a bubble of guilt in my chest – I have wasted time looking at the others. Of course Mackley is our boy.

'We need to get Joshua Mackley back in here,' I continue. 'We can arrest and charge him for the drugs – at least then we can hold him and that'll buy us time until we have something more concrete to tie him to Denny's murder. Get him in this afternoon, charge him, and tomorrow we'll try speaking to him again.'

'Already on it,' Dunwoody says. 'I left Naomi Ross with a constable, told him not to leave her until Mackley gets home or until she can lead us to him.'

'Dunwoody,' I say. 'If it wouldn't be unprofessional, I'd stick my tongue down your throat.'

Mack

2nd January 2020, afternoon

I click to answer Naomi's phone call.

'Mack,' she says. 'Where are you?'

'Promenade. Walking. Clearing my head.'

'Whereabouts?'

I look around, clutching my phone to my ear. 'Opposite Murphy's, actually.'

I hear Naomi mumbling to someone in the background, commotion, scuffling, noise.

She comes back on, 'I'm sorry, Mack.'

'What for?'

I hear a catch in her breath.

I keep walking, a little more determinedly than before.

I have covered around eight miles today, I think. Just walking from one end of the beach to the other and back, hands in my pockets and shoulders hunched against the cold. It is always quiet, nearly dead, in Vetobridge from October until April. You could almost set your watch by it. The second weekend in September signifies the start of autumn, the end of the season, when the few tourists that explore Vetobridge over the summer start to pack up their caravans and drive back to wherever life exists outside of our town, wherever children go to schools without 'Sea' in the name. Strangely, it is always the sleepy, empty Vetobridge of winter that I love the most. Sitting on a bench on the promenade eating chips, you can be anywhere. If you squint. Wrap up warm enough and

Vetobridge is Australia. Probably. I'm sure the sand is the same. I've done some of my best thinking on this beach in the middle of winter.

After Mum died, I wrote the most flipping awful, terrible song I've ever written, and I wrote it sitting on the exact bench I can see just across the sand from me.

'The police are here,' Naomi says eventually. 'They found your … They found *a bag* with some pills in it. I told them the truth, that it's nothing to do with me.'

I stop walking. I think I can hear police sirens in the distance already.

It was called 'Freedom', the song, and everyone in the band and Naomi and even Jude said it was so beautiful and *poignant*. That's how I know none of them actually understands music. They knew it was a song about my dead mum, so they went into it thinking it was going to be beautiful and sad but it actually wasn't. It was about feeling so tied down to someone that you know you have to love, but you don't.

Keeley didn't say anything about the song, and that's how I know she understood it.

Which made me wonder how she could grasp that so easily but be so wrong about Pete.

I was right when I told Jude around forty people would show up to Keeley's birthday party. It doesn't sound like that many, but with a small living room, an even smaller kitchen and a Den as the main party areas, the house soon filled up. Bodies squashed together like beans in a jar, coated in sweat, bottles mainlining for mouths, girls holding their phones at arm's length, the music from my amplifier making the air in the room bounce and vibrate.

I was pretty drunk by nine o'clock and suggested that Premorbid set up in the living room and play a few songs. Keeley, who was wearing two birthday tiaras and carrying around a magnum of champagne, was all for it, and Naomi and I started to plug in the instruments. We didn't have Kyle's keyboard, but he usually carried a bodhrán about and he was happy to perch on the end of the sofa with that, his eyes closed as though he were in the midst of something life changing. We didn't have Roy's drums either, but he kind of beatboxed his way through 'Red Skies' while Naomi sang and Paddy and I strummed our guitars.

Some of the girls from Keeley's class were rolling their eyes at one another, but most of the guests seemed to like it, and even requested an encore once the song was over.

Keeley and Jude were speaking seriously in the corner, not listening, having heard us perform and practise dozens of times before. The only others not listening were two men in the corner that I didn't recognise, both wearing the same Vans shoes and speaking earnestly to one another. They both kept glancing around, as though afraid someone would see them.

After our third song, I hid my guitar behind the sideboard and let the guests claw at the microphone stand. A screeching match began between two girls, and finally one prised it from the other and began a pitchy rendition of a song I thought I knew from a recent film musical. The reaction to this was more light-hearted – people laughed and booed good-naturedly, and soon everyone was taking it in turns to grab the microphone and sing along to the iPod songs.

I went into the kitchen, pulling Naomi with me.

It was only a little quieter in here, and my ears were starting to hurt from the volume of the music.

Birthday presents and bottles of drink had been placed on the tiny kitchen table, so many that you couldn't see the chips and scratches of the wood underneath.

I selected a bottle of gin and poured glasses for myself and Naomi, adding a little lemonade. We clinked glasses as she settled on the countertop.

I said, 'You sounded great tonight.'

'So did you,' Naomi said. 'I think the ginger girl standing in the doorway really fancied you.'

I chuckled. 'Can't blame her.'

Brains and Roy came in, deep in animated conversation, and ignored us as they lifted beers from the table.

'Fucking loves his bodhrán, our Kyle,' Roy was saying. He pointed at the back door. 'Who's that?'

We all turned to the door, half dirty-white plastic and half glass. A tanned face grinned in at us through the glass, its head covered in a Union Jack.

'Whoever it is, tell him to get that filth off his head,' said Brains.

I opened the back door and let Pete D inside.

'Hello, fuckers!' He bounced around me and lifted a half-empty bottle of Bud from the bench. 'You look surprised to see me, considering you invited me …'

I could tell he had already had quite a bit to drink. His breath smelled of booze and his eyes were bloodshot. He was wearing jeans and a dark-coloured T-shirt down which he had spilled something, the Union Jack tied clumsily around his forehead. He smelled unpleasantly of a deep smoke, something more than cigarettes.

I realise grudgingly that, despite the state of him, he was probably still the best-looking man in the room.

'Where have you been, you melter?' Brains asked, trying to pull at the flag and earning himself a good-natured shove from Pete.

'You smell like fire,' said Naomi. 'Did you put a lighter to your nose hairs again?'

'Nah, bonfire,' he replied. 'Bands and shit.'

'You don't care about all of that,' Naomi said, rolling her eyes. 'You just like the booze and the craic.'

'Don't we all, Nomes. Don't we all. There's no one under fifty who lives in this country who actually gives a shit. We just love the craic. Feeling part of something, you know?' Pete finished his beer and reached for a second, unopened bottle on the table. 'Where's your wee sis?' he asked without looking at me. 'I hear she's looking a go on me to make her a woman.'

'Who told you that?' I asked warily. 'I just said she wanted to meet you.'

He didn't need to answer my question: Brains and Roy were laughing and nudging each other like children in the corner of the kitchen, clearly delighted with themselves.

'She just wants to meet you,' I repeated. 'She's eighteen today.'

'She wants your cock to meet her mouth,' Brains piped up from the corner. We looked over and he waggled his eyebrows. Somehow, he had managed to spill chocolate cake all down his T-shirt, even though the cake hadn't been cut yet.

'She likes it rough, our birthday girl,' Roy added. 'I've never been there myself but I know plenty who have.'

'Me too,' said Brains. 'She's wild, I heard. Likes it really rough and isn't afraid to do a bit of work.'

'Can we maybe wait for me to not be in the room before we have this detailed discussion about my sister's sex life?'

'Half-sister,' Roy said. 'To be technical. It's not that weird.'

'Dirty bitch,' Brains giggled.

'Oi,' I said a little more seriously. 'Watch it.'

I was fairly sure that the things people said about Keeley were just that. Just things people said. As far as I knew, she'd never had a boyfriend, and she'd certainly never brought anyone home.

'Which one is she, then, Katie?' Pete was craning his neck into the living room, peering over heads.

'Keeley,' Naomi and I said in unison.

'Wee blonde thing near the window,' Brains said, pointing to where Keeley and Jude were picking a song on Naomi's iPod. 'With the nice arse.'

'She mustn't have seen you yet, or she'd be in like a shot,' I said.

Pete made a kind of roaring in the back of his throat, spat into the sink and grimaced. 'I'll make sure little sis has a nice birthday, Mack.' He winked at me.

'Pete, while I have you here –'

He downed the end of his second beer. 'What?'

'When are we going to get filming?' I asked. 'For the video for *All Things Lost*? You've been promising for months and I haven't even seen you with a camera yet. I was thinking we rent out the funfair at night. I can see us on the teacups in a dream sequence. Do you think you could do that? Pete?'

Pete had stopped listening quite a while before, and I knew this but continued to speak. He was watching the two guys in matching Vans in the corner of the living room beyond, who now sat with their arms around each other, laughing with a girl and sipping beers.

'Why did you invite a load of fags?' Pete's tone was not scathing. If anything, he sounded genuinely curious and conversational.

'Stop that,' Naomi said. 'Don't be a dick.'

'Speaking of dick.' Pete set his empty bottle by the sink, then made a pantomime of tying the flag over his head like a habit. He knotted it under his chin to keep it in place. 'No time to waste, fellas. Lady.' He grinned nastily at Naomi and made his way through the crowd in the living room.

'Prick,' Naomi mumbled, shaking her head and jumping down from the countertop.

I shrugged. 'Let's go Sixes?'

I lifted a plastic sandwich bag from the cupboard and held it up, smiling at her. Her face softened and she followed me into the living room, leaving Brains and Roy examining a cut on the former's finger and looking confused.

I asked a sick-looking girl in a red dress to budge up so Naomi could sit on the edge of the sofa. She obliged, then immediately sprang up and ran towards the kitchen, a hand over her mouth, barely holding in the vomit that was trying to escape.

I emptied the pill packet on to the arm of the sofa and passed one to Naomi. She waited for me to take up my own, then we smiled at each other and put them in our mouths. Naomi kissed me, once, on the lips before she swallowed. Our lucky kiss.

I turned around to face the room.

'Keeley?' I shouted. The music was loud, very loud, but she appeared at my shoulder a moment later, very drunk but smiling and laughing.

'Happy Birthday,' I said, holding out a single Six in the palm of my hand.

'What happened to *they aren't ready yet*?' she asked. Her impression of me was uncanny, even in her drunk state.

The music seemed to vibrate my whole body.

'Special circumstances,' Naomi said. 'Did you see the other surprise Mack got for you?'

Keeley grinned and put the pill into her mouth. 'The Cortina? Yeah, I love it.'

I opened my mouth to explain that Naomi had meant Pete, but Keeley shouted over the music, 'Where's Jude?'

We both shrugged and shook our heads. Then a girl I vaguely recognised as Kim, or maybe Kate, from Keeley's drama club, grabbed her by the arm and started speaking excitedly into her ear.

'Think it's time we put something good on,' Naomi said. She went to the iPod and picked the band Dark Dark Dark. Some of the guests wrinkled their noses or booed at the sudden change of pace, the lack of bass, but Paddy whooped loudly and Kyle started to sing along, which made the rest of the guests laugh.

My Six had started to take effect already, though I couldn't have said for sure if I'd taken it five or twenty minutes ago. My vision seemed vibrant, the sofa was jumping, the picture on the wall was jumping, Naomi was jumping.

Naomi really was jumping. She jumped with every word of the song, but still somehow out of time.

The two guys with the same shoes were kissing in the corner, their nerves forgotten. I watched them and wondered how anyone could ever disapprove of something so beautiful.

Brains had my guitar in his arms and I reached out to take it from him, but suddenly he was very far away. I laughed at how far away he had managed to get in the split second it took me to raise my arm.

I turned to tell Naomi but she had gone. I kept laughing, hard. How did she get away so quickly?

I was speaking to someone that I thought was Naomi but who, when I really looked, had the wrong colour of hair and a small scar across her eyebrow. I laughed in her face and went into the kitchen.

Naomi was sitting at the table, her arms outstretched to me.

She had been waiting for me as I had been waiting for her my whole life.

'Let's go to bed?' she asked. She slid her hand into mine and we pushed through the crowd and went upstairs.

'If I didn't have you, I wouldn't have anything,' I said. It was supposed to be a compliment, one of those profound things that you say when you're drunk and you want somebody to know how much they mean to you, but my voice sounded sad when I said it. I tried to explain better. 'I had Murphy, and he was like my best friend in the world. Don't tell Brains. But then he died, and then Mum died and you're all I have in the world.'

'Don't let your sister hear you saying that.' Naomi grinned. We were halfway up the stairs. She pushed me against the wall and kissed me, hard.

'But you're the only point,' I tried to say. She pushed my words away with another kiss.

Upstairs was quiet and, I thought, empty.

Until I pushed open the door to my room.

Here on the promenade, I can hear sirens for sure now.

I stand motionless, staring across at the empty arcade where I'd had the best days of my life. The metal shutters haven't come up since Murphy died.

A police car pulls up on the kerb right at Murphy's and two officers get out. I barely register as they cross the road and come towards me.

'Joshua Mackley?'

'They're all my drugs,' I say. 'Nobody else's. Nothing to do with Naomi. She didn't know they were there. Are you going to arrest me now?' I suck in the first long, real breath I've had in two days. How good it feels to have said that.

They do just that, arrest me.

A mother with a pram who had been walking in our direction stops in her tracks and hastily turns the pram around, her mouth agape. A group of young men stand across the street, craning their necks to see me better.

The handcuffs are cool and solid. There is comfort in knowing I won't have to think again after this.

The constable is rhyming off some words I've heard on TV, and I'm nodding constantly.

I understand, I understand.

Please just take me away.

Jude

2nd January 2020, evening

Dad seems overjoyed to have me at the dinner table with them. Since Keeley managed to get the day shift in work, she and I have been making spaghetti or curry together at the Mackleys' or eating leftovers at a table in the bar in the Clandy. If Pete was there, or if she was out with him, I'd make a sandwich at home and insist I wasn't hungry. With the exception of Christmas Day, I can't remember the last time I ate with my family.

Dad has cooked a pasta dish with a tomato sauce and has referred to it at least three times as 'Jude's favourite'. I vaguely remember enjoying it once or twice as a child.

There is some stilted conversation at the dinner table, but mostly the clinking of Mum's wine glass, the scrape of forks. Mason is chasing a piece of onion around his plate, glancing surreptitiously at Mum, hoping she doesn't catch him and start ranting about starving Africans.

Mum and Dad are, for once, oblivious to him.

'Nice to have us all together,' says Dad. When nobody, not even Mum tries to reply, he adds, 'Have you both got homework?'

Mason has successfully moved three pieces of onion to the far side of his bowl, out of Mum's eyeline. He grins and says, 'I only had two homeworks. Finished them both. Max wants to know if I can go to his house this weekend.'

'I'm sure you can,' Dad says, going to the sink to refill his water. 'We'll need to see … what's happening closer to the time.'

'You mean if they catch whoever killed Pete?' Mason asks.

Mum sets down her glass. I want her to smash it.

'It was on the news yesterday,' he says, shrugging. He goes back to his pasta.

'What did it say?' I ask before Mum can steer the conversation away from this.

'Oh, they didn't name him,' Mason says, delighted to be involved. 'Just called him a twenty-eight-year-old man. Said police were interviewing potential suspects. Are you a suspect, Jude?'

'Mason,' Dad says. I don't think either of them has ever properly shouted at Mason – probably his slow legs make them feel guilty – but there is a definite warning tone in Dad's voice as he comes back to the table. He resumes his meal, one eye on Mason.

'No,' I say.

'Is it drugs?' Mason asks. 'Is that why he was killed?'

Dad sets his fork down at the exact second Mum picks up her wine glass again. She holds it over her mouth like she is trying to hide herself or keep her words inside.

'Not at the table, Mason,' Dad says.

'When, then? Why not tell me here, while we're all together? I need to know. Everyone knows the "man" died in Wits End and I'll look like an absolute dick if I don't know –'

'Mason!' Dad shouts. 'That is enough.'

There is silence as we each go back to our plates in turn. After a few moments of scraping, I say, 'I'm not sure about Keeley and Mack. Neither of them has bothered calling me to tell me what's going on. I don't know anything more than you do. But I'm not a suspect. At least, I don't think so.'

Mason nods solemnly, happy for the bite of information.

'In the morning,' Mum gushes suddenly. 'I was thinking we could all join in and help take down the Christmas decorations. What do you think?'

'Sounds riveting,' says Mason, picking at a piece of onion that has lodged in his teeth.

I stay at the kitchen table after dinner and take out my English coursework, telling Mum – and myself – that I have one more essay to finish by Monday.

She seems satisfied and tops up her wine glass before leaving the kitchen.

I last less than ten minutes before I push my books aside and pull my laptop towards me.

I have typed in WITS END MURDER before I can really think about what I am doing.

I click on the top result, which was added ten hours before.

After a brief synopsis of the story, the writer focuses on how semi-famous Pete was and how the social media world will be affected. The webpage is a student news website and is littered with typos and flashing advertisements on either side. There are a few photographs from Pete's Facebook page where, the captions tell me, he was known as 'Pete D Official'. I scroll quickly past the photos.

Ten hours ago there had been no arrests.

I have a cold trickling feeling in my stomach that is alleviated only a little by this. No arrests is the best I could hope for at this point. I can sleep tonight.

I take out my phone and text Keeley again.

What's happening? Where are you? Ring me ASAP x

I look back at the screen. A thumbnail picture of Pete's face smiles at me, goading, all his white teeth on show. It is the same picture Keeley showed me, I think, when she announced she was meeting him in the flesh for the first time.

It was late August.

Bright, hot sunshine. Everything so bright. One week of glorious, easy freedom left before school started again. Sixth form. A new start. I would be different, I thought. Everything would be fine. I would forget Keeley's birthday party and become someone entirely new. A new and better Jude.

We were parked up on the promenade, lying on the bonnet of the Cortina like something from a film. Her blonde against the red of the car was striking and beautiful. She shook back her head and let loose waves ripple down her back, eyes closed, face skyward. I knew how soft her hair would be if I reached out to stroke it. This would make the perfect photograph, I thought. If ever the perfect image could exist, it would exist with her, here, on the car, right now.

'Drink up,' she demanded without opening her eyes.

I had a beer in my hand, from which I was taking odd, dutiful sips, and Keeley had her phone in hers. She had been texting all day, almost constantly, but had started rolling her eyes at the blank screen in the last hour or so. Whichever boy she had chosen that month wasn't replying to her. I didn't ask his name.

'Drink,' she said again. 'We're celebrating, remember?'

Keeley had passed her driving test after only seven lessons and – though I would not admit it to her – I was shocked by how good and sensible she was behind the wheel. I thought maybe the Cortina had literally driven the recklessness from her – she wasn't going to spoil such an iconic, beautiful car.

I took an obedient sip of warm Coors Light. It was much too fizzy, and the aftertaste made me retch.

'Is that Beth and Kim?' Keeley said suddenly. I nearly dropped my bottle of beer, snapping my head around violently to where Keeley was pointing. 'We should invite them over.'

'If you like,' I mumbled, glancing down at my outfit. Keeley had called right after my shower, beeping the horn of the Cortina in a manic song that made Mum sigh audibly, and shouting, 'Come on, I passed! I passed! Let's go.'

I had thrown on the nearest pair of shorts I could find and an old T-shirt that was a little bit too short and showed a line of my stomach, all without really thinking, wanting only to hug her and congratulate her. I had shoved my wet hair into a plait between Wits End and McDonald's and it still hadn't fully dried, though we had been driving around all day. Beth and Kim would have a lot to say about that. My heart beat faster.

Keeley sipped her Fanta and continued to look, but she didn't call to the two figures on the beach.

Sure enough, as they got closer, I realised it was Beth and Kim from our year at school. They were stumbling down the beach, both wearing ridiculously high, multi-coloured wedges and matching sun hats. They were talking quite seriously.

I lay back on the Cortina and sucked in my stomach, hoping they wouldn't spot us. Keeley was more conspicuous than me in her neon orange bikini top and tiny denim shorts, but the girls did not look away from each other.

With a fresh thrill of horror, I realised I had a small patch of unshaved stubble on my right shin that I must have missed in the shower. My eyes snaked to Keeley's perfect, tanned legs, smooth as they always were. Hair never seemed to grow anywhere but on Keeley's head.

'When we live together, I promise I will share all my beers with you, but only if you hurry up and drink that one.'

Her words made my eyes fly open. She had closed her own eyes again, but she was smiling. She hadn't joined in our game for months.

'And … we can take it in turns to do the cooking and drink the beer,' I said a little hesitantly, in case her words were a one-off. 'Or maybe wine.'

'Oh, of course,' she said. 'And we can pick a different colour theme for every room. Pink for both our bedrooms, grey and purple for the living room –'

'Black and white for the kitchen.'

'Yes. Now that I can drive, we can take a run to IKEA and start getting our furniture.'

My heart pounded, my stomach sick with excitement. 'Your room can be pink,' I said. 'But I think mine should be …'

Keeley sat up suddenly, fixing her hair around her shoulders and pressing the backs of her hands against her flushed cheeks. 'They've seen us, babe, I'm sorry.'

I realised she had been talking us through playing house to distract me from Beth and Kim who, of course, were now only metres away.

Keeley's here, I reminded myself. They're not going to do anything.

'Nice car, girl,' said Beth, as they came to a halt on the sand in front of us. 'I know you told me at your birthday party but what's it called again?'

'It's a Cortina,' Keeley said. Her tone was the epitome of nonchalance, but I knew she was thrilled to get the compliment. 'Just something to wreck about in.'

'Hi, Judey,' said Kim, smiling broadly at me. 'Are you out taking piccies for your art project?'

I felt a blush climb to my cheeks. My camera lay in between us, in the shade of my shadow on the bonnet. Kim had been in my art class last year. She had sat behind me and watched all I had done, commenting on everything from my handwriting to my brush strokes.

'She's obviously done with that project,' Keeley said. 'Very soon there will be dozens of her photographs in every magazine in the country. It was A-star material.'

Kim raised her eyebrows: this was not the answer she had been hoping for. 'So glad it all went well … And I loved the theme. Dozens of pictures of Keeley, how …'

She seemed to search for the right word. I heard Beth mutter, clear as anything, *gay*, and they both laughed.

Keeley was oblivious. Her phone had finally beeped with a reply and her thumbs were moving furiously, long nails sliding over the keys of my dad's old BlackBerry phone. Only on Keeley could such an old phone look so good.

'What are you two up to?' Beth asked.

I waited for Keeley to respond, but she was still tapping incessantly. I cleared my throat and said, 'Keeley got her driving test this morning so we just thought we'd go for a bit of a drive.'

'Sure, we'd love to!' Beth said. 'You're so kind to invite us.'

Kim giggled. They were not drunk but seemed full of energy or sugar.

Keeley slid her phone screen down and looked up, eyebrows coming together. 'What?'

'Jude invited us to come for a drive with you,' Kim said.

Keeley smiled slightly. She knew I would never do that.

'If you like,' she said. 'But we have to be back for nine because …' She trailed off and I was extraordinarily grateful that she did not say *because Jude has a curfew.*

'Fine,' said Beth. 'But I have to go in the front because I get travel-sick.' She and Kim shared a smirk.

Keeley slid off the bonnet and chucked her empty cup into a nearby bin. I stumbled a little as I stepped down, clinking my beer bottle against the side of the car as I did so.

Keeley's sharp intake of breath made me flinch and Kim and Beth laughed openly.

'It's fine,' I said quickly, running my fingers over the car. 'No marks.'

'Just be careful,' Keeley said, trying to keep the annoyance from her voice. She pulled her crop top on over her bikini, opened the car door and got in. I hastily moved to lift my CDs – Westlife, Pink, Abba – from the passenger footwell, along with my Marvel hoodie.

Beth stood at my back, almost pressing into me as she watched me scurry to collect all my things in one arm while keeping the camera safe in the other.

Kim had already taken the seat behind Keeley and was drumming her fingernails on the headrest in front of her.

'It's kind of old,' Kim stated as I slid in next to her.

'It's vintage, you fucking spastic,' Beth said, perching herself on the passenger seat, long legs crossed elegantly.

I must have twitched at the word, because Kim mumbled, 'Don't say that, Jude's brother is disabled.'

'He's not!' I said, surprising even myself with the vigour of my words. That someone might think Mason mentally disabled made my cheeks burn harder than ever.

'He isn't disabled like that,' Beth said. 'He's just got something wrong with his legs.'

'It's called Duchenne Muscular Dystrophy and it's a genetic condition that causes the muscles to weaken over time. It's more common in boys. Mason copes remarkably for someone who has been in a wheelchair for nearly all his life.'

If I had said it, I would have been thrown eye rolls and tuts and sighs. In Keeley's deep, calm voice, the explanation sounded like a voiceover on a documentary. Informed, clear and not to be argued with. I looked to her, grateful, but she was focused on watching a reversing car in her rear-view mirror. Her pink cheeks made her look breathless and pretty, like she had just woken up from a nap.

The sun was starting to go down as Keeley drove us away from the promenade.

Beth's seat was pressed right back against my legs, but I didn't want to ask her to move in case she started an argument and it bothered Keeley.

'How do I put the window down?' Kim asked doubtfully. 'There's no button.'

'It's manual,' I explained. I reached across her to turn the handle, and she jerked back against her seat, as though afraid my arm would graze against her.

'No, no, it's fine!' she said quickly. 'I actually don't want to put it down. Might wreck my hair.'

Beth was talking incessantly. Keeley was driving faster now than she had earlier, and the movements were not as thoughtful as before. Beth hadn't put her seatbelt on and I wanted Keeley to ask her to.

'What about you?' Kim asked Keeley, when Beth had finished a particularly graphic story about her summer romance with a boy that she had been calling 'El-yut'. 'You were seeing Owen in the year above before we got off for summer, right?'

'Frigid,' Keeley said simply. 'Was all over before it had begun, that one. How did you two do in your exams?'

I was the only one who noticed the rapid shift in the conversation. I wondered if she had pushed the subject away from sex to save me any potential embarrassment, or to save herself. As much as she went on dates and did a lot of texting, I was 85 per cent sure Keeley was still a virgin.

On our left, we passed the rock pools – I was so concentrated watching Keeley that I forgot to look out at them and only remembered at the very last second. When we were younger, the rock pools had a car park of their own and the area was really popular with tourists. We loved it, and some of my happiest memories are of me and Keeley running between pools and lifting up tiny silver fish with our bare hands. A few years ago, a girl hit her head off one of the boulders and drowned, right in front of about ten families and her own mum and dad, and the whole place was closed for the investigation and never reopened.

We were driving higher and higher, the Mournes getting clearer and closer. The sea, below us, winked in the fading light, and I was happy to stare out of the window, ignoring the others and hoping they would continue to ignore me.

'Five Bs and five Cs,' Beth said. 'Not too bad.'

'Two As, four Bs, four Cs,' said Kim. 'What did you get?'

'I did fine,' Keeley said. 'A few As, a few Bs and a D.'

'The only D you got this summer,' Kim said.

The three of them laughed.

In actual fact, Keeley had got six A stars, three As, one B and one D. Her D was in RE, because the class was on a Friday afternoon, and she kept skipping it to go to work behind the bar in the Clandy. It hadn't mattered, the D. She still did better than my two A stars, four As and four Bs.

Keeley drove until we were out of Vetobridge, on the scenic route that would eventually take us, in a very roundabout way, to Belfast. Beth put on the radio and the three of them sang along to a chart song. I recognised the chorus, something about shotguns, as Keeley had been singing it all summer. Keeley's phone continued to bleep every few minutes, and I could see she was itching to check her texts. I wanted to offer but didn't think she'd want it read aloud in front of the others.

'Who is gagging for you?' Beth asked, as though reading my mind. She lifted Keeley's phone from the space between their seats.

I expected Keeley to snatch the phone back, but she kept her eyes on the road and smiled slightly.

'Hold on ...' Beth said. 'This says Pete D. It's not *the* Pete D, is it? The one who never showed up at your party?'

'Yeah,' Keeley said. 'We've been texting for a few weeks. Mack gave me his number. Well, I got his number off Mack's phone. Same diff. He seemed terrified when I first messaged him, actually, like I was going to go bunny boiler on him for not coming.'

Right in my ear, Kim squealed. 'Oh my god, Keeley you are *so* lucky. Pete D is literally the closest thing we have to a celebrity.'

'He is *literally* a celebrity,' said Beth. 'He has fifteen thousand views on his latest video, and he's up to nearly fifty thousand followers. Have you seen the video he made about climate change?'

'Climate change?' Kim asked doubtfully.

'It's sexy now,' Beth said. 'He seems to be done with shitty small-time bands – oh, no offence to Mack – and he's focusing on bigger issues now. The last four videos he's posted have just been of him talking to the camera and honestly he is so …'

'Engaging?' Kim asked.

'Charismatic,' Beth said.

'And hot,' Keeley added. 'And he's coming over to mine tonight.'

Kim and Beth squealed in unison.

My whole body had frozen. I stared at the back of Beth's head and tried to focus on her badly sewn extensions. There were white chunks of dry shampoo stuck to her roots.

I could hear my blood pumping in my ears.

'I'd honestly let him do anything he wanted with me,' Kim was saying. 'He's gorgeous.'

'I'd let him pin me to a bed and blindfold me and gag me,' Beth said.

I didn't hear Kim's retort.

My throat burned and I felt bile rising right from my chest and into my mouth. I fumbled uselessly at the latch on the door but wasn't sure what I would do if it opened – we were driving too fast. I couldn't open my mouth to tell Keeley to stop. My eyes started to stream with the effort of keeping the vomit in my mouth.

I leant forward and retched on to the floor of the car, covering my shoes, my hoodie, my camera, in a foamy, light-coloured liquid. Chunks of my McDonald's burger stuck in my throat and I coughed hard to unblock my windpipe.

Kim was properly screaming, and Beth was peering around her seat, her face a mask of horror.

Keeley slowed down and put one hand on my head in an attempt to pull my plaited hair back from the mess. Finally, she pulled up on a kerb.

I fumbled with the door, unlatched my seatbelt and stumbled out of the car. I staggered a few feet away and threw up again. My tears were hot on my face, pain hot in the back of my throat.

She was next to me in seconds.

'Get it up,' she murmured. 'All of it. No point trying to keep it in now.'

'Your car,' I choked.

'Doesn't matter.' Her tone was kind enough but from the corner of my eye, I saw her glance back at it, her face creased in worry.

I wiped my eyes on the back of my hand, shivering and shaking. A black Corsa zoomed past, beeping its horn manically. A boy shouted something indecipherable from the window.

'I'm sorry,' I said. 'They're going to think I'm an idiot.'

'They're idiots,' she whispered. I smiled obediently and took the tissue she was holding out to me.

'Beer and sun,' I said, unable to look her in the eye. 'That's why I was sick. Is it?'

'Must be,' said Keeley.

While one of her hands was on my shoulder, the other was gripping her phone and she typed into it, a small smile on her face. She turned the screen to face me. 'This is him, Pete, look –'

I leant forward and was sick again.

Now, in the kitchen, the webpage I have been staring at refreshes and a new headline appears. My insides register what I am reading before my brain does, and they turn to liquid.

ARREST IN PETE D CASE?

I stare at the words, hover the cursor over them.

The article doesn't give a name.

I tap my fingers on the kitchen table, three taps for my index finger, three taps for my middle finger, and mouth the words *keep us safe* with every beat. I repeat this until Dad comes into the kitchen and suggests that we play the new trivia game that Mason got for Christmas.

We sit around the coffee table in the good living room and roll a dice and answer questions, each of us deliberately ignoring the police tape that, were we to squint down the green, could be seen from the window. I sit cross-legged on the floor with my back to the window, but the hairs on the back of my neck stand up as though someone is watching me. I imagine the police tape flapping in the wind, a flimsy strip of yellow plastic separating me completely from the world that existed before.

Detective Inspector Chris Rice

2nd January 2020, evening

I close the front door behind me and stick the key in the lock.

The flat is cold and, now that I have been away from it for two full days and a night, stinks of old curry and stale air. I can't remember when I last opened a window.

I put the Project Twenty file on the sofa and take a beer from the fridge. Joshua Mackley is in a cell and is facing a custodial sentence for possession with intent to distribute.

After two long swigs of beer, I finally let myself exhale.

It is evenings like this that I miss Rebecca and Aisling most. Non-specific, weekday evenings mid-case, when the girls would be watching TV together, and I would be snoozing in my armchair in our house – *our* house – in Holywood. I would sleep through entire shows and wake with a jolt at the ad breaks. A look at both of them, checking they were still there, making sure they hadn't been just a wonderful dream, and I would be snoring again. Reminding me that real life – real, gorgeously ordinary life – existed outside of police reports and interviews and fingerprints.

I open up my emails on my laptop and play the Spar CCTV video that Edgecomb sent me. I watch it four times, focusing on a different part of the screen on each play. The last night of Mackley's recognisable life, I think, and the last few hours of Denny's.

I leave the tape playing and go to the fridge for a second beer. I keep watching the footage while I sip. There is something calming, comforting, in the slightly vibrating feed. Every now and then the display clicks, making me blink with it, and once every ten minutes or so, the lights of a car can be seen driving past the shop window.

When the tape finally runs black, I exit the video and click on the second attachment to Edgecomb's email: the Jamesons' CCTV tape.

I have already heard everything that is on it, but again there is something comforting in watching for myself. Watching and knowing what is about to happen, what is going to come.

Mack and Naomi are the last to leave the house. They come through the back door, one after the other, Mack leading his girlfriend by the hand, the black sports bag over his shoulder. She hurries to keep up with him. Thirty-nine minutes past two in the morning.

On the sofa, four more bottles and a Chinese takeaway later, I reach my free hand over to open the Project Twenty file. The typed interview transcripts for Keeley, Jude and Mack have been placed at the front, with handwritten A4 pages accompanying them. Jess's writing and my own. I run my eye over the interviews, and then our notes, not reading sentences, merely picking out words. *Friends. School. Nineteen. Keeley. Earring. Last year. Keeley. Jaw. Party. Drugs. Door. Relationship. Brother. Keeley.*

I flick through pages: Edgecomb's CCTV photographs, like technicolour spot-the-differences; a hand-drawn house plan of 166 Wits End; a photograph of the tiny kitchen paring knife, with rulers at right angles. Then photographs of Keeley's face. I pause at these, one hand raised in mid-air, the beer almost kissing my bottom lip. The photographs are labelled in Jess's neat print, telling me they have been taken from Jude's Instagram page. *Used for GCSE art project entitled 'She and I'. Received A* grade.*

There are twelve photos in all, some black and white, some in colour, some using the special effect where only one colour comes through amidst greyscale. I flick quickly through them. My favourite is a close-up of Keeley's face with her pale blue eyes the only colour. The pictures are all basically the same, I think at first. All headshots, all void of expression.

Then I go back to the first picture and start to flick through them again, more slowly. In the third, there is a tiny, almost imperceptible spot on Keeley's forehead. In the sixth, her hair has been pulled back into a ponytail, and her whole face seems to lift. By the seventh picture, I realise that the expressions are different too. The seventh looks a little forced, while the others look natural. I flick through the rest and pause on the twelfth. My stomach jolts. The twelfth picture is not of Keeley. It is of Jude.

I hurriedly put the pictures back in order and make my way through them one last time. On this third time, I finally see it. Somewhere around the fifth, sixth and seventh pictures, Keeley's features start to morph into Jude's. By the final picture, it is entirely Jude. The same expression, the exact same pose. Just the same amount of blank space behind the head. The changes so subtle in each photograph that I hadn't noticed at all the slight darkening of the hair, the movement of the jaw, the tiny upturn of the nose. Some kind of camera trickery and some very clever editing.

My phone rings and I jolt upright. I fiddle in my pocket and extract it after six rings.

'Hi. Yes. Dunwoody?' I have to shake my head to focus, both girls' faces clear in my mind.

'Hi, Sir. I couldn't find you at the office earlier, just thought I'd update you on Tim's Pizza.'

'Of course.'

'A guy called Michael Parish delivered a pizza to Naomi Ross's address in Boar's Brae at two minutes to three on Wednesday morning. He knows for sure because they have to enter into an app when it's been delivered. It was his last run of the night and he went straight home afterwards. He says the two of them seemed drunk, or maybe something else, but that they were friendly enough and handed over the money and said thanks. No blood on their clothes, not acting strangely. I got you that pepperoni that you wanted. It's on your desk.'

'Yeah, sorry, I had to go. Were you able to find out what time they ordered it?'

'I did.' I hear Dunwoody rummaging around for something. A notebook, maybe, or, knowing him, a scrap of paper. He puts the phone back to his ear. '2.41. Immediately after they left 166 Wits End. Ordered on the app, so we know for sure.' When I do not respond, Dunwoody adds, 'What are you thinking?'

‘I’m thinking …’ I take a deep breath then, instead of speaking, a swig of beer. When I have swallowed, I finish, ‘They ordered the pizza to give themselves an alibi of sorts.’

‘I think you’re right,’ Dunwoody says. ‘I suppose in their drugged-up heads, they couldn’t have murdered someone in Wits End if they were munching pizza in Boar’s Brae. They were probably thinking it would be good to have a witness who saw them both acting perfectly normally at the time Denny was being sliced.’

I wince at his choice of word. ‘Yes. OK … good work. With that timing, they must have ordered en route to her house … Thank you, Charlie. See you tomorrow.’

I settle back on my favourite photograph – of Keeley, I am still sure – and sip my beer. My mind is a myriad of hazy images.

My eyes well up only a little bit by the seventh beer. Rebecca would tell me I’ve had enough.

Rebecca, Rebecca.

The last thing I think, before my eyes close on Keeley Mackley’s face, is that Joshua Mackley has a lot to answer for in creating this horrible mess for his sister.

It is as simple as that.

Keeley

3rd January 2020, morning

I haven't said a word to Naomi since Mack's arrest last night. What could I possibly say to her? She couldn't have given Mack up easier if she'd tried.

I try to ignore the voice in my head that wonders if I would have done something different.

Though I'm not speaking to her, I am happy she hasn't tried to kick me out of her house. She called the Clandy yesterday to explain that neither of us would be in to work for a while, so we are trapped together in her tiny space in silence. I am thankful she mostly keeps to her room.

I switch on my phone. I've been keeping it off to keep it charged. There is one message from Jude, sent last night.

What's happening? Where are you? Ring me ASAP x

I sigh to myself, feeling emptier than ever and wishing I'd left it alone.

After lying on Naomi's sofa for most of the morning, I decide I really have to wash my clothes. I can't knock on her bedroom door to ask for another loan of a jumper, can I?

I take the hoodie I wore to the police station – Jude's, I've since realised, a *JJ* sewn neatly on to the label – and put it into the washing machine.

We each got a hoodie with the Seaview High crest on our first day of sixth form. If this is Jude's, I have no idea where mine is now, though I suppose it doesn't matter. I haven't attended that school in nearly a year. How easy it would be if, on Monday, I was going back to sit in a classroom and be taught things. I had loved and looked forward to school the way most people did the school holidays. In fact, my flirtation with sixth form was the happiest time of my life.

Our AS-level year was tough but interesting and teachers handed me back my tests with high scores circled in red pen. Drama, maths, biology and physics. We were doing a whole statistics module in maths which was inherently fascinating and, somehow, had made me love those classes more than the drama practicals. I had learned what an actuary was and was privately thinking that if I did well enough, I might even be able to pursue a career in that if the acting was too hard to get into. It was a hazy, blurry dream that seemed part of a distant future, but thinking about it made me feel warm and excited. Sitting in an office wearing work clothes, having a lunch hour, looking forward to the weekend. Being normal. It could happen. Playing house but in real life. If anyone asked me, I still said, 'Oh, an actress', because that's what I had always said. I didn't think anyone would take me seriously if I mentioned an office job. Mackleys didn't do office jobs, did they?

My status of 'Pete D's girlfriend' enclosed me in a golden bubble as I walked the halls in my new green blazer that first autumn term. We hadn't had the girlfriend/boyfriend conversation yet – that would come much later, but so many people had seen us driving around together, sitting at a secluded table in the Clandy together, that 'Pete D's girlfriend' had become my social media tag, and Pete hadn't made any attempt to correct anyone. Younger girls smiled at me, and if I smiled back they gasped and looked at one another. Even boys thought it was cool – Pete was into 'cool' drugs, but he was likeable and cool himself in a way that my brother never had been.

The only thing that wasn't perfect then was Jude.

She had been a *little* bit moody and quite distant for most of the summer and, though I had decided to justify it to myself as jealousy over my new relationship with Pete, I knew in the back of my mind that her funny attitude had started before I ever met Pete.

'Leave her alone,' Mack advised when I brought it up with him. 'She's a teenager. You were moody when you were sixteen, it's just hormones. Just be there for her.'

I didn't remember ever being moody at sixteen, but I took his advice and let it go and was nice to her when she was being funny.

She was mostly herself at home and after school, despite her point-blank refusal to spend time with me if Pete was around. It was when we went back to school with our new sixth-former status that I really started to notice. She always seemed like she was in a rush to get away if I held a hand up to her in the corridor, and while she had moaned constantly when we had to be separated for classes for our GCSEs, she seemed relieved to say goodbye to me in the mornings to take her English, history and art AS-level classes.

But she seemed willing enough to sit at our usual table in the canteen at lunchtime, and at the desk next to mine during study periods, so these quickly became the only times I saw her during school hours. We chatted normally enough: about school, about our classmates, about the latest cheesy CDs Roddy had jokingly handed down to us from his vast collection, but there was always something just a little bit *off* about her until we got home. She would glance around, unable to relax, or would laugh just a fraction of a second too late, until we stood up to go to our separate classes.

During one such study period two weeks into the term, I offered to dye Jude's hair for her again. The blonde was fading quickly and her darker roots had grown a few inches over the summer, but she refused quite determinedly.

'I'm over it,' she insisted as her phone vibrated in her pocket. 'I don't want to be blonde any more, blonde is your thing – it suits you but it doesn't suit me.' She took out her phone, looked at the screen and put it back in her pocket again.

I'd done all of my homework and didn't feel like reading, so I swung back in my chair, one hand clinging to the desk, and let my eyes wander over to the side of the study hall taken up by the drama club. I had suggested to Jude that she come with me so I could sit with the rest of my class, but she refused that too. That day, I found myself wishing I was sitting with them instead. Beth and the others always seemed to be in fits of giggles over something or other, usually looking at someone's phone.

Jude's phone buzzed again, then again. Then three times in a row. She kept her eyes on the textbook in front of her, but I noticed they didn't seem to be moving across the page. She has a secret boyfriend, I thought to myself. She has a secret boyfriend who is really ugly and she's ashamed to tell me about him.

I jumped as Beth let out a barking laugh from the far side of the room. The laugh brought with it a memory of a drive we'd all had together over the summer. Jude's nervousness of Beth and Kim, the way she had *actually thrown up* just being in the car with them. I knew it was because she was afraid they were going to take me away from her, which is why I insisted on making the odd casual jibe about them within earshot of Jude – *Did you see Kim's new haircut? Awful. And Beth was doing my head in in drama earlier* – and on making our joint presence visible in the canteen. It was my way of saying *Nobody is going to steal me from you, I'm your best friend, look at me insulting these girls, look at us sitting together*. Her painful shyness, the shyness she had just been starting to break free from in our mid-adolescence, seemed to have come back with a vigour in recent months, and I wondered if it was being *seen* at all that stopped her shouting across busy corridors to me.

'Oh, please just let me dye it!' I said suddenly. 'Please, I'm so bored. I can nip out and get the box of dye now and we can do it tonight!' I reached across the aisle between our desks to run my fingers through her hair. Jude jumped as though electrocuted and pulled away from me, eyes wide in alarm, as if I'd done something embarrassing.

By the end of September, Linda had taken her to have her hair professionally stripped, and though she looked like my Jude again, she still didn't act like her.

In the first week of November, I paid for my panini at the lunch counter and made for our usual table by the window. Jude was already there waiting for me, hunched over her packed sandwiches and apple. As I negotiated my tray around a crowd of squealing first years, I saw Beth approach our table. She spoke to Jude for a moment, in a fairly friendly way, it seemed, then went back to her own table where her friends were laughing uproariously.

Jude's shoulders seemed to sink as I came closer.

'What was that?' I asked, indicating Beth. I lifted a handful of crisps from my tray and set them on the tinfoil of Jude's sandwich, as always.

'Nothing,' Jude muttered. She took a crisp but I could tell it was automatic. 'She's talking shit. As usual.'

I looked over at the table. Allan Casey, the only non-gay boy in our Drama Club (though I had heard rumours otherwise), had his arm around Beth's shoulder but was staring over at our table, grinning widely. Kim and a black-haired girl whose name I could never remember were clutching their sides with laughter, each holding their phones. Their eyes kept flicking to us.

I looked back at Jude. 'Is this something online?'

Jude shrugged, but she had stopped eating her lunch, one hand paused in the act of flattening her sandwich. She looked paler than usual.

'Well, check,' I said.

'Why do you care?'

'Because … because, Jude, it looks like they're laughing at *us*.' What I really meant was '*at you*', but it felt too harsh to say.

'She told me to check Instagram,' Jude mumbled. 'I haven't yet. It'll just be something stupid they've posted about me. How was biology?'

Without responding, I reached across the table and into the outside pocket of Jude's blazer. She made a half-hearted attempt to swipe her phone from me as I bounced back down on my seat, but I was too quick. I tapped in her password and opened up the app.

Jude had been tagged in a photograph that had been very effectively Photoshopped. It was Jude's face – taken, I thought, from a photo she had posted of the two of us a few Christmases ago – and it was my face – taken from my most recent school photo – but the images had been expertly cut and stuck on the naked bodies of two women that could only exist in male fantasy porn. The two bodies were tangled together, fingers probing between each other's legs.

My first instinct was to snort with laughter. 'I wonder which one of them made this. Their talents are wasted; they should be graphic designers.'

'What?' Jude's voice was high, panicked.

I turned her phone around to show her. She didn't laugh. She didn't react at all.

I looked at the phone again. The photo had been 'liked' forty times, even though it had only been posted ten minutes before. The caption read *Jude Jameson Loves Fanny* and used a variety of colourful hashtags. I rolled my eyes. 'For fuck sake, that's original.' I turned towards Beth's table and shouted, 'Hilarious, guys. Really clever.'

The group roared with laughter and a few of them clapped. Around the canteen, I noticed some more heads starting to turn towards us, nervous smiles, whispers. Everyone was looking down at their phones.

'Don't let it bother you,' I said easily, handing Jude back her phone. 'We're just their latest targets. We had to have our turn sometime.' I took a bite of my panini and wiped my hot-sauced hands on my skirt.

When I looked up, Jude was staring at me. 'Their latest targets?' she repeated. 'Keeley, are you fucking serious?'

I choked slightly at the anger in her tone. 'J, don't worry about it. It's just a joke. They'll laugh about it for today and forget about it by tomorrow.'

'No, they won't, and *you* are not the target here. It's me. It's always been me. Not everything is about you.'

'Sorry,' I said, bemused. 'I thought it was a little about me. Given that the picture has my face on it.'

'It isn't you they're laughing at.' Jude's teeth were gritted. 'It's not your name in the caption, is it? They've been making lesbian comments at me for *years*, even more so this term than ever. I've had dozens of messages, really graphic stuff. Everyone has been saying it behind my back since the start of the year, some to my face. Now it's there online for everyone to see. They think I'm … I dunno. In love with you or something. Obsessed with you. They think I try and get with you.'

I spluttered a laugh. 'Jude, that's ridiculous. Nobody thinks that. Who has been saying that?'

'Everyone!' She was nearly shouting now. Those at the closest tables were listening, their mouths slightly open in awe. Others were craning their necks to have a look. 'Everyone, all the time! They haven't left me alone for weeks!'

'I didn't know,' I mumbled, looking around. My amusement had gone cold in my throat. 'Jude, keep your voice down. Eat your sandwich. I'm sorry, I didn't know.'

'Of course you didn't know, you're too busy hauled up in your room with *him*. With that prick you call your boyfriend. That stupid, horrible *cunt*!'

She stood so abruptly that my water cup toppled and soaked the rest of my lunch. She grabbed her bag and swung it over her shoulder before half-running to the door. A few people cheered.

Allan Casey shouted, 'Trouble in paradise? A lovers' tiff?' He snickered and pulled a tin of tobacco from his blazer pocket. Beth, freed from his grasp, stood, smoothed her uniform and came over to take Jude's vacated seat.

'Hi,' she said. 'So sorry if our wee joke offended you. It was meant to be a prank on Judey. You were just collateral, I'm afraid. But I know you can take a joke.'

Still reeling from Jude's anger, and her use of a word I had never heard from that mouth, I blinked. 'Yeah,' I said. 'Wasn't funny though, was it? You've upset her.'

'We're sorry.' Beth tossed her hair back and made an exaggerated eye-rolling gesture. 'In all honesty, it wasn't me. I told them all it was childish. I'll ask them to take it down. Listen, we wondered if you were up for a little *soirée* at my house on Saturday night? Just a select few. You can totally bring Pete D, though.'

'Working,' I said. My chest felt numb. I couldn't remember Jude ever shouting at me before.

'After, then,' Beth said, unfazed. 'We're all dying to meet Pete IRL. Just … and I don't mean this in a bitchy way, but it'd be better if you didn't bring Jude.' She looked at the spot where Jude had disappeared and made a point of sighing loudly, as though in despair. 'She doesn't really get our sense of humour.'

Jude wasn't petty enough to blank me and I wasn't petty enough to drive off without her after school that day. So it was that I was waiting in the car park with the Cortina running at half-past three, texting Pete. He had seen the picture online too and had made some happily suggestive comments about it.

I glanced up in time to see Jude coming around the corner of the English block. She looked wary at first, as though unsure if I would be waiting, but relaxed as she came closer. She opened up the passenger door and put her bag in the footwell before sliding inside.

'What time does your shift start?' she asked quietly. She knew very well I started at six every Monday. I thought this was her way of breaking the tension.

'Six,' I said. I switched on the ignition and pulled out of the spot.

The thing was that, because we never argued, never fought, never shouted at one another, we had no make-up ritual. In our twelve years of inseparability, there had never been need for a plan like this. There were no rules about who should apologise or when. I felt like Jude was completely in the wrong, but it was clear from her body language, the fact she was almost totally turned away from me in the car and didn't speak, that she thought I was somehow to blame for a prank pulled by a few girls I used to be friends with. Come to think of it … the reason I wasn't more friendly with Beth and Kim and those ones *was* because of Jude. She had been overly jealous of me going to parties with them or going to Beth's house after school for years before this. I had only stopped doing things with them outside of school because it was making things so awkward with Jude. But it had been nice, on those few occasions, to have friends that I could talk to about boys. Something Jude had little or nothing to say about.

We were driving through Vetobridge town centre in no time, the promenade and subsequent beach on our right, Murphy's Arcade on our left. I was still thinking about a party at Kim Lennon's house the year before when, with a jolt, I realised Jude had said something.

'What?' I ask.

'I'm reminding you about tomorrow,' Jude said. 'You're staying behind after school for Open Night, aren't you?'

'Oh, shit. Yeah.' I had forgotten about that. Mr Tweed had asked me to help out in the physics lab on Open Night, showing nervous ten-year-olds the trick where you rub a balloon on your jumper and make everyone's hair stick up. 'Are you OK to get a lift home with your mum?'

'She's taking Mason to physio and Dad's working. I'll get home somehow.'

I glanced at her. The jutting jawbone I could trace with my eyes closed seemed set. It struck me then that maybe the reason she had taken the photograph so badly was because there was some truth in it. Was she gay? Could she have been gay this whole time and I hadn't noticed?

I hadn't thought about it before and supposed it made sense. She had never had a boyfriend, had never shown the least bit of interest in any boy that I knew of, squirmed if I tried to talk to her about Pete.

'You know you can tell me anything,' I found myself saying.

'Like what?'

'I dunno. Anything. You can tell me anything at all.'

I kept my eyes on the road but felt her looking at me. After a moment, she took a deep breath.

A football bounced out on to the road in front of me, and I slammed on the brakes just in time to see a small child try to dodge out from behind a parked car to chase after it. The child's mother threw both arms out to pull it back and made an apologetic sort of motion with one hand.

We had both thrown our arms across each other in a blind panic and drew back in on ourselves as the mother, with the child by the hand, quickly dipped out into the road and back the way she had come, football in her arms, motioning her apology to us with her head the whole time.

'Do you have to get straight home?' Jude asked as I sped up again. 'Or do you want to go and get smoothies? I've got money on me.'

'I'm seeing Pete for an hour before work,' I said, trying to sound apologetic. I couldn't stop the smile creeping on to my face. 'Maybe on Wednesday?' Jude made a sound that could have been a tut or a murmur of consent. I added, 'Did you get your history results back?'

'Yeah. Forty.'

'Out of?'

'Forty per cent.'

'What? That's shit.'

'I know it's shit.'

'Did you not understand it?'

'No, not a word.'

'Oh. Well, at least it wasn't a real exam. You'll have plenty of time to brush up. Big jump, from GCSE, isn't it?'

She made the tutting murmur again.

Pete's Honda Civic was parked in our driveway when we got home. I pulled up on the kerb and we got out.

'Thanks for the lift,' Jude mumbled. 'See you tomorrow.'

'Do you want to come in?' I asked, my fingers crossed that she would say no.

She shook her head, pulling her school bag across her body, and was gone behind the house and up the green before I had opened the front door.

Pete was in the kitchen.

'There she is!' he said with exaggerated bravo. 'The hottest lesbian in Vetobridge. Get your cameras out, lads, from what I've seen online today she could rip off her clothes at any minute!'

I rolled my eyes and pecked him on the lips. 'Not funny,' I said. 'Jude's really upset.'

'She's a bit sensitive, though, isn't she?' Pete seemed to shrug by moving his whole body. 'It's just a joke. A hot one.'

'Is Mack here?'

'No.' He grinned at me, his teeth shining, his thick eyebrows waggling. My heart surged as if straining to get out of my chest to touch him.

Being in love was not at all what I expected and at the same time I felt like it had always been there, lying asleep at the bottom of my stomach, awakening only when Pete was within touching distance. How was there ever a time when I didn't know about the tiny scar over his eyebrow? How did I get through eighteen years of life without ever having felt the pointed tip of his tongue? I had discovered a new colour – nobody had hair that colour, surely?

Why wasn't everyone in love with Pete? Even straight men? Had I been dead before Pete? Would I be dead if he left me?

It was not like loving Jude. At the beginning, I thought that meant it wasn't love at all, but lust, but the more time went on – and it had been three whole months – the surer I was. This was hard and fierce, it made me want to bite through my own lip, whereas loving Jude was easy and clean and familiar and it smelled like home. Until now, nobody had ever seen me the way Pete did. Even my own mother had never seen my naked body in adolescence or adulthood.

I wanted him to squeeze my shoulders until the bones snapped, to dig his nails into my softest parts, to thrust until I severed. That was love too, I thought. The things that made people blush so much they weren't sung about, were rarely shown on TV and never as a hallmark of true, deep love. I couldn't believe people didn't walk around with grins permanently pinned to their faces. Maybe nobody had felt it quite like me.

I'd never have admitted my feelings to Pete, of course. We'd only just started seeing one another. It was enough just to feel them.

'She's really upset,' I repeated.

Pete had pulled me into a hug and was kissing at my neck. 'Huh?'

'Jude. I think something's up with her; she took all of that stuff today way too bad.'

'She's a kid, it'll be hormones,' Pete murmured into my neck.

I frowned and pulled away from him. 'I'm being serious. I think she's a bit … a bit jealous of us. She's never had to share me with anyone before, I think she feels a bit left out.'

Pete, looking crestfallen that the kissing had stopped, shrugged again.

'I think I should invite her over,' I said, chewing the inside of my lip. 'Give you a proper introduction. This isn't going to work if Jude isn't OK with it.'

Pete narrowed his eyes, but knew better than to say anything.

I texted Jude and asked her to come over as quickly as possible so that is, of course, what she did.

She cautiously tapped on the back door and opened it.

When she saw I was standing next to Pete, she froze. She stared at a spot on my school tie, refusing to step beyond the doorway.

‘What’s wrong?’ Her voice was too high.

‘Nothing,’ I said quickly. ‘Nothing, I just wanted to properly introduce you two. Jude … this is Pete. Pete, this is my best friend, Jude.’

She loved it when I said *my best friend, Jude*. I waited for a bashful smile, a blush maybe? I waited for her to at least throw a smile at him.

But she didn’t.

When I looked at Pete, he too was staring determinedly at a spot on the kitchen floor. I thought there was the tiniest blush on his cheeks, something I hadn’t seen before. Did he think she was good-looking?

I snorted a laugh, feigning normalcy amid the awkwardness. ‘You two fucking weirdos. Can you at least say hello? Jude is shy but you’re not, babe.’

Pete cleared his throat and raised his eyes to Jude. ‘Hi,’ he said.

Her eyes flashed to his and I watched a look between them that I could never replicate. Like an agreement, maybe.

‘Hi,’ she said quietly.

She was gone two minutes later.

Here in Naomi’s kitchen, my phone, still in my hand, begins to ring.

I answer the unfamiliar number.

‘Hello? Is that Keeley Mackley?’

‘Yeah?’

‘Miss Mackley, this is Detective Magill at Oldry Police Station. We have a set of keys belonging to you that you can come and claim anytime. The investigation of your house in Wits End is finished.’

It is only when the washing machine beeps to indicate the cycle is over that I realise I have sat on the floor in front of it for a full half hour, mind whirring: full of Pete and Jude and that look between them.

Jude

11th July 2018

On the morning of Keeley's eighteenth birthday, I wake up smiling.

She has been waiting her whole life to turn eighteen, she says. I think this is probably an exaggeration, as she always seemed perfectly content at sixteen, seventeen. It's me who should be looking forward to being eighteen, me who has a mum who stands in the way of everything.

It is me who will embrace freedom in January 2020.

My good mood lasts only until I get out of bed. I have texted Keeley, received an excited response and a selfie in which she pouts and wears a birthday crown.

'Aren't you ready yet?' Mum asks when I come downstairs in my pyjamas.

She is perched on the edge of the sofa in the good living room, curling her eyelashes, looking into a hand-held mirror. She is wearing her white blouse and pink fitted trousers, her make-up heavy but very pretty.

'I'm going over after breakfast,' I say.

She lets the mirror fall to her side and looks at me. 'What are you talking about?'

'What are *you* talking about?'

'We're all going for lunch with Granny. Mason is nearly ready, go and get dressed.'

'Lunch with Granny?' I repeat. 'Since when? It's Keeley's birthday, I'm going over there now.'

Mum sighs. 'It's her birthday all day, you can see her later.' She goes back to curling her eyelashes.

I have been telling her my plans all week. No, all *year*.

'I'm going over now,' I say. 'Soon. I have to help her set up.'

Mum snorts. 'It's a teenage party, Jude, not an investiture.'

'Why are you always trying to ruin everything for me?' I am shouting suddenly. 'Why don't you want me to be happy?'

'Oh, don't be ridiculous,' she says lightly. 'We'll have a quick bite to eat with Granny and then you can go off to your little party later … If you're good.'

'I have had these plans for weeks!' I say, trying to keep my voice under control, my eyes from filling. 'Years, basically. You've known about them. I have to go over now. I don't have time for Granny.'

'If Granny dies tomorrow, you'll be very sorry you said that.'

'What's happening?' Dad pokes his head around the door and looks from one to the other. 'Granny isn't dying, is she?'

'Dad,' I say, practically jumping on him. 'Mum is being a complete bitch, she won't let me go to Keeley's house even though it's her birthday and I've been planning this forever and I have to go over, we have plans. I have to go now –'

'I'm letting you go to a party,' Mum says drily. 'And you're calling me a bitch?'

'Dad,' I say. 'Talk to her.'

'*Her*,' Mum repeats. 'You're really not going about this the right way, Jude. I don't think you should go to this party at all.'

'Well, Linda.' Dad is clearly uncomfortable. His giant hands wring together as he looks from wife to daughter. He looks as though he wishes he hadn't put his head around the door at all. 'Jude has been talking about this for a long time … she is very excited for it. And she worked so hard for her exams.'

Mum glares at him. 'Fine.' She snaps her make-up bag closed. 'But just remember where we live. We're right across the road. I can come over and drag you home, you know, if things start getting out of hand.'

She stands and brushes past me, her heels click-clicking.

'Eighteen!' Dad says suddenly, to lighten the tension. 'Can't believe it. Give her our card, won't you? And tell her a big happy birthday from me.'

'I will. Thanks, Dad.'

'Be safe tonight, OK, love? I know you will be. You're a sensible girl.'

He pats me on the shoulder and shuffles away.

Hours later, the argument with Mum is still ringing in my ears. I hear the last words she said, *I can come over and drag you home, you know*, and I shiver in fear and anger.

'Forget about it,' Keeley commands. 'And keep still or I'll get peroxide in your eyes, you silly goose.'

She doesn't let me look in the mirror until she is totally done. Hair dried, curled and sprayed, make-up finished and patted down with loose powder.

Her eyes are on my cheeks, then my eyelids, then my hair. She is smiling. Real and proper. My eyes stay on her face the whole time.

'Well?' I ask.

'Come and see for yourself.' She takes my hand and we go together to the bathroom. It is covered in ruined, bleached towels, plastic gloves and empty boxes of hair dye. When I look in the mirror, I think I've never seen a room more beautiful.

I look like her. I really do.

I'm maybe half a size bigger, with slightly smaller boobs, but our faces, and now our hair, look the same. They *are* the same. She stands slightly behind me, eyes wide, all her teeth on display. The exact same height, if I stretch just an inch or two.

'What do you think?'

'I look … like you. Do I look like you?'

Keeley cocks her head to the side and I watch in the mirror as she looks me up and down. 'I suppose you do,' she says, as though she has never thought of this before.

I beam at her in the mirror.

'Go down and show Mack,' she says. 'Make sure he isn't stoned yet. I still have to curl my own hair.'

Keeley's dress rides up my thighs and I use both hands to push it down as I make for the door. The empty champagne bottle is perched at the top of the stairs, as if we are waiting for some in-house recycling collection.

'Quit pulling the dress!' she hisses. Then she softens, 'Just try and enjoy yourself tonight, please. Remember what we talked about.'

I can already feel myself sweating with nerves and excitement. I know my cheeks are burning but Keeley has warned me not to even *think* about touching my face.

This is the first party I've actually been allowed to go to (well, kind of allowed to go to), the first party with no curfew (Mum *promised* after months of goading). The first time I won't have to pretend to be sober afterwards. The first time I can let go and actually enjoy myself. We have agreed that Keeley will check in with me every hour, but that we should both mingle and talk to other people.

'People are going to start arriving soon,' she continues. 'Have another drink before they get here. And relax. You look amazing.'

I can't stop smiling at that.

The party goes exactly how I have always imagined a proper teenage party will go: there are loud games of beer pong; someone is sick in the kitchen sink; I speak to girls who have ignored me since we left primary school and they seem to be interested in what I have to say. People compliment my hair, my dress, my nails. Beth and Kim are there, skulking in a corner and muttering to one another, scowling at me, but I ignore them. They aren't going to hurl insults at me here: this is my territory. Keeley is here. I am safe from them for now.

I am comfortable.

I find Keeley over by the iPod speaker and she grins at me.

'Are you having a good time?' she asks. She is very drunk and her tongue is stained blue. She puts both her arms around me and pushes her cheek against mine.

'The best,' I say honestly. 'I've had five Bacardi Breezers.'

She laughs. The sound is muffled by her head pressed against my ear.

'You're so funny. Have a drink of this – I got four bottles of champagne as presents, can you believe it?'

I take the bottle she is offering and have an obedient sip. The Breezers seemed to sober me up after the earlier champagne and I am happy that I am feeling clear-headed. I want to remember the night.

The guests are jumping, dancing, singing, screaming over the music. It is a rap song I don't recognise. The music is everywhere, in my head and inside my body. I grin at her and she grins back and kisses me on the cheek.

'I love you,' she says. 'You're my best friend in the whole world.'

'I love you too,' I say. 'And you're mine. Forever.'

'And ever and ever and ever and ever.'

We both laugh and pull apart. She disappears into the crowd. I lean against the wall, suddenly feeling dizzy. The last gulp of fizz was a mistake. Between the champagne, the vodka shot Brains convinced me to do with him and the sugary alcopops, my stomach churns and my head feels like it is vibrating.

I stumble up the stairs, past two girls who are crying into one another's shoulders, and come to a halt outside the bathroom. A boy with thick-rimmed glasses stands outside. He nods his head at me and smiles. I do the same, then remember about my dress and hastily pull it towards my knees.

'I think someone's taking something in there,' he says, indicating the bathroom. 'I've been standing here for ten minutes. Do you go to Seaview High?'

'Yeah,' I say. 'I'm Jude.' I want to add *I'm Keeley's best friend*, but she has told me to try and be cool, so I say nothing more.

'I'm Johnny,' says the boy. 'I like your yellow dress.'

'Oh, thanks. It's not mine.'

He furrows his brow at me, but laughs. He opens his mouth to say something more when the bathroom door opens and Paddy Devlin comes out. Paddy either ignores me or doesn't recognise me as he brushes past to go downstairs. The boy grins at me, then goes into the bathroom and locks the door.

My head spins. I don't think I will be sick, but my stomach is lifting and I have to close my eyes to stop myself falling over. I kick off my – Keeley's – heels and sit down against the wall to the bathroom.

Maybe when the boy comes out, we will talk some more.

I wonder if he is good-looking, if Keeley would be pleased.

When I open my eyes again, there is a new person in front of me. Or rather, I hope it is a person. All I can see is a red, white and blue pattern. My vision swims and I close my eyes again.

'Are you OK?' the person asks. A deep, lovely voice.

'Yeah,' I say. 'Just dizzy. I'm fine.' I open my eyes again.

He is beautiful and he is smiling at me. The red, white and blue pattern resolves itself into a Union Jack. Has he tied it around his head? His skin is tanned and his teeth are white, and I think immediately that he must be a model or an actor. People like this don't live in Vetobridge. I have never seen anyone who looks like this. I feel myself blush.

'Are you sure?' he asks. 'Maybe you just need a refill.'

I feel myself laughing against my will.

I am so drunk.

'Maybe I do,' I say. It comes out more flirtatiously than I thought it would.

'What are you drinking, then?' He stands and empties a bottle of beer he is clutching into his mouth. His hands are so big I can't read the label. He is so tall that he blocks out all the light. A rugby player, then, maybe? Keeley didn't mention she was inviting a rugby player. Maybe he is a friend of Mack's, or the older brother of someone from our class.

'Bacardi … and coke,' I say, too embarrassed to ask for the alcopop. 'Please.'

He grins at me and goes back downstairs.

The bass of the newest rap song is up so loud it is impossible to hear the lyrics. The whole house shakes. The guests downstairs rap at the tops of their voices, with mixed levels of ability and lyrical knowledge. I glance downstairs: even the crying girls have gone back to the party.

Johnny leaves the bathroom and smiles at me again. He pauses as though he is going to talk some more when –

'For you, Madame.' The Union Jack boy is back, and he hands me a pint glass full of a pale brown liquid. He pulls the flag from around his head and rouses his hair. He smells like shampoo and smoke.

The bespectacled Johnny goes back downstairs.

'What's with the flag?' I ask. My eyes burn at the smell of the drink, but I take a sip anyway. 'And what is the alcohol-to-mixer percentage here?'

He grins mischievously at me. 'That's for you to guess.'

I giggle. 'More than 50/50. Mostly alcohol.'

'Mmm, OK. You got me. It's about 60 per cent alcohol.'

'I can't drink that!' I say, laughing now.

'You can sip at it! Trust me, I'm not that interesting; you might need it. Are you having a good night?'

'Yeah,' I say. 'Are you?'

'Yeah.'

I almost leave a gap in the conversation for Keeley to speak. When I realise she is nowhere to be seen, I flounder, but only for a second. 'I hate this awful music,' I say, pointing downstairs. 'Who picked this?'

'Some girl with a tattoo of a flower on her wrist.'

'Oh. That's Polly.'

'Polly has awful taste in music.'

'She does.'

'What kind of music do you like, then?'

'Well ...' I think about it. I take a sip of the Bacardi. It burns my throat but I swallow it down. 'I suppose I like Mack's kind of music.'

'Oh, you have to say that!'

'I don't. I really mean it!'

'Sure.' He grins again, showing me his beautiful teeth. 'What about Darling in Skins? Have you heard of them?'

I furrow my brow. 'I've definitely heard of them ... Darling in Skins. Are they Danish?'

'Swedish! Close.'

'Oh! I know who you mean. Look!'

I stand quickly and push my pint glass at him. He takes it in his free hand and clutches his beer in the other, looking bemused. I trip a little as I open the door to Mack's room. I move inside so the boy can follow me and close the door behind us.

'There!' I say. I point to the poster on the back of the door. Sure enough, four figures dressed in black, with lots of eyeliner on, glare back at us. 'Darling in Skins' is written in silver on the bottom.

'Hey!' the boy says. 'That's cool. Has Mack been to see them?'

'Nah,' I say. 'He got the poster online, I think.' I take my drink back from him and sip it. My throat burns less this time, somehow, but I sit down on Mack's bed to be sure I won't keel over. 'What's your name?' I think it is the first time I have asked a boy his name in my life.

He smiles as if we are sharing a joke, so I smile back.

'Peter,' he says.

Detective Inspector Chris Rice

3rd January 2020, morning

'Sir?'

I am sitting in my office. It is just after seven and my head is pounding. I am staring at a spot of damp on the ceiling and vaguely hoping that something heavy from the office above will fall through the floor and crush me. The very cold pizza Dunwoody bought for me yesterday is almost finished, crusts and all.

The Project Twenty file sits unopened on my desk, an orange stain on the cover, the origin of which I can't quite remember. When I lean forward to sniff at it, I detect sweet and sour sauce.

'Do you want some breakfast?' I hold the pizza box out to Edgecomb who stands in the doorway.

Edgecomb shakes her head.

'Sure? It's quite good.' I put the box back down. Then I put my forehead down on the desk and enjoy the cool.

'I checked in with Beth McKenna, Sir.'

I raise my head from the table and stare at her. 'Sorry, Edie, who?'

'Beth McKenna. She was in Jude and Keeley's form class. The girl whose jaw was broken. You asked me to look into it … ?'

I snap to attention. 'God, yes, of course.'

I motion to the chair opposite me and Edgecomb sits down with a grateful smile.

'So, initially, I couldn't get hold of Beth, so I thought I'd go and speak to the headmistress, a woman called Joan Sparks. She lives in Oldry, not too far from me. Anyway, I asked her about Jude and Keeley, and at the start she was nice as pie about both of them, talking about their grades and their *nice friendship*. I had to remind her that Keeley got excluded and she clammed up at that, claiming she didn't allow violence in her school. I asked why the police hadn't been called … after all, that's intentional GBH. She broke the girl's fucking *jaw*, for Christ's sake. That got Joan Sparks talking. She seemed to think she was about to get in trouble. She said she wanted to call the police, that that was her intention, but then she called Beth's parents, and *they* were the ones who insisted the police didn't get involved.'

I stare. 'Their kid's jaw gets broken and they *don't* want to involve the police?'

Edgecomb nods seriously. 'I pushed her, insisted she tell me. Finally, she confirmed that Beth and a few others were bullying Jude during her GCSE years and in lower sixth, until the incident.'

'Bullying her, how?'

'In every way you could possibly imagine, Sir.' Edgecomb removes a loose sheet of paper from her notebook and hands it to me. 'Sparks didn't have a file on it. Apparently she was as clueless as everybody else until the jaw-breaking. Nothing had ever been reported. Jude was bullied for over two years and nobody but her tormentors knew a thing about it. They did some sick stuff to her.'

I glance down at the sheet of paper. There are dates in the margins, next to the neatly written paragraphs. Most of the dates have question marks next to them or have 'approx' written underneath.

'If there was no record, where did you get this?' I ask.

'I made it,' Edgecomb says. 'Took me all last night. I finally got hold of Beth and her mate Kim Lennon. They were so keen to make sure I knew they had nothing to do with any murder that they practically sang. I made sure to keep bringing it back to Peter Denny to put the fear of God into them both, even though we obviously know they weren't involved. Told them if they held anything back, they would be obstructing the investigation. I sat with them until after midnight, asking about the bullying, making them go through their phones and social media. Beth's mum was nearly throwing up, some of the detail. I hope you haven't eaten anything recently because you will too. Kim just cried the whole time. I would have felt sorry for her if I wasn't listening to the most horrifying account of bullying I've ever heard.'

Edgecomb's fat, careful handwriting swims in front of my burning eyes. She has colour-coded the incidents. There is a key at the top: green for cyber, yellow for verbal, red for physical.

The first side of the page is mostly yellow, with a little green. The reverse of the page is a veritable sea of all three colours. The red paragraphs are longest, the most detailed.

'It started in their fourth year ...' Edgecomb is speaking quietly, as though out of respect, and I feel a rush of affection for her. ' ... I won't go into details, Sir. Everything important that you need to know is in that file.'

I flip the page over to begin reading at the start, but Edgecomb isn't done.

'The most interesting thing I found out,' she says, 'is that the bullying ended as soon as Beth's jaw was broken. March 2019. Beth and Kim had locked Jude in a toilet cubicle with Kim's brother's pet tarantula ... When Keeley came in and made them let her out, Jude went mad at the girls. It was Jude who broke Beth's jaw.'

I stare at her. 'What did you say?'

'You heard me. Jude started punching her, apparently. She got her on the floor and, according to Beth, stomped on the side of her face and broke her jaw. Beth says if Keeley Mackley hadn't pulled her off ...'

'So why the hell did Keeley Mackley get excluded for something she didn't do?' I demand.

'That's what I wondered. A teacher heard Kim screaming and came in, and Keeley immediately said it was her who had done it. Kim was confused but, since Beth wasn't arguing –'

'She was too busy holding her jaw to her face.'

'– she didn't think to correct it. Keeley calmly followed the teacher to the headmistress, taking full responsibility for the injury. Kim claimed she hadn't seen anything. Jude was silent. Beth later agreed it had been Keeley because, apparently, she didn't want the whole school to hear that a *runt like Jude* had injured her so badly.

When Beth's parents heard from Jude and Keeley that the only reason there had been a fight was that their daughter had locked another girl in a toilet and had been bullying her for years, they agreed not to press any charges, provided that Keeley was expelled immediately. The school were so embarrassed that the bullying had been going on for so long right under their noses that they just expelled her and agreed to forget all about it.'

'They washed their hands of the whole thing,' I murmur. My mind is racing.

'Do you want me to go and tell the team?' Edgecomb asks, standing.

'I'll tell them later,' I say. 'I'll have a look over this and I'll bring everybody up to speed tomorrow once I've got my head around it all. Thank you so much for this, Edie. Why don't you head home and get some sleep? I think you've earned it.'

She makes for the door of my office but stops. 'I know she caused a serious injury to that girl,' she says quietly. 'But I can't help but feel incredibly sorry for Jude Jameson in all of this. She suffered in silence for so long. Until things got so bad that she snapped.'

'I feel sorry for her too,' I admit. 'But that doesn't mean …'

'Yeah. You know, Miss Sparks and Jude's art teacher, they agreed on one thing. They said that Jude left at the end of fifth year doing well, seeming like a normal, smart teenager. Despite the bullying, she was *almost* herself. Maybe that's why nobody noticed. Then she came back to sixth form and she was completely different. She wasn't paying attention, she seemed unhappy, she wasn't handing in work. She hasn't been passing any exams, this year and last. Sparks more or less admitted that they've only let her stay on because of the bullying. They feel guilty. Both teachers told me that they thought that that summer – 2018 it would have been – had changed her. They said the Jude who came back to lower sixth was not the person who'd left two months before. Like a different person entirely.'

I pull myself together enough to give the briefing at half-past eight.

'Joshua Mackley is in custody,' I announce, as soon as the door shuts behind Dunwoody. A few heads nod appreciatively. 'I think we're finally going to get to the bottom of what happened on Tuesday night.'

'I found his drug stash yesterday,' Browne says quickly. 'We're able to keep him in on that while we –'

'Congrats on doing the job you're paid to do,' Jess says to Browne, deadpan.

'We're going to charge him with possession with intent to sell,' I say, throwing Jess a look. 'It's not his first offence and there were more than enough pills in that gym bag for the charge. Did they find a stud earring in the Den?'

A few people look at one another. One or two frown or shake their heads.

'OK. Anything more I should know from forensics or the house search?'

Most heads look towards Colson, who stands up. 'Not much. All blood was the victim's, all contained in the garage.'

'Three sets of fingerprints on the knife,' Jess interrupts. 'Apart from the victim's. Lab work came back this morning. Joshua Mackley's, Keeley Mackley's and an isolated thumbprint belonging to Jude Jameson.'

'Fair enough,' I murmur. 'Didn't Keeley say they sometimes cut their pills? It would make sense for them to have used whatever they found lying around in a kitchen drawer. They were all so off their tits they could each have done exactly that on Tuesday night and *they* wouldn't even know.'

'The fingerprints don't rule out Naomi Ross,' Jess says. 'Not by any means. She might have worn gloves or wiped her own prints.'

'You asked us to look for anything drug-related in the house,' Colson continues, as though she has not been interrupted. 'We know now there was nothing like that; they moved everything before we were called, but we did find a prescription slip under Joshua Mackley's mattress. It's probably not important, but it has the name Naomi Ross on it. For a single Levonelle.'

'Levonelle?' I repeat, my face blank. 'What's that?'

'Morning after pill,' Jess and Colson answer in unison.

'Oh. Aren't those pretty common?'

'Yeah, you can get them over the counter, usually,' says Jess. 'Or you can get a prescription one for free.'

'Naomi Ross and Joshua Mackley have been together for nine years,' pipes up Clarke. 'That probably isn't too significant.'

'It's the date that is interesting,' says Colson. She holds up a green and white sheet that has been placed in a clear plastic bag. A few heads crane to look. Jess and I, at the front, don't bother to squint.

'The 12th of July 2018,' says Colson. She shakes her red hair back from her shoulders, and I can tell she has been itching to share this piece of information. 'The same day Joshua Mackley beat up Peter Denny. Apart from anything else, it indicates that Mackley hasn't washed his bed sheets in eighteen months ...'

Something in this seems to tingle in my stomach, like a memory I can't quite grab. Jess and I glance at one another. Her expression is thoughtful, but unsure.

'Perhaps too many drinks were had and protection was ... overlooked,' I say. 'I don't think it's relevant, Mairead, but good spot. At least we know the search was thorough.'

Colson nods, unoffended. 'The other thing is we've tested clothing from our four suspects – no traces of blood anywhere that we can find. Joshua Mackley came to the station in the same clothes he was wearing on New Year's Eve, which we verified using the video that Browne found online. We've tested Naomi Ross's clothing too. Neither Jude Jameson nor Keeley Mackley was actually seen on the screen, so we do only have their word for what they were wearing on Tuesday night. To be sure, we tested the dresses they *claimed* to have on and then we tested all the other women's dresses we found in 166 Wits End. All the guests agree they were both in dresses, but nobody can be clear on colours or style. Either way, nothing. No blood. Whoever stabbed Denny was either very careful or, if it was one of the younger girls, managed to get rid of the offending articles before we searched the house.'

'Impossible,' announces Dunwoody, whose uncharacteristic quietness had been starting to alarm me. 'Both the younger girls were escorted from the house in police cars first thing on Wednesday morning. The CCTV shows clearly that neither of them left that house between Tuesday afternoon and then.'

'It might have just been missed in the search,' suggests Magill. 'Hidden under a floorboard, shoved behind the fridge.'

'Or one of the girls could have given Joshua or Naomi their dress to dispose of when they left for Boar's Brae,' Jess says quietly. 'They could have dumped it in a bin on their walk to Naomi's place, right? Or hidden it in a bush …'

'It takes seven minutes to walk from Wits End to Boar's Brae,' says Dunwoody. 'Me and Raymond checked that out yesterday. You could do it in four if you were rushing. We know Mackley and Ross left Wits End at twenty to three and Michael Parish delivered a pizza to them at two minutes to three. If they disposed of anything, they did it quickly.'

'They both had most of the next day to dispose of clothing,' Jess says. 'Remember, we didn't speak to either of them until Wednesday afternoon.'

'They would have wanted rid of it as soon as possible,' Dunwoody says. 'I'd put money on it they got rid of it in those seven minutes, on the walk to Ross's house, if they got rid of it at all.'

'Seven minutes isn't a lot of time to dispose of a dress,' I murmur. 'Not properly. So if they did, they've thrown it over a wall or in a hedge or something. Dunwoody, you and Smith go back again – this time check bins, check behind walls, check everywhere. We're looking for … most likely a dress. I just hope the bins haven't been collected yet.'

'Nah,' Smith offers from his seat in the corner. 'Bins that end of town won't be done again until Monday. I'm on the same day as them.'

'The person who stabbed Peter Denny might just have been careful,' Jess reminds me. 'There might not be any bloody clothes.'

'We need to find something,' I murmur. 'Mackley isn't admitting to anything.'

'Maybe his night in the cells has loosened his tongue,' Jess says.

'If we're looking for a dress,' Smith repeats, 'does that mean you think one of the girls did the stabbing? Either Keeley or Jude?'

'We're still focusing on Joshua Mackley,' Jess says. 'Right, Sir?'

Every head turns to look at me.

I stare hard at a spot on the floor, my brow furrowed. When I don't respond immediately, Jess says, 'He has previous beef with Peter Denny. Hurt him not eighteen months ago. He's a junkie. Denny was cheating on his sister. It makes the most sense that it was him.'

'Or that he helped, or is covering up for someone,' Smith offers.

'I think we should talk to the girls again,' I say finally. The sentence sounds right, and a few of the team nod, like it is warming the air around us. It is the right answer I have been hopscotching around since Wednesday morning. 'Starting with Jude,' I continue. 'I can do that later today, before we speak to Mackley. Then I'd like to talk to Naomi Ross myself.'

My office is cold.

I set my plastic bag on the desk and keep my coat on as I remove the hot burrito from inside. After I have swallowed down a few bites of chicken and sour cream and hung up my coat, I pick up the handwritten sheets from Edgecomb and begin to read in chronological order.

After half a page, my stomach is churning and I have set the burrito back in its tinfoil.

When I get to the bottom of the second page, I push the tinfoil across the length of my desk until it plops into the wastepaper basket below.

This is one report I have no desire to reread.

What started as some relatively harmless name-calling – *lezzer, pussy-licker* – had moved from the school corridors to social media. There are a few hazy lines about prank calls made to Jude's phone and the Jamesons' home phone. *Sixteen to twenty times?* Edgecomb has written next to this. Apparently Beth and Kim cannot agree how many times they did this. Private messages, anonymous phone calls, voicemails. Edgecomb has done a good job of making the girls talk. Pictures on social media, edited, Photoshopped. One incident of destroying an art project, one of pushing Jude into a wall – *She only scratched her face*, one of the girls has said of the incident. My blood feels hot. One attempt to steal a camera. Another art project destroyed. Coursework deleted from a school computer. A coffee in a styrofoam cup poured into Jude's lap as she sat in the study hall with earphones in.

A red-coded paragraph near the end of the second page tells of an incident in November 2018, just a few months before Beth's jaw was broken, when the two girls and two others, unnamed, cornered Jude after school one day, *in the alley that connects the Secret Place to the promenade*, held her down and put raw chicken in her mouth. *Packet from Tesco.* Edgecomb's handwriting is shakier here. *Filmed on a mobile phone. More than one?*

Edgecomb has underlined the last line of this paragraph: *We thought it would be funny.*

Jude

3rd January 2020, afternoon

I type into my phone, *How long does it take to go stir crazy?* But I can't find a definite answer.

The last time I spent this much time in my room was when I was fifteen and I got strep throat and had to stay at home for a full week. I could hardly keep my head up, everything hurt so much, and the doctor that Mum took me to see said it was highly contagious and that I shouldn't be around anyone, full stop. School was out of the question. I was worried – it is insane how much you miss by being off school for just one week.

I took ill on the Sunday, went to the doctor with Mum on Monday morning and texted Keeley to bring me my homework that Monday night. Mum answered the door. I was lying on the sofa with a hot-water bottle and two packets of antibiotics at my feet. They had a murmured conversation in the hall, and when Mum came back in, Keeley wasn't with her.

Mum dropped a few sheets of paper and a book on to the sofa beside me.

'Where's Keeley?' I asked.

'She had to nip on,' Mum said, not meeting my eye. She resumed her seat in the armchair. 'She said she doesn't want to get sick and I don't blame her. Are you feeling up to trying your maths homework?'

If I had felt like it before, I certainly didn't after that. I felt sick to my stomach. Keeley didn't want to see me, just because my throat was infected? The time she got food poisoning, I sat on the floor of the bathroom, holding her hair for a full day and night.

Then my whole body went cold. Of course. A day at school without me meant Keeley would have had to find someone else to walk to class with, someone else to eat lunch with. And who would she pick? Who would be desperate to have her in their gang? Beth and her dopey mates. I could just see them now, standing in the lunch queue talking about boys and make-up and drugs they'd tried; all the things Keeley liked to talk about of which I knew nothing. They'd probably spent the first few periods chatting casually and getting to be friends again, but I was sure that by the end of the day, they'd been pecking her head and making her all uncomfortable about me again. The words *lesbian bitch* flashed in my head for a second before I shook them out. They'd been texting me variations of those words for weeks. I clenched my fists and promised I wouldn't cry.

She probably hadn't thought about me all day. It was probably an effort for her to walk across the green to give me my homework.

I took my hot-water bottle and the papers from the sofa and marched upstairs, feeling hot tears prick my eyes. Mum called after me but I ignored her. I kept the tears in until I was safely on the second floor.

I lay on my bed and imagined Beth McKenna. I wanted to pull out her teeth, cut off her hair with a knife. Smash her huge forehead and big boobs into the ground. I imagined punching her as hard as I could. I punched my pillow but it was too soft to be satisfying. All it took was a stupid throat infection to push Keeley into Beth's chubby, waiting arms.

She'll sit next to Beth in all our classes now, I thought. Kim will have to come next to me.

My phone bleeped from the pocket of my dressing gown and I pulled it out, wiping my eyes on my sleeve. It was a message from Keeley.

Text me when your silly mother is in bed and I'll come up. She tried to tell me you were too sick for company LOL. Hope your wee throat is better. Such a shite day without you. Love you x

It was like waking up. It was like I had fallen into a very raw, real nightmare, and suddenly I opened my eyes and took a deep breath. My relief was such that I felt weak and dizzy and I almost laughed out loud.

Thought you were avoiding me! I'm so stupid. Come up now? I'm in my room xx

I stood on tiptoes under the skylight, waiting for her.

She came into view after two minutes, jogging across the green in her school uniform and a black hoodie. Her hair was loose and trailed behind her in the wind, and I thought she had a kink in it from when she had it in a ponytail for HE class that afternoon. I couldn't possibly see that from where I was, of course; it was just a feeling.

When she got close to the house, she went around to the right so she didn't trigger the sensor light. I watched her put one of her school pumps on the first wooden beam of the gate, then the second, then the third. She stepped on to the top of the gate like a tightrope walker, arms outstretched and not even a little nervous. For someone so thin and gangly, she was incredibly graceful. She lifted a leg and tested the slate on the roof over Dad's study. It had been years since either one of us had had to sneak in or out this way, and I knew she was making sure it would still hold her weight. It must have passed the test, because moments later she was outside my window, arms still outstretched but beaming at me.

'Hold on!' I called. I motioned for her to stop. She did so, peering at me, bemused.

I ran to get my camera, turned it on and ran back to the window. I felt the cool plastic against my palms and knelt on the ground, looking up into the starry night. I positioned myself and the lens so that the window was in the middle, the black sky everywhere, Keeley's arms outstretched as though still balancing, though she was safe on the roof now. Used to being asked to pose, she stood stock-still, exactly as I had wanted her to.

I clicked.

My heart beat fast, my pain gone. Adrenalin.

I clicked again.

I leant back to look at the digital display.

Perfect.

I moved to open the window and she clambered in. The least graceful part of her journey was her awkward landing on the window seat, both legs in the air, but she still managed to look good while she did it.

'I thought we'd outgrown this,' Keeley said, a little out of breath. She looked out across the roof and seemed to marvel at her own feat. Her forehead shone with perspiration, but the rest of her face was flawless: eyes bright and cheeks flushed. She had the kink in her hair, like I'd known she would.

'Me too,' I said. 'Thank you for bringing me my homework.'

Keeley rolled her eyes. 'I actually brought you something much more exciting. I didn't think Linda would approve.'

She unzipped her hoodie and felt in her inside blazer pocket. She flipped out a packet of Regal Kingsize and threw them to me.

I caught them just before they hit the floor and laughed. 'This will be good for my throat.'

'How is your throat? Let's see it.'

I opened my mouth obediently and Keeley peered in, an expression of mild curiosity that did not change when she saw the thick, white spots on my tonsils and tongue.

'Huh,' she said. She has always had a morbid fascination with anything ugly, bloody, sticky, gross. She wants to have a good, long look. She nodded in what seemed to be approval. 'Well, that is certainly infected.'

'Thank you for your assessment, Doctor Mackley.'

She laughed her loud, wild laugh and I shushed her, pointing my finger down. She put a hand over her mouth and twirled around in a circle, moving towards my bed.

'School was shit today.' She flopped herself down on my bed on her back. 'It dragged. I actually went to the library at lunch. Did you know we had a library?'

'I've heard of it.'

'A whole room. Stacks of books.'

‘Imagine that.’

‘It’s pretty cool, actually.’

I grinned at her and took the cellophane from my cigarette packet. ‘Did you read something?’

‘I did. I started a novel that was called …’

I went to the open window to light up. I took a deep drag of the cigarette and felt every muscle in my body relax. I sunk into the window seat, so grateful that Keeley had known exactly what I needed when I didn’t know myself.

‘ … Her husband wants to have an affair. Or maybe he’s already had it. I can’t really remember, but it was powerful. The writing was really good, I think you’d like it.’

‘That’s the best book recommendation I’ve ever heard.’

She giggled and threw her arms and legs out, starfishing on the bed and staring at the ceiling.

‘We could have a ten-person orgy in this bed of yours,’ she declared, not for the first time.

I looked over at her. Sure enough, there was probably enough room for both of us to completely starfish and never touch. She was bouncing her right leg up and down, and she let her shoe fly off and hit the wall opposite the bed. She giggled at that too, she was in a giggly mood. Her sock had ridden down, and I could just about see the scar on her shin – a pale white reminder of the first time we ever got drunk, on holiday in Spain, when she fell on the beach boardwalk and got a long, thin cut on her leg that bled for hours before we realised.

I puffed the last of my cigarette out of the window, ground the butt on the outside windowsill and pulled my head back inside.

I went to the bed and lay down next to her. She turned on her side to face me and looked at me properly for the first time. Her eyes narrowed. ‘Have you been crying?’

I felt heat rise to my cheeks. ‘No.’

‘Jude Jameson, don’t tell me lies. Is it really that sore?’

‘No, it’s not that.’

‘Oh my god, you said you thought I was avoiding you … You actually thought that? What the hell did you think had happened in the space of twenty-four hours, you sensitive little dodo?’ She ran her fingers across my cheek, staring at me. 'Why did you think that?'

I stared right back for so long that it would have been weird to answer her question once I jolted and came back to life. Her hand stayed on my cheek.

'I'm highly contagious,' I said, tapping her hand. 'We probably shouldn't be this close.'

Keeley sat up to pull off her blazer. 'We probably shouldn't be this close,' she agreed.

I found out later that Mum had come up to check on me before she went to bed and found us both fast asleep on top of the blankets, Keeley's chin hooked over my shoulder.

Of course, Keeley woke up the next day with an extremely painful strep throat, and we spent the week in my room, watching films and eating ice cream. We both missed an entire week of learning about index notation in maths and neither of us ever managed to grasp it.

It was one of the best weeks of my life.

'Jude?'

Mum is calling me from outside my bedroom door. I turn on my side and close my eyes, feigning sleep.

'Jude,' she whispers. She has let herself in and stands at the top of the four little stairs up to my bed. 'Detective Rice is on the phone. He wants to know if he can come and have a chat.'

I sit bolt upright. 'Now? Today? But it's already …' I hit the button on my phone. 'Can it wait until tomorrow?' It sounds as pathetic a question out loud as it did in my head.

Mum has the landline in her hand, covering the receiver. 'I think we should let him come over,' she says. 'I don't want it to look suspicious if we say no.'

'Did he say why he needs to talk to me again? I've already told him everything.'

'No, he didn't say. Just that he needs some help with something.'

'Mum, I really don't –'

'Come on, get dressed. He probably just wants you to identify something so we can put this whole matter to bed.'

This little murder.

Mum has been in a good mood for the past two days, and I know that it is because this is the least she has seen of Keeley for years. I, on the other hand, have not spent this much time apart from Keeley in my entire remembered life. I feel her absence like a dull pain in my head.

'I don't want to,' I say.

'I don't care what you want!' Mum hisses, suddenly angry.

My mouth, which had been open to protest further, closes in abrupt shock.

Mum puts the receiver back to her ear. 'Yes, Detective Rice? We'd love for you to come over. We'll see you in an hour.'

Detective Inspector Chris Rice

3rd January 2020, afternoon

'Thank you for agreeing to see me, Jude. Mrs Jameson.' I nod at them each in turn. 'I just had one or two more questions, trying to get a few things wrapped up.'

'What's happening with Keeley?' Jude asks. Today, she wears a woollen jumper with a hole on the left sleeve. She has her thumb resting in the hole and picks at the thread around it. Linda Jameson's eyes keep flicking to it disapprovingly.

'We haven't spoken to Keeley today,' I say.

'So she hasn't been arrested?'

Jess and I glance at one another.

'What makes you think she's been arrested?' Jess asks.

'I saw online that somebody has. Is it Mack?'

'It's you we want to talk to now, Jude.'

We are standing in the hall of their house. The floors sparkle. The angel ornaments make me feel distinctly uncomfortable.

'Let's go to the dining room,' Linda Jameson suggests. 'It's just through the kitchen, back here, Detectives.'

Jude is no longer drumming her fingers on the table or moving her mouth, the way she was the first day we met her. In her home, her safe place, Jude is alert and comfortable, neat hair framing her determined face. Apart from the anxiety she shows in still picking at her sleeve, she looks focused. Exactly what we hoped for.

'I want to see Keeley.'

Jess and I sit opposite Jude, as though conducting a job interview. The dining room is a myriad of white and silver reflections; nothing seems solid.

'I'm sure you will soon,' I say. 'It's her we wanted to ask about, actually. I'll just get to the point. Why didn't you tell us Keeley argued with Pete on the night he was murdered?'

This catches her off guard, but only a little. Behind her, Linda Jameson freezes in the act of straightening a perfectly straight picture on the wall, pretending she is not listening.

'I didn't think it was important,' Jude says quickly.

'You didn't think it was important that there was a violent argument between Keeley and her boyfriend just hours, minutes, before he was murdered?' Jess seems to have come to the end of her tether.

'That was nothing,' Jude says. 'They were usually violent and they had a lot of arguments.'

The three of us stare at one another. Jude seems to realise the significance of what she has said and closes her mouth determinedly.

'They were violent?' I ask. 'That's … that's interesting. You didn't think to mention that to us?'

'Keeley didn't hurt him,' she says softly. 'Not … not like *that* anyway. She didn't kill him. They just … Just sometimes.'

'We heard the end of one of their arguments in a video,' Jess says. 'It sounded aggressive. She said some pretty damning things.'

'Saying and doing are very different,' says Jude.

Linda stands looking at us now, her back to the picture frame which is, only now, off-centre. The picture inside is not a photograph, but a generic painted landscape. Like the picture that comes in the frame.

'That's true,' Jess agrees. 'But it still would have been helpful if you'd been honest with us from the start. That way we wouldn't have been focusing on the wrong suspects, following up the wrong leads. We might have found Pete's killer by now and we wouldn't be here bothering you and your family.'

'It's no trouble,' Linda says in a murmur. An automatic reaction, I think.

'Do you know what the fight was about?' I ask. 'It would be great if you could tell us.'

'You said you heard it.'

'We'd like to hear it from you.'

In a voice so quiet we have to lean forward to catch it, Jude begins to speak.

'I went into the kitchen to get something. Pete was in the corner of the room, talking really quietly. I didn't see him at first. He was talking to a girl. I knew that right away. He was saying he missed her, he couldn't wait to see her. Then he said something like "*I'll leave her as soon as I can.*" He said he couldn't wait for them to be together.' Jude takes a deep breath. 'Then he turned and saw me. He wasn't stupid enough to ask me to keep what I'd heard from Keeley. I went straight into the living room and told her everything.'

'And she believed you?' Jess asks, eyebrows raised.

'What?' Jude demands. 'Of course.'

'Well, I just thought … this is her first long-term boyfriend. You're used to it being just the two of you. Maybe Keeley thought you had made that up about Pete to get her to dump him. So it could just be the two of you again.'

Jess is teasing her. I feel as uncomfortable as Linda looks.

Jude's cheeks are pinker when she responds. 'Well, Keeley isn't as stupid as you then. She knew I was telling the truth. The two of them had a fight in the kitchen. I tried to calm Keeley down but … she was angry. Naomi tried to help as well but we were going to end up getting hit, so we left them to it. It was nothing new.' This last, more defiant. 'They hit each other and pushed each other all the time. They had stuff to fight about, it was one of those relationships.'

'What else did they have to fight about?' I ask.

'Well …' Jude looks around the dining room as though the answer will pop up from behind the white sideboard. I look at it too. I have a feeling that the drawers would be empty if we were to take a look. 'Drugs!' she says suddenly. 'They fought about drugs. Keeley didn't like that he did them and was trying to get him to stop. She wanted him to give up dealing, as well. They fought about that.'

'Keeley wanted Pete to stop selling drugs …' Jess says. I see her glance sideways at me, unwilling to give away how important this might be. 'The drugs that her brother makes. The drugs that make them the money they need to get by.'

'Yeah,' Jude says. 'I think she was making progress too; he told her he was going to stop. But then, he was also planning to leave her. So I guess none of us really knew anything about Pete at all.'

Jess is nodding carefully. 'That's interesting. I think it's only fair we tell you … We have Joshua Mackley in custody.'

Jude swallows but otherwise does not react. 'And?'

'Are you surprised by that?'

'No. Yes. Why is he in custody?'

'He moved a large quantity of drugs from his house to his girlfriend's house on Wednesday morning. No matter what happens in this investigation, he's going to be going to prison for at least a few years.'

Jude mumbles something under her breath that sounds like *shit*. Linda does not react.

'I wanted to ask you something else,' I say. 'What can you tell me about Beth McKenna?'

If Jess is surprised by the sudden swerve, she hides it well. I haven't yet showed her the colour-coded pages Edgecomb gave me.

Jude's face hardens.

'Beth McKenna is a girl from Jude's school,' Linda says quickly. 'Why are you asking about her? Do you think she might have something to do with … ? Was she at the party?'

'No,' I say, in response to the last question. 'This is a separate thing. What can you tell me about her, Jude?'

'She and a few of her friends said some very nasty things about Jude on the *Internet*.' Linda's arms are folded so tightly she struggles to keep her balance as she plonks herself on the seat next to Jude. 'But this was months ago.'

'They bullied you.' I don't phrase it like a question. I keep my eyes steady and on Jude's face.

'GCSE years and for a while at the start of sixth form,' Linda says. 'So not for months, now. There hasn't been anything like that since. We were quick to put a stop to it.'

'After two and a half years,' I say.

'As soon as we found out.' Linda's tone dares me to argue.

'Why are you asking?' Jude says. She has stopped picking at her sleeve. I think I can see a pulse in her neck.

'It might be relevant,' I say. 'What happened to stop the bullying?'

'Oh, that's easy,' Linda says. 'Just ask Keeley Mackley. As usual she intervened instead of asking for help from an adult. She punched her, the ringleader, Beth. Broke her *jaw*. I've known the McKennas since the girls were in primary school, and I would never have suspected this from a family of such … calibre. Do you know Mr McKenna is an orthodontist? The best in Vetobridge. And Mrs McKenna is an interior designer. They have a beautiful home. How a daughter of theirs ever became a … a *bully*. It's completely beyond me. It must have been a lapse in judgement. A phase. Beth was always a nice girl. Maybe she was going through something. Anyway, all of that is over now. We put a stop to it.'

'Keeley Mackley put a stop to it,' I correct. 'You only found out after she broke this girl's jaw.' I turn to Jude and ask softly, 'Do you want to tell me about that? Maybe … maybe it wasn't Keeley? Maybe you want to tell me who it was.'

'What?' It is Linda who speaks, but Jess looks at me in much the same way.

Only Jude does not react.

We are each silent for the longest time.

A clock chimes in the hall. An old-fashioned clock, I think. A fancy wood, a fancy face that is dusted every day. A glance down at my own watch tells me the clock is off by at least ten minutes.

'No comment,' Jude says. 'I can say "no comment", can't I? I have nothing else to say. Are we done?'

I am unable to hide my sigh. 'Yes. OK.'

Jess stands and leads the way back through the kitchen. Jude quickly follows her, pushing in her dining room chair.

'Mrs Jameson,' I say, pulling my coat around me as best I can. 'Your picture is askew.' I nod to it.

Linda turns around slowly, as if dreading what she is about to see, then barks an awkward, single-noted laugh. 'So it is. Thank you. So it is.'

At the front door, Jess snaps her fingers as though she has just remembered something. 'Oh, Jude. We'd like to take your phone.'

We rehearsed this in the car, asking casually as though it had almost slipped both our minds.

'What?' It sounds like a yelp.

'Just procedure. If you give your permission, that'd be really helpful. Otherwise we can come back later with a warrant and take it then. Up to you.'

Linda, who has followed us out to the hall, says, 'You need her phone? Why?'

'Procedure,' I agree. 'It'd be really helpful. Thanks.'

'What if Keeley needs me?' Jude asks.

'She lives across the road, darling,' Linda says, her voice unhampered by affection. 'She'll find you. Yes, Detectives. You have Jude's permission. It's upstairs in your room?'

Without waiting for an answer, Linda begins to climb the stairs. Jess follows.

Left alone in the hall, Jude and I don't look at one another. I want to say something.

'I saw a photo of you at the rock pools.' It is not exactly what I had hoped would come out, but it is fine, neutral territory.

'Yeah,' Jude says. 'We used to love it. Haven't been in ages.'

'We used to take our daughter,' I say. 'Haven't been in ages.'

'Is she afraid to go since that girl died there?'

I stare at her. My mouth is suddenly very dry. 'No,' I say after a pause. 'She isn't afraid of that. We can't go any more. Not with Rebecca. She … Well. Rebecca isn't … she isn't with us. She isn't with us any more. She's –' It is not what I wanted to say, not how I wanted to word it. What is she? I look around wildly. 'She's …'

Jude's eyes are wide. She nods as though she understands and says quickly, 'Oh, right. I'm sorry. Sorry.'

We hear voices from upstairs and both look up at the ceiling gratefully.

'Phone's probably slipped down the back of my bed,' Jude says after a moment. 'I'll just go and …' She trails off, then follows the other two up the stairs.

I stand for a few minutes glancing around the hall, sniffing as phlegm threatens to drip on to the shiny floor.

'You're supposed to blow your nose into a tissue.' I turn on the spot. A skinny boy with a mop of black hair has just come from what I assume is the living room. He has two crutches, one under each arm, and he is grinning at me. 'That's what my mum says, anyway. I suppose you're an adult so you can do whatever you want. And you're a detective.'

'I am,' I say. I grin back at him. 'You must be Mason. I've heard about you.'

'Do you know who did it yet?' He looks only a little like his family: he is darker, but the cheekbones are the same as Jude's. He wears Spiderman pyjamas and is barefoot. His legs seem to bend awkwardly at the knee.

'Not yet,' I say. 'Still early days. Need to make sure we're being thorough.'

'You've arrested someone, it said on the news.'

'We have.'

'Who?'

' … I can't really tell you.'

'Why are you asking Jude more questions? Do you think she did it?'

'No,' I say instantly. 'I'm sure your sister is perfectly innocent. We just have to ask her a few things, to help us piece together what happened.'

'She isn't innocent.' Mason tuts a laugh. 'She's horrible.'

I try and blink away my surprise. 'Why?'

'She just … is.'

I nod as if I understand. Then a sudden thought occurs. 'Mason, do you remember what your sister was wearing on Tuesday night?'

Mason furrows his thick eyebrows. 'You mean at the party? I have no idea. She left here early and was just in … jeans or something, I don't know.'

'Oh, of course.'

'She always borrows Keeley's stuff.'

'Yes, I've heard.'

'They're obsessed with each other.'

'I've heard that, too. Why is Jude horrible?'

Mason raises one of the crutches in the air so he can scratch his nose. 'Dunno. Just is.'

'She seems really nice to me,' I say, frowning as though shrugging him off. I turn away from him.

'Well, she isn't. You don't know everything about her.'

I keep quiet, my back to the boy, pretending to examine the intricate design on the inside of the front door.

'She used to hurt me. A lot. She pushed me down from upstairs a few years ago and I broke my arm. Pushed me from upstairs down that, my lift.'

Before I can respond or react in any way, I hear voices, then footsteps coming down the stairs.

When I turn to Mason, I see only the back of his head disappearing back into the living room.

'How do you want to play this?' Jess asks. We have decided, wordlessly, to take the lift the three floors up to Room G, where Naomi Ross is waiting for us. I think perhaps Jess is under the impression I am not capable of taking the stairs.

We are standing, both looking at the backlit up arrow on the wall next to the single lift. We can hear it, somewhere above us, creaking down, slowly. The lift is ancient. I think of Mason Jameson being pushed down his own lift. If he had landed differently, he might have been killed.

'We'll just ask her about Mack,' I say. 'Maybe she saw him kill Pete and hasn't said anything until now because she's scared. Wouldn't blame her.'

'She could be involved,' Jess says. 'She helped him move the drugs from the house; she must have wondered why they were doing that.'

'Mack says she didn't help,' I correct her. 'It was him carrying that gym bag back to her house; she might have thought it was a change of clothes or something.'

'Yeah, he seems like that kind of forward-thinking guy. I'm sure that's what she thought. After nine years together.'

It is only now, looking at the arrow next to the lift, listening to Jess, that something in the back of my mind clicks into place. Like I have been standing on one leg and have just remembered I can set the other down. Relief mixed with numbness.

When we get to the room, I can barely wait to set up the tape before I say, 'Naomi, where did you say you were on the 12th of July 2018?'

'My sister got married on the 14th,' Naomi says. 'The Saturday. I flew over on the 12th. Early in the morning. Is this about the fight again? I had no idea Mack and Pete fought until one of your detectives told me. Honestly.'

She has very black hair, cut short and with a fringe, and piercing green eyes. Her nose is long but suits her long face. She is skinny – flat chest, tiny, child-like forearms. She wears no make-up and is holding her hands in her lap, palms up. She seems calm, as if she wants to answer our questions.

'So, you left early on the morning of the 12th?'

'Yeah.'

'What time were you in the airport?'

'Ten, probably.'

'So you left at, what, 9 a.m.?'

'I'd stayed at Mack's the night before and had to go home to get my case. We were getting a taxi from my sister's mate's house so I would have left mine ... half-eight?'

'The 12th of July is a public holiday,' I say.

Naomi blinks. 'So?'

Jess has seen where this is going. I can almost feel her cursing herself inwardly. We exchange a glance.

I speak to and pause the tape and Jess leaves the room.

Naomi's eyes are round and panicked. I know her confusion is genuine.

When Jess returns ten minutes later, she is carrying the clear plastic envelope with the single slip inside. I reset the tape and explain to it what Jess is holding.

'Do you know what this is?' Jess asks.

Naomi leans forward. Her serious fringe does not move a single hair. She mumbles something.

'Sorry?' Jess asks. She actually puts a hand to her ear, as if to hear better.

'Prescription slip,' Naomi repeats.

'Can you read the name and date from the top there, please?'

Naomi scowls at Jess.

Unfazed, Jess reels, '12th of July 2018, Miss N Ross, 8b Boar's Brae, Vetobridge, County Down, Northern Ireland. That's you, isn't it? How were you able to pick up a prescription from a chemist in Vetobridge when you were in Spain?' When still Naomi says nothing, she carries on. 'Can you read the name of the drug that was supplied for Miss N Ross on this date?'

Jess sounds like a prosecution barrister in the midst of a trial. I lean back in my chair and let her continue.

'Levonelle,' Jess says, when still Naomi does not answer. 'Morning after pill. You spoke to a doctor, probably from the airport, I'm guessing, and got emergency contraception delivered to a pharmacy. When you weren't in the country to pick it up or take it. Why did you do that? Or have you lied about Spain, completely?'

'No,' Naomi says quickly. 'Well. I don't know what to tell you. I … I can't remember. This was years ago. How am I meant to remember what happened years ago?'

'You seemed very sure of the facts just a minute ago,' I say.

'How is this even relevant?'

'We're investigating a murder,' says Jess. 'Your boyfriend is in custody and we are trying to establish whether or not you are a liar.'

'I'm not.'

'Prove it. What's the deal with the prescription?'

'What has Mack said?'

'It's you we're speaking to.'

'I think you should speak to Mack.'

'Why?'

Naomi looks to me, her eyes wide, appealing. I keep my arms folded and say nothing, not trusting myself to blurt out the questions I have in a coherent manner. The tingling sensation in my stomach is back.

'I want to speak to Mack first,' she says finally. Her voice is firm. She, too, leans back in her seat and exhales.

'You don't get to call the shots, Miss Ross,' Jess says. She is trying not to grit her teeth. 'We are police officers and we are questioning you about a murder. You don't get to tell us you'll get back to us.'

'I'm not speaking until I've seen Mack.'

'You know we can arrest you? If you're keeping something to yourself that might be –'

'Arrest me, then.' Naomi even throws her hands up a little.

Jess looks at me.

When nobody speaks for a few moments, Naomi says, 'Look. I'm not hiding anything from you. I just think some things will be better coming from Mack. I'm not as … *involved* in all of this as he is. I want to see him, I need to talk to him.'

'Miss Ross,' Jess says with a sigh. 'You must understand that we can't let you speak to Mack at the moment; we can't let you discuss any part of this case while he is a suspect.'

'Not about the case,' Naomi says. 'That's not what I want to talk to him about. It's just … I need to break up with him. I know what that sounds like, but for what it's worth I really, really don't think Mack could kill anyone. No matter how many drugs he'd had. He just isn't capable of anything like that.' She pushes back her fringe and seems to struggle with something before she says, so quietly that Jess and I lean in towards her,

'On Tuesday night he went to get us another drink, but he came back with all the pills. He put them all in a bag, started running about the house like a madman, clearing stuff up, and he wouldn't tell me why.'

'And what time was that?' I ask, speaking as softly as her so I don't break the spell.

'Dunno. After two. Maybe closer to half.'

'*Like a madman*,' I repeat. 'Why do you think he –'

'I know it looks suspicious as hell,' Naomi says, louder and more assured now. 'But Keeley was still in the house. There's no way he would have just left her there, to get the blame, if he had stabbed Pete. There's just no way. So, I know it can't have been him. But he must have known Pete was dead, right? Otherwise why the rush to leave with the drugs?' She lets her head drop as though it is too heavy for her neck. 'We've been together ages. I'm the Jude to his Keeley, I suppose you could say.

'There were things we wanted to do with our lives. We wanted to travel, to live somewhere where there's more to do in the evenings than just sit on someone's mum's old sofa and take pills and listen to the same music we've liked since we were sixteen. When we met, Mack was doing a business course, did you know that? He was going to be an entrepreneur. Gave it up, of course. The classes clashed with his very important schedule of taking coke and playing the guitar. He's stuck here, he's stuck falling asleep on old sofas and having the same conversations week in week out. But I'm not. I still want to travel, I still want to … I can't do any of that if I have a boyfriend who is in jail.' She lifts her head again and looks from Jess to me. 'I think we all knew it would end like this. It always felt like we were living on borrowed time. Even when things were really good, we knew eventually it would all catch up. Do you know what I mean? And I'm not saying I'm any better than him, I've fucked up too, I'm just saying if I'd known somebody had been stabbed … I would have called an ambulance. And I really thought he would too.

'Do you think there's any way I could see Mack? Tomorrow, maybe? I just want to tell him it's over.'

We arrange for Naomi to meet Mack under supervision the following afternoon, and with that promised, I see her back downstairs. Just before we get to the doors, she turns to face me. I almost walk into her, I am so focused.

'Am I horrible?' she asks. 'Am I really horrible for breaking up with someone who is probably going to prison for murder, even when I know he is innocent of that?'

I do not look at her. Instead, I use my pass to open the door and it buzzes obediently. Naomi's shoulders seem to sag, but she hitches her bag on to one and leaves the station.

If she is walking away from Mack, I think, as I press the button for the lift again, she is not the Jude to his Keeley.

'Got some info that might interest you,' Pogo says, his mouth chewing on air.

My heart beats a little faster.

We are sitting on opposite sides of a bench that overlooks a children's play park. We haven't looked at one another yet, and I haven't said a word. The hairs on my arms are standing up, not entirely because of the cold.

'Denny was never a rival dealer,' Pogo continues. 'He started selling my boys some new thing maybe two years ago. Little white pills that impact you in one of six different ways, depending on a few factors. I've had it and honestly, it is seriously good. It's basically comedown-free. My boys are devastated Denny is gone; they're going to have to stick to their own stashes of coke, now. They're all terrified. They think if this was a drug murder, they'll be next.'

I look at him. He wears a sports jacket and tracksuit bottoms and looks like he hasn't shaved for a few weeks. 'My heart bleeds for them,' I say. 'Did you find out anything about July 2018 and Mack?'

Pogo glances around surreptitiously. 'Yeah. I asked them about that date and they all remembered; they knew what you meant. So, two summers ago, like you said, Denny had been selling to them for a few months. He came around to see the boys and sometimes they took these Sixes together, sometimes they just had a drink. This was before I was really involved with this particular group. Anyway, Denny showed up one night, really late, in a state. Drunk, off his face and crying, apparently. Says he's made a mistake and he's proper shitting himself because he thinks the police are going to be on to him. The boys were questioning him, obviously. If he was wanted by the police, they didn't want him hanging around. They got nervous. If the police wanted Denny for drugs, they wouldn't have to go too far to find his buyers. So they pester him with questions, asking him what the hell had happened, what he'd done. He just kept saying, *I fucked up, I fucked up*. Was it drugs, the boys asked? He was shaking, could hardly speak, but eventually they worked out it wasn't drugs. They got nothing else out of him, and eventually he sobered up a bit and fell asleep.

'Then he showed up again two nights later, beaten to a pulp. He'd brawled outside a pub, he said. Not a big deal, it happened on the 12th of July. The boys remembered the date because he had a Union Jack in his back pocket which was soaked in blood. He'd used it to bandage himself up the night before. Said he'd just spent the night in a police cell and didn't want to go home to his own house until his injuries calmed down a bit ... They asked him what he'd done.' Pogo looks at me for the first time, and I know he is gauging my reaction. 'Do you know what he'd done?'

'Do you?' I ask impatiently. I can think of only one thing that would explain the prescription, the confusion over dates, Jaxon's unofficial theory about the stab wound.

'No. He'd been to a party on the night before the 12th, though. The night he was crying. It was at Mack's place. Something happened. And on the 12th, then, Mack sees him in a bar and starts on him. They argue, take it outside, and Mack beats Denny to within an inch of his life. Denny said he thought Mack was going to kill him, and he might have done, if the police hadn't broken them up.

'As far as the boys know, Mack wasn't charged. Denny didn't want to pursue it, for whatever reason. They spent that night in the cells and then just carried on with things. I suppose neither of them wanted the police in their lives. Nothing more was ever said about whatever Denny had done that angered Mack so much.

'I asked the boys if they could guess what it was. They guessed the same thing I would but ...'

I don't bother to fill the silence, this time. There is no point asking Pogo how he is, no point in making small talk.

He doesn't even say goodbye. Just sits for a few minutes, staring across the park, then stands up and walks away. He knows he has told me all that he needs to.

I sit on the bench for a long time after Pogo has gone, my brain whirring and my body strangely numb from more than cold.

Then I pull out my phone and call Keeley Mackley's number.

Keeley

3rd January 2020, evening

I am lying on Naomi's sofa, blanket pulled up to my chin, staring at the TV that I've forgotten to switch on.

My phone rings. I glance at the screen, expecting it to be Jude who has been unusually quiet this evening, but click to answer the unrecognised number.

'Keeley? Hi. It's Chris Rice, here.'

'Oh, hi, Chris.'

Chris? I wince at myself and sit up, blanket falling.

'Did you get your keys back?'

They sit on Naomi's coffee table in front of me. 'Yeah.'

'You're home safe?'

'No, I … I decided not to go back just yet. Staying with my brother's girlfriend.' When he doesn't say anything else, I add. 'How's Mack?'

The detective heaves a sigh. 'Can't really talk about him but … We'll look after him, I promise. I'm going to speak to him again this evening and I'll make sure he's OK. Listen, I just wanted to run something past you. Can you think back and remember as best you can for me, when *exactly* you met Peter Denny?'

I furrow my brow. 'I told you I … Summer 2018.'

'Can you be specific for me, Keeley? This might be important.'

I think hard for a moment.

'Was it at your eighteenth birthday party?' Rice asks. 'Did he come to your eighteenth birthday party?'

'No, he … He was invited but he never showed up. The very end of August was when we first met.'

'And when did Jude meet him for the first time?'

A beat.

'Well, after that. I introduced them … I could probably get you the date; it was the day before the school's Open Night. October, I think. No, early November. November 2018.'

Rice sighs as though I have disappointed him. 'Thank you, Keeley,' he says. 'That's been really helpful.'

What the hell was that all about?

I remember them meeting, that look between them. I remember driving home from Open Night the next day too, and seeing Jude trudging along the promenade.

Her school bag was hanging off one shoulder, hair covering her face.

I slowed to a halt just as the rain started and rolled down my window. I beeped the horn.

'Jude!' I called. Like somebody had turned up a switch, the rain became heavy and loud.

She turned, squinted, then came towards the car. I rolled up my window, teeth chattering.

'Why are you getting back so late?' I asked the second the passenger door opened. 'Don't tell me you had to stay for Open Night too, did you? You should have waited for me! It's a six-mile walk, surely?'

Jude slid into the seat next to me, shivering. 'Got held up at school.'

She was drenched, her hair sticking to her scalp. Her face was red, like it had been rubbed on carpet, and her eyeliner had almost totally come off. She had a long ladder in her school tights and, I noticed as I reached over to sweep what looked like a streak of mud from her school shirt, one of the buttons on her new blazer was missing.

'You look a mess,' I said. 'What's … ?'

'N-nothing. Tripped earlier. Fuck, it's cold.' She busied herself adjusting the heat settings.

'You OK?'

'Yeah. Can you just drive? Please.'

I drove us home, Jude shaking long after the car had heated up.

How the bloody hell had I not seen it then?

It was months before I found out what had happened, and then only by pure accident.

It was a Thursday.

I spotted Kim up ahead of me in a corridor before third period and sprinted to catch her up. She had invited me that morning to another *Beth McKenna Soirée* at the weekend, and I wanted to let her know I was coming. Pete and I finally were official, committed, *exclusive*, and I was dying to see the looks on their faces when I pulled up at Beth's house on the arm of the most famous person in Vetobridge.

Kim didn't hear me, and I ended up following her towards the bathroom outside the Technology corridor – famously unused because the window didn't close properly and so your bum was always freezing when you tried to have a pee.

I could hear Beth laughing as soon as I got within a few feet. I opened the door and stared.

'Have you done it already?' Kim asked. 'I wanted you to wait for me. If we lose that thing, Jack says he'll strangle me with his bare hands.'

'Shut up! I'm recording.' Beth was wiping her eyes with one hand – she had real tears of mirth rolling down her face – and holding her phone with the other. She was standing on top of the cistern of the nearest toilet, only her head visible over the top of the cubicle.

I could hear crying. A pitiful moan and choked sobs. For just a moment my blood ran cold, but I wouldn't have been able to pinpoint exactly why.

'Make sure it doesn't get away,' Kim said uneasily. She pushed open the door to Beth's stall and vanished from sight for a second, only to reappear as a bobbing head a foot or so below Beth's. She stood on the toilet seat, I guessed.

'What are you doing?' I asked.

They turned in unison, Beth nearly toppling from her perch, having to grab Kim's shoulder for support.

'Keeley?' came a high-pitched squeal from the second cubicle. A voice I knew better than my own.

'Jude? What's going on, are you –'

'Get them to let me out!' she shouted. 'Make them let me out.'

I said nothing, only stared – mouth closed in a tight line – at Beth.

Beth sighed and jostled at Kim. The two of them moved awkwardly, a lot of tutting and swearing in their attempt to get down from their perches without injuring themselves.

My hands were shaking.

'Just a joke,' Beth said seriously to me, as I came around to the front of the cubicles to join them.

I noticed then that her school tie was not around her neck. Instead, the tie had been rolled thin and threaded between the two parts of the lock of Jude's cubicle from the outside.

'She can't get out?' I demanded. 'Are you serious, you've actually locked her in there? Undo it. Now!'

Beth did as she was told, the smile still on her face, though less assured now. She pushed open the door and Jude stumbled out, face ashen and tear-stained. She moved as close to the far wall as she could and pressed her back to it.

'What the hell are you playing at?' I shouted. When Beth only smirked and looked at her phone, I wheeled around to face Kim. 'What's this about?'

Kim looked to her friend for help. When none came, she seemed to falter. 'It was a prank,' she explained. She lifted a large plastic Tupperware container from the side of the nearest sink and dashed into the cubicle Jude had vacated.

Confused, I went to Jude who was shaking, her face wet.

'I told you,' she managed as I put one hand on her cheek. 'It's not you. It's always been me. For ages. Years.'

'He's my brother's,' Kim said.

I turned. In the Tupperware she had caught a giant spider – a tarantula, maybe. Brown and hairy, its legs moving up and down, pushing at the side of the container. I leapt back and felt Jude do the same.

'Get it away!' Jude screamed.

Beth snorted. She still had the phone pointed at Jude.

I imagined, for one glorious second, gripping her by the hairline and pulling with all my might until the skin of her face peeled off and I could crumple it in my hand and spit on it. As I was thinking this, I felt Jude pulling forward, towards the very thing that had frightened her so much.

I had no warning.

Evidently, neither did Beth.

Jude spoke in a hushed, almost excited voice for ten minutes, detailing the various texts, threats and abuse she had received over the past two and a half years. We both kept one eye on the door to Miss Sparks's office, shutting our mouths abruptly if a teacher or another student walked by. People looked at us. Word had spread.

I sat, legs stretched out in front of me, on one of the two chairs outside the main office. Jude paced the floor in front of me while she spoke. We were waiting for Miss Sparks to hear our side of what had happened and to hear Jude out about the bullying. Beth's mum, blonde and big-toothed Mrs McKenna, her husband having gone with Beth to the hospital, was in the office now.

'They got me on my way home a while back,' Jude said. 'Trying to get me to eat raw chicken.'

'They *what*?'

'I didn't. At least, I don't think I swallowed any. They've pushed me about a bit before but never anything like that. It was the day you picked me up, in November, the day of Open Night. Somebody was filming it too.'

'What? Hold on, *what*?'

'Disgusting. I know. They wouldn't let me go for ages.'

'I can't believe I made you go for that drive with them last summer. Why didn't you tell me any of this?' I tried to sound concerned, but my exasperation was audible. 'And don't say because I seemed too *busy* with Pete because that's only been a few months and this has been going on for years.'

'Not as badly as this. I didn't want you to get involved, I was …' Jude seemed to search for the right word. I got the distinct impression she was relieved to be talking about this. 'Embarrassed. About the things they were saying. It seems mad, thinking about it now.'

'It is mad. I can't wait to tell everyone the way Beth's jaw clicked when you kicked it in. Or when I did, rather.'

'What?' Jude asked. There was a shred of anxiety in her voice now. 'You're not going to keep that up, are you?'

'Of course I am. You can't get in trouble for standing up for yourself. We can say it was me who hit her.'

'They'll kick you out.' Her voice was more panicked than I had ever heard it. 'What about your exams?'

Being an actuary was a stupid idea anyway, wasn't it? I'd never have made it. It didn't seem important anyway, not in light of this.

'It's fine,' I said. 'I've said it now. What do they call it? Self-defence? I was self-defending you, we'll say.'

'You can't take the blame for something you didn't do!' Jude insisted, a thick edge to her voice that was a sure sign of tears to come. 'You can't! It's not fair. They might want to get the police. You might be arrested. It was me and I'll tell them!'

'Sit down,' I said firmly.

She sat down next to me.

I reached out and gripped both her wrists, pulling her to me. 'You have to stick to the story,' I said. 'I came into the bathroom and saw they had locked you in the cubicle. I knew they had been bullying you for years and I snapped. I threw a few punches at Beth, got her on the ground and kicked her. OK? Say it.'

Jude choked and tears started to spill on to her cheeks.

'It's over,' I whispered urgently. 'This is it. They won't touch you any more, not now they've seen what you're capable of, what happens to people who fuck with Jude Jameson. I'm just sorry you didn't tell me sooner. I'm sorry I didn't notice sooner. I'm so sorry, Jude. Now, what happened in there?'

She tried to blink away her tears but they kept falling, thick and fast. 'If you're not here, it'll be worse. The lesbian stuff might stop but the rest might be worse.'

'It won't be worse; it's over. You stopped it. What happened in there?'

She took a deep breath. She looked exhausted. How had I not noticed this? How had I put her fear of Beth and Kim down to a stupid, childish jealousy?

'You punched and kicked Beth,' she mumbled. 'Because she had locked me in a cubicle with a spider.'

'A fucking tarantula, let's not underplay it.'

'A fucking tarantula.' She smiled amid her tears.

'I'm going to sort this and you won't get in trouble. I just want one thing from you, now that everything is out in the open. Now that we're being completely honest with each other. OK?'

'I'm sorry I didn't tell you,' she said quickly.

I closed my eyes. 'That's OK. Some things hurt too much to talk about. I just want you to do something for me, OK?'

She eyed me warily.

'I want you to give Pete a chance,' I said. 'I love him, Jude.'

'You what?'

We looked at one another until her eyes slipped away, on to the floor, her mouth slightly open.

'I love him,' I repeated. 'I haven't told him yet, obviously. He'd run a mile. I'm in love with him. So it's really important to me that the two people I love the most can get along. You weren't exactly friendly when I tried to introduce you both, and you're always in a rush to leave if he's around. We've been together, what, six months now? I'm just asking you to spend a bit of time getting to know him. Come with us when we go places. I think you'd like him. He's funny. If I love you both, you're bound to like one another, right?'

Jude didn't look convinced. She cradled her left wrist against her chest and didn't say anything. She sniffed.

'I just want you to try,' I said. 'For me.'

'OK,' she said quietly. A final, single tear rolled down her cheek. 'For you.'

Here on Naomi's sofa, my phone still clutched in my hand, I realise it is Jude's eighteenth birthday the day after tomorrow. I haven't even got a present for her; I was going to get something this week.

I have let her down so much.

What the hell am I doing?

I scroll to Jude's number and press dial, suddenly desperate.

This person's phone is switched off.

Detective Inspector Chris Rice

3rd January 2020, night

My head is pounding and my stomach grumbling, but to take myself out of my office for painkillers or food seems cowardly. I need to speak to someone, to have someone hear my theory, share with me this horrible, heart-wrenching last piece of the jigsaw, but the rest of the team have gone home. I know later I will be grateful for this opportunity to get my head in order.

Our most recent interview with Mack has revealed nothing but, as I now know, this is unsurprising. *No comment. No idea. They're my drugs, Naomi has nothing to do with it. No comment.* It had been hard to keep up the questioning, knowing he was innocent of the murder at least.

I have written everything down by hand as carefully as I can on an A4 sheet and put it in the front of the Project Twenty file. The process of writing it helped me reason each point and I know for certain, now, that I am right.

I just have no idea what I should do about it.

I know what Jess will say. The word protocol will come up, she'll quote some piece of law, she'll frown at me and show me the single wrinkle between her eyebrows and say, 'Why are you hesitating?'

I set the file to the side and switch on my computer. I tap through emails until I get to the right one. I play the live video taken on Brian Reed's phone. I am not even thinking about it as I watch. I have seen it so many times that I can recount it word for word.

'*It'll sound stupid without the bass.*'

'I'd like to dedicate this to …'

I watch the video to the end, then click repeat. I watch it again. Click repeat.

A scratch on Jude's cheek.

Repeat.

Girls laughing.

Click.

A mouth full of raw chicken.

Click.

Peter Denny.

Tears.

I click again just as Brains is standing to leave the living room. For just a split second, the phone camera flips so that the TV is in focus. In the reflection of the huge blank screen, three figures can be seen.

Naomi Ross, short hair and a woolly jumper. Brains himself, a blur in motion. Jude on his other side. The image is blurry, facial expressions cannot be read, but it is clear enough.

The dress Jude wears is dark, maybe even black, and the sleeves are long. She told us she wore a lilac, silky piece with short sleeves. There is something else that jars about her as well, but I can't quite decide what it is. Something in the reflection that just doesn't quite fit. I think of Jude the first day we met her, in the interview room in the station, sleeves pulled over her hands, pale face peeking out from the curtain of straight, clean hair.

Now, more than ever, I want to speak to someone. It should be Jess, I know.

Something stops me picking up the phone. As well as being a dedicated and hard-working detective, I have to remember that Jess is also someone's girlfriend, someone's cohabitant, the other half of someone's bed. She won't want a phone call from me at this time.

Other people have more components to their day than police work.

I think of calling Aisling. Would she even pick up this late?

And then it hits me – the only person about whose opinion I actually care.

The one and only voice I want to hear.

Mack

3rd January 2020, night

They lead me back to my cell after the second interview.

It is almost bigger than Keeley's bedroom.

Disjointed phrases are swimming around in my head, and I'm not sure if I said them to the police, if I thought them, or if they are parts of conversations I had a long time ago.

My drugs. Nobody else. I said that to the police, surely? They kept looking at me as though they could see a film of my thoughts playing inside my head, and that made me nervous, so I kept thinking about the beach and refused to think of anything else, until they sighed and just left me to it. The social worker they have paired me with – for reasons I listened to but can't quite remember – kept looking at his watch and sighing, even though it only lasted for an hour or so. Or did it?

My cheek is bleeding and I can't stop scratching my face.

I do remember one thing the big detective, the Rice man, said.

'Naomi Ross wants to come and see you tomorrow,' he murmured, near the end of the interview. 'You're amenable?'

'Yes,' I gasped. 'Yes, please.'

I get to see her to explain. She probably wants to apologise for telling the police where to find me.

I can't wait to tell her that I forgive her.

I sit down on the bed – just as comfortable as my own, I think – and kick off my shoes, thinking of Naomi's face and feeling a tired smile on my own.

I met Naomi the first time Colly Murphy asked me to deliver a package of cocaine wrapped in Christmas paper.

She was behind the reception desk at the Clandy. She had a sharp face and bony features, with straight black hair that was cut severely to her chin. Her face was subservient to a pair of large, thick-framed glasses, and I thought I'd never seen anyone as beautiful in my life.

'What do you want?' she asked. She was peering over the desk and eyeing my trainers. I glanced behind me and realised I'd walked sand all through the lobby.

'I need to see Saul. Please.'

'He isn't about. Want me to take a message?'

'Oh.' My heart sank. 'I've come from Colly Murphy. I have something for Saul.'

'Oh *that*. Murphy hasn't sent you before,' she said. She chewed a piece of gum. 'I think I recognise you from the arcade. While I have you here, can you get me the number of the big fella who plays the slots on a Friday? I'd definitely fuck him.'

I stared at her. I'd heard women talk like that before, of course, but this girl worked at the *Clandy*, the poshest place in Vetobridge bar none. She was a receptionist, she wore *glasses*. She was in a different league from all the girls I knew. I peered at her more closely. She was not as old as I had assumed at first glance. In fact, without the glasses and the sensible blue blouse, I'd have guessed her to be the same age as me.

As I learned later, she was.

'What's your name?' she asked.

'Mack,' I said. It was the first time I had introduced myself as such, even though everyone in my life, my own sister included, had embraced the change of name – Murphy's suggestion – without question.

'I'm Naomi,' she said simply. 'And Saul's not in any fit state to take that. Come into the back with me; I don't think we should stand here with a bag of coke wrapped in Christmas paper, do you? Bad face for business, you know. Family-friendly Sundays and all that. Are you listening to me, Mack?'

The way she said my name made me forget about the sand.

She went into the little room behind the desk and I followed, closing the door after me.

'Saul's basically passed out in one of the rooms. Stag do at the weekend, totally fucked, has barely moved off the bed since.'

I had seen my Mum like that before but had no idea that there were others. I tried to keep my expression neutral.

'Want to do it with me?' Naomi asked.

I stared. 'Do it with you?'

'The coke,' Naomi explained. 'Not sex.'

'Oh.' I was so relieved by this answer that I let out a shaky laugh. 'I don't do cocaine. But thanks for the offer.'

Naomi rolled her eyes. 'Coke is the best, most enjoyable thing ever. You've never experienced anything like it. Saul's fucked because of the drink, not the coke. Poor bastard.' She frowned with real pity then.

'Why is he a poor bastard?' I asked. In any other circumstances, talking about someone like that would have made me feel guilty and uncomfortable. Something in Naomi's casualness had calmed me and given me confidence. 'It's his own fault surely?'

'Is it? He's addicted to booze, so I suppose it depends if you think addicts are sick or weak.'

With a jolt, I realised that she was looking at me to answer. 'Oh, I'm not sure. Sick, maybe?'

'Nah, they're weak,' Naomi said decisively. I had failed her test. She turned to me. 'So, are you up for it?'

'Coke?'

'Yes. Not sex.'

'Right. Well, I don't know. Murphy has asked me to give it to Saul and I don't want to let him down. Maybe I should just leave it here for him?'

'Fuck that. Tell your mate Murphy that you gave it to Saul and then just give Murphy twenty quid of your own. When Saul comes round, I'll tell him he paid you himself and took it all before he passed out. He won't know the difference.'

I thought, then, that Naomi was a little cruel, a little cold and very pretty.

When I hesitated, Naomi said, 'You can stay and watch if you don't want to have any.'

She stuck her head out the door that led to the reception desk. Satisfied that no customers were waiting, she came back in and tore the paper from the package. She took off her glasses and set them on the top of the sideboard in front of her.

I joined her, obviously.

There was never any formal conversation, never an exchange where we used the word 'boyfriend' or 'girlfriend', but that was what we were from the moment I let Naomi Ross put her little finger in my mouth and rub the powder over my gums.

She was smart, funny and mildly depressed, and I was in love with her almost immediately. She must have seen something in me beyond my own naivety that I hadn't ever seen myself.

And with Naomi came drugs. Lots of them. A feeling like flying and running and winning a race all at once; something to do, something to focus on, something to work for and towards.

It felt right, even the mornings after, as long as Naomi was by my side.

But now, the metal door opens with a drawn-out squeak and a guard sets a tray of food on the ground. He doesn't say a word and neither do I.

How long will Naomi wait for me?

I have no idea how long I will get for the drugs … a few years, maybe? As long as I'm out before we're thirty, I think, she will wait.

Which means I can't go down for Pete. I can't leave her for that long.

I will have to tell the truth.

No matter what the consequences.

Detective Inspector Chris Rice

4th January 2020, afternoon

'Mackley said anything yet?' I ask before the door closes behind Smith.

The afternoon briefing. A half-full incident room. Colson, Browne, Smith, Magill, Jess and me.

'Nada,' says Colson. 'Just keeps going on about the drugs. He's sweating buckets though. Think this is the longest he's gone without any gear for a long time, by the looks of him.'

'Poor kid,' mutters Browne. 'Poor stupid fucking kid.'

I still haven't decided how much I am going to tell the team and am hoping to take guidance from them.

'Colson, do you know if we found a black dress at the house?'

All heads turn to me. Colson, standing in the space between three desks that almost form a square around her, moves her hands in a kind of dance at waist height, scanning the pages in front of her. 'I – I don't know. *Black* dress? I can check. Let me …'

'What about yesterday?' I ask, turning to Smith. 'Did you find anything en route to Boar's Brae?'

Smith shakes his head. 'Nothing. Looked hard.'

'Sir,' says Browne. 'I'm sorry for asking but, why are we looking for a dress? You never really explained. We're trying to find something to tie Joshua Mackley to this and you are going on about a dress. It would help if we knew why.'

'Yeah,' agrees Magill. 'You must think the girls are involved, is that it? Do you know something we don't?'

'No,' I say quickly. 'No, I don't.' I heave myself on to a nearby chair and sit down. Across the room, her laptop on her knee, Jess tilts her head to the side in a friendly gesture.

Colson continues to thumb through evidence on the desks.

The three men stand leaning against desks, arms folded or their hands in their pockets. Smith has pulled an orange from his bag and is trying to bite it just right so that he can peel it.

'I don't know anything for sure,' I continue carefully. 'I just … have a feeling. The first time Jess and I spoke to the girls, it felt as if they … It felt like they were lying. Even now that the shock has worn off, Jude doesn't seem remotely sad that Pete is dead and even on that first morning, when it was still new, Keeley wasn't acting like someone whose boyfriend had just been murdered. She was … light. Nice. Jokey, nearly.'

'She certainly wasn't like that when I drove her to the station,' Smith says. He too has pulled out a chair, and he sits down now, to get a better angle on his orange. He is speaking casually, almost thoughtlessly. 'Screamed the whole way here. Cried so much I had to let her out of the car to be sick.'

The already quiet room becomes completely silent. Jess stops tapping at her computer. Colson freezes halfway through shuffling a pile of paper. Browne and Magill look at one another, then finally come to settle on the same vision as the rest of us: Smith brushing some orange peel to the side of a desk and wiping his hands on his trousers.

Before he can separate the segments, he looks up. His eyes widen. 'What?' he asks.

'What did you just say?' I ask.

'Just … Just that I drove Keeley –'

'To the station on Wednesday,' says Jess. 'Yeah, you've told us nine times. You let her out of the car? I assume you went with her?'

Smith furrows his eyebrows and looks to the orange as though it will help him. 'Well, I had just pulled in at the side of the road. I couldn't get out.'

'But Dunwoody got out of the car?' Jess demands. 'Dunwoody got out with her?'

Smith looks at me, his face ashen.

'Answer her,' I say, my voice a low rumble.

'Dunwoody is squeamish ...'

I don't wait to hear the rest of his scrabbling defence. 'Sergeant Curran, take this dunce and make him show you exactly where Keeley Mackley got out of the car. Magill, phone the lab and let them know we'll have something for them in the next two hours and we need it fast-tracked.'

'Are you going to help facilitate the meeting between Naomi Ross and Mackley?' Jess asks.

'No,' I say. 'I'll get a constable. I've got an appointment that can't wait.'

'Oh,' says Jess. 'You didn't say?'

'It's not related to the case,' I say quickly. 'I'll be back as soon as I can.'

'Right.' Her voice is not clipped exactly, but she turns away almost immediately and busies herself in tapping on her phone.

I'll make it up to her later, I think.

I catch sight of myself in the black screen of a broken laptop and make an attempt to push back the hair I have left, smoothing it over my ears as though it will make all the difference in the world. I straighten my tie, mouth dry.

My heart hammers watching the thick iron door.

There is a long, low buzzing sound as it opens.

Rebecca is the second person to come through it. She beams when she sees me.

My hands are sweating and the headache I've had since Wednesday still hasn't quite subsided, but after deciding with whom to share my theory, I slept more last night than I have in the last week. I even managed a bowl of porridge before the briefing.

I want her to think I am sticking to the diet plan she made me.

We hug for as long as we can, until the nearest guard coughs pointedly. We break apart and Rebecca sits down opposite me.

'Two visits in the same week?' She narrows her eyes. 'What's wrong, Dad?'

'I can't visit my own daughter on a random Saturday?'

'Depends. Have you stuck to your diet this week?' She pokes the flap of stomach that rests on the table in front of us, but she is smiling.

She is wearing the same jumper she had on when I visited her on New Year's Eve, but she has washed her hair and the sight of her lifts my heart.

'I can hardly talk,' she says, patting her own tiny stomach. She takes after Aisling in her size. 'They've fed us rightly in here over the festive period. Can't complain. It's still nothing like Mum's turkey dinner.'

'I am sticking to the plan,' I say. 'It was a very thoughtful gift, thank you.'

'No problem. Now you have … two years and four months to lose about seven stone. I'll be weighing you the second I get out of here.'

'Seven stone? I'll be the size of Peter Dinklage.'

'Har, har,' Rebecca says. Her smile becomes wan and she cocks her head to the side. 'What's wrong? You didn't do your Peter Dinklage impression.'

'You said it was cruel.'

'It is. Don't avoid the question. What's wrong?'

I take a deep breath and sigh it out. 'I just wanted to talk to you.'

'To talk to me, or to talk *at* me?'

I smile. 'Well, both. I have a bit of a weird case on at the minute.'

Rebecca waits patiently as I sip the weak tea I made for something to do with my hands.

Rebecca will have been in Seekbank Prison for three years in May. When she was seventeen, she drove her car into a tree, upon whose branches a seven-year-old boy had been climbing. He fell from the tree in shock at the squeal of brakes and was crushed between the tree and the car.

His friend was screaming, shrieking, crying. Rebecca was limp in the driver's seat, hair falling over her face, matted with blood from where her forehead had slammed the steering wheel upon impact.

These things were described to us later by a kind police constable I recognised but had never worked with.

First, there was only the overpowering, heart-soaring relief that she was not dead.

Aisling's happy tears, my own fists clenched, saying thank you, thank you, to I know not whom. Nodding to nurses as they hurried past, wanting to encourage them. The fact that, actually, Rebecca was not hurt at all, besides a lump on her forehead and a few cuts. That beautiful, concrete fact we clung to with gritted teeth and pounding hearts, but which directly contrasted with the grave stares on the faces of a second police officer and a white-coated doctor as they put their heads close together and whispered.

'Can we see her?' I demanded of the second officer when he came close enough to hear us.

He sighed a little. 'The boy didn't make it,' he said. 'He was pronounced dead just now.'

'Boy?' said Aisling, her voice a high-pitched shriek. 'What boy? She was on her way back from hockey practice on her own; there was no boy.'

The officer's expression changed. 'The boy Miss Rice hit with her car … She came off the road and veered into a tree. A seven-year-old boy was killed. I'm sorry, I thought you had been told.'

The relief was still there, for me. It was a bubble in my chest, protected by my ribcage, and it could not be punctured. His words meant very little to me.

'But Rebecca is fine?' I asked.

The police officer nodded. 'So the doctor says.'

Rebecca got five years for causing death by dangerous driving.

Our solicitor was as aghast as we were. We had tried so hard for the charge of 'careless' driving, not 'dangerous'. The difference between those two words changed everything, and instead of a fine and a driving ban – which seemed a tiny, unimportant price to pay for what had happened – Rebecca was sent to Seekbank. The judge looked at her single speeding ticket – for doing 37 in a 30 – and genuinely rolled his eyes. The sentence was so harsh because he was making a point. All parties involved had acknowledged that Rebecca was very unlikely to reoffend. Nevertheless, he wanted the well-publicised case to be a lesson to all restricted drivers, and that is exactly what happened. He said he hoped all novice drivers would take note of what happens when people get overconfident behind the wheel.

Aisling, who had stood up for the judgment, sat down abruptly at the words 'without parole' and never really got herself back up again.

While I had made a point of visiting Rebecca at least once a week since, even after my move to Loughbricksea, Aisling had visited her only three or four times in the last two and a half years.

'She just doesn't want to accept it,' Rebecca told me once. 'She wants to go about her normal life and pretend it isn't happening. Wants to act like I'm at home waiting for her to get back from the Sunday shop, not wasting away in here.'

'She just can't adjust,' I said. 'You're right. Once you're out, everything can go back to normal.'

'Oh yeah, five years isn't so long. And I suppose you two will just get back together and we can move back to Holywood, and everything will be the same?'

I squirmed uncomfortably. It hadn't been my intention to tell Rebecca about our separation, but she asked after her mum so often that I couldn't hide the fact that I was no longer living with her. The thing was that, while I could understand how Aisling was feeling – distraught, embarrassed, ashamed, angry – I felt nothing more powerfully than I felt the fierce, unwavering desire to protect Rebecca.

I wouldn't have anyone ask pityingly after the boy. I shrugged and refused to enter into conversation about it. I did not speak if someone asked me how fast she was driving, only stared at people until they got the right idea.

Aisling sent cards to the boy's family. I cursed the day he was born. Why did he have to play in *that* tree? Why couldn't he have been inside, playing on an iPad like a normal boy?

Sometimes, when I was really bitter and missing Rebecca, I would think, why didn't the car before hers plough into him? Why not the car after?

It was April, so we couldn't blame ice, though I had suggested it to the solicitor in a moment of desperation. We couldn't claim anything, couldn't blame anyone else. Rebecca had simply been driving too fast on a country lane, hadn't slowed enough for a bend, hadn't been thinking clearly for all of a few seconds.

It is strange that something so fast, so instantaneous, could make everything that followed so slow and still.

'Dad?' I blink and she is in front of me. Twenty and tall and red-haired and somehow perfect.

Why couldn't the car before hers have hit that stupid kid?

'What's wrong?' she asks. 'Tell me about your weird case.'

I look around, making sure we aren't being overheard. 'A girl … Seventeen, nearly eighteen. Might have stabbed her best mate's boyfriend to death.'

Her lips, dry and chapped, open only slightly. She always wanted to hear about my cases and used to follow me around the house after work, asking me to describe murder scenes in as much depth as I could remember, begging me to show her my files. She was going to join the PSNI when she finished her A-levels. I could prep her for the tests; she would pass, fly through her uniform days, make it all the way up, surpass me, by then aged eighty, still an Inspector, clinging to my job like a life raft. Though if Rebecca had been able to finish her A-levels, if all of that had happened: would I have stayed in my job or retired? I'm not sure I'll ever know.

Chief Superintendent Rebecca Rice had a nice ring to it.

Low-security prisoner Rebecca Rice raises her eyebrows. 'So, what's the problem? You think she might be innocent?'

'The opposite,' I say. 'I'm pretty sure she's guilty; it's my team who have set their sights on another man.'

'But it's not him?'

I puff out my cheeks and let the air out through my mouth. 'There's some circumstantial evidence … and a motive, I suppose. And he has previous. Judges and juries love previous.'

I think of her speeding ticket and the judge's eyeroll.

'I suppose there is a chance it could be him,' I say. 'But I just found out yesterday that my girl might have a very good reason for wanting the guy dead … and it would make sense if she had done it.'

Rebecca frowns and leans back in the plastic seat, extending her long neck so her chin points to the ceiling. Her thinking pose. She swings back into position after a few seconds and says seriously, 'I don't think it matters much that she *wanted* him dead. I don't know if having a good reason for killing someone justifies it.'

'I know that,' I say a little impatiently. 'Obviously. I'm not saying she should have. I'm not saying it was the right thing to do, I'm saying … It's done now.'

I can't help but feel that my point has ended lamely. I'm not even sure if I have made the point I wanted to make. I put my hands around my cold tea mug for something to do.

'It's done now,' Rebecca agrees. She sucks at her teeth thoughtfully. 'So you're wondering what the point in sending a seventeen-year-old girl to prison for it would be?'

Coming from Rebecca, in her cool, matter-of-fact tone that has only intensified during her stay in Seekbank, the idea sounds ridiculous. I feel heat rise in my cheeks.

'I'm being a silly, sentimental old man,' I say. I reach across the table and hold her hand.

She grips mine back and says rather fondly, 'Yes, you are. There is only what happened.'

We have finished with the subject and I am glad to sit, my hand on hers, not thinking of anything for a moment.

I watch the people at the table next to ours. A woman in a stained pink jumper and tracksuit bottoms sits on the same side as me. A younger woman, her daughter, I think, mumbles consolingly to her, an endless stream of narrative. I know the mother is not listening, is not paying attention. Her eyes are sunken, almost haunted, and I wonder if it is prison that has given her this look, or her life before it. Her daughter wears dark-rimmed glasses, the kind that I've seen non-visually-impaired young people wear as a fashion statement. I can picture her at her job – as an accountant, or an estate agent, maybe – smiling at her clients and adjusting those glasses on her nose.

I want to lean across and whisper to her, tell her to hold her mother's hand. Her touch might be all she needs to get her through whatever private horrors she has back in her cell.

We speak for nearly two hours longer – going around in circles, saying the same things we've said a dozen times before, but enjoying saying them all the same, our hands clasped together and our eyes locked on one another.

The guard, who has been walking the aisles of tables and has reached ours, mumbles, 'About time to wrap up, folks.'

We stand and hug, tightly.

The mother and daughter at the table next to us stand too and, to my surprise, after their hug, it is the daughter who follows the guard to the door that leads back to the cells. The mother makes her way to the visitors' exit and I follow her. She is not the prisoner, but the visitor. Her pretty, bespectacled daughter is the prisoner.

There is what happened … and then there is what you can make people believe.

How much else have I assumed?

Jude

11th July 2018

Peter is funny. He makes me laugh twice, three times. He leans back on the bed and rests on his elbows. He is interested in me. I tell him some things about my life, but not much, and he talks openly about everything, anything he can think of. Music, drinking, Catholics and Protestants. I smile and nod and enjoy it.

I forget about keeping Keeley's dress from riding up and concentrate on the conversation, unable to keep the smile off my face.

Peter goes downstairs to get another beer and I realise, with a flutter to my heart, that I am enjoying myself without Keeley. Should I be checking in with her about now? She is going to be so proud of me … She'd be even prouder if I manage to kiss Peter; she wouldn't care about the missed check-in then. My head swims a little at the thought.

Dark Dark Dark is playing downstairs. The familiar song is beautiful and calming. I am still smiling.

When Peter comes back, he sits closer to me than before. My stomach tingles. He sets his beer on Mack's bedside table and leans over to kiss me. It is less frightening than I have always imagined it would be. I think it helps that he has obviously done this before: I simply follow what he does. Open my mouth when it feels like I should, move my tongue when he isn't. It is nice, it feels good. But it is a little boring and after a few minutes I pull away, happy that there is no embarrassing trail of saliva connecting our mouths the way I once saw in a film.

He grins at me and reaches for a swig of his beer.

'Do you want this?'

'Yeah,' I say, and he hands me the Bacardi.

After I set the glass back down, he moves on top of me.

Weight. Heat.

'Wait,' I say. 'Don't.'

Dark Dark Dark has stopped. Keeley has finally managed to negotiate the speakers to put on our song, 'Alone' by Heart. She is downstairs wondering where I am.

Keeley. Keeley. Keeley.

If we have anything, any connection, if she loves me at all, she will hear me screaming for her in my head. She will come running.

'Don't,' I say again, into his lips.

He doesn't hear me, or he pretends he doesn't. I start to wonder if I've even said it out loud.

'They told me you like it rough,' he breathes, smiling. That beautiful smile that, now, sends a shiver of fear down my spine.

My heart races. 'Who?'

I feel him smile against my neck, and I try and push back as far as I can into the bed, my arms and legs stiff and numb.

'All of them,' he murmurs. More kisses to my neck. Wetter.

No.

If Keeley can't hear me, maybe Mum will.

Mum.

Mum, come and ruin the party, come in and get me like you said you would. Come and find me and march me out and embarrass me.

A tear rolls down my cheek, because I know that even if I pray and beg and shout for her in my head, she would never hurt me like that.

Nobody is coming to find me.

'Happy Birthday,' he says.

I feel like someone has poured ice all over my body.

There are a million things I could say. I could laugh: after all, this has all been one big misunderstanding. I could shout. I could call for Keeley, I could call for Mack, I could call for anyone. I could just scream.

But I don't. I don't want anyone to find us like this.

'No,' I whisper to him. 'No, no.'

I am determined that he should realise his mistake. He doesn't mean any harm; he thinks I am someone else. So, what's happening doesn't really count. This isn't real. It's my fault for not making it clear. I never introduced myself. I didn't even say my name. Of course he didn't just know who I was. Why would anyone know who I was? I am nobody.

His fingers are on my leg. I turn my head to the side to try and make it clear that I want to keep drinking and talking.

Weight.

'Wait.'

I even try to reach for my glass. His weight pins me to the bed and I cannot move.

'Come on,' he murmurs. Kisses. 'Don't be like that.'

When it is over I stand up, my legs shaking. I pull Keeley's dress down as much as I can and head for the door, but it flies open before I can get to it.

'Oh, wow, sorry!'

It is Mack and Naomi. I don't even blush, I just stare. I catch sight of myself in the mirror that hangs beside the door. My hair, perfectly curled before, is frizzy and tatty and my eye make-up, the make-up that Keeley spent an hour on and that she told me I mustn't ruin, has smudged all across my face and on to my cheeks.

I don't stop to think about it – I shove past them into the hall and make for the bathroom. The door is locked, I pound on it.

'Fuck off!' someone calls from inside. 'We're a bit busy!'

I turn to Keeley's room.

Mack steps in front of me, eyes huge from more than drugs. In that brief second, he looks like the little boy I've seen in photographs but was too late to meet. 'Jude. Jesus Christ – did you – ?'

'I need to find Keeley,' I mumble. I turn around suddenly, meaning to go downstairs, but I stagger and stumble forward.

Mack reaches out and catches me just in time. He half walks, half carries me to Keeley's room. I am glad that it is empty of other guests.

She is still partying downstairs, still having the best night of her life. She has no idea.

The thought makes me angry.

'Jude, what happened? Did he try something?'

Mack's horror-stricken face. His panic. All because he thinks Pete has *tried* something. I want to laugh and cry and scream at him all at once.

The police. That is what you are supposed to do.

'You have to call the police,' I say, voice shaking. 'But I need Keeley first. Go now, Mack.'

'The police?' Mack's mouth falls open. 'Jude, what the fuck just happened? Did you sleep with Pete? How do you know him?'

It is too many questions. I don't know the right answers to any of them.

I am suddenly very aware of a pain that starts deep in my stomach and twists downwards, right into my legs.

I lean forward and retch but swallow the liquid that comes up. My throat aches.

'Oh, fuck,' Mack whispers. He slams Keeley's door shut. The music is only a little muffled.

'Jude?' His tone is gentle, the one Mum uses when she is speaking to Keeley. 'Did you have sex with Pete?'

I nod. I have no energy to blush. I want him to shut up and get Keeley. I want him to leave the room, let me be on my own until she gets here. I cannot get her myself; I cannot walk through the party. A single, thin line of moisture runs down the inside of my leg. I cannot tell what it is. It erases the fake tan as it goes.

I sit on Keeley's bed.

'Jude, he's twenty-seven. Did you know that? Why did you … ? Keeley's interested in him, that's the guy she's been going on about. That's Pete D, the music video guy.'

I look up, scandalised. 'What? Mack, I didn't know. I didn't want to. I said no.'

He stands, rigid, understanding finally dawning on his face.

The door opens. It is Naomi. Her eyes are wide, her mouth a thin, straight line. In the few seconds before she closes the door after her, I see the back of Pete's head, shaking, as he goes downstairs. He is doing up his belt. I retch once more and this time am sick on Keeley's carpet. It is entirely liquid. My eyes and throat burn.

'Jude …'

Naomi hasn't spoken to me much before, or at least not only to me. We've only ever been together in a group, so she never got the chance. I look at her face now and take her in for what feels like the first time. Her eyes, very green and round, are full of concern, her shiny black fringe sticking to her forehead with sweat from all the dancing, all the drugs. She is the only girl not wearing a dress: she wears a plain T-shirt and tight jeans and sandals, and she looks better than anyone.

I think, ridiculously, of how beautiful she must be when she is naked.

She kneels beside me, not caring about the little puddle of sick she is almost touching. She brushes my hair out of my eyes and takes both my hands. I try to pull them away, but she is insistent, tugs hard. My tears fall harder, thicker, faster, my cheeks burning now.

'Jude, I think this was a misunderstanding. He thought you were …' She doesn't have to finish.

Mack has both hands on his head, pulling at his hair. He has begun to pace as much as one can pace in the doorway of a tiny box room.

'Can you call the police?' I ask softly. I know this is what must be done, someone will have to do it at some point, and I don't want it to be me. 'Can you get Keeley, please?'

Naomi squeezes my hands tightly and takes a breath. 'Darling,' she says. 'We can't.'

'I need her,' I say. I am unable to raise my voice. My legs will not stop shaking. Everything hurts.

'Keeley, yeah. We can get Keeley soon. I meant the police. We can't get the police here. You understand that, don't you?'

Mack stops dead, one hand on the wall, the other halfway through raking his mop of hair back from his forehead.

'Why not?' I ask.

Naomi and Mack share a look.

'Jude … Think about it.' Naomi gestures around Keeley's room as if this is an answer. I look from the pink bedspread to the small hole in the wall, to the bare bulb. My overnight bag pushed into a corner. The empty bottle. 'There are a lot of drugs in this house,'

Naomi continues. 'And a lot of very stoned people who cannot afford to spend any more of their lives behind bars. You know about the Sixes? The quantities we've all been helping to produce, helping to shift … We'd be in serious trouble. We cannot have the police coming here. Not tonight.'

'So … what?' My voice is small and sounds more curious than desperate. She cannot be suggesting what I think she is suggesting.

'I'm sorry, Jude.' Mack cannot look at me as he says this. 'It's not an option.'

'Get Keeley,' I say again. Keeley will be able to talk sense into both of them.

Naomi looks to Mack again and for the first time, she seems frightened. They are thinking the same as me. Keeley will not stand for this; she will make us all do the right thing.

Mack struggles with something: he looks as though he is trying to swallow something too large for his throat. Then he says, 'Fine. We'll get Keeley for you. But don't blame us if she's angry with you for what you did.'

'What Mack means,' Naomi says quickly, 'is that maybe you shouldn't tell Keeley.' Now she can no longer meet my eye either. 'She only has your word for what happened just now, right? She might think you did it on purpose. You know how much she likes him.'

I stare at her, then shake my head and look to Mack. 'But I wouldn't do that. Of course I wouldn't, I couldn't. Keeley knows I wouldn't.'

'She's only got your word for it,' Naomi says.

'Mack.' It is my last, desperate chance.

Somewhere in the back of my mind, in a locked drawer, there is a thought. She might not believe me. She might hate me. There is a chance, a tiny chance … that she would never speak to me again.

Mack is speaking quietly, but not to me. 'I'll go and get one in the morning.'

'It's a bank holiday,' Naomi whispers to him. 'They're all closed, open for prescription pick-up only. I'll phone for one in the morning when I get to the airport. You go and get it.'

'Right. Jude. Jude? Are you listening to me? Come on your own and find me tomorrow and we'll get you sorted.'

I stare at him. I have no idea what he is talking about. I feel my shoulders sag. I don't want to hear any more.

I pull back the cover on the bed and slot myself inside. I shut my eyes tightly and wish I could cover my ears the same.

'Jude,' Mack says again. 'I'm so sorry.'

'Sorry,' Naomi mumbles.

I sense her standing and they both leave. They close the door softly.

The music continues to vibrate the room.

I tap my fingers on the palm of my hand in a rhythm, thinking with every beat, *She cannot know. She cannot know. She cannot know.*

I lie, shaking, in the same position all night until the morning, my fingers tapping on my palm, my stomach in knots, my eyes wide open.

Mack

4th January 2020, afternoon

This is the worst feeling in the world.

Far worse than the worst comedown imaginable, worse than when I shattered my ankle jumping off the roof of the Den when I was eleven. Worse than Mum. Worse than even Murphy.

I just don't think we can make this work, Naomi said.

She hadn't come to apologise; she had come to break up with me.

Suddenly this bed, this shit metal frame with no headboard, isn't as comfortable as mine. It's like sitting on concrete. This room isn't the same size as Keeley's, not even nearly. What was I thinking?

It takes the feeling of wet on my fingers for me to realise I have scratched my cheek so hard it is bleeding. I stare at my fingers, seeing only red, my whole arm shaking, my heart pounding. But I do not scratch my cheek again.

The door opens, the long squeak I have come to associate with the arrival of food, of another human presence. The same guard as yesterday has brought the lunch that I missed while I was at my meeting with Naomi.

He stops when he sees my fingers, poised in a half-crouch, ready to set the tray on the ground. When he realises where the blood has come from, he seems to shrug to himself and straightens up again.

'Can you get Detective Rice for me, please?' I ask. My voice, both the very fact that I am speaking and my calm tone, surprises me. 'I really need to speak to him. It's about my case.'

My case. I sound like a young barrister, I think for one bizarre moment.

You really don't, the guard's expression tells me.

He looks at me, then leaves without saying anything, locking the door behind him. I think this means he has ignored my request, but he is back in less than half an hour.

The long squeak.

The same broad shoulders in the doorway.

'Detective Rice is on a personal errand,' he informs me. 'But I spoke to Sergeant Curran over the phone and she says she is willing to talk to you. She'll come and get you when she's free.'

When she's free. These people have been so desperate to get me to talk for four days, and when I finally decide I'm ready to give them answers, they can't even be bothered to see me?

The guard leaves without another word.

I wish I had a full gym bag full of Sixes, an off-licence full of something clear and strong and burning. I wish I had my guitar so I could rewrite the lyrics of every mildly optimistic song I've ever written. Thinking about my guitar makes me think about Naomi and I have to push the thought away.

I think of Brains instead, possibly being questioned about the drugs even now, of Keeley, going back to Wits End to live there without me. The one thing I'd promised myself was that, even if I was useless, even if I couldn't practically help her in any way, at least I'd *be* there. At least she wouldn't be alone.

I think of Pete in one of those ice boxes in a wall, a towel draped over his waist.

And that makes me think of Jude, and where she might be.

I spring up from my bed so quickly that I trip over the tray of untouched food that has now gone cold. I fall towards the door and begin to hammer it with all my might, shouting 'I need to speak to someone! Please? Please! Detective Rice!'

Flecks of blood spatter across the door.

Linda

4th January 2020, afternoon

The table is set: four perfect, circular place settings, four crystal wine glasses, my red and white centrepiece from Christmas glinting in the fairy lights I have draped around it. The glass table is shiny and free from fingerprints, the chairs painted the exact same grey as the walls.

I stand for a few moments simply looking at the table. The neat symmetry calms me. The dining room is the most ordered, and therefore my favourite, room. I pat my hair and take a deep breath. I count to ten, release and smile at the table.

Jude comes into the kitchen and I go to her. She has made more of an effort than she has all week – jeans instead of leggings, a blouse instead of a jumper. She still wears a pair of pink trainers on her feet that I do not recall ever having purchased.

'What have you made?' she asks. 'It smells nice.' Her hair is brushed for the first time in days, and, despite the trainers, I am strangely touched that she has more or less done as I asked.

'Breaded brie to start!' I say excitedly. I point to the oven as if we will be able to see through its opaque front. 'With cranberry sauce. Followed by beef Wellington with blackcurrant jam gravy. Then birthday cake. Home-made. Of course.'

She doesn't smile, but she doesn't turn her nose up either. 'One of Nigella's, that beef thing, is it?' she asks.

'Jamie's,' I say. 'Do you want a glass of wine?'

If she is surprised at this, my first ever offer of alcohol, she does not show it.

'No, thanks,' she says. She sits at the breakfast bar.

'You can have one, if you want. I know it won't be your first alcohol ever but that's OK. I know you've pretty much been behaving like an adult for a while now. It's fine. We can start again, if you'd like. You and me. Start again as adults with no secrets. Be … friends.'

I am not sure where this rush of embarrassed love has come from, but it hangs limply in the air between us all the same, and I am unable to retract it. Instead I stare at her, lips slightly pursed, willing her to answer.

'OK …' she says, after a moment. 'But I don't want any wine. Thanks. I don't really … Well, I don't like drinking, really. I don't like losing control.'

'Quite right,' I say, and I go to the fridge and take out a new bottle of Chardonnay. 'You're quite right, Jude.' I pour myself a large measure into one of the crystal glasses and, at that, Jude finally smiles.

I take a sip of my drink, suddenly feeling awkward. Jude looks around the kitchen as if she can't think of anything to say, either.

'I thought we'd eat early,' I say, clutching to fill the silence. 'Your dad needs a few hours this evening to plan his classes for Monday, and I thought you and Mason would want an early night too. Big day, Monday. Your last six months of school ever. I can't believe how quickly it's gone.'

She nods, half-heartedly, her eyes on my wine glass.

'I'll just go and get your birthday present!' I say suddenly. 'You can open it after dinner.'

She seems relieved to see me go.

'Well, that was just gorgeous, Linda,' Roddy says. He leans across the table and pecks me on the cheek. 'Wasn't that nice, kids?'

'Thanks, Mum,' says Mason. 'Can I go on the Xbox now?'

'Not yet,' I say. 'We haven't had cake yet.'

'More food?' Mason asks dully. 'It's like Christmas Day again.'

Roddy and I laugh. He stands up and takes a stacked pile of plates into the kitchen. 'More wine, Lin?' he calls.

I accept and hold my glass out gratefully. 'Maybe Jude should open her present before dessert,' I suggest.

I reach to the empty chair at the head of the table and take a pink-wrapped box from it. I hand it and the accompanying card diagonally across to her.

She takes it with an attempt at a smile. 'Thanks, both of you.'

'It's from me too!' Mason says.

'I didn't notice you contributing any pocket money,' I say, pretending to swipe him across the head.

Jude opens the package to reveal a new mobile phone.

'It's the one you wanted for Christmas!' I say. 'We only pretended we had forgotten. We had to save something for your birthday.'

She is grinning. 'Thanks, Mum.'

'Is it the right one?' I ask, though I know it is.

'It's perfect, thanks.'

She takes it from the box and switches it on.

'I have it all charged for you,' I say. 'And I've saved all of our numbers into it. You can use that one and the new number, now that you're an adult.'

'I suppose,' she agrees. 'I'll just add some of my contacts in from my other phone when I get it back from the police.'

'When they bring back your other phone, I'll just take it,' I say. I take a determined sip of wine and keep my voice light, airy. 'I'll donate it to a charity shop. I'll take the SIM card out, don't worry.'

Still smiling, Jude narrows her eyes at the screen. 'You haven't put Keeley's number in this. I'll just get it off your phone.'

'There's not really any need for that,' I say. 'Is there? Roddy, why don't you get the cake from the fridge.'

'It better not be chocolate,' Mason says.

'But you love chocolate,' says Roddy.

'I obviously need Keeley's number. Can I borrow your phone?'

'I've had chocolate every day for every meal since the start of December.'

'Well, that's an exaggeration, Mason.'

'Not really.'

'No, you don't need my phone.'

'Where is it?'

'It's not an exaggeration. There's chocolate in my cereal and everything.'

'This is a nice sponge cake that your mum has made. It looks gorgeous!'

'Is it in your bedroom? Mum, answer me.'

'I'll just have a small slice.'

'Where. Is. Your. Phone?'

'We'll light the candles and let Jude cut it.'

'Yes, Roddy, let's sing happy birthday.'

'It's in your bedroom, isn't it?'

Jude stands so quickly that the table legs squeak across the polished wooden floor. I stand just as abruptly and follow her out.

Roddy and Mason say nothing.

I catch her in the hall and pull her back by the arm.

'You don't need my phone,' I hiss. 'You don't need to speak to her. The detectives seem to think it's a good idea if you don't speak to or see Keeley at all while they're investigating and I agree.'

'Are you a detective now and all?' she asks.

I blink hard and take a deep breath. Count to ten, release.

'Jude, I know you've had a stressful few days, but please don't take it out on me.'

She stands at the bottom of the stairs, her neck craned behind her to look at me, her left hand on the banister as if she is about to climb up. She doesn't move.

Her eyes bore into me. Behind her head, on the wall, is her Primary Five photograph, the same eyes staring out, but smiling. Clean uniform, shiny hair pulled back into a ponytail, not a single hair out of place. She is still my girl, I think desperately. She's in there somewhere.

'You must know this is for the best,' I say. 'You must know that you don't belong in … in that scene. With them. We're not like them. Talk to me, Jude.'

'Why?' she spits. 'What's the point? You obviously have Keeley down as a killer. Maybe she planned it, threw the party as a cover, stabbed him, hard, made sure to watch the blood drain out of him. Maybe she got off on it.'

'Stop it!'

We are both angry but have enough control of ourselves to keep our voices at furious whispers. I glance back towards the kitchen, part of me wanting Roddy to come after us, part of me dreading just that.

'Why?' Jude demands in the furious whisper. 'That's what you're thinking. You think she's a murderer, you actually think my best friend is a fucking murderer. You've never liked her, you've always been worried about her dirty feet on your good white fucking floors!'

I've slapped her across the face before I can stop myself. The sound is loud, but Roddy doesn't come to investigate. He is speaking loudly to Mason, his tone full of a forced animation.

Jude doesn't flinch at the slap, just closes her eyes briefly, too stunned to react.

'I do think she's a killer,' I say, my voice coming out harsh, spitting. 'Of course I do. Or at least that her brother is and she is covering for him. I don't know, I don't *care* which. Her waste-of-space boyfriend has just turned up *dead* in her garage. That girl has form for breaking the rules. Drinking, smoking, taking drugs since she was a child, breaking a girl's *jaw*, getting *excluded from school.* That dead boy was a bad egg, by the sounds of him, but that suits her just fine.

'You've wasted all your best years, Jude, trailing around after her like a puppy, copying everything she does, being obsessed with her. You can't see it. You haven't got the full picture, you're in too close. Keeley is probably a killer, Jude. She's a murderer. She *stabbed that man until he died*, and she is going to go to prison for it. Why can't you see that? Why can't you see how sick this whole thing is? I hope she rots in a cell; I hope she has years to think about what she's done.'

I don't know what I expected from her. It certainly wasn't the slow smile that creeps up her face. She is shaking her head, eyes wide and manic like I'm embarrassing myself beyond belief.

'You don't have all the answers this time, *Mum*,' she says. 'You don't know anything about it. She isn't a killer. She is none of the things you think she is – you've had a picture in your head since we were kids and you cannot let that go. Keeley didn't touch Pete on Tuesday night. I know that for a fact. I know that because it was me. I killed him. I stabbed him in his chest. And you know what ...' Her eyes are dancing. She is enjoying the effect of her words. 'I'd fucking do it again.'

She moves from the stairs towards the front door and lifts her coat from the hook. She is so calm, her actions wholly considered. Her hands do not shake.

She closes the door so quietly that I wish she'd slammed it.

Detective Inspector Chris Rice

4th January 2020, evening

It is after six when I step out of Seekbank and into the freezing evening air. My phone, returned to me by a pudgy woman with rosy cheeks, takes a few minutes to load up. I have started the car and turned the heat right up before my notifications appear on screen. Two missed calls from an unknown number, four missed calls from Jess, a voicemail notification and a text. I click on the text, which is from Jess.

Call me. Super not happy.

My stomach flips. I call her back.

'Jess?'

'Sir.'

'What is it, what's wrong?'

'You haven't spoken to McCrane yet, then?' Her voice, usually confident, authoritative, is hesitant. Maybe even irritated. She is moving – out of the incident room and into the corridor, I think – and her breath sounds like one long sigh. 'Ugh. Sir. It's a mess.'

'Why?' I demand. 'What the hell is going on?'

'McCrane just left the incident room about ten minutes ago. He asked for an update, asked where you were … I said you were off investigating a lead, but when I couldn't give him anything more than that, he had a go at me, telling me I was bullshitting. Some people have mentioned to him that you've been AWOL and uncontactable throughout the case. He put Browne on the spot about what exactly was being done, who was in custody, who was being charged and … well, Morris had to be honest, Sir. He told him everything. McCrane's really angry about how the investigation has been run, I've never seen him like that. He said something about how you've ruined another detective's undercover op –'

'He what?'

'I'm not sure. He said you were seen in a park with someone you shouldn't have been with? Then he asked me when you first went to the crime scene and …'

Jess trails off.

'And?' I ask. My head is resting on my left palm. I have no feeling left.

'I had to tell him you'd never been. I had to tell the truth. What else could I tell him but the truth?'

Neither of us speaks for a moment.

'So, what does this mean?' I ask finally.

'I think you need to call McCrane.'

'What does it mean, Jess? I'm a big boy, I can handle it.'

'He's taken you off the case. He wants to speak to you in an official capacity on Monday morning.' There is definite acrimony in her voice when she adds, 'He said he hasn't made his mind up about me yet; he might reassign me too. I'm going to speak to Joshua Mackley now, but that might be the last thing I do on this case. McCrane is sending Polson to take over.'

We stay on the phone for a full minute. Both of us breathing almost normally, not saying a word. I imagine her in my office now, her pretty eyes narrowed, wanting to tip over my lamp, dent my desk. She won't. Women like Jess are spilling over with dignity.

'What about the dress?' I ask finally.

'Yep. Got it. It looks clean but it's at the lab. Don't suppose you're planning on sharing with us what it means?'

'And what about the earring?'

She doesn't try to hide her sharp sigh that turns to a bark of a laugh. 'Earring? What earring? There is no earring. There was never an earring. What's going on with you?'

I sit in the car park for several minutes after she hangs up, not thinking of anything in particular. The Project Twenty file, on which I have made my meticulous handwritten notes detailing my theory – the theory I know, now, must be acted upon – sits on the passenger seat.

I will ask Jess to come to the front of the building so she can take it from me. I don't think I can bear going inside, seeing the team's faces. I won't have to say anything – everything is there, in the file, and Jess is smart, much smarter than me. She will figure it all out for herself.

The wheels of the Punto struggle on the ice in the car park, but I ram the accelerator and begin my slippery journey back to the station.

Realising I haven't listened to my voicemail – undoubtedly from McCrane – I tap once and put the message on loudspeaker.

Message received today at five forty-one p.m.

Detective Rice? This is Linda Jameson. From Wits End.

She no longer sounds like the gushing sycophant we met in the police station a few days before. There is no attempt at breezy insouciance. Her voice is lowered, as though she does not want to be overheard, and it cracks. She sounds simultaneously dazed and seriously concerned. I am so surprised to hear her voice instead of McCrane's that I miss the first few words of what she says.

… But I need your help. It's Jude. She's left and I don't know where she's gone or what she'll do. I know this isn't what you meant when you said we could call you any time but … please call me back.

The tyres of the Punto screech as I brake, hard. A driver indicating to enter the Seekbank car park bleeps their horn but I ignore it. I make a U-turn so that I can take a shortcut to Vetobridge, grateful that the evening roads are quiet.

I tap to call Linda back. It takes her several rings, but finally she answers, sounding breathless.

'Mrs Jameson. It's Chris Rice. I'll be in Wits End in forty minutes. What's happened with Jude?'

Linda takes a breath. 'Just … come, Detective. I'll tell you when you get here. Please hurry.'

Any notions I had of calling McCrane or going to the station have evaporated.

It is not until I am well on to the carriageway that the peculiarity of her words dawns on me. *Linda Jameson … From Wits End.* Not *Linda Jameson, Jude's mum.*

She has opened the front door and stands on the veranda, a thin beige cardigan pulled around her. She is shivering. I park in the empty driveway and hurry up the steps.

'She's left,' Linda says. 'She said some horrible things and now she's gone. She wasn't herself, wasn't making any sense. I don't know what's got into her. It's been a hard week for all of us, a really stressful time. We were having a nice family meal tonight– it's her eighteenth birthday tomorrow but we wanted to celebrate tonight because the kids are back to school on Monday and we wanted to get them back into their routine …' She finally stops for breath.

'Mrs Jameson –'

'Linda.'

'Linda. Where is your husband? Is he out looking for Jude?'

She tugs at the sleeves of the cardigan, and pulls it around herself more tightly, as though she is trying to make herself disappear. 'No. He doesn't know she's gone. I told him she wasn't feeling well and he's taken Mason to the 24-hour pharmacy in Oldry to get some painkillers for her. She can't take aspirin and that's all we have in the house, luckily. I told him to get some ice cream on the way home. It buys us half an hour.'

I stare at her.

'Come in, Detective.' She seems to gather herself and leads me through the open front door. My feet click on the shiny tiles inside.

The house is uncomfortably warm, a sharp change from the cold outside. The hall seems smaller now – lit only by a few soft lamps – than it did yesterday. The ceramic angels on the sideboard look as though they are staring away from us determinedly. I try not to look at the glass lift.

She leads me to the kitchen. There are empty plates stacked by the sink and one of the stools at the breakfast bar is out at an angle, as though pushed back in haste. Apart from that, the room looks like a show home, everything shiny and clean, just as it did the first time we visited.

Linda places a hand on the breakfast bar and seems to think for a moment. Then she turns to face me and her expression has changed. She looks fierce, angry. 'Why haven't you arrested Keeley Mackley yet?' I can tell she is struggling to keep her voice level.

'The investigation is ongoing and I can't reveal any details to you at the moment,' I rhyme off. 'What's going on, Linda?'

She seems to toy with something for a moment, then she heaves a sigh. She sits on the vacated stool and indicates that I can take another. I eye it and decide it would likely not hold my weight.

'Jude has got it into her head that that boy –'

'Peter Denny?'

'Him. That she somehow had something to do with his death. She basically told me tonight that she stabbed him herself.' Linda snorts. 'Obviously we know Jude would never do that. She's covering up for Keeley. It's obvious to me now. At the start I couldn't get past the fact that you had arrested Joshua – I thought you must know something I didn't. But it is clear he and Jude are simply covering for Keeley. If you knew them, you'd understand. I don't know why Keeley did it but that's the only explanation for why Jude would come out with such nonsense. I'm just … afraid. I'm afraid she'll say that, or something similar, in front of someone who will take her seriously. I don't want her to get into trouble for no reason. You need to arrest Keeley. Soon.'

Linda takes a tissue from up her sleeve and wipes at her eyes, though I can see no tears.

I think it is safe to take a seat at the table by the window and I do so.

'Linda …' I say quietly. 'Did you know Jude failed her AS-level exams last year?'

This makes her stop in the act of wiping at fake tears. She looks over at me.

'What? No, she didn't. She got three As. She's predicted to get three As when she takes her real exams this summer.'

'No As. She got a D and two Us,' I say. 'One of my colleagues spoke with the headmistress on Thursday, and she told her Jude also failed the mock exams she had before Christmas. Jude wouldn't know about that yet of course. She'll be finding out on Monday when she goes back to school.'

If she goes back, I hear in my head.

'This is nonsense.' Linda shakes her head and moves her shoulders back, defiant. 'The school would have told us if that were true.'

I remember Edgecomb's file, innocently nestled among the rest of Project Twenty. 'They tried to arrange meetings with you last year, according to Miss Sparks. Jude told them it wasn't a good time for you because you were in hospital with your son.'

Linda's mouth forms a perfect O. She stares at me. 'We haven't been in the hospital with Mason for … nearly three years. Apart from his check-ups. He's healthy, he's fine. His physiotherapist comes to the house now …'

'Jude gave them your new mobile number then, and Miss Sparks says she spoke to you herself … twice.'

She blinks, not understanding.

'My best guess is that she spoke twice to Keeley Mackley who, I'm not ashamed to say, has her impression of you perfected. It's uncanny. Jude won't be getting any A-levels. She won't be going to university in September.'

She is silent. I can see her mind whirring.

'You know everything about Keeley Mackley and her family, don't you, Linda?' My voice is light. 'You're very … observant. You know things about the people your children spend their time with. Don't you?'

Linda sits up straighter. She fixes her hair behind her ears where it has fallen from a bun. 'Please don't judge me for my past mistakes, Mr Rice. I was against Keeley Mackley from the start.'

We are both silent for a moment.

The tap drips every couple of seconds. A few streets away, a car revs loudly and we both listen until it drives away.

'Do you have children, Detective?'

I swallow, thinking of Rebecca in her tiny room. More like a university dormitory than a prison cell, from the way she describes it, but still not right. Still not her home, not with me.

'Yes,' I say. 'One daughter.'

'Then how would you feel if you knew, from when your daughter was five years old, that she was no longer yours? That someone had taken her from you, that you were nothing at all in comparison? If you saw her every day, if you did your best for her, but you never got her best smiles, her real laughs? If you did everything and got nothing in return?'

They are not real questions, so I give her no answer.

'Perhaps we didn't help,' Linda continues. 'Perhaps, in some ways, we added to the problem. Roddy and I, we treated them like they were one person, sometimes. From early on. Like they were two halves of a whole. I remember, they were still in primary school, and we'd just bought our first adapted car for Mason. A black, shiny thing. Ford, maybe. Like a minivan. It cost us a lot of money, but it was perfect for Mason. We were delighted. We'd just brought the car home that day – the girls were playing something outside. They used to play a game involving complicated treasure maps; it took them all over the garden and the green … They were playing for ages, and when we came out to get Jude that evening, there was a huge scrape right along the edge of the car, done with a stone from the drive. It spelt their initials, JK.

'Thinking about it now, I know it was Keeley. Jude knew better than to damage property. But we acted like it was the both of them.

'I remember Roddy calling me out and saying, *Look what they've done to the car. They.* Not Keeley, not Jude. Both of them. At no point did we think to ask whose hand had picked up the stone. But they didn't argue, just took us shouting at them both, heads hung. I suppose our thinking, then, was that if *she* had done it, then *she* had done it too. Even if Jude didn't scrape the car, she had let Keeley do it. I think our logic was that not stopping her was bad enough to warrant the punishment.'

She runs her hands through her hair.

I glance at my watch.

'She stank of trouble from the first time I laid eyes on her,' Linda says. Her voice sounds faraway now. She is staring at a spot on the shiny tiles as though she has forgotten I am even there. 'Is that mad to say about a child? That I think, deep down, I always knew something like this would happen? There was a little flashing light in my head, every day, all the time, since the day Keeley Mackley first jumped off our garden wall. Jude was going to be the most perfect girl, you know. She was going to read her books and help me with her brother. When she was old enough, she and I would share a bottle of wine after a Saturday's shopping. She'd meet a nice boy and get married at thirty, and they'd live no further away than the far end of Vetobridge and have three or four kids. We'd see them every Sunday. My perfect family, my perfect girl.' There are real tears in her eyes now, though her voice is steady and calm. 'Keeley stole my daughter from me because she had nothing. She had no one else. She preyed on Jude because Jude has always been weak. I will never forgive her for what she's done. That horrible … orphan … tramp. I will never forgive her for what she's turned Jude into. My daughter is not a girl who goes to druggie parties and takes the blame for murders she didn't commit. This is Keeley in her head. This is Keeley speaking, this is not her.'

I try to keep my own voice as steady. 'Mrs Jameson, Keeley and your daughter have been friends since Jude was four. Do you really expect me to believe she's turned out like this because of Keeley? You're so *observant*, but you didn't even notice your own kid was failing school.'

Her face looks like I have punched it.

I stand and make as if to leave, thinking I am done, but then I turn back to her, saying, 'I don't think Jude is anywhere near as innocent as you imagine she is. She hasn't been led astray; this is who she is. And I'll tell you something else— No, listen to me, Mrs Jameson. I've been doing this for a long time, I've interviewed countless young women and do you know what I think? I think Keeley Mackley is happy, when she's not coming to terms with the murder of her boyfriend, that is, and I think Jude is one of the most miserable teenagers I have ever met. She has been failing. Failing everything. She has been upset and scared and depressed, and you haven't even seen it. She broke a girl's jaw last spring. That's right, not Keeley, Jude. I spoke to your son just yesterday and he says Jude has been violent towards him too. Don't try and deny it, I heard this from him. You can't put words into your children's mouths any more. To top it all off, I've just told you Jude's future is a mess, I've told you that she broke a girl's jaw and hurt your son, and she told you herself that on Tuesday night she killed someone … and

I know that you're choking, wanting to talk to me about Keeley Mackley. Keeley is still your focus. Just as much as she is Jude's.'

My heart is beating quickly. The words are spewing from my mouth before I can stop them. 'You're so quick to pick up on problems in everyone else's lives, but your daughter's been living under your roof, eating dinner at your table, pretending to be the little girl Mummy wanted and hating the terrified woman she is becoming. The things that have been happening to her. She wasn't just being called names by a few girls in school, you know, she was being tortured. You didn't even bat an eye. Every day for two and a half years she was tortured until she took it upon herself to fight back because nobody else was going to fight for her. And who took the blame for that? Keeley Mackley. She gave up her future; she altered her *whole life* to protect Jude.

'I know you've tried, Mrs Jameson. God knows, that much is obvious. In your own way, you've loved her harder than anyone. But you need to have a long, hard look in the mirror and come to terms with the fact that this … *orphan tramp*, as you call her, has been a better mother to your child than you ever have been.'

She looks at me, eyes wide, like I've just pulled a stun gun on her. For the first time, I can see a family resemblance. She has Jude's nose, her eyebrows. Now, the same terrified eyes.

'Now, if you don't mind,' I say, turning again to walk away, 'I'm going to find your daughter before she does some more harm. To herself or to someone else.'

I leave her sitting on the high stool at the breakfast bar, one hand on her chest like she's in pain, the other outstretched towards me as if she is going to call me back.

She doesn't.

Jude

4th January 2020, evening

It is my intention to start walking as fast as I can into Vetobridge town centre. I have nearly one hundred pounds in my bank account, and that will pay for at least one night in the Clandy at short notice. Though it is dark, it is barely half-past five, and I feel safe enough walking the two miles or so to the hotel.

I have reached the green at the other side of the road before I look up.

The light in Keeley's bedroom is on. The window seems to sparkle, illuminating the street so that it looks beautiful.

My heart lifts.

Keeley is home.

The back door is unlocked. I open it and call out for her tentatively. There is silence for a few seconds, and then I hear footsteps – unmistakably hers – coming down the stairs.

The kitchen is dark, and the shadows from the fridge, the bread bin, everything, are enough to keep my focus so that I do not have to look through the plastic pane in front of me into the Den.

Then she stands in front of me, real and there and *Keeley*. Her hair needs washing and there is no concealer covering the circles under her eyes, as dark as cigarette ash, but she is *here* and I step a little closer so I can breathe her in.

'I was so worried,' I say. I breathe an audible sigh of relief. 'I'm so glad to see you.' When she only looks at me, expression unreadable, I add: 'Is Mack … ?'

She shakes her head. 'They're holding him. They found a bag of drugs and they're charging him. They're going to give him jail time. Naomi and I think they're being so harsh because they're trying to get something to charge him with killing Pete.'

'Is that where you've been?' I ask. 'At Naomi's? Did the police make you stay away all this time?'

'Didn't you hear what I said?' She shakes her head again. 'They gave me back our keys on Thursday. I just stayed at Naomi's because …' She looks away. 'Jude, I don't have long. I just came to get some clothes and my car.'

'You haven't been replying to my messages,' I say. I try not to sound too accusing, but my attempt at casualness makes my voice break and the last syllable hangs in the air, too loudly in the quiet kitchen. 'The police took my phone yesterday but I thought you would have called the house or …'

Keeley nips her bottom lip. 'I don't know if we should be talking at the minute. Detective Rice has made that clear and he's been really nice to me and to Mack. I don't want to throw that in his face.'

'So we won't talk about the case,' I say. I can hear the desperation in my voice and make no attempt to hide it. 'Let's just stay here and we can talk about something else and forget about it all. We can just be us.'

'Forget about it all?' She looks stunned. 'Jude … no.'

'Why? We can have a drink, if you want. Just sit and –'

'Jude. Stop it.'

My heart is beating so fast I am sure she can hear it.

'Naomi is at the station right this second, breaking up with Mack because she thinks he had something to do with it,' she says. 'Naomi is all he has, that's it. How does that make you feel, Jude? She's leaving him. Washing her hands of all of this. You want to talk?' She is fiercer now. 'OK, we can talk. But not here …' She looks at the door to the Den. 'Let's go for a drive.'

The Cortina keys are already in her hand. She turns on her heel and makes her way through the house. I close the back door behind me and hurry after her.

I know where she is going, though she does not say it. She doesn't say anything at all. We sit in silence. She turns a corner, sharply, and I bump against the passenger door, glancing furtively at her. I know what she is going to say when we finally stop and I have no idea how I should answer.

After fifteen minutes, she pulls up on a kerb next to a long row of hedges that line a steep hill. She jerks the handbrake up and has taken off her seatbelt and opened her door before I can say a word.

The rock pools are about a mile and a half from the main beach and promenade, and they can be accessed only by walking the length of the beach, across a mountain of stones and boulders, or by parking on the hill and forcing your way through a gap in the trees that years of lazy teenagers have created. The car park for the rock pools has been padlocked shut since the girl drowned.

I put up the hood of my coat to stop my hair catching twigs as I pick my way down the hill of thick trees. More than once my foot slips and I whimper in fright.

The darkness is so close.

Keeley runs on, oblivious to my discomfort, a slight pink outline in the dark.

When we get to the edge of the trees, she stops so suddenly that I walk into her and have to grab her to stop us both falling over.

We are in a clearing of sand and grass, with two dark swells of water in the middle that make up the two rock pools. There are clusters of huge boulders around the pools, and I am sure I am exaggerating by thinking I can still see the dead girl's blood on one of the rocks.

Keeley spins around to face me, her face set.

'Why, Jude? Why did you do it?'

I blink at her. My breath fogs between us. The moon is high and I can see her every feature as if it were the middle of the day.

'You were out of it,' is all I can say. 'You wouldn't wake up.'

Keeley closes her eyes for the briefest moment, as though she would like to punch me but does not have the strength. Then she turns again and makes for the rock pool. I have to jog to keep up with her long strides.

'I can explain,' I say. 'You took a Six and it knocked you out. I knew you weren't going to wake up.'

She sits on the nearest boulder and pulls her knees up to her chest, her eyes on the pool.

I can't think of how to continue with the next part of the story and am glad when she speaks.

'They found my dress,' she says. 'The one you were wearing. Just a while ago. I don't know how they worked it out. I don't know why they were even looking, I mean … they think it's Mack now. Right? I had the dress in the pocket of my hoodie when we left the house, when we were being taken to the station to make our first statements. I knew I had to get rid of it before they searched me, so I pretended I had to be sick just as we got into Oldry, and I hid it in a hedge at the side of the road. They only found it today.

'I was lucky. I was going with Naomi to the station to visit Mack and we happened to drive past them: two police cars, parked at the exact spot where I'd hidden the dress. I got out of the car at the station and called a taxi to take me home. The police are going to be looking for me soon. I'm going to need to get away while I think about what the *fuck* I'm going to say when they ask why Pete's blood is all over my dress.'

'I thought you washed it,' I say numbly. It is the only thing I can think of in the world that makes sense.

'I did,' she said. 'But it's not enough to get rid of all the traces. You've seen TV shows, Jude.'

Her voice is so bitter, so dismissive, that my brain is struggling to accept she is speaking to me. Of course she is stressed, I reason, she might be arrested. I know I am the surrogate of her anger and not the intended target: she is angry about the situation, not at me.

'Go on then,' she says quietly. 'Tell me why.'

I move to sit on the rock next to her, my eyes not leaving her face.

'Tell me how much you remember,' I say.

'I remember the fight, now. It came back to me once the shock had worn off. I remember Pete was on the phone with that girl,

Leah. And you heard them talking. I read his texts. He was going to dump me for her … And then we fought, me and Pete. We really fought.'

'I've never seen you like that,' I murmur.

'I was angry. I took one of Mack's Sixes and you and I went to the Den. I cut it in half with … with the vegetable knife from the kitchen drawer. I took one half. You didn't take yours, did you?'

I shake my head, slowly. 'You took yours,' I say. 'And then you had another drink. The pill calmed you down instead of hyping you up. You were making sense, a lot more sense than before, saying that it was over with Pete and it was for the best. You took the other half of the pill. Then you wanted to sleep. I tried to get you to come up to bed but you took off your dress and just lay on the sofa in the Den. You were asleep in seconds. Passed out. He came into the Den … then.' My voice, hollow and matter of fact until now, wavers just a little. Keeley's eyes are locked on mine. 'He was off his face. He must have had something else after you fought. He wouldn't leave, seemed to think you'd had a stupid fight over nothing. I kept telling him to go but he wouldn't listen. And then he was touching you. Pulling at your underwear, touching you while you weren't even conscious and I thought he was going to …'

Now, I cannot bring myself to look at her.

'The knife you'd used to cut the Six was still on the table. I lifted it, just to point it at him, scare him, I don't know. I wanted him to leave you alone. To leave. He wouldn't.'

A single tear rolls down my cheek. It is more the frustration that I am not explaining myself properly than it is sadness. Keeley makes no attempt to comfort me.

'You have to believe me,' I say. 'When I say that I thought he was going to try it. To try and … and have sex with you, I had to do something. He was so sure I'd move away if he came closer, but I didn't. I stayed beside you, I wasn't going to leave you.'

'He was my boyfriend, Jude. He was just touching me.' Her voice is flat.

My pulse quickens, anger stirring deep in my stomach. 'Don't say it like that,' I say sharply. 'Don't act like it would have been OK because he was your boyfriend, because you'd done it before. You weren't there – you weren't consciously there; you have no idea. You don't know what he's capable of. I know he would have forced himself on you. I'm glad I was there.'

I want her to ask me for more. She only stares.

'He just sort of stumbled into the corner, then,' I say. 'And after a while he stopped breathing.'

This makes her start. She has been motionless for minutes, but this makes her look at me differently. 'After a while?' she repeats.

I blush scarlet.

'So you just … you let him fight for breath?' I can tell she is struggling to keep her voice calm. 'You just left him on the floor of the Den? Gasping and spluttering? Is that what you're telling me?'

'I didn't want to leave you.'

'You could have *phoned*. You could have shouted. You could have got an ambulance.'

'I was scared.'

'You could have got Mack. He could have taken him to a hospital and said he found him at the side of the road, you could have done *something*! Pete didn't have to die because you made one stupid, drunken mistake.'

Though it doesn't seem the right moment to say it, I feel I must say something, so I mumble, 'I wasn't drunk.'

She stares. 'What? Of course you were. Don't be silly, you …'

'I had two ciders. Nothing more. And that was early on. I haven't been drunk since your eighteenth birthday.'

Her mouth seems to fumble around some word, a question, just out of reach. Whatever it was slips away in the dark.

Detective Inspector Chris Rice

4th January 2020, evening

My first stop is the right stop.

I park at the side of the road, pulling in as much as I can. A car speeding past beeps its horn at me as it has to veer into the right lane to get around. I don't bother looking up.

Keeley Mackley's Ford Cortina is parked just up ahead, unmistakable in the orange glow of the street lamps. She has done a much better job of moving in off the road than I have. She continues to impress me.

My door slams shut in the wind. The bitter air pinches my cheeks and neck.

I trot along the pavement until it thins out and is replaced by road. I look behind me to make sure there are no cars and start the ascent up the hill. Down to my left, boats bob in the harbour. There are no lights, now, no sound but the waves.

My breathing becomes more and more shallow as the road becomes steeper. I have to stop halfway up and take a breath.

When I finally arrive at the break in the fence, I step through, pulling my coat around me tightly so the low-hanging branches do not snag it.

I walk for less than five minutes before I see them.

They are sitting in the clearing, on the same patch of sand by the rock pools where they once posed for a picture. Where Rebecca and I posed for a similar picture for Aisling.

They are side by side and I cannot tell which is which. They both have their hoods up. Then the one on the left tugs her hood down and runs her hand through her hair, and I see it is Keeley.

Keeley's legs are stretched out in front of her and Jude's are pulled up to her chest. Jude's chin rests on her knees. I do not think they are speaking.

They both turn around as I come nearer. Their faces are lit by the moon and its reflection on the water, and they appear ghostly.

Neither of them is surprised to see me.

It strikes me that this is the first time I have seen them together outside of photographs. I cannot explain why, but they complement one another perfectly. Tendrils of Keeley's hair are floating in the wind, obscuring Jude's expression for a moment. When they fall, I see that she, like Keeley, looks calm and settled.

Keeley brings her hand up to rest on Jude's knee for just a second. They do not look at each other, but something passes between them, and in a moment, Keeley stands up and walks towards me.

I give her a cigarette and she takes it.

'Why did you tell everyone you broke Beth McKenna's jaw?'

Her face doesn't change. She lets me light the cigarette, leaning down, holding her hair back, her eyelashes almost brushing my hand. She takes a small drag and I see her face screw up, just for a second, with disgust.

'Jude would have been expelled,' she says, after a moment. 'And her life is going somewhere. She has the brain to go to uni and get a first. She can do anything she wants whereas … Well, what am I going to do?'

'That's bullshit,' I say calmly. She looks at me. Moonlight bounces off her beautiful cheekbones. 'She's failing every single subject. And I know you know that because she got you to phone the school and pretend to be Linda Jameson. So don't bullshit me, Keeley. Why did you say it was you when it wasn't?'

She glances towards Jude and I know she is thinking, deciding whether or not to accept that the game is up. When she looks back, there is the ghost of a smile playing on her lips. The cigarette hangs limply from her hand, forgotten.

'I told them it was me because it wasn't me,' she says simply. 'It wasn't me. But it should have been.'

It should have been.

'It all came out after the fact,' Keeley continues. 'About the bullying. Have you heard what they did to her, Chris?'

'I've heard.' My stomach churns as I think of the raw chicken incident.

'And I had no idea. All of it was going on right under my nose and I didn't know a thing about it. If they hadn't been fucking her around, she would have been fine. She could have done anything. That's why I took the rap for breaking that silly bitch's jaw. It wasn't me … but it should have been. If I didn't help her, if I didn't know … the least I could do was make sure she didn't get into trouble for stopping it.'

I nod at the ground, making a circle in the sand with my foot.

'I thought you were coming here to ask me about the dress,' Keeley says.

I look up.

'You found the dress,' she says. 'The one I hid on the way to the station on Wednesday morning. I assumed you were going to ask me about that.'

I take a deep breath and consider. I do not have the energy to ask how she knows we found it.

'Are you going to arrest me, Chris?' There is the slightest hint of flirtation in her voice when she says it. Unmistakable this time. Her eyebrows are raised, her eyes wide and playing with me. Her head is cocked to the side and I can see, then, why someone might want to do something so terrible if it meant keeping her face just like this.

But then I see her delicate throat vibrate as she swallows in fear. She isn't fooling me.

I shake my head and look back to where she had been sitting. Jude waits by their spot at the rock pool, watching me. She knows I am here only to see her.

I come to a halt in front of Jude and pull my cigarettes out from my pocket again. Keeley hasn't followed me and I am glad. I offer the packet to Jude and she takes one, mumbling thanks. I take a second that I don't want.

'Your mum's worried about you,' I say. 'She called and asked me to find you.'

She says nothing.

'I've been asking a lot of questions,' I say. 'Going round and round, investigating every possibility. Trying to work out what the hell happened on Tuesday night. I've had a lot of very interesting conversations, Jude. Are you sure there's nothing else you want to tell me?'

The fear I have seen in her eyes has vanished entirely. She stares at a place a few feet behind me, her mouth set, her right arm curled around her chest, the other holding the cigarette.

'Thing is, Jude,' I say, taking a puff of my own and savouring the feeling in my chest. 'Somebody has to go to prison for what happened to Pete. We aren't just going to stop looking and put the file in the cellar. It doesn't work like that. Someone has to pay for what happened to him. If we make exceptions, if we decide that someone had a good reason for killing him, and just call it "case closed" … we're spitting in the face of truth, in the face of … justice. There's no grey area here. There is only a murder. There is only a victim and a murderer. You know how that has to go.'

I look off into the distance, trying for mysterious. I know she can see through me.

'I understand,' she says quietly. 'Without truth … justice, we're no better than animals. We're as evolved as a bird who can't bloody fly.'

'Exactly.' I take another puff, trying to hide my confusion. 'I'll be honest with you, Jude. At the minute, my colleagues think Keeley looks like our most likely suspect.'

I feel her eyes snap to me, but I keep looking ahead. I need her to believe the lie.

'Motive. She'd just found out her boyfriend was cheating on her. Means. She used a vegetable knife from her kitchen drawer, a knife that is covered with her fingerprints and Pete's blood. Gumption. She's not exactly a shrinking violet, your Keeley. She's ballsy. Feisty. They were violent with each other. She fought with him minutes before he died. And today … well, today, we found a piece of evidence that Keeley tried to hide from us and it makes her look very, very guilty.'

I wait to see if she will respond. When she doesn't, I add: 'They think it *could* be Mack. He's not coping well in a cell with no drugs but he still hasn't admitted anything to us, which leads us to believe he just might be innocent. As I say, the jury is out but … I promise you, by the end of this week, we'll have at least one of you in custody, being charged with Pete's murder. You can mark me on that. And if I had to put money on it – and I am a gambling man – I'd say it'll be Keeley. My bosses are pushing me to arrest her too.'

Jude takes a drag from her cigarette. She doesn't crinkle her nose like Keeley did, she lets it fill her lungs. She holds it there, and then she lets it out. It suits her: she looks grave and older and beautiful with it.

The smoke has cleared her head.

'If it was an accident,' she says finally. 'Or, you know, manslaughter. What would someone be looking at?'

I suck my teeth, pretend to consider. 'No pre-med. Heat of the moment, crime of passion. Momentary loss of control. One single stab wound … No previous. If someone just lifted the first thing they saw and reacted to, say, a threat … I'd say a manslaughter charge is likely enough.'

'How long?'

'Five. Six, maybe. Less with good behaviour.'

She stares in the direction of the sea, swaying. The cigarette dangles from her left hand.

'It's not that long,' I say. 'Five years isn't forever. Five years is nothing. Not in terms of a whole life.'

It is true.

I imagine Jude up in court, sentenced, and placed in the same correctional facility as Rebecca. Maybe they would even be friends, maybe they would look out for one another. They could eat lunch side by side and count down the days for one another, telling each other what they were most looking forward to. 'A pint with my dad,' Rebecca might say. 'I'm looking forward to being old enough to go into the pub with my dad.'

I think of the Project Twenty file, sitting in the footwell of my car, photographs and maps and typed statements all spilling out, covered in sweet and sour sauce. The photograph that had been taken on this very beach, in almost this very same spot, only eight years before. The girls in the photo, naturally tanned, smiling. Smiles that reach their eyes and keep on going. Skinny arms hooked around necks, hips touching.

Five years is nothing. It's easy for me to say, I'm an old man now. What does it matter if I'm sixty-three or sixty-eight? Five years for these girls … If they missed five years of each other, could they ever go back? One on the outside, one on the inside. Who would change the most?

I realise that thinking about the photograph has pushed the smell of the salt into my nostrils, for real this time. Instead of the high moon behind the trees in front of us, I see a sun high above us, just as it shone in their eyes that day. I can even see Roddy Jameson taking the photograph, delighted that his girls were so happy. My stomach jolts. Here is another little girl who is being taken away from her dad.

The length of time doesn't matter.

Jude won't be placed with Rebecca.

Rebecca isn't dangerous, but Jude just might be.

I look to Jude, but she is still staring out to the sea, defeated. For one bizarre moment, I want to reach out and hug her, tell her that I know, but that everything will be fine. Her dad will understand, he will forgive her.

But it isn't her dad Jude is thinking about.

It never has been.

'Whatever happened in that house,' I say finally. 'In that damn Den … I know it was an accident. Or there might even have been a really good reason for it. If I could pull a tramp off the street and get him to confess, I'd do it. Promise him three meals every day, a comfortable bed … If I could do it, I would. Just to get this fucking case over with, just to make it all stop. But I can't do that. You know I can't do that.

'I'm going to go home and get some rest, now. If anyone wanted to call me to tell me anything, I'd try to help them as best I could. If anyone wanted to wait until tomorrow, and come and have a truthful conversation with me, one on one … as an adult now, without any parents … Well, my phone is always on. Why don't you take tonight to be with Keeley? Speak to your mum and dad. Let's not allow any more lives to be ruined, eh, Jude?'

She doesn't say what I think she will. 'How did you know to look for a dress?' she asks. 'You were looking for evidence against Mack but you knew to look for a dress. Why?'

'Your hair,' I say. That gets her full attention. 'When we took your phone, I looked through it and saw a picture you'd taken with Keeley during the day of the party. Your hair was all …' I gesture at my own practically bald head. 'Big and curly, on New Year's Eve. When we spoke to you on New Year's Day, it was different. Straight. So I knew you'd had a shower before we got there, though you said you called the police as soon as you'd woken up. And in the video that Brian Reed took, I saw your reflection in the TV. You told us your dress was lilac and short-sleeved, but the one you wore in the video was dark with long sleeves.'

I don't bother telling her that a part of me had wanted to look for a dress from the minute I had laid eyes on her.

I walk back to my car, feeling sore, sick and exhausted. Nearly four days running on empty, without any proper sleep and with nothing but fried food and cheap porridge, I feel like I am swishing around, 80 per cent coffee. My stomach has bloated, my head is fuzzy, and I feel heavy and sore. That's it, I tell myself. After this case, no more. No smoking, regular exercise, no more junk food.

How many times have I promised myself this?

I cannot bring myself to look at the Cortina as I pass it.

Moonlight glints off my own Punto and renders it a sparkling, navy pool. I almost run my fingers along the roof to make sure it is still solid, will still hold my weight.

I pull my coat around me more tightly so that I can step into the car, and with a sinking heart I realise that it no longer fits as it used to.

It must have shrunk in the wash.

I have just turned on the engine when my phone rings.

Jude

4th January 2020, evening

As Rice walks away from me, I hear Keeley walk towards me. I sit back down on the rock.

'Why didn't he arrest me?' she says in my ear. 'What did he say?'

I turn to face her. 'He knows it's me.'

Keeley looks confused. She sits next to me.

'I told my mum,' I say. 'Just before I came to see you tonight. Not the details, but I told her I did it.'

'Why did you tell her, of all people?'

'She kept saying it must have been you. I couldn't stand hearing it. She must've told Rice.'

'She won't have,' Keeley says. 'She's your mum, your blood. She won't hand you in. Besides, she probably thinks you said it in the heat of the moment to protect me or something. He would have arrested you there, if he knew.'

'Nah. I'm going to jail, Keeley.' It is almost a relief to say it. I am less afraid now than I have been for months, years. The words sound clean and smooth. They roll off my tongue like the right notes. The perfect answer.

Keeley's eyes are closed, and I am glad, for once, that she isn't saying anything. Her anger seems to have drifted away with Rice.

We sit there for a long time, listening to the sound of the waves somewhere behind us, far away but loud. A single seagull laughs to a companion somewhere above our heads. Keeley has straightened her legs and the tip of one of her trainers is dipping into the water.

I wonder when I'll next get to hear the sea, but the thought doesn't cause me any pain. Keeley's hair blows across her face in the wind and she pulls up her hood in an attempt to restrain it.

'What am I supposed to do without you?' Keeley says at last.

'I think … I think we're all exactly where we're supposed to be. All of us.'

She turns to face me. She is so close our noses are nearly touching. Her eyes are dry and bright, just like on the morning it all happened. I will remember her face, every inch of it. I will remember every freckle and the exact lines on her irises and I will remember the precise shade of her hair. I will not need my photographs to remember. I will draw her from memory, exactly. I remember something she said to me, a long time ago, so clearly it is as if she has just repeated it. *Some things hurt too much to talk about.*

Don't I know it, Keeley. Don't I know it.

I think back to Wednesday morning.

Keeley waking to my alarm. Seeing the knife.

I see myself standing, shivering beside the bath as it filled with cold water. The heat hadn't been on all night and I knew I would freeze as soon as I put a toe into it. I was almost looking forward to it. Perhaps then I would wake up.

I remember Keeley coming back into the bathroom with a jumper and a pair of her jeans in her arms.

'J, it's going to overflow.' She spoke softly and moved to turn off the tap. Water lapped dangerously close to the sides. She set the bundle of clothes on the closed lid of the toilet, and I saw a pair of socks and some underwear on top of the pile. I felt my eyes well up against my will. She'd thought of everything.

'Shh.' Keeley lifted the hem of my dress and started to tug it upwards. I put my arms up in the air, obediently, like a child, and felt a slight tug on my ear as she lifted it off over my head. The back of one of my earrings had come free and it fell into the bath with a tiny *plop*. She didn't notice.

'We don't have much time,' she murmured. She reached around me to unclip my bra, let it fall to the floor. 'Get in. I know it's cold but we need to be quick in case somebody comes.'

She meant Mack. She wanted this all done before he got back so he didn't have to involve himself.

I wondered if I should explain.

Shaking harder than ever, I turned away from her to remove my underwear and climbed into the bath. The cold was so extreme that I was instantly made numb. I took deep breaths, trying to stop my shuddering.

'Do your hands, they're the worst,' Keeley said, inspecting the dress. The pattern of the silver and black sequins across the front of the dress was such that I couldn't see anything on it, but I knew it must be there. I wiped my hands over it more than once. Blood.

The word was enough to make my stomach flip.

I submerged both my hands in the freezing water and let wisps of pink unlatch themselves from my knuckles and melt away into the bath.

'Scrub,' Keeley instructed. 'I'm going to sponge this off as best I can.'

She left again, clutching the dress tightly but holding it as far away as she could from her own skin. She still hadn't put on her clothes. It was the 1st of January, and we were both either naked or almost naked, running around with no heating on, me shivering in a cold bath. I nearly laughed.

Instead, I looked down and began to scrub at my hands and face. I squirted some of Keeley's shower gel over my knuckles and massaged it as hard as I could. I was thankful that the little mirror above the chipped sink opposite me was too high for me to see my reflection.

She came back a few minutes later without the dress, carrying a small jug instead. She knelt at the side of the bath and began to wet my hair using the jug.

'You've got some on the ends,' she explained.

I knew 'some' must refer to blood, but it seemed sensible to refrain from saying the word.

'All of that effort I put in and you only got a few hours out of those curls last night,' she said.

I smiled obediently at the joke. Her own hair was still very curly, though a little fuzzy on one side where she had slept on it.

She shampooed my hair carefully, keeping one hand flat above my eyebrows to avoid it dripping into my eyes. I continued to shake, making half-hearted attempts to scrub my hands. Her touch was so gentle that my eyes filled with tears again and she mistook them.

'Everything is OK, darling,' she murmured. 'I'm nearly done, then I'll get you dried and warm. We can call the police and they'll get everything sorted. We're going to be OK.'

'Keeley.' Whispering her name I thought might break me altogether.

'What?'

'Keeley, I'm sorry. I'm so sorry.'

Her hand stopped on the base of my skull, poised in the act of rinsing suds. 'Don't,' she said. 'We don't know what happened. We both slept in my bed. I woke up this morning and went downstairs and …'

'Yes,' I said. 'OK.'

Her reserve faltered for only a minute. She put her head down so that it was nearly touching my soaking arm and took a deep breath. I waited, thinking she was about to start crying. Then she resumed the careful washing of my hair, her face set.

When I stepped out on to the thin bathmat and Keeley wrapped her towel around me – the same towel I used yesterday, I thought, which smelled of damp and shampoo – she took a hairbrush and began to comb my hair. I watched the pale pink water drain from the bath. My earring lay next to the plughole, swishing this way and that as the bath drained.

Keeley held my head so she didn't have to pull too hard.

With the very last dregs of the bath, the earring caught in the water and escaped down the plughole and out of sight.

Here, at the rock pool, I realise we haven't said anything for a long time.

There is a moment when I think she is going to kiss me. She is staring at my mouth, and she hasn't pulled away, even though we are sitting too close to see one another properly. I remember Mum's speech about being too close to see the whole picture. That's why Keeley doesn't know, I think. She's too close, she doesn't see it. She doesn't realise. She can't tell what's happened to me and I have never told her. It is not her fault.

Her lips part.

Then her phone rings.

She leans back to reach into the pocket of her jeans. She answers, throwing me a puzzled look.

'Hello? Yeah …'

When she gets off the phone, I think, I'll tell her. I'll tell her everything, in as much detail as I can remember. She will believe me. She will forgive me, she will understand, and I can go to prison and she can wait for me. And when I get out, we can play house for real.

I look around the clearing and try to imagine we are children again. All I can see is Keeley running. Running, always running, hair flying, nose dripping, jacket soaring at either side of her skinny body. Constantly in motion, a whirlwind of colour and sound. While I wanted to play, to make-believe, Keeley just wanted to run. While I wanted a tree to be our castle, the rock pools to be the moat, the leaves were just leaves to her, and all the more wonderful for it. She found the remarkable in the everyday, in everything. Everything made her happy, she didn't have to pretend or try. She played along for me and only me, but I knew she was happiest when we were covered in mud, or drenched from jumping in puddles, twigs in our hair, giggling at that, at this real, tangible life between our fingers and nothing more.

'That was Naomi …' I realise she has hung up and is speaking to me. Keeley's voice sounds far away, as if it is she who is on the other end of the phone. She is looking straight ahead, and not at me. 'She said Mack's … Mack has …'

In the split second before she speaks, I realise that I know exactly what she is going to say. Like I have known it all along.

'He confessed to killing Pete.'

Keeley

May 2022

This month has been hot so far and is predicted to get even hotter as we sprint towards June at full speed. A bird – I have no idea what kind, who really knows what kind? – tweets happily from a tree at the edge of the courtyard, and I find myself smiling in its direction as I tell Mack –

'I sold your guitars to buy myself a new car.'

He stops walking abruptly. 'Well, don't sugar-coat it, Keeley.'

I stop walking too. 'The Cortina gave up.'

'No way.'

'I know, only forty years old. I'm sorry. I'll buy you new guitars eventually.'

'I won't need them for a while.'

'Good. Gives me time to save up.'

Mack smiles at this and turns his head towards the sky. With the sun shining down on him like this, I can see every line on his face and, though he is paler than ever, his skin looks clear and his cheeks a little fuller. He has grown a beard that suits him more than I would have guessed, but somehow, he still looks like a little boy. I think he always will to me. He certainly doesn't look like someone to whom you would attach the crime *voluntary manslaughter*.

This is the first chance we've had to take a walk in the grounds so far this year – it rained the entire time during my April visit – and I'm enjoying the half dozen lazy laps we've taken around the decorative fountain. The staff stay back, either sitting on benches or standing by the doors, also enjoying the sunshine, but flicking their eyes over the residents (*I'm a resident, not a prisoner*, Mack says).

'I sold them to a guy in Droless who found me on Gumtree,' I find myself telling Mack. I want to say more, to explain that I have been messaging the man ever since and that he has suggested we meet up. I haven't agreed to anything yet, but with every message I find myself wanting to throw caution to the wind and do just that.

'That's OK,' Mack says. 'I don't mind. Love the new hair, by the way.'

He throws his hand in the air in the vague direction of my head. I cut my hair just above my shoulders last week and he's the first person to comment on it.

We do another lap in silence, then both decide to collapse on to a bench at the same moment.

'Ella Denny came to see me,' Mack says suddenly.

I open my mouth to ask who this is, then freeze. 'Ella Denny?' I repeat. 'Pete's sister?'

Because there was no trial – well, no proper trial with a jury like you see in films – we never had to see Ella Denny, or Pete's parents. Mack said he did it and the judge spoke to him about his rights and he agreed and that was it. Ten years. Rehab, assessment and then prison; or rehab, assessment, rehab. No parole. It seemed like the best outcome at the time. The family liaison who explained all of this to me kept using the term *diminished responsibility*. I asked Kyle about that afterwards, and he seemed to think they'd gone easy on Mack because his brain was so addled from eight years of drug addiction.

'Yeah,' Mack says. 'She's just turned eighteen so she came to see me by herself. Facilitated by the Centre, all very formal and very …' Mack trails off and I can tell he is thinking. I wonder what he does now, when he has the urge to write a song and spew out all his thoughts.

'What did she say?' I ask, trying to take this in but feeling numb. I haven't said Pete's name in such a long time that it sounded foreign coming from my mouth.

'Wanted answers,' Mack says. 'Couldn't give her any, really. I'm not the person they need to be asking.'

I have no idea what to say. I look away from him to watch the fountain: the constant rise and fall of water is comforting, the sound like polite clapping at a classical concert.

'So what *did* you say?' I ask eventually.

'I just said I was sorry for the way things worked out,' Mack says.

He puts his hands in his pockets and stretches his legs out in front of him. If this weren't the grounds of the Redstone Secure Rehabilitation Centre, we would be brother and sister, both slightly freckled, having a chat on a bench on a sunny day. An ice cream each wouldn't look out of place.

'Still picking up loads of overtime?' Mack asks.

I glance at him, wondering if this is a dig – my excuse for not visiting Redstone more often has been that I'm taking every shift the Clandy will give me, which is completely true and completely necessary.

I have a plan, but I need to save money to enact my plan.

Plus Redstone is over eighty miles away from Vetobridge.

'Still loads,' I say. 'How's *choir practice* going?' I grin at him and waggle my eyebrows.

'It's going well, actually, my narrow-minded sister.' Mack smiles indulgently. 'We have a Summer Concert sometime in July, did I tell you that? You'll come?'

'Unless you've magically become four hundred times better at singing, no.'

'I'm still not great,' he admits with a grimace. 'But I'm practising loads. Hey, it's music, at least. I was never much of a singer.'

A flicker of Naomi hangs in the air between us and I cast around for something to say, but when I look back at him, he is staring serenely at the fountain like he hasn't a care in the world.

With the slight plumping of his cheeks has come a sense of calm I haven't known in my brother before. Though I know he is innocent of murder, I cannot help but think he feels justice has been done in sending him here – he certainly never fought it. He speaks evenly and without emotion at all times now. It is disconcerting.

We talk for a while longer and, as soon as it is appropriate for me to leave, I hug him.

'You'll be OK?' I ask. The same thing I always ask just before I go.

Mack pulls on a lock of my hair and smiles. 'Yes, I'll be OK. It's steak and kidney pie tonight.' When I don't look convinced, he adds, 'We're all exactly where we're supposed to be, Keeley.'

It is only after I have signed myself out and made my way to the visitors' car park that I wonder if he is including Pete in this.

I drive home from Redstone feeling much the same way I always do after these visits – exhausted from forcing myself to smile and act normal, and wanting, more than anything, to speak to Jude. The old Jude.

You have more to lose than me, Mack told me in a whisper, a week after he confessed. I think that means he thinks I stabbed my own boyfriend and was too scared of prison to confess. I'll let him think that because – though I would never admit this – he is right. Without Naomi, all he has is me. And I am not enough to want to live for. He would have gone away for a few years anyway, even if they only had the drugs on him, so what's a few more?

That's what I have to keep telling myself, though I don't believe it for a second.

I indicate and pull on to the motorway that will take me back to Vetobridge. No lane changes until past Oldry and, frustratingly, nothing to distract me from my thoughts.

I sail past Oldry Police Station in record time, keeping my eyes determinedly on the road ahead of me.

Nothing ever came of the dress, but I still don't want to look at the spot where I hid it. They asked me about it and I shrugged. They asked Mack about it and he said he vaguely remembered trying to mop up some of the blood with it. There were no further questions. That piece was not the right shape to fit, and so it was ignored and the other pieces stretched to fill the spaces.

I park up behind the other car in the driveway, then automatically glance up the green behind the house. I can just about see the Jamesons' house – or, I suppose, what used to be the Jamesons' house.

Roddy still lives there, but I don't see him much. He's lost a lot of weight and seems to be doing a lot of walking. Sometimes I'll look out of my bedroom window and he'll be marching across the green, a sports watch on his wrist and a determination to his steps.

Inside, I throw my keys into a bowl we've placed on the sideboard in the hall. They jingle against hers.

Jude moved into 166 with me. She and I are playing house for real.

We cleaned up the house. Not just cleaned it, we actually fixed it up. I'd say it would sell for a lot now, if we wanted it to. We opened windows that hadn't been opened in years, and we painted the bedrooms, and I moved into Mack's old room and Jude moved into mine. When I was clearing out my cupboard and making a bag for the charity shop, I came across a digital camera. I plugged it into an old phone charger and a few minutes later the screen lit up. There were only three photographs on it – one beach shot, a pretty sunset in the centre, and two of me. In both I am lying with my eyes closed on a sunbed, my face a little burnt and my hair nearly white instead of blonde. I squinted to try and work out where we had been. I looked maybe eleven or twelve. Our Spain holiday, it must have been. I deleted the pictures and added the camera to the charity-shop bag. Then I plastered up the hole in my bedroom wall in less than ten minutes and spent hours shaking my head afterwards and saying, 'All these years I could have fixed it just like that?'

We don't talk about the Den. We never go in there, and as far as we are concerned, the door will stay locked until we sell up.

'You're home early,' I call, trying to sound happy about it.

'Yeah!' Her voice comes from the kitchen so that, of course, is where my feet take me.

What if you looked at your shadow and it was an entirely different shape than you thought it was? What if you realised you'd been looking at it from the wrong angle your entire life?

She stands with her back to me, stirring sauce on the hob. Her hair reaches her waist, now. 'Fancy Bolognese? I know it's boring.'

'Boring is perfect,' I say, meaning it. I slide myself on to the bench of our new table. 'How come you're early?'

'Skipped my last class,' Jude says. 'Got good news.' She spins around to face me and I see she is beaming. There hasn't been a lot of beaming between us lately.

She has been doing a photography course at the college and working in a tiny shop in town that is literally called ArtsNCrafts. She doesn't have models in her photos now; it's all nature scenes and landscapes, the odd still life. They're good pictures, I think, though I've never really had an eye for any of the creative stuff. She works hard, she does well. When we do spend time together, it's on mundane domestic tasks. I can't remember the last long conversation we had, or the last time we had a proper laugh together.

She takes her phone from her pocket, makes a few clicks and pushes it into my hand.

I take it, feeling my pulse quicken.

Dear Miss Jameson, the email reads, *We are delighted to welcome you to our BA (Hons) Commercial Photography YEAR ONE. We were very impressed with your portfolio application and especially enjoyed the piece 'She and I'.*

I stop reading and look up. 'You got in?' I ask. 'Jude, oh my god!'

'It's not Belfast Hope,' she says quickly. 'They haven't got back to me yet. It's another university. A place in England.' Her eyes slip away from me, the moment of happiness evaporated.

'You told your mum?' I imagine Linda, now living in Derry with Mason in her sister's house. Jude finally a university student, the girl Linda always wanted.

'Nah, not yet.'

My heart hammers. I can't tell if it's fear or excitement that has me sweating. 'And you're going to go? You'll take it, the place?'

'Well, I should. Shouldn't I?'

'Yes.' For a moment I think I will tell her about my own plan. I hesitate over this for so long that she turns back to the hob and continues cooking.

'Alex got into the same one,' she says. To any other ears, this would sound casual. To mine, so in tune with every nuance of nearly every word she's ever said, the nonchalance sounds forced. 'At least I'd have a friend there.'

Alex is the name of someone on her course. She's mentioned him once or twice, in passing, but I've not met him yet. The few times his name has come up, I've watched her face carefully for signs that this is a potential boyfriend, but if it is, she's keeping it to herself for now.

'And Alex,' I say after a moment. 'He's definitely going to take the place in England?'

'She,' Jude corrects. 'Alex is a she. And yes.'

I had just closed my eyes to rest them, but they snap open again.

'Spaghetti or penne?' she asks.

I have a night off from the Clandy, so after dinner I suggest we do our food shop for the week.

We get into my recently acquired second-hand Clio, towards which I feel no affection, and I drive us to Tesco.

Staring at a packet of chocolate biscuits on a shelf, I remember to tell Jude –

'Chris Rice came into the bar the other day.'

She stops, five paces ahead of me, and swings the trolley around so we can face each other.

'Chris Rice,' I repeat. 'That detective who –'

'I know.' Jude gives a little laugh through her nose. 'I know who he is.'

I smile back.

It was the previous Sunday. Chris seemed relaxed.

'You full-time here now?' he asked, as I poured him a pint of Harp. He was possibly thinner as well, I thought, though he was in a T-shirt and jeans and I'd only ever seen him in a suit so it was hard to tell.

'Just for now,' I said. Then I told him what I hadn't had the chance to tell anyone else yet. 'I'm going back to do my A-levels, actually, so I need to save up now so I can go part-time from September. I'm going to do law, eventually.'

'Law?' His eyebrows shot up, but not unkindly.

'I'm not thick,' I reminded him.

'That you're not.' He grinned at me, so that his eyes nearly disappeared.

I gave him the pint and the glass of wine he'd ordered and he went back to his table.

Now, I say to Jude, 'I asked him if he was a sugar daddy now that he's retired – he was with a girl not much older than us, but it was just his daughter *apparently*. Rebecca or something.'

Jude, in the act of reaching for something on a high shelf, freezes. She turns to look at me, her arm still outstretched, her brow furrowed.

'What?' I ask, alarmed.

Then she smiles slowly, and before I know it, she is laughing. Properly laughing, eyes bright and wide, head tilted back. She laughs so hard tears begin to spill down her cheeks. A woman with a sleeping baby on the front seat of her trolley throws Jude a look, and I begin to laugh too, bewildered.

In the car park afterwards, with two bags each, I have a sudden urge to run.

'One …' I say. 'Two …' I look at her and she blinks at me in confusion. Then she takes my keys from my hand to click the Clio open.

If Mack were to comment on this, he might say that all our lives we were running towards something, when we played our game, and now that we're there, there's nothing else to run towards. I'm trying to think about things more, trying to put myself in Mack's shoes, but I'm not sure if I like it. The last words he spoke to me at the Centre are still rolling through my head. *We're all exactly where we're supposed to be.* I feel like I've heard them before.

As though reading my mind, Jude says, 'Oh, I didn't ask about Mack?'

'Fine,' I say. I have no desire to tell her about his visitor.

'Did you tell him about Naomi?'

Brains informed us last week that she is living with someone in a flat in Belfast. She gave up the Clandy shortly after Mack's confession and hasn't spoken to me since.

'I hope Naomi's really happy,' Jude said. I was surprised, because I'm pretty sure they never even had a conversation, but maybe this is her new attitude to life now. Maybe she wants all of us, everyone, to be happy.

'Nah,' I say in response to Jude's question. 'He doesn't need to know.'

Jude fusses with the boot, putting our bags in, and I get into the car. Without any conscious thought, I take my phone from my pocket and open up my chat with the Gumtree guy. Stephen.

I'm free on Sunday evening, if you still fancy that drink? X I type. I press send before I can follow the thought through and put my phone back in my pocket.

Jude opens the passenger door and holds something out towards me.

I take it. It's a Creme Egg.

'Jude ...' I have one hand on the steering wheel and the other on the gearstick, the Creme Egg tucked tightly against my palm. I have suddenly remembered where I've heard Mack's words before, and I don't think I can wait until we get home to have this conversation.

'What?' she asks.

I turn to face her. She is all eyes and cheekbones and hair, one hand reaching behind her for her seatbelt. I know her face better than I know my own.

She has always been much more beautiful than me.

'I think we should go for a drive,' I say. 'And I'd like you to tell me exactly what happened between you and Pete and Mack. All of it.'

If she is surprised, she doesn't show it. Instead, with not even a sigh or a glance away, she nods.

I put the car into gear and make for the rock pools.

I'll keep trying to make her laugh. No matter what she is about to tell me. It made me feel good, that little girl laugh in Tesco, like she was still in there somewhere. Like she was still the girl who beams at me from the rock pool photo that sits on our sideboard, taken the day before she scratched our initials on to her dad's new car. The girl I have grieved hardest for.

I pull on to the main road, parallel with the promenade, and speed up.

Epilogue

Jude

1st January 2020, early morning

The digital display reads ten past two in the morning. It glows, sickly. Keeley is passed out next to me. Her eyes are already beginning to lose their redness, her skin is no longer blotchy. The house is quieter than ever – most people must have gone home. I adjust myself on the sofa, pummelling the pillow to get more comfortable. I know I won't sleep tonight, of course I won't. But at least I can lie next to her and try.

Their fight rings in my ears. Is this it, is it really over? Is he out of our lives for good? His face when Keeley punched his chest, when he pulled at her wrist. I cannot let myself hope. She could wake up in the morning and forget the whole thing; she could forgive him entirely … I know, more surely than I have ever known anything, that she will.

He will never, never be gone.

I lean my head back on the arm of the sofa and time my breaths, ten seconds in, hold, ten seconds out. I tap out our rhythm on my palm.

The door of the Den opens with a low creek. I open one eye, ready to tell Brains or Ian that this room is out of bounds for anyone else, we have claimed it. It is not Brains.

It is Pete.

My mouth goes dry.

We have not been alone since …

I look towards Keeley, wondering if I can shake her awake, wondering how many drinks she has mixed with her Six and if it was too many to wake her.

Pete is whispering something. I freeze, still feigning sleep, but he is whispering to Keeley.

He is very, very drunk. And very stoned, if earlier is anything to go by.

His words are slurring and he is teetering to one side as he tries to get close to Keeley on the sofa.

'K … Kee-Kee. I'm sorry. I'm sorry.' I can't tell if he is about to laugh or cry.

I sit up. I have no plan, but I know I have to get him to leave.

'Go away,' I say softly. He looks up, eyes unfocused, until he sees me. He makes a half-laugh by sputtering air out from between his lips and shakes his head, dismissing me entirely. He sits on the concrete floor next to the sofa.

'Kee-Kee. Come on, baby.' He is pawing at Keeley's arms, her hair. 'I'm sorry. Baby, wake up and talk to me. We can sort this out.'

He looks like a child, sitting there with his legs crossed and his lips pouting, a wet stain down his T-shirt. I can smell vomit from it, mingling with his aftershave.

The same aftershave as that night.

My stomach lurches.

'Go away,' I say again, more firmly this time.

He ignores me entirely and continues to paw at Keeley's bare arm, but he will not wake her and he must, he *must* know that. I wonder if I should find more Sixes, offer them to him, try and make him overdose. The thought makes my skin tingle with pleasure, and a jolt buzzes through my solar plexus.

But he is more used to the drugs than Keeley is. They seem to have slurred his speech and made him giggly – he is smiling now, running his hands over her stomach. He is smiling, smiling, smiling.

I grope around for my phone with the intention of calling Mack, but the Den is dark and I cannot find it. I don't want to leave Keeley alone with Pete. Then my hand finds the paring knife from earlier, the one Keeley used to cut the Six for us. I touch the tip of the blade with my index finger and press.

When I look back, Pete has stood up and is making a muddled attempt at undoing his belt. He is still crooning to Keeley, who lies on her back, mouth slightly open, oblivious.

'Stop it,' I say. I am surprised at how strong my voice sounds when it comes out.

Pete looks towards me and his eyes widen in amusement at the sight of the knife. 'Look what she's got,' he mumbles. 'Put that down … Go back to the party. I need to talk to my girlfriend, just us alone. I need to get her back.'

His belt is undone and he is trying to work the button on his jeans.

I sit up straighter, knife held out in front of me like a magic wand.

'Stop pointing that at me,' he mumbles. 'Fuck sake.'

I look down at my hand, curious.

'Fucking stop it.' His voice is louder now, more serious. It sounds as though he has almost sobered up. He has stopped fumbling with his jeans and has turned to face me, caught between annoyance and amusement. 'Fucking put that down, you dopey bitch.'

I don't move. My hand is steady, outstretched towards him. I stand from the sofa and take a step back from him, towards the roll-up Den door. The knife is pointing directly at him.

'Go away,' I say. 'Leave us alone.'

His eyes wander from the knife to my eyes and he snorts.

'If you knew how to stay out of things, we wouldn't have this problem,' he says quietly. 'Are you happy you told her about Leah? Does she seem happy to you? If you only knew how to leave me and Keeley alone … You never told her about us either, did you?'

His words are floating through the air, I can see them written down in gold, swirly letters in my peripheral vision. I need to tap my palm to keep us safe but the knife is in my way. If I drop the knife, Pete will have the upper hand. I need to keep us safe. I need to keep us safe from him.

He is talking, mumbling, smiling. 'You're a little girl,' I manage to make out. He laughs to himself and reaches over to stroke Keeley's cheek. 'Wake up, Kee. We have to make up. You know how we make up.'

He tugs at Keeley's underwear, attempting to pull it down.

I am next to him in two steps. He turns his body halfway around, going to shun me away again. Then his expression changes to one of mild curiosity. We look at one another, then look down in complete unison to my left hand. Still it grips the blade of the paring knife. Feeling my fingernails digging into my palm around it is the only thing I can feel for sure. The blade of the knife is hidden in Pete's T-shirt, and something hot flows out fast on to my fingers, on to the floor.

I do not know how it happened. I do not know if he turned into it, or if I pushed it in.

It does not matter either way. I have done it now, and I let go.

Let go.

Pete takes a step backwards. The knife stays where it is; he has his hand pressed against it. Then he takes another step. Then another. He steps, stumbles, backwards and to the side, until he has reached the roll-up door. He makes a strange kind of noise, like he is trying to exclaim. His nose is bleeding heavily. I think it must have been bleeding when he came in, I just didn't notice. He pulls at the knife and it comes easily out with a quick, wet sound. He stares at it in his hand for a moment, his expression still curious. He seems to hold it out towards me, and for one wild moment, I go to take it.

I stop and he lets it fall. It lands on the floor of the Den, between us.

He slides down the wall into a sitting position.

In the immediate aftermath, I look towards the kitchen.

Mack's face in the pane of plastic. No expression at all.

He is standing at the drinks table, his back to the kitchen window, and I can see a bottle in his hand.

He looks me in the eye for the longest time. It feels good just to look at him, to wait for him to make the first move. There is no pressure, here. There is no worry. I'll just wait and see what Mack does. He can decide. Whatever he decides, we will do. It is not up to me. I don't have to do anything. My heart is beating quickly, but it is not unpleasant. I will just look at Mack, and Mack will decide what to do. I stare and stare and stare.

Then he nods slowly, and moves away, back into the house.

I wipe my bloody hand on my dress and sit on the sofa at Keeley's feet. Still she sleeps, the deep, unawakenable sleep of the drugged. I roll her on to her side so I can lie next to her, and put my arm around her waist, the big spoon. I want to move closer so I can feel her spine between my breasts, along my stomach, so I can touch the solid reality of her, but I am careful not to let the wet of the dress touch her skin. She sighs in her sleep and her hand finds mine.

I lie there, motionless, eyes closed.

I match my breathing to hers until we are one.

In the corner of the Den, Pete makes a half-choking, half-laughing sound. He is murmuring to himself.

And then he is silent.

I realise after a few hours that I will have to go and get us a blanket. The thought of leaving her, even only for a few minutes, almost makes me gag, but I steady myself. I will go and get us a blanket, and I will watch over her while she sleeps, and nobody will take me away from her. Not ever. And maybe, when things are a little different, I can sleep again.

We are safe now.

Acknowledgements

Thank you to my wonderful agent, Charlotte Seymour. Without your promise to read my first novel, it probably wouldn't yet exist. Your professionalism and determination to find my book a good home is appreciated more than any words can say.

A thousand gushing thank yous to my editor, Sara Helen Binney. You put more effort and love into fixing and bettering *She and I* than I ever could have hoped for, and I feel very lucky to have you on my side, colour-coding spreadsheets.

A big cheers also to Dr Darran McCann who, in 2019, had the confidence to publish a short story of mine that got the ball rolling for this journey. I am grateful for this and to have been taught by you.

Thanks to my mum and dad. You know why.

And John – you're welcome.

A Note on the Author

Hannah King is a writer from County Down, where she lives with her partner and their dogs. *She and I* is her first novel.

A Note on the Type

The text of this book is set Adobe Garamond. It is one of several versions of Garamond based on the designs of Claude Garamond. It is thought that Garamond based his font on Bembo, cut in 1495 by Francesco Griffo in collaboration with the Italian printer Aldus Manutius. Garamond types were first used in books printed in Paris around 1532. Many of the present-day versions of this type are based on the *Typi Academiae* of Jean Jannon cut in Sedan in 1615.

Claude Garamond was born in Paris in 1480. He learned how to cut type from his father and by the age of fifteen he was able to fashion steel punches the size of a pica with great precision. At the age of sixty he was commissioned by King Francis I to design a Greek alphabet, and for this he was given the honourable title of royal type founder. He died in 1561.

Ever After High™

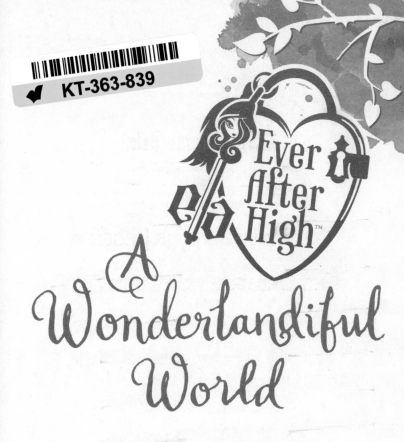

A Wonderlandiful World

BY SHANNON HALE

LITTLE, BROWN BOOKS FOR YOUNG READERS
www.lbkids.co.uk

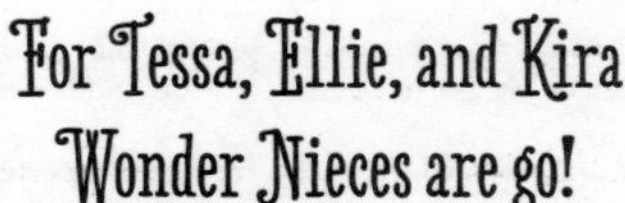

For Tessa, Ellie, and Kira
Wonder Nieces are go!

Contents

PROLOGUE
1

CHAPTER 1
When in Doubt, Shout! 3

CHAPTER 2
The Lone Tree on the Hill 24

CHAPTER 3
Maddie Converses Politely with the Narrator 35

CHAPTER 4
The Tragedy of Aquilona 37

CHAPTER 5
A Baby Bandersnatch 49

CHAPTER 6
Maddie Tries to Just
Listen Quietly 62

CHAPTER 7
A Twisted Kind of Wonder 68

CHAPTER 8
Wonder Worms Are Go! 71

CHAPTER 9
Storybooker Share Slam! 80

CHAPTER 10
Reasonable by Accident 89

CHAPTER 11
A Wobble of Uncertainty 100

CHAPTER 12
Wonderland Found Me 109

CHAPTER 13
Trapped! 123

CHAPTER 14
The Narrator Takes a Sick Day 138

CHAPTER 15
Swamp Juice in Your Teacup 143

CHAPTER 16
Running from Deadly Terror 165

CHAPTER 17
Tales of Wandering Un-Books 172

CHAPTER 18
More Vorpal 185

CHAPTER 19
Yellow Wallpaper 197

CHAPTER 20
THE VORPAL SWORD AWAITS 214

CHAPTER 21
BEWARE EMPATHY! 230

CHAPTER 22
HEDGEHOG CROQUET 236

CHAPTER 23
A RULER OF NOTHING 254

CHAPTER 24
MADNESS IS LIFE 263

CHAPTER 25
FRIENDS WOULD BE ACES 269

CHAPTER 26
ACCIDENTALLY BECOMING FRIENDS 285

EPILOGUE
295

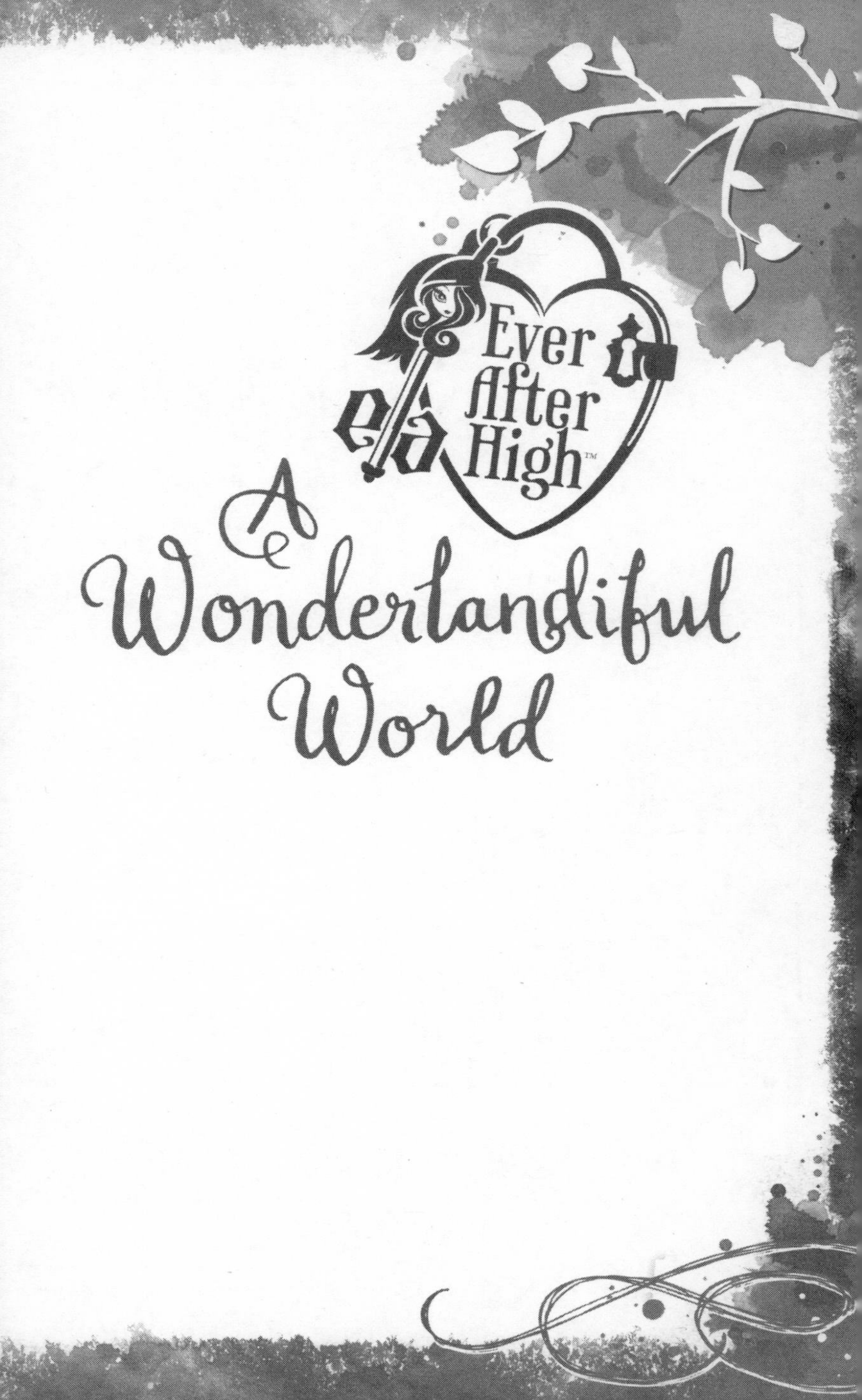
Ever After High™
A Wonderlandiful World

Prologue of Doom!

How many years had the great Jabberwock spent trapped in that tiny glass Uni Cairn prison? It had been impossible to keep track in the shimmery, drowsy darkness, with no sun setting, no clock ticking, no sheep counting. After the foolish, slivy little creatures had accidentally cracked open the Uni Cairn, the Jabberwock had fled its prison.

It curled up in the mountains and intended to rest for ages. Sleep. Soak power back into its fearsome bones.

But then, the sound of breaking glass.

Not just any glass. And not another Uni Cairn. No, somewhere, an immensely powerful magic mirror shattered. The sound exploded through all of Ever After, fast and sharp like arrows. Deep in the Dark Mountains, the sound struck the sleeping beast. Nudged it. Woke it.

Awake far too early for its liking, the Jabberwock screamed its disapproval. The trees around it shook, bent, and splintered. But they shook, bent, and splintered in a completely normal way. Everything here was far too sensical. Wrong. Flat. Right-side-out. And that was infuriating.

Ever After would know its rage. It would punish the stones, the seas, and the very earth for not being as wonderlandiful as its homeland.

But first, the Jabberwock would eat. It was very, very hungry.

CHAPTER 1

When in Doubt, Shout!

Lizzie Hearts, the princess of Hearts, daughter of the Queen of Hearts, heir to the throne of Wonderland's Card Castle, captain of the Ever After High Croquet Team, and hedgehog enthusiast, was holding a knife. It wasn't sharp, barely sharp enough to shout "Off with your butter!" Well, perhaps sharp enough to use on a very small man made entirely of butter. Yes, she could use this knife to behead a tiny butter man. If such a thing existed.

"Don't tell me you are packing a butter knife," Duchess Swan said as she practiced her twirls around their dorm room. Duchess, daughter of the Swan Queen, was usually dancing. Even while sleeping, she kept her toes pointed.

Lizzie stuffed the butter knife into her red-and-gold-checkered skirt pocket and felt her cheeks turn a royal flush red. In Wonderland, having a butter knife at all times just made sense—after all, one never knew when one might come upon some butter. But what made sense in Wonderland rarely made sense in Ever After. Lizzie often felt as confused as an egg full of bats.

"It's a *field trip*, for fairy's sake," Duchess was saying, doing pliés while stuffing a silver tiara and a feathery gown into her backpack. "Don't you know how to pack for a field trip?" Duchess added a pair of black satin ballet slippers. "Why, when I..."

Duchess continued to talk, but Lizzie had stopped listening. Her mother had taught her that Not Listening was a very important skill for a queen. Lizzie's hand was still in her deep skirt pocket, and she closed it around her treasured deck of playing cards. Her mother had given it to her before Lizzie escaped from Wonderland with Kitty Cheshire, Madeline Hatter, and a few others. She slid one card out of the deck and read the note scrawled by her mother's hand.

❤

Worms speak, indeed they do,
but not to such as me and you.
All they ever say is "mud mud food,"
so you need not listen good.
Practice Not Listening to worms today.
And by worms, I mean people.

❤

On each card in the deck her mother had written advice for Lizzie, designed to make her a better queen, often combined with information about how the world worked. Or how it *should* work. Even though she'd been at Ever After High for some time, Lizzie still felt incapable of understanding all the strange and infuriatingly reasonable ways of the school. Such as what one packed for a field trip.

". . . a feather! Can you believe that?" Duchess was saying while brushing her long black, white, and lavender hair. Lizzie raised her hand for silence, which did not come. "And it wasn't even white, not really! It was painted, like with some kind of—"

"*Off with her head!*" Lizzie shouted.

Duchess paused, mouth open.

"Explain this field trip," Lizzie demanded.

Another of her mother's cards advised:

♥

Never ever ever ever ever ever ever ever admit
there's something you don't know.
Because you know everything.
You may have just forgotten
a piece of the everything.
Also, don't tell anyone you forgot.

♥

So Lizzie added, "Not that I don't remember exactly where Headmaster Grimm said we're going and why. I just want to see if you know. Naturally, it's not just a trip to a field. Um . . . right?"

Duchess sighed. "This is a Winds trip. Each year we visit one of the Four Winds. The West Wind was last year, remember?"

Unfortunately, Lizzie remembered that trip to the beach very well. She hadn't minded the West Wind himself, even though he kept calling everyone "dude." He hadn't looked like actual wind at all, just a man in swim trunks whose blue hair was constantly flapping in a wind no one else could feel. But the after part—the "fun" part—still gave Lizzie shudders.

The students had brought swimming gear, run in and out of the water, and thrown balls over nets as if such activities were completely normal. Meanwhile, Lizzie had sat on the sand while wrapped in her flamingo-feather-trimmed cloak, sweating. If she'd asked anyone to explain what one was supposed to do on an Ever After beach, they would know she didn't know everything—and, therefore, that she wasn't ready yet to be the Queen of Hearts. And she would disappoint her mother and fail Wonderland. So she had just sat there. Sweating. And looking as much like a queen as possible.

She fingered her feathered cloak now, unsure whether she should pack it again.

Duchess was still talking. "...his name was Zephyrus, you know? Such a nice guy for a Wind. I was thinking that Zephyrus would be such a lovely name for my destined prince. Or Ryan."

Lizzie prepped herself for more Not Listening but found she didn't quite have the energy for it.

"I think I hear a hedgehog in trouble," Lizzie said. In a queenly manner—chin up and lips stiff—she walked to the ornate, heart-shaped door on her red-and-golden side of the dorm room. The door was just her height, and, to Duchess's perpetual irritation, Lizzie was the only one who could open it. But Duchess couldn't complain. After all, the magical door had been installed by special permission from Headmaster Grimm himself.

"*Excuse* me?" Duchess said. "I was in the middle of saying something."

"You're excused," Lizzie said, and walked through the door, shutting it firmly behind her.

At first there was a chilly nothing. Lizzie's pale skin prickled with mother-goosebumps as she waited for the magic. In the time it took to inhale once, a honey-scented fog rose up, swirled, and flushed away. At her back was the door, but it wasn't attached to a wall. Lizzie was no longer in the school, transported to the edge of the school grounds and into her own personal garden.

Lizzie exhaled and felt herself relax from heavy gold crown to gold-heeled red shoes. The air in the Wonderland Grove, scented by Wonderland plants and flowers, brought to mind wet bubble gum, cold fizzy soda, and half-eaten Turkish Delight.

Lizzie strolled the crystal gravel path between well-ordered flower beds, carefully pruned bushes, and perfectly shaped trees. She let her fingers trail over leaves and flowers, greeting with a touch the flora she had planted and tended. Their magic was dimmed in Ever After—the yellow polka-dotted mushrooms that popped up between tree roots couldn't change your size, for example—but at least they all looked and smelled like home. Lizzie closed her eyes and smiled. Here, she didn't have to worry if people were watching her to see if she was acting like the proper queen her mother wanted her to be.

A squeal cut through the air. Lizzie ran to the small shack where she kept gardening tools, croquet accessories, and a few hundred spare packs of Wonderlandian playing cards. Her pet hedgehog, Shuffle, was dangling from its roof by one tiny paw. Lizzie grabbed her and stroked the prickly beast as she shivered in terror.

"Apparently I was right about there being a hedgehog in trouble," she said. "How did you get all the way up there, Shuffle-bug?'

The hedgehog said nothing, because in Ever After, hedgehogs did not talk. No hedgehogs that Lizzie had seen, anyway, and she was quite observant of all things hedgehog. In Wonderland, a hedgehog—or anything, really—might talk one day and not the next, but the talking was always possible. In Ever After, things were what they were, little changing, little speaking (Duchess being a notable exception). So she had to just imagine Shuffle expressing her thanks for the rescue, go on to gush about how much she loved Lizzie, and then give her a recipe for a delicious marshmallow-lime cobbler.

"*Roink*," said Shuffle.

"Well, yes, I suppose you do talk," said Lizzie. "Just not the way I do."

"*Roink*," whispered Shuffle.

Lizzie smiled. "*Roink*," she whispered back.

"*Tweet*," said a sparrow from the top of the shed.

A finch landed next to it.

"*Tweet*," the finch said, and the sparrow nodded at it approvingly.

A robin fluttered down to join the group. "*Tweet*," said the robin.

"I don't speak Tweet," Lizzie said.

"*TWEET*," all three birds said in unison.

"Shoo," Lizzie said, waving a hand at the tiny flock. "Go away."

The sparrow cocked its head at her.

"Look, I've got nothing against birds," Lizzie said. "It's just that in Ever After, you guys tend to bring other, larger, more demanding things with you."

In the distance, somewhere between the last Wonderlandish plant and the official school grounds, someone shouted, "Lizzie!"

"And that"—Lizzie sighed—"is exactly what I'm talking about."

Apple White, the co-president of the Royal Student Council, was running toward her in impractical red-and-gold high heels. Like Lizzie, Apple was destined to become a queen. But Apple was *nice*. It made Lizzie uncomfortable. Hadn't the Queen of Hearts warned her daughter about what is expected of a queen?

♥

A queen stands and shouts in hollow rooms
when feeling faint,
for she is her own echo.

She is the thing that stands between
the been and the seen,
and pushes either side wide.
A queen stands for herself,
and by herself, and on her legs.
For legs are what make her stand.
But not four legs. Or forelegs.
She also stands for land. Her land. Wonderland.
Without land, one wonders where one would stand.
Especially queens.
In summary: Push. Shout. Stand. Be a queen.

❤

"Lizzie!" Apple called again, waving now, even though Lizzie was well aware of her own name, so repeating it like that seemed unnecessary. Perhaps it was an Ever After thing. She should try it out, to make the Ever Afterlings feel more comfortable.

"Apple!" Lizzie shouted, watching Apple jog the last few yards toward her.

"Hey," Apple said, a little out of breath but with absolutely no evidence of sweat, her perfect blond curls flowing around her plump cheeks and ready smile.

"Apple!" Lizzie shouted again.

"Yeah," Apple said, clearly a little confused about something, but Lizzie felt it wasn't worth worrying about.

"Apple!" Lizzie said again, because the third time's a charm.

"Hey, I tried to find you in your room, but you weren't there, and Duchess wouldn't tell me anything." Apple held out a hand, and the finch flitted down to perch on her finger, the sparrow and robin landing lightly on her shoulders.

"She didn't tell you *anything*?" Lizzie asked. "I find that remarkable. She's always telling things, whether one wants to hear them or not."

Apple laughed. "Yes, well, but she didn't tell me anything about where you were. I guess I didn't pay attention to the rest."

Lizzie nodded. Apple must have gotten the Not Listening lesson from her mother, too. Perhaps they were more similar than Lizzie had thought.

"Anyhoo," Apple said, "I sent my sweet little bird friends to find you so that I could offer you a most hexcellent opportunity to connect with the student body, be fairy helpful, and have an incredible shared experience!"

Then again, perhaps Apple and Lizzie were just as different from each other as Lizzie had originally supposed.

"I'm busy," Lizzie said.

Apple walked past her, taking in the Grove. "This is amazing! How many different species have you planted?"

"Twenty-two," Lizzie said, her voice softening against her will, "if you count the two types of flux-berry bushes, three different Wondodendron bushes, and several subspecies of Venus Fairy Traps."

Apple crouched by a fluxberry bush, gaping as the berries changed color before her eyes. "You should totally show this place off. I think people have the wrong idea about you."

"What idea do they have?" Lizzie asked.

"Oh, I don't know, like you're often yelling, talking about chopping off heads, and altogether imperious," Apple said, petting the furry purple Wondodendron leaves.

That sounded about right to Lizzie. Loud and imperious was how books about Wonderland usually described the Queen of Hearts. Perhaps she was doing an okay job of turning into Mother after all.

So why did the thought make her feel like the last kitten left in the local village's FREE KITTENS! box?

"But you're way softer than that," Apple said, leaning over to sniff a six-headed bellflower. "I mean, you must have a soft heart and an amazing amount of patience to create and tend a garden like this! In here, it's like I'm seeing the real Lizzie."

The real Lizzie? She had clearly let her guard down for Apple to say something like that. Feeling suddenly too visible and Not Perfect Enough, she put on her queen face.

"I do not have time for whatever helpy-sharey thing you have come to enlist me in, and trying to flatter me with interest in my Grove will not change my—"

"Oooh!" Apple squealed. "Hedgehogs! You have cute little hedgehogs in here!"

"Yes," Lizzie said, grabbing one of the little creatures. She started to pet it but stopped, not wanting to appear too soft. "They make excellent weapons." Lizzie tossed the hedgehog at the garden shed. Wonderlandian hedgehogs were nearly indestructible on the quill side. That's what made them such excellent croquet balls.

“Oh! Poor little thing!” Apple gasped, running to where the hedgehog was now stuck to the shed’s wall, its quills embedded in the wood. It gave Lizzie a little wave. Lizzie waved back. Clearly, Apple White didn’t know *everything* after all if she thought a Wonderlandian hedgehog could get hurt from a little hurling.

“Are you okay, little guy?” Apple said, prying the beast free.

It plopped to the ground and ambled into the nearest bush.

“It looks like he is okay.” Apple turned to Lizzie. “How could you? You—” Her eyebrows lifted with a thought. “Well, you are *destined* to sort of be a villain, aren’t you? I can’t fault you for following your destiny.”

“If you haven’t packed for the field trip, Apple, I think now would be a good time,” Lizzie said, her discomfort growing.

“Yes! Of course! The field trip!” Apple went through the motions of dusting herself off, even though she had absolutely no dirt on her. “That’s why I came! Headmaster Grimm needs you in the

Royal Student Council Room—for the, as you said, helpy-sharey thing."

"Oh!" Lizzie ran to the heart-shaped door that led back to her dorm room. "I'll meet you there."

Apple followed her. "I'll just—"

Lizzie whirled. "You'll just *nothing*!" No one but her had ever gone through the heart-shaped door.

Apple widened her eyes. She seemed almost afraid. And that was what Lizzie wanted, wasn't it? For people to be afraid of her?

Advice from one of her mother's cards:

❤

It is better to be gloved than bearded,
and better to be fearded than loved.

❤

Lizzie pulled on her black lace-hemmed gloves tighter. She affixed her most fearsome expression on her face and said to Apple, "You go on foot. I will meet you there."

She entered her dorm room and slammed the magic door behind her. Perhaps her mother would be proud. But instead of buzzing with power and joy, Lizzie felt a little lonely, as perhaps a hedgehog dangling from a garden shed might, no one near to hear its squeak.

Lizzie power-walked through the corridor, under the school's pillar trees, and down the stone steps. What could Headmaster Grimm want? She hadn't broken any rules, had she? One never knew in this un-peculiar land. After all, Maddie had nearly been banished just for trying to celebrate the Swappersnatch Gyre. True, the Uni Cairn had tragically broken right at her feet, releasing the Jabberwock, but that hadn't been Maddie's fault. Besides, Baba Yaga said the Jabberwock would likely curl up on a mountaintop somewhere far away and sleep for years.

Just as Lizzie reached the Royal Student Council Room door, Apple flew in through a window. That is, about a hundred songbirds carried her through and set her down beside Lizzie. With wings and beaks, they arranged her hair and clothes in perfect order before flying off.

"Thank you, my feathered friends!" Apple called after them. She smiled at Lizzie as if nothing uncomfortable had passed between them and opened the door.

The headmaster was pacing on the Student Council's dais, checking his gold pocket watch. He had a firm face, steel-gray hair, and an impressive gray suit. All that grayness seemed to declare to Lizzie, *I am serious!* Beside him, Daring Charming leaned against a desk, checking his teeth in the reflection of his sword. His blond hair was combed back and gelled to within an inch of its life. Briar Beauty lay on the floor between them, dressed in hot pink and snoring sweetly. What was going on?

Timely advice from one of Lizzie's mother's cards:

♥

When in doubt, shout!

♥

"WHAT IS THIS ABOUT, HEADMASTER GRIMM?" Lizzie shouted.

Grimm winced and rubbed his ears. "Er, yes. Well, Miss Hearts, I need your help."

Aha! The shouting had worked! Her mother was a genius.

Daring swooped into a royal bow and said, "Be still, my heart! A fair princess has arrived!" And, strangely, he was looking at Lizzie, not Apple.

Daring's complimentary, showy stuff seemed to set the Ever After girls' lashes aflutter, but Lizzie raised an eyebrow.

"If your heart were still, Mr. Charming," she said, "then you would be dead."

"Excuse me?" Daring asked.

"You said 'be still, my heart,' thereby commanding your heart to stop beating," said Lizzie. "If your heart is obedient, I expect you to drop dead at my feet."

Daring stared at Lizzie. He opened his mouth and seemed surprised when a chuckle escaped it. Lizzie smirked. She didn't often hear Daring Charming chuckle.

Apple pulled some papers out from under Briar's sleeping form and handed them to Lizzie.

"'*The Tragedy of Aquilona*,'" Lizzie read. "'A play by Milton Grimm.'"

"The performance will be a delightful and surprising part of our field trip to the North Wind tomorrow," Grimm said. "However, our Aquilona has never actually practiced her part, because at every rehearsal, the actress..." Grimm nodded to Briar snoring sweetly on the floor. "We need a replacement."

A chill skipped down Lizzie's spine. Prance about in an attitude of drama before a bunch of commoners? Surely her mother would not approve. People performed for a queen, not she for them.

But she remembered a piece of her mother's playing-card advice:

♥

If you want something done right,
you must do it yourself.

♥

Of course, her mother had followed up that advice with:

♥

So make sure you personally order servants
all by yourself to do what you want done.

♥

Pfft. Not a single servant in all of Ever After waited upon her. She was constantly having to do stuff herself. Stuff like thronework. And pillow fluffing. And hedgehog hurling.

"Why me?" Lizzie asked.

"You are a Royal," Grimm said. "For this part, we need a loyal Royal. *Ahem.* Rhyme intended."

"But the field trip is tomorrow already," said Lizzie.

Apple took her hand. Instinctively, Lizzie pulled it away. She wasn't used to being touched. Apple didn't seem the least troubled.

"Lizzie, what does it say outside the Castleteria?" Apple asked. "The little yellow sign by the door that was put up last week."

"'All students are henceforth required to forgo any and all activities of war, conflict, combat, and indeed all projectile-based activities upon entering this facility,'" Lizzie quoted. "'Comestibles taking to the air by means magical or otherwise—'"

"Wow," Daring interrupted.

"You were right, Ms. White," Headmaster Grimm said.

"About what?" Lizzie asked.

"About you," Apple said. "You can memorize stuff royally fast."

Lizzie shrugged. She did have all fifty-two of her mother's cards memorized. And lots of other stuff, too, like rules and poems and recipes for weapons-grade scones. A good memory was essential for a ruler of Wonderland. In such a topsy-turvy place, someone had to remember what things were, what they were not, and what they might possibly become.

"Here." Apple took the script from Lizzie and scribbled a new first line of the play:

Aquilona: Off with her head!

"Start that way," Apple said.

Lizzie smiled, just a little.

CHAPTER 2

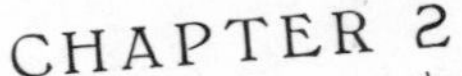

The Lone Tree on the Hill

Cedar Wood stood on the lakeshore, wiggling her toes nervously in the sand. They made little creaking noises when they moved, like a tree bending with the wind. Cedar glanced around to see if anyone noticed. Hopper Croakington II stood next to her in frog form, tapping his webbed foot in the water, staring back at the path for his racing partner, Daring Charming, to appear. He noticed Cedar looking at him and smiled.

"Pip-pip, my little wooden foe," he said. "Good luck! It must feel daunting to compete against a Charming and a Croakington, but worry not! This is just the qualifying race. You can lose with dignity."

Cedar nodded and tried to keep her mind blank. Being cursed to speak only the truth came with a side effect: sometimes blurting out whatever was in her head at any moment.

"One question, though," Hopper said, his voice dropping in volume. "A bit personal, though. Do you mind?"

"No," Cedar said, and then, despite her best efforts, added, "I mean, I would mind if it's something awkward, because then I'd have to tell you the truth."

Hopper blinked. "Right. So—"

Kitty Cheshire flickered into visibility next to him, saying nothing.

"Er... hello, Kitty. That is, as I was saying, Cedar." His eyes twitched back to Kitty, who clearly made him nervous. Kitty just kept smiling like always.

"Yes, Hopper?" Cedar prompted.

The son of the Frog Prince rallied. "Yes, I was going to ask: Do you float? As in, being made of wood, do you have to make an effort not to sink, or does it come naturally?"

"I naturally float," she said.

"Get ready, Cedar!" a voice called from behind.

Cerise Hood was running down the cobblestone path leading to the lake, red hood covering up her white-streaked dark brown hair, red cape flapping behind her. She seemed built for athletics—tall and broad; strong, solid thighs; and intense eyes focused on her destination.

"Where the deuce is Daring?" Hopper grumbled. "He's supposed to be fast!"

Cedar's toes wiggled more frantically. She patted herself, checking to make sure she was ready for her practice swim. Her dark, wavy hair was tucked into a bunch of braids. Her swimsuit was, almost literally, a *suit*. It started high at her neck and extended all the way to her wrists and ankles. She hadn't had time to smear on her waterproofing lotion this morning, and she needed to avoid swollen joints.

"It could be that Daring found a damsel in distress in one of the trees along the path," Kitty said.

"What?" sputtered Hopper.

"It could be that I accidentally left a blond wig in

one of those trees," Kitty said, examining her nails. "It could also be that I screamed 'help' from up there, you know, before popping over here."

Cedar jogged closer to the water as Cerise ran up beside her, handing off the tightly wound waterproof relay scroll.

"I have it!" said Cedar, gripping the relay scroll. "So do I just—"

"Yes!" said Cerise. "Jump in!"

Cedar dived into the lake. She didn't even submerge, her body easily floating on the water. She supposed the water was chilly, but cold didn't bother her. Or heat. Or anything really—well, except for fire. And axes. And wood chippers. And woodpeckers, beavers, termites...

"Swim!" Cerise shouted from shore, keeping pace with Cedar on land.

Cedar swam.

"You guys are already two minutes ahead of last year's relay winners," Raven Queen called out from the opposite shore. Dressed all in purple and black with silver-studded knee-high boots, Raven didn't resemble any coach Cedar had seen before. But she'd stuck an Ever After High baseball cap onto her purple-and-black locks to look more sporty.

Cedar held up a wooden thumb and kept kicking. With Raven as their coach, Cerise and Cedar's relay team naturally became known as the "Rebel" team. Since Legacy Day, everything was becoming "Rebel" this and "Royal" that. Raven had refused to sign the Storybook of Legends and promise to become the Evil Queen like her mother, and now it seemed everyone had to take sides. Apple White, who had been devastated by Raven's refusal to sign, now led the Royals, those who wanted their fairytale destinies and pledged to someday live out their inherited stories exactly as scripted. The Rebels were following Raven's lead, vowing to write their own destinies, no matter what path their parents took.

Cedar's story wasn't as bad as some, but as the next Pinocchio, she was supposed to make lots of bad choices that would bring heartache to her kind, loving father before eventually getting turned into a real girl. To Cedar, that story never felt "just right," as Blondie Lockes would say.

"Go, Cedar, go!" a voice called from directly above her. Cedar flipped onto her back to see Cupid hovering, her pink hair billowing in the breeze made by her flapping feathered wings.

"You are amazing," Cupid said. "I'm wicked bad in the water. But you make swimming look enchantingly easy."

"It is easy," Cedar said, and then, "I wish I hadn't said that. It sounds boasty, and that's not what I mean at all." She paused. "I also wish I hadn't said that."

Cupid giggled.

"Cupid, leave her alone," shouted Cerise from the shore. "She's trying to go fast, and you're distracting her!"

"Right! Sorry! Swim enchantingly, easily on!"

Cupid flitted off, and Cedar turned back onto her stomach, paddling with all her might. Cerise was counting on her, and Cedar really hated disappointing people. It made her feel terrible, but because of her honesty "blessing" from the Blue-Haired Fairy, she was compelled to *tell* people exactly how she felt. Cedar was a fan of the truth in general, but by the godmother's wand, was it ever awkward having to volunteer the truth *all* the time! It kind of made you a weirdo.

"Shore!" and "Rock!" two people yelled at the same time, so it sounded like "Shock!" Cedar looked up midstroke and was in fact shocked as her head slammed into a large stone on the lakeshore.

Feet splashed into the water, hands helping her up and out onto the sand.

"Are you okay?" Raven asked.

"Fine, good," Cedar said. "Just embarrassed."

"There's nothing to be embarrassed about," Raven said. "You guys are still, like, a minute ahead of the best recorded time, and all you have left is the biking part."

"Where's Sparrow?" Cerise said, scanning the lakeside path.

Cedar spotted fresh bicycle tracks.

"Looks like he was here but took off," Cedar said.

"This is a disaster," said Cerise with an irritated huff and puff.

Cedar ducked her head. "Sorry." Raven had suggested that Cedar partner with Cerise and Sparrow Hood for the Glass Slipper's annual Tiara-thalon, an opportunity to get out of her art studio and make more friends. But here she was spoiling it from the start.

Raven put her hand on Cedar's shoulder. "Cerise isn't mad at you."

"What?" Cerise said, voice cracking a little. "No, no, Cedar. I'm sorry. I'm just mad at myself for thinking that I could count on Sparrow."

Dexter Charming, the younger of the Charming brothers at the school, pedaled on his royal-blue mountain bike to the group of wet, grumpy, and rebellious girls.

"Hey, what's upon-ing?" Dexter asked, skidding to a halt. "Is your practice run over? I wanted to see if I could keep pace with Sparrow."

"Looks like Sparrow got bored waiting and took off," Raven said.

"Tragic ending," Dexter said, adjusting his thick-rimmed glasses. "Do you need to borrow my bike?"

"Yeah, we do," Cedar said, unable to keep her thoughts from bursting out. "If our team's biker doesn't cross the finish line by noon, then we won't qualify to compete in the Tiara-thalon. But... you're a Royal. I wouldn't think that a Royal would want to help Team Rebel."

Dexter shrugged. "Who cares? I mean, maybe

you care. I mean, maybe I should care…but I don't know. I feel like things are getting out of control around here, and can't a Royal still like a Rebel?…Or not *like* like, or maybe *like* like—I don't know what I'm talking about. But you can still borrow my bike for your practice and for the race itself, if you want."

Raven smiled at Dexter, and Cedar thought she saw him blush.

"Will you ride it, Raven?" Cedar asked.

"I would…" Raven examined her boots. "Should have worn my studded sneakers."

Dexter said, "I'll do it for you, Raven."

"Really?" said Cerise. "For the…er…Rebel team?"

Dexter rubbed his brown hair as if trying to smooth it flat, but it stood straight up in front. "Maybe our team will show some people that the whole Rebel and Royal thing doesn't have to be that big of a deal."

Cedar handed him the relay scroll, still wet from the lake, and he took off. Fast.

"He's good," Cedar said, watching Dexter pick up speed.

"Yes," Raven said. "Yes, he is."

"Hey, Raven," Cedar said. "Do you *like* like Dexter?"

Cerise made a muffled grunt that turned into a cough, and Raven blinked.

There was a moment of silence, and Cedar wasn't entirely sure what was going on. It could be that Raven didn't want to answer, because Cedar, being who she was, would end up telling everyone. People only shared stuff with Cedar once everyone else already knew. Even standing there under the candy-blue sky, part of a relay team, Cedar felt locked up and alone.

No one was talking, and that made Cedar lonelier than ever. Into the silence, Cedar said, "I don't want to be the lone tree on the hill."

Raven wrapped her arms around Cedar in a tight hug. "No worries, little sapling," she said. "I will always be your forest."

Cedar smiled. She noticed the creaking noise her face made whenever it carved itself into a different expression, and pulled away from Raven, not wanting her to hear it, too.

"Speaking of forests," Cedar said. "We've got a

field trip tomorrow, to the Dark Mountains, right? I'm running low on paints, and I was hoping to gather some berries there to make more. Will you guys help?"

"Totally," Cerise said.

"Sure thing," said Raven, and then her brow furrowed. "Unless Apple needs me first. She has some surprise something she's doing at the field trip that she said she might need help with if Briar falls asleep."

"That's okay," Cedar said, and it was true, but there was still a part of her that felt just the tiniest bit un-okay. There always was.

CHAPTER 3

MADDIE ~~CONVERSES POLITELY WITH~~ THE NARRATOR Interrupts

THE MORNING OF THE FIELD TRIP DAWNED AS yellow-gold as leprechaun treasure.

Ooh, Narrator, that's a pretty image! Well, if leprechaun treasure is pretty. Is it? I haven't seen any before. Oooh! What if leprechaun treasure is actually, like, something really, really gross? That wouldn't be pretty.

Madeline Hatter, you know I can't talk to you.

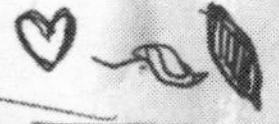

Characters aren't supposed to be able to hear the Narrator, and it's so awkward for me that you can.

Mmhm, but that's called a simile, isn't it, Narrator? When you say that something is like something else to paint a picture in the reader's mind? The sun was like an egg frying on the sky, or the tea was as hot as dragon's fire, or the crab juggled like a six-legged man?

Yes, a simile, exactly. But I must get back to the narration. Many things are about to happen—

Ooh! What things? Tell, tell!

Well, the drama will really start when a frightening—wait! You're not going to get me to spoil the story, Maddie, not this time!

Aw, Narrator, you're cute as a whole bag of buttons. You're as cleverful as books that read themselves. This simile game is fun! You're as invisibilish as a ghost playing hide-and-seek. You're—

Shh. No more interruptions, please. I must return to the narration. *Ahem*.

CHAPTER 4

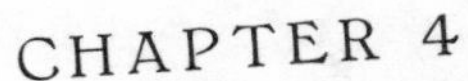

THE TRAGEDY OF ~~AQUILONA~~ Lizzie

THE MORNING OF THE FIELD TRIP DAWNED AS yellow-gold as leprechaun treasure. The great castle of Ever After High seemed gilded with the light. Songbirds swooped and sang, butterflies danced with fairies, goblins yawned and crept into the cellar to sleep.

In her dorm, Lizzie dressed carefully, as always, arranging her red-and-black hair under her crown. She peered at her mirror, painting a red heart around her left eye. Her mother bore a heart-shaped birthmark. Lizzie was born without the birthmark, so she drew one on each day to be a little more like her mother.

She slipped her pack of playing cards into her pocket and didn't bother to take anything else. Except for the butter knife. You could never be sure.

A field trip day was a bubbling cauldron of excitement. The corridors were raucous, the laughter constant. By the time Lizzie marched and shouted her way through the school and out to the wishing well, there was an enormous line. She could tell which students were going to visit the West Wind by their attire—all swimsuits and flip-flops, reeking of coconut sunscreen. In front of Lizzie, two fairy-godmothers-in-training prattled on endlessly about the supposedly spectacular hollowed-out mountain palace the East Wind lived in.

At last it was Lizzie's turn.

"The North Wind," Lizzie said to the fairy godmother directing traffic at the wishing well. She waved her wand, and Lizzie jumped in. After a rush of sparkly darkness and freezing-hot breezes, Lizzie hopped out of another wishing well in the Dark Mountains beyond the Dark Forest. She looked around for a royal sedan chair carried by four servants (preferably card soldiers), but when none appeared, she was forced to trudge up the mountainside like the rest of her class.

"Hey, Lizzie!" Madeline Hatter hopped up on one foot. Maddie was dressed in layers of turquoise and purple, which matched her hair colors. Her striped and polka-dotted skirts flounced with each hop. "Hop with me!"

Maddie held out her hand. Lizzie's hand twitched, almost reaching back. But readily her mind called up her mother's advice:

♥

A ship is only as floaty as its leakiest timber,
and friends are the leakiest timber of all.
Sail not on the Friend Ship, Lizzie,
lest you drown in an ocean of tears!

♥

"A princess of Wonderland never hops," said Lizzie.

She walked through the forests of the mountain path alone.

No blue-skinned North Wind (in swimming trunks or otherwise) waited at the top of the mountain. Instead an amphitheater of log benches faced a small stage.

"Ooh, are we watching a play?" said Maddie. "Tea-riffic!"

"This is just right," said Blondie Lockes, settling onto a bench alongside other Royals, including Briar Beauty and Holly O'Hair.

Lizzie started for the backstage. Behind the curtain, Apple and Daring were slipping on costumes over their clothes.

"Break an egg," Lizzie said to Apple.

"Excuse me?" Humphrey Dumpty squeaked as he passed by, his white-pale cheeks turning so pink he seemed to be dyed.

"It's *leg*," Apple whispered. "Break a *leg*."

"Oh," said Lizzie. "That's actually much better."

"Now, students, quiet down, please," Headmaster Grimm was saying on the other side of the curtain. "You're probably wondering, 'Where is the North Wind, and what is this beautiful forest amphitheater?' And perhaps even, 'I bet Headmaster Grimm is skilled in the theater arts, and when will we see an example of his genius?' "

Someone in the audience shouted something Lizzie couldn't make out.

"No, Mr. Hood, you will not be able to meet and speak with the North Wind, as you did last year with the West Wind—or the *beach dude*, as you call him. The Winds *are* part of the magnificent heritage and history in Ever After. But the reason why you can't speak with the North Wind herself is a tragedy, one I fear you *all* need to hear, especially now."

Lizzie straightened her crown. It wasn't her tall gold one with ruby red hearts that just screamed "Wonderland" (sometimes literally). This was the costume crown of Princess Aquilona, and while a shoddy representation of true royalty, it was still a crown and should be respectably oriented.

"To best communicate why the North Wind, though present, can no longer speak with humans, I have written a play," said the headmaster. "Behold, *The Tragedy of Aquilona*, performed by the Ever After High Royal Players!"

The curtain rose to thunderous applause. Faybelle Thorn shouted "Boo!" so loudly and brightly it sounded like a cheer. Lizzie, flustered, yelled the first line of the play that Apple had written for her, and the crowd silenced.

Grimm lifted his arm up grandly and intoned, "Long ago, Boreas, the great North Wind, ruled the mountaintops."

The headmaster's voice was suddenly high-pitched and trembly, like someone trying to sing soprano who really shouldn't.

"Why is he talking like that?" Lizzie heard Maddie whisper loudly from the audience. "Is someone choking him?"

Daring marched forward with his typical easy-going yet kingly demeanor. He was dressed in a white billowy wind costume that didn't completely cover his muscles. Some of the girls in the audience squealed.

"I, Boreas, rule the winds of the North!" Daring announced.

"The nature of wind is to be wild," Grimm said.

Apple rushed onstage in a fringed blue cloak. The audience applauded, several shouting, "Apple White! It's Apple White!"

"I am the wild wind," Apple howled. A few

birds in the surrounding forest sang out in happy response.

"Shh, she's not talking to you," Maddie whispered at the birds.

"But Boreas was the shepherd of all the winds of the North, directing them hither and yon," Grimm continued in a tight, squeaky voice.

"I shepherd you," Daring said, pointing at Apple. "Go hither! And yon!"

Someone in the audience actually did yawn at this point. Lizzie had to admit the lines Grimm had written were a little flat.

"Boreas's companion in his great work was his daughter, Princess Aquilona," Grimm said.

"I am Princess Aquilona," Lizzie said, her fists on her hips.

The line was longer, but Lizzie deemed it too boring to finish. The headmaster waited for the rest, but Lizzie just folded her arms.

Grimm cleared his throat. "Princess Aquilona was destined to take on her father's responsibilities, but she refused."

"I will not take on your responsibilities," Lizzie said, pointing at Daring.

Daring opened his mouth in a parody of shock. "Ridiculous! It is your destiny! To deny your destiny would destroy everything!"

"Then I shall leave forever and go where the North winds cannot travel!"

The audience gasped. Lizzie smiled. Maybe this strutting-about-a-stage business wasn't so bad. She glanced at the anxious face of Headmaster Grimm for inspiration and decided to make up a few more lines. "I will not be the daughter who does nothing but watch her wrinkled father writhe with the agony of age and death, your voice slowly becoming more nasal and oddly high-pitched, as if you were being strangled by a possum or a really weak octopus or something."

Daring pressed his lips together, valiantly attempting to hold back a laugh, and ultimately failing.

He covered his face with his hands, and Lizzie knew she must do something to save the play.

"Do not blubber so, Father. When you stop weeping, I will be gone," Lizzie said.

Headmaster Grimm cleared his throat and lowered his voice to its natural pitch.

"And so, Aquilona ran away to be selfish,

ignoring her great destiny so she could do whatever selfish things she wanted. Selfishly." Headmaster Grimm looked significantly at Raven Queen, who was sitting in the back row of the amphitheater. Raven rolled her eyes.

"Meanwhile," Grimm continued, "Boreas got old."

Daring pulled a white beard from his pocket, stuck it to his face, and began to shuffle around.

"And died," said the headmaster.

"I die!" Daring collapsed to the floor in a heap.

"Without a shepherd, the winds tore up trees and hassled hills."

Apple, her wind cloak flapping, danced around, spinning and leaping across the stage, shouting "*Whoosh*" and "*Boom*" and "*Rustle rustle rustle*."

"The winds, wanting a shepherd, blew all the way to Aquilona. But Aquilona was too selfish to claim her destiny, as previously mentioned."

Apple and Lizzie spun in the circles they had practiced, but Lizzie was not as good at remembering steps as words, and the choreographed dance turned into a sprawling slap-fight. From the floor, "dead" Boreas started to chuckle.

Lizzie shrugged into a ragged blue cloak like Apple's.

"In her struggle against the wind, Aquilona was stripped of her body, becoming wind herself," said Grimm. "She had no body after that, and without a mouth, you can't talk. And that is sad. And it was her own fault. So be warned: Those who run from their own destiny just might be chased down and turned into wind." He cleared his throat again and added grandly, "Or something! The end."

The headmaster began to applaud, and about half the audience followed his lead. The other half just silently glared, so Lizzie glared back until the curtain fell.

Daring laughed, his fake beard wiggling. "'A really weak octopus?' I just about lost it out there!"

"You did lose it," Lizzie said.

"Great job improvising, Lizzie," Apple said. "Turning his laughter into tears was perfect."

"Yes, turning laughter into tears is a skill I learned from my mother."

"I think your mother would have loved your performance," Apple said, patting Lizzie on the shoulder and heading off the stage. Lizzie held her breath, surprised by a knot of emotion in her throat.

Daring followed Apple. Lizzie heard him mutter "strangled by a possum" under his breath, letting out another chuckle.

Lizzie stayed in the quiet behind the curtain, fingering her ragged blue cloak. She was a princess separated from her kingdom, just like Aquilona. All portals between Ever After and Wonderland had been magically sealed ever since Raven's mother, the Evil Queen, went royally off script and infected it with some magical contagion. If the greedy witch hadn't rebelled and tried to take over everyone else's story, Lizzie would be home right now.

Unlike Aquilona, Lizzie yearned for her destiny. But cut off as she was, how could she become like her magnificent mother? If only she could be so scary and large and...and loud! If only she could live with Mother at home, where everything made its own kind of wonderlandiful sense, and rabbits talked and people didn't unless they were offering you cake and tea, Your Highness.

What if she was trapped in Ever After forever after? One day her mother would need Lizzie to take over, and if she couldn't get back...would a pack of wild playing cards worm their way into Ever After and steal away her body, just like the winds did to Aquilona? Would they carry Lizzie back, bodiless and mouthless, as insubstantial as a wind? The thought was terrifying.

She wished she had brought her hedgehog, Shuffle, with her. Even if it was unqueenly, just then Lizzie really needed a cuddle.

CHAPTER 5

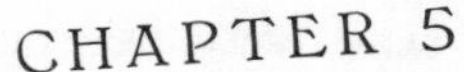

A BABY BANDERSNATCH

When the curtain lowered, Cedar was holding her wooden hands before her, though she couldn't bring herself to clap.

"Um, that was a bit obvious, and I can't lie," Cedar said.

"Yep," said Raven Queen, her shoulders slumped.

Cedar dropped her hands. "Headmaster Grimm might as well have called the play *This Story Is a Warning to All Rebels about the Evil Consequences of Not Fulfilling Your Destiny—I'm Looking at You, Raven Queen.*"

Raven nodded. But she un-slumped her shoulders. "I'm not going to let him get me down anymore. I *am* okay with myself and my destiny-less future, and I'm ninety percent sure that I won't be turned into wind if I don't turn evil and try to poison Apple. Even so, I could really use a laugh about now. I'm going to go find Maddie. Be right back."

Raven sprang away.

On the bench in front of Cedar, Blondie Lockes whispered something to Briar Beauty. Briar snorted, bending at the waist and wiping laugh tears from under her pink crownglasses. Blondie giggled, hiccuping. Just hearing her friends laugh brought a creaky smile to Cedar's face.

"Hey, what are you guys laughing about?" Cedar asked, plopping down beside them, her legs clicking against the hard bench.

"Well, Blondie was just telling me—" Briar began, but Blondie elbowed her. "*Oof!* Blondie, what are you . . ."

Blondie nodded in Cedar's direction, opening her eyes wide in warning.

"Oh, right," said Briar. "Um, nothing, Cedar.

Never mind. I just...sorry, girl, I'd better not repeat it to you. You understand."

"Sure, I understand." Whatever it was, it was a secret. "Although I get why no one wants to share secrets with me, when you do that, I still feel whittled to my heartwood. Sorry! I couldn't help saying that. And also, Blondie, there's a huge black cricket stuck in your curls. Sorry, couldn't help that, either! Never mind. I'm going."

Cedar ran off, Blondie's horrified shrieks fading behind her.

A few minutes later, Raven found Cedar knee-deep in the scratchiest, meanest, most villainous blackberry bramble Cedar had ever found.

"What's up, Cedar?" Raven asked.

Cedar wiped her dry wooden cheeks. She felt like she was crying. A knot of sadness tightened in her chest where her heart would be, running up into her head with a burning, uncomfortable heat. But no tears fell from her carved eyes. It was just her magic-enhanced imagination.

"Oh, you know," Cedar said, shrugging as if it were unimportant. "Puppet girl is cursed to blab, so *real* girls can't confide in puppet girl, yadda yadda yadda."

"I'm sorry, Cedar," said Raven. "But . . . hey, why are you in the middle of a blackberry bush?"

Cedar held up a handful of dark purple berries. "For paints, remember? I like to make my own. The colors are rich and natural and uneven and unexpected and just luscious! I found some black walnuts—their shells make beautiful black paint—and I even found some turmeric for yellow."

She reached into the thicket for a fat berry, so ripe it was black. Thorns big as shark teeth scratched at her brown arms, but Cedar didn't feel a thing. She didn't even feel a thing as something lurking inside the bramble took offense at her probing arm and attacked. When she lifted her hand up again, the something was stuck to her. Furry and fat, like a dog-sized guinea pig, the thing's two rows of teeth-big-as-thorns were now clamped to her forearm.

"Oh," said Cedar.

"Whoa!" Raven stumbled back with her hands out, as if ready to cast a spell. "What *is* that?"

Cedar shook her arm, but the beastie didn't

budge. A pale green gas leaked from its nether end, and the girls turned their heads and gagged.

"That... smells... like a *very* bad ending!" said Raven.

Cedar nodded. She *could* smell things (unfortunately, at the moment)—or at least, the magic that made her alive enhanced her ability to *imagine* smells, just as it allowed her to imagine joy and sadness, fear and excitement. But the magical imagination didn't allow her to experience sickness or pain—not even from the bite of the toothy creature clamped to her wooden arm. Still, that didn't mean she wanted to keep it there.

She fought her way out of the blackberry bramble, and they ran back toward the amphitheater.

"Headmaster Grimm! Madam Baba Yaga! Help!" Raven called out.

"Um... something appears to be biting my arm," Cedar said softly. "I didn't want to make a fuss, but..."

"What is that creature?" the headmaster said, his normally robust voice a mere whisper.

Baba Yaga floated forward, sitting cross-legged on her levitating stool. Her fierce eyes and determined nose and chin made her seem formidable. She pushed her tangled gray hair out of her face and squinted. "It looks like a bandersnatch, but that's impossible. There are no bandersnatches in Ever After."

Baba Yaga took a deep sniff of the pale green gas and then smacked her lips as if trying to identify a peculiar taste. Cedar winced. She heard Raven behind her trying not to gag too loudly.

"It *smells* like a bandersnatch," said Baba Yaga. "Or perhaps a thing wearing bandersnatch perfume."

"Yeah, that's sure to be the hot new scent this spring," said Briar, her nose plugged. "Bandersnatch perfume—for those special occasions when you want everyone to run away screaming."

"Um...could you maybe pry it off my arm?" Cedar asked.

"Hold your piglets, Ms. Wood. I'm still investigating," said the old sorceress.

Cedar nodded. And considered maybe lying down and dying on the spot. All her classmates were staring at her. And she had a smelly, sticky beastie clamped on her arm. Cedar imagined the warm prickle of a blush in her cheeks, but she knew her cheeks remained the same shade of warm brown.

"Doesn't that hurt?" she heard someone whisper.

"Those teeth are, like, an inch long," someone else whispered.

"Yeah, but she's, you know, made of wood."

"I never realized she was *that* weird."

"No kidding."

Cedar closed her eyes. Maybe if she tried really hard, she could grow into a tree and disappear behind a wall of leaves. Or maybe if she tried even harder, she could wish herself real like everyone else.

Please, please, please, Blue-Haired Fairy, please make me real now. Please don't make me wait any longer or follow a choiceless destiny to get my Happily Ever After. I just want to be normal. Please . . .

"Aha!" Baba Yaga shouted, startling Cedar's eyes open. The old sorceress mumbled a spell, then shot mustard-yellow light from her hands, and the bandersnatch began to vibrate. With a noise like a soufflé popping in the oven, the bandersnatch transformed.

"Oh!" said Ashlynn Ella. "A fuzzy, cuddly bear cub! Look at you, sweetie pie!"

She pranced forward and began to pet the cub. Which was still clamped to Cedar's arm.

"The question is," said Baba Yaga, "why was a bear cub transformed into a baby bandersnatch?"

"It's so cute!" said Ashlynn. "What are you saying, cutie sweetie-bear? I can't hear you when you've got an arm in your mouth."

"Uh..." said Cedar.

"But...isn't a bear cub, I don't know, dangerous or something?" Raven asked.

"Not nearly so dangerous as your basic fire-breathing dragon," said Daring, "of which I've battled dozens."

Several girls sighed dreamily.

"Who's scared of a teddy bear?" said Faybelle Thorn.

"I am and not embarrassed to admit it," said Hunter Huntsman, putting his fists on his hips. His hair—styled in a sort of relaxed Mohawk—rippled in the breeze. "A bear cub is extremely dangerous not for itself but for who is nearby."

"Like it's mother?" Apple squeaked, staring at something in the distance.

"Exactly, Apple, like the cub's mother," said Hunter. "Um...Ash, you should probably leave it alone. If its mother is nearby, she might misunderstand and fear we're harming her cub."

"Nonsense," said Ashlynn, scratching behind the cub's ears. "I'd just explain to her the situation."

"In my experience," Daring said, sharpening his sword on a rock, "a mother bear mauls first and listens to lengthy explanations second."

"Uh..." said Cedar again. Baby bear/bandersnatch drool had covered her arm and was dripping into a puddle at her feet.

"Hey, bear," whispered Blondie, crouching down and whispering in its ear. "Where's the porridge? You and your folks have an unsupervised porridge-filled cabin stashed nearby? Come on, talk."

"Why a baby bandersnatch?" Baba Yaga was asking herself, tapping the wart on her chin with her finger.

"We should let the little fella go," Hunter said. "The momma bear could be mighty angry."

"Or she could, oh, I don't know, also be transformed into a bandersnatch?" suggested Apple.

Apple pointed. Cedar looked.

A momma-bear-sized bandersnatch was lumbering

toward them, drool oozing out of her spiky-toothed jaw, trails of curling green gas sputtering from her nether end, generally resembling a giant people-eating guinea pig that was having a really bad day.

She stood on her hind legs and grunt-roared.

"Off with its head!" shouted Lizzie.

Daring drew his sword with a flash of steel and an equally brilliant flash of a white-toothed smile.

"I'm just the prince for the job," he said.

Lizzie smiled in surprise that someone was actually taking her seriously. Daring winked.

Students screamed and ran, but Cedar still had a bear cub latched to her arm. She yanked at it. "Come on, teddy-weddy, just let go of me, please."

"Fear not," said Daring. "I'll protect you!"

"As will I!" Hunter loosed the ax from his belt and struck the Huntsman-To-the-Rescue Pose, fists on hips, shoulders thrown back, feet apart. From nowhere, trumpets blasted a heroic fanfare. Hunter nodded to the magical trumpet tune. He had, no doubt, heard it many times in his life.

"Headmaster, I don't like this," said Baba Yaga, sniffing the air.

"Don't be alarmed, fair—uh, noble sorceress," said Hunter. "We are well-schooled in defending damsels—uh, anyone—from ferocious beasts."

The trees around the momma bandersnatch shook. Yellow eyes lit up the shadows, and a herd of bandersnatches lumbered out. Cedar counted . . . nine, ten, eleven . . . *fourteen* full-size bandersnatches, eyes glowing, mouths drooling, nethers gassing.

"Yes, that's what I don't like," Baba Yaga muttered.

Students began to scream.

"Magic is afoot!" cried Professor Jack B. Nimble.

Baba Yaga cast a magical barrier, encaging the bevy of bandersnatches inside a sparking yellow dome. The bandersnatches grunt-roared and clawed at the magical cage, sparks flying from their paws. Cedar wondered if the cage would hold.

"Students, get out of here!" Headmaster Grimm shouted.

"Help?" Cedar whispered.

"Let! Go!" said Raven. She zapped the bear cub with a bolt of purple magic, and the cub squeaked and opened its jaws. Cedar set it down, and it galloped back toward the momma bandersnatch.

And still the bandersnatches advanced, the magical dome sparking and twinkling, its yellow color fading.

"Go straight to Ever After High and do not leave that building until we return!" the headmaster shouted.

Mr. Badwolf dropped to all fours and transformed into his wolf shape, growling, his black lips trembling. He turned to howl something over his shoulder.

"Okay!" Cerise Hood answered back. She grabbed Raven's and Cedar's hands. "We need to get out of here. Now."

Cedar had never run so fast, partly because she was fleeing a mountaintop crawling with strange, growling, sticky, pungent monsters, but mostly because Cerise Hood was dragging her along at her own speed. And by the Blue-Haired Fairy's wand, that girl could run.

Madeline Hatter was skipping beside them.

"How are you skipping so fast?" Cedar asked, her words shaking with the force of her pounding feet.

"I don't know," Maddie said, bounding along, not at all out of breath. "I'd never tried speed-skipping before, but I thought this was the perfect time for it. I am now making a point to not ask you if speed-skipping is impossible in Ever After, because if it is, Cedar will have to tell me the truth and then it might stop working. So, what's going on, anyway?"

"We're not really sure," said Raven.

"Oh, good," said Maddie. "It's a relief when everyone else is as confuse-boggled as I am. I feel so cozy, like a bundle of puppies in a box."

"That's cozy?" Cerise huffed.

Maddie giggled. "It is if you're one of the puppies. And if you're confuse-boggled, of course. If you *know* you're in a box, then you start thinking things like 'why am I in a box?' and 'who put me here?' It just makes you nervous. I, for one, am glad we don't know we're in a box."

"*Oh*," Cedar said in a small voice. She didn't feel cozy at all.

CHAPTER 6

MADDIE ~~TRIES~~ FAILS TO JUST LISTEN QUIETLY

THE JOURNEY DOWN THE MOUNTAINSIDE was fraught with peril, mostly in the form of Briar Beauty. Apple White naturally took the lead, searching for sensible paths through thickets and down ledges. But Briar, her best friend forever after, was constantly picking more "interesting" paths.

"Come on, this way looks fun!" she said, grabbing Apple's hand and nearly vaulting with her over a cliff.

"Briar," said Apple, "perhaps a good goal would be not only to make it down the mountain, but also make it down alive."

"Don't be such a snooze." Briar lifted her crown-glasses to look her friend in the eye. "We're fleeing a bloat of bandersnatches, hurtling ourselves over unfamiliar terrain in a gasping fight for our very lives. This is, like, the best chapter ever after."

Briar grabbed a clutch vine and swung over a boulder.

Blondie Lockes held up her MirrorPad, filming Briar's daring moves and the dark shadows of the forest, and narrating in an ominous voice. This adventure was going to make a hexcellent episode of her MirrorCast show.

Madeline Hatter, as the only character who could hear the Narrator, was listening intently to the narration. But she did *not* interrupt. Because she had promised so faithfully she would not interrupt anymore.

That's right, cutie-patootie Narrator. You'll get no interrupting from me!

Ashlynn and Hunter kept "accidentally" brushing against each other as they walked, the backs of their fingers knocking together, their knuckles grasping, until Duchess Swan finally yelled, "Oh, just hold hands, already! Everyone knows you're dating!"

Humphrey Dumpty mumbled rhymes to himself as he walked—or wobbled, actually, his thin legs trembling dangerously with each step. For the field trip, he'd completely encased himself in a thick coat of Bubble Wrap. Just in case.

Raven Queen and Dexter Charming chatted as they jogged through the woods, playing a game called What's More Evil?

"A pinecone is more evil than a pine needle," Raven said.

"Really?" Dexter said. "What about pine needle versus pine sap?"

"Um, pine sap," said Raven. "So what's more evil, pine sap or squirrel?"

"Squirrel, definitely," said Dexter.

Kitty Cheshire was—

"Wishing to remain private, thank you," said Kitty.

Oh! I didn't realize Kitty could hear me, too!

"Me neither!" said Maddie. "That's breakfast-tastic, Kitty!"

Kitty hissed.

Very well. *Ahem.* Lizzie Hearts kept to the front of the group, keeping pace with Apple, correcting all her decisions, and declaring things like "This way!" and "That way!" and "By the way!"

"Relax, Lizzie," said Briar. "Apple is in charge, and she's leading us just fine."

"One does not order a crown princess of Wonderland to relax!" said Lizzie.

"This isn't Wonderland, so stop trying to rule."

Lizzie stiffened everywhere—her shoulders, her spine, and especially her upper lip—and wished very hard she had an army of card soldiers at her command.

Madeline Hatter had begun playing leapfrog with Hopper Croakington II. Or so she thought. Hopper wasn't actually playing.

He's not? Oh, thank you, Narrator. That's why

he keeps glaring with the beady eyes and pouty lip and grumbles of "Why do you keep vaulting over my head?"

Maddie! You were doing so well at not interrupting.

Why, thank you, Narrator, dear, and that is why I'm barely interrupting at all. I learn so much about narration by listening to you, you know, such as how you're using this travel time to give us updates on all the main characters, revealing more about them through descriptions of what they're doing. How cleverful!

Thank you. It's a basic technique I learned in Narration School. But I really shouldn't—

I know, I know, no more with the barging and the pestering and the mouth flippy-flapping. Narrate on! Ooh, wait, one quickish question first.

Maddie, you know I can't answer your questions.

Well, it's just that a baby bear was bandersnatched, and either the big bears were bandersnatched, too, or there were actual true bandersnatches back there. And a bandersnatch is a Wonderlandian beast! So what are they doing in Ever After?

Um...

You know, don't you?

Er...

Come on, just a hint. You're so good at accidentally giving me teensy-weensy-bleensy hints.

Not this time! This Narrator refuses to be tricked! This Narrator is a shining example of rule-following technique! So, let's fast forward.... The group finally reached bottom, made their way to the nearest wishing well, and wishing-welled it back to Ever After High. Okay, then, next chapter!

CHAPTER 7

~~A Twisted Kind of Wonder~~ RUN!

The great Jabberwock, terror of Wonderland, was still grumpy. It had been having such a frabjous dream of buttered bandersnatches when that crashing, smashing, bitter-bashing sound of a broken magic mirror had torn it away. Now it was awake and trapped in Ever After, a land entirely without bandersnatches, buttered or otherwise.

The bears had tasted too sweet, not nearly crunchy enough, and more like meat than madness. After the Jabberwock's magic melted away their bear-ness and filled in the holes with bandersnatch-ness, the taste had improved, though they still got stuck in the Jabberwock's gullet.

Too long it had been caged, trapped, and cut off from Wonderland. Its magic needed recharging.

The Jabberwock leaped from treetop to treetop. It could fly, but flight was exhausting in the thin air of this not-home place, and it was still tired. It yawned angrily, breath stinking of decaying magic and the meat of false bandersnatches.

The beast had gotten lost from Wonderland long ago, but its bowels were still pulsing with wonder, though a rotting, twisted kind of wonder. Its hot breath slurped and crawled out of its mouth, transforming whatever it touched. The Jabberwock exhaled, and the tree bending beneath its weight brightened to a vivid green and sprouted pumpkins instead of pinecones. The tree was not exactly what it would have been in Wonderland, but at least it was closer. Could the beast alter this un-peculiar land entirely? Make it more like home? No, not without more power.

The Jabberwock caught a whiff of tiny Alice-things fleeing the far edge of the forest. It smiled, its gray lips curling around a huge set of buckteeth.

The Card, the Cat, and the Hatter were nearby. It could smell them. It could feel the fresh Wonder emanating from their bodies. Wonder it would need if it was to shape this world to its liking.

The Jabberwock heaved up and took flight. Its massive, batlike wings shook the air, its deep purple shadow sending the forest creatures shivering into holes. It dived, mouth open, claws out ready to seize, when suddenly the Card, the Cat, and the Hatter disappeared into a wishing well. Vanished. Too fast, as if the story they were in had suddenly sped up, pages flipping faster than the narration should allow.

The Jabberwock reeled in the air, skronking with rage. It would stalk these Wonderlings. It would follow them wherever they went, and one by one it would squeeze every last drop of Wonder from their bones.

And then, maybe, it would eat them.

CHAPTER 8

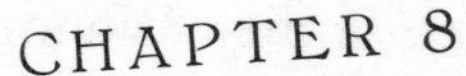

Wonder ~~Worms~~ People Are Go!

Worms!" Lizzie yelled the moment she emerged from the wishing well on the grounds of Ever After High.

"What?" said Cedar.

"Where?" said Apple with a small shudder.

"Gross!" yelled Blondie.

"Yay!" said Maddie.

"Um," said Raven, "what worms, Lizzie?"

"And by worms, I mean people!" Lizzie shouted, hoping the strength of her mother's words would clarify things. She noticed that the confused stares only got confused-er.

"And by people," Lizzie continued, "I mean *Wonder* people. Er...I mean Kitty and Maddie. The Wonderlandians."

"Wonder Worms are go!" shouted Maddie, striking an action pose and then wiggling toward Lizzie. "Lady Catworm!" Maddie called to Kitty Cheshire, who hadn't moved an inch. "Make haste! We have been summoned!"

Kitty shrugged and disappeared, reappearing beside Lizzie.

"Hatworm and Catworm at your service, O Lizard Queen," Maddie said, giving Lizzie a wiggly bow.

"Don't call me that," Lizzie and Kitty said in unison.

Maddie straightened from the wormy stance. "Fine, party poops. What's the story?"

"I have something to discuss with both of you," Lizzie said, turning her back on them. "Let's go to the Grove."

"To the Grove, Catworm!" Maddie shouted heroically, and was rewarded with a hiss just as Kitty popped out of sight.

Lizzie breathed in as they left the school grounds and crossed into the Grove. Some days the rich, candied scents made her heart feel light and floaty as bubble birds. Sometimes the smells made her feel achy for home, as heavy and slow as a steel scarecrow. Today she felt nervous and jittery as if she had swallowed handfuls of live hornets.

Which she hadn't, just to clarify. One never knew with Lizzie.

"Citizens of Wonderland," Lizzie began.

Kitty looked over her shoulder, as if expecting more people to be there.

"As the representatives of our world in exile, it is our responsibility . . ." Lizzie was already bored with her own speech. She sighed. "Look, there were bandersnatches up there. I am certain that when we escaped Wonderland with the White Queen and Maddie's dad, no bandersnatches sneaked out with us." Were the ways to Wonderland reopening? Or had the bandersnatches found a secret way out and come looking for the lost Wonderlandian princess? Hope shivered in Lizzie.

Kitty purred, "I know of something else Wonderlandian here without permission."

"She means the Jabberwock," Maddie whispered.

"No, I don't!" Kitty's pale purple hair seemed fluffier, standing on end at the mention of the monster. She hissed, "Don't say its name out loud! I just meant the jubjub bird I was chasing on the mountaintop during that riddle-diculous play."

"A jubjub bird, too? Maybe we should talk to the White Queen," Maddie said.

"Very well," Lizzie said. "I'm glad I was able to get you to that conclusion. We will find the White Queen and demand of her an explanation."

"Or we could just ask," Maddie said.

"Or we could just ask!" Lizzie shouted as if it were a battle cry, pointing her scepter at the school.

They headed to the White Queen's office. Empty. They investigated the faculty lunchroom. Void. They peeked into likely classrooms. Nil. Then they began to get creative.

Sometime later, Maddie flung open the last stall door in the teachers' restroom. "*Aha!*" she shouted, but no one was there.

"She's hiding from us," Lizzie said. "The White Queen must know something and knows that we know she knows and wants to keep the knowing from us."

"But how can she if we already know she knows?" Maddie asked.

"The *extra* knowing," Lizzie said, nodding wisely. "The knowing about why there are bandersnatches and jubjub birds. Not the knowing that she knows."

"Oh," said Maddie. "So she's hiding from us. Good hiding."

"Too good!" Lizzie shouted. "I won't allow it! People can't just disappear!"

At that, Kitty disappeared.

"Present company excepted, of course," Lizzie muttered.

Kitty reappeared sitting on the bathroom counter. "Searching for the White Queen has been fun and all, especially the bit where Lizzie got stuck in the crawl space, but you'll never find her. You've probably noticed there are lots of people not at the school today."

"I assumed they were hiding like the White Queen," Maddie said, "to make this game of hide-and-seek more fun."

"She wasn't playing hide-and-seek," said Kitty.

Maddie threw up her hands. "Am I expected to keep track of every game and who is and isn't playing all the time?"

"The faculty and most of the students are still on their field trips," Kitty said, pulling out her MirrorPhone to check her teeth. "Only our group came back early."

"I know that, of course. I just wanted to make sure you knew it, too." Lizzie's eyes narrowed. "But you didn't see fit to tell us this before because . . . ?"

"Because watching you two run about like madwomen is fun."

"She does have a point," Maddie said.

Lizzie dialed the White Queen on her MirrorPhone. No answer. Her voice mail picked up.

"*I am busy right now*," said the White Queen's recorded voice. "*Please call back ten minutes ago*."

The door to the restroom pushed open.

"Here you are!" said Briar. "Everyone's meeting in Apple and Raven's dorm room. Some of the students are hextremely upset about what happened on the mountain, and Apple thought some soothing talk could help."

"Okay!" Maddie said, un-straightening her hat and hopping out the door.

"Soothing talk?" Kitty asked. "Royals and Rebels together, sharing nonjudgmental and openhearted opinions?"

"Totally," Briar said.

"I'm there," Kitty said, fading until all but her mouth remained. "There's bound to be a tasty fight," the smiling mouth said, and then it, too, disappeared.

"I don't see how sitting around babbling could be soothing, let alone productive," Lizzie said.

"Come on, Lizzie," said Briar. "I'll be there, so it's sure to be a blast!"

Briar was always throwing parties where Lizzie would stand awkwardly in the corner, shouting things like "Fetch me a flamingo!" or "Stand back, peasant!" in reply to any small talk. Mother would declare all those bumbling partygoers beneath the Princess of Hearts and not worth her time, and yet Lizzie spent those parties secretly, silently, carefully wishing that she were one of the girls on the dance floor, laughing with Briar. Lizzie opened her mouth to tell Briar that but found herself shouting, "Off with your head!"

“Okay, then. See you fairy soon,” Briar said, throwing down a skateboard and skating down the corridor.

Lizzie drew a card from her mother’s deck. Her mother’s words would give her strength, courage, and direction.

♥

Already Been Chewed food (hereafter referred to as ABC food) can appear appetizing, but not for such as you. Eat no ABC food today.

♥

Hmph. That didn’t seem particularly applicable. Lizzie flipped through a few more.

♥

Frogs are mostly faces.
Notice a frog today and make a face.

♥

ON WITH ITS HEAD!
JK. ☺ Behead something today!

♥

Rugs are the unnatural spawn of Rabbits and Hugs. Beware rugs. (Could also be Rubber and Bugs. In any case, BEWARE RUGS!)

♥

Sometimes it took Lizzie a while to figure out how her mother's wisdom applied to her current situation. This was one of those times. She slid the cards back into their well-worn box, checked to see that no one was watching, and hugged it to her chest.

"I'm trying, Mother," she whispered. "I'm trying to be like you."

She crossed her eyes twice and made a wish that bandersnatches were just the beginning. That Wonderland *was* coming to her. All of it. And soon her mother would be there to pull Lizzie into her huge embrace and assure her she was doing all right.

CHAPTER 9

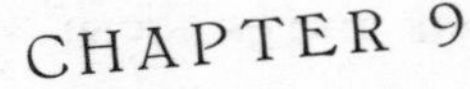

STORYBOOKER SHARE SLAM!

When Cedar arrived at Raven and Apple's room, most of the other students from her field trip were already seated on lounges and chairs or on pillows on the floor, everyone arranged in a circle. Several dozen scented candles burned, filling the room with the smell of baked apple pie.

Lizzie Hearts entered beside her.

"Kind of a strange day, huh?" Cedar said.

"Strange days may be here to stay, and not to—"

Lizzie stopped suddenly and stared intensely at Cedar. "What rhymes with '*go away*'?"

Cedar shrugged and walked away. She rarely understood what Lizzie was talking about, but clearly she didn't want or need friends, let alone a chat with the puppet girl.

Raven was in urgent conversation with Apple, so Cedar sat on a couch beside Humphrey Dumpty and Poppy O'Hair.

"Hey," they said.

"Hey," said Cedar.

Cedar crossed her arms, trying to hide the bandersnatch teeth marks. She'd sand those off as soon as she got a chance.

"I love that color," said Poppy, indicating the sky-blue paint staining Cedar's fingertips, left over from a recent art project. "Art is one of my favorite subjects."

"Mine, too!" said Cedar. "I love painting."

"I'm into the verbal arts myself," said Humphrey. "I'll treat you to a little freestyle rap. Um...just give me a minute...."

"I'm interested in sculpture," said Poppy. "Maybe

because my hands have so much practice styling hair. Do you like my new do?"

Poppy's hair grew royally fast, and she was always experimenting with new styles. Today it was a turquoise faux-hawk.

"Oh . . . well, it's kind of alarming," said Cedar.

Poppy blinked.

"Sorry!" said Cedar. "I didn't want to say that! I totally respect your individual style, even if I think you look like a bird built a nest on your head."

Poppy blinked twice. "Sorry!" said Cedar again.

"Got it!" Humphrey said. He began to rap, his extremely white hands gesturing in rapid motions.

Yo, Cedar and Poppy,
the talk's sounding choppy.
Don't wanna hop, T'
likes both of you guys,
so trade the lows for the highs,
say we stow the unwise.
Call a truce before war.
Let that snoozin' dog snore,
and opt for the choosin'
to not talk about hair, fair?

Humphrey smiled, as if certain he had just solved everything. Poppy looked confused, as if she wasn't sure whether to be upset.

"Sorry," Cedar whispered.

Apple stood at the head of the room and the talking quieted.

"Welcome, friends," said Apple. "Ever since Legacy Day, I have so enjoyed meeting together for our Storybooker Share Slams to discuss our Rebel situation—"

"And Royal," said Raven.

"... And Royal," said Apple, nodding. "But today we have even more serious matters to discuss."

"Yeah, what in Ever After was that play?" Sparrow said.

"That vas art!" said Helga Crumb, shaking her fist in the air.

"*Ja*, you are right, my cousin Helga," said Gus Crumb. "Headmaster Grimm is a genius!"

Apple cleared her throat. "I meant the appearance of the bandersnatches."

"Wait, did that play have anything to do with the bandersnatches?" asked Blondie, recording everything with her MirrorPad.

“Monsters appearing outside of their stories is the sort of catastrophe that happens when *people* don’t follow their *destiny*,” said Faybelle Thorn, glaring at Raven.

“I don’t like it,” said Nathan Nutcracker, sitting on the mantel. His jaw chattered, making a clicking sound. “I don’t like it at all.”

“A queen!” Lizzie shouted. “A queen is only as big as her fishbowl, so be careful not to behead too much of your water!”

Apple tilted her head, her lips pursed, as if trying very hard to take the statement seriously. “What do you mean, Lizzie?”

Lizzie slipped a card back into her pocket. “Ah... never mind. In context it doesn’t really seem to apply.”

“Why does *everything* have to go back to being a Royal or a Rebel?” Cerise said.

“Because these crazy, off-script things didn’t use to happen before...” Apple glanced kindly at Raven.

“I don’t see how my not signing the Storybook of Legends made bandersnatches appear on a mountaintop,” said Raven.

"Well, I'll tell you one thing," said Faybelle. "It sure didn't help."

"Wait a splinter!" said Cedar, standing up. "Don't go blaming Raven. She was right to not sign."

Faybelle stood up, too, flipping her ponytail over her shoulder. "I don't get you, little Miss Pinocchio. Why are you a Rebel anyway? If I were you, I'd follow my script so I could get to the Happily Ever After and finally be *real*."

Nate Nutcracker gasped. Raven clenched her fists. Cedar met Faybelle's gaze.

"You're right, if I don't follow my destiny, I might be trapped in this wooden body forever—but even worse would be to be trapped in a choiceless life. If I can't lie, if I'm cursed to blurt out whatever I think even if I don't want to, then I can't *really* choose." She glanced at Poppy and then quickly away, afraid she might let slip another horrid opinion about her hair. "I think being a Rebel means you get to cut the strings and choose your story. And nothing is more important to me than choice."

"Hear! Hear!" said Maddie. "Though—and this isn't a criticism—I'd have enjoyed what you said more with a cup of tea." Maddie looked down at her hand, which was holding a cup of tea. "Oh! Well this is perfect now. Call off the hounds! Call off the king's men! I found my tea!"

"Rebel, Royal, bleh," said Kitty, examining her nails. "If you don't care where you want to end up, it doesn't matter which road you take."

"I don't know everything, but I know that choices are complicated," said Cedar. "Every choice we make affects other people. So if you're not sure where you want to end up, should you just hold still, choosing nothing?"

"Or should you leap ahead anyway," said Briar, "making bold choices and accepting where they take you?"

"And if they take you over a cliff?" asked Apple.

"If your destiny happens at the bottom of a cliff, then yes," said Briar.

"One should always know beforehand exactly what should happen, how it should happen, and then make it happen," said Lizzie.

"Look!" Cerise shouted, pointing.

A bunny was hopping up the face of Apple's grandfather clock. The clock chimed one, and the bunny ran down again. Cedar felt her mouth hang open. Such behavior wasn't uncommon for Ever After mice, but a bunny?

"Whoa," Dexter said, adjusting his glasses as if he couldn't believe what he'd just seen.

"Hickory dickory dock," Cerise whispered.

"Raven, did you do that?" Apple asked.

Raven shook her head. "I wouldn't even know what spell to use."

Cedar couldn't help saying aloud, "When the bunny reached the top, I swear it paused to check the time."

"What-ever-after," said Faybelle with an eye roll.

"Ha-ha!" said Lizzie, brandishing her scepter. "When is a mouse like a bunny?"

"Well," said Ashlynn kindly, "both are fluffy and cute and small and cute—"

"No," said Lizzie. She cleared her throat and looked at everyone significantly. "When is a mouse like a bunny? And when is a bear like a bandersnatch? Off-put? This is precisely my point!"

Cedar sighed. Lizzie's not making sense was the most normal thing about this day.

Apple wrangled the conversation back to bandersnatches and the headmaster's instructions to stay at the school, but Cedar kept her gaze on her hands, chipping off the blue paint. Perhaps if she managed not to notice anything, she might not blurt out something awkward and hurtful and lose any more friends.

CHAPTER 10

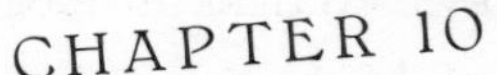

Reasonable by Accident

When Apple dismissed them, Lizzie was so full of thoughts she forgot to shout "Off with your head!" before leaving the room. Lizzie *knew* bunnies. She wouldn't exactly say she liked them—they were much too fluffy and softish and un-hedgehog-y—but she was royally *aware* of them. At no point had she sensed a bunny in Apple and Raven's room, despite the big-eared bouncer she'd seen with her eyes.

Lizzie's stately walk down the corridor nearly tripped into a skip. A giddy kind of excitement wiggled inside her, as if her stomach were a bag of popcorn in midpop. Bandersnatches! Jubjub birds! Bunnies that are obsessed with clocks! Were some of her subjects wriggling their way out of Wonderland and flocking to their princess? She took a deep breath and heard an extra inhale besides her own.

"It is unseemly to hide from your future queen," Lizzie said.

"Fine," said Kitty, slinking out of thin air. "Though I might have said 'un*seen*ly.'"

"What happened to that bunny rabbit?" Lizzie shouted.

"You mean the clock-climbing mouse that had somehow been transformed into a bunny?" said Kitty.

"Yes! Don't you *care* that you don't know how it happened? I would like to know, and am troubled by the fact that I do not!"

"Calm down, Princess Freak-Out." Kitty's smile weakened. "Now that you mention it, I'm *troubled*, too."

Unbeknownst to the Wonderlandians (except for Kitty, who can hear this narration right now but pretends not to), both Lizzie and Kitty had just used the word *troubled* for the first time in their lives.

"*Grrrr*," Kitty growled.

Maddie was on her way to find a place that needed to be hopped on. But upon overhearing the Narrator mention things of a *troubling* nature, she hurried back down the hall to her fellow Wonderlandians.

"I'm concerned," said Maddie, and then immediately covered her mouth. "Oh no! It's happening to me, too!"

"What is?" Lizzie asked.

"I said I'm *concerned*," Maddie said. "Not 'kilter-tipped' or 'taut-hearted' or even 'wormy-worried'! 'Concerned' is even worse than 'troubled'! It's Ever Afterlish! It's *boring*," she whispered now, hand to the side of her mouth. "It's bland, heart-sapping plain-talk!"

Kitty shrugged. "It's not unlikely that enough time spent in a different place would introduce drift in your natural speech patterns." Kitty's eyes went wide, and then she, too, covered her mouth.

"See!" Maddie said, pointing at Kitty. "You said 'introduce drift—' "

Kitty interrupted. "Don't repeat it!"

"It," said Maddie.

"Not it," said Lizzie and Kitty in unison, and with that simple bit of madness, they realized all was not lost.

"That's a relief," Maddie said. "The Narrator just said we realized all was not lost. Now we need to find what actually *is* lost, and then everything will be fine again."

Lizzie wondered if something wasn't lost so much as found. Perhaps Wonderland had found her at last.

"Ooh, Lizzie, you think Wonderland is coming to Ever After?" Maddie asked.

"How did you know what I..." Lizzie started.

"The Narrator sometimes mentions what you're thinking."

"Nattering nosy nabob," Lizzie muttered. "Since you have no respect for royal privacy, tell us exactly what is going on, Nut-Bundled Know-It-All Narrator! Tell us why there are bandersnatches and jubjub birds and mice disguised in bunny-ness, and why Maddie is 'concerned' and Kitty is 'introducing drift'!"

No one said anything for a moment, except the Narrator, who didn't *say* anything, since this sentence was not audible to all parties.

"Did the Narrator tell you anything?" Lizzie asked.

"Nothing helpish or revealy," Maddie said. "It's a Narrator rule. They're not supposed to interact with the people in their story. Though you can trick them sometimes."

About that last part Maddie was completely wrong. At least with regards to this upstanding, rule-abiding Narrator.

"We need help," Lizzie said, stumbling over the words. She remembered one of her mother's cards:

♥

Worms NEED *things. But a princess such as you*
ORDERS *things. Today, put your things in order*
by ordering things to be what they are.
And then, for fun, order them to be
what they are not.

♥

Lizzie sighed. "We're having far too many reasonable thoughts to be able to figure out anything on our own."

"I'm sure Apple and Raven—" Maddie started to say, but Lizzie banged her scepter on the wall.

"They're reasonable even in the best of times! No, we need Wonder and riddles and sideways explanations. That's the kind of sense that will make sense of nonsense."

"I have a helpful suggestion," Maddie said. "But I'm afraid to say it because it might be *reasonable* by accident."

"Try saying it while standing on your head," Kitty suggested.

"Hat-tastic idea, Kitty!" Maddie bent over, balancing the rim of her teacup hat on the floor, and then flung her legs up into the air. "That's better. Anyway, we could go talk to Giles Grimm. The headmaster's brother? He lives in secret rooms beneath the library and only ever speaks in Riddlish."

Lizzie often visited the library, paging through books that reminded her of home—not because the books spoke or flew or read themselves backward, but because they had tales and pictures of Wonderland. It was nice to be reminded that she did have a home, a real home, a setting.

She followed Maddie and Kitty into the library,

through the stacks of books, out of the school entirely, past the sports fields, around a tree three times, back into the library, through a wall, down a narrow, dark, and properly eerie corridor, and into the Vault of Lost Tales.

"There wasn't a more direct route?" Lizzie asked.

"Probably," Maddie said, and gestured to the pile of rags sitting at a desk. "This is Giles. Hi, Giles!"

The pile of rags stood, and Lizzie realized it was a man wearing extremely raggedy clothes, so she thought she could be excused for mistaking him for refuse.

"Hello, er..." Lizzie said, searching her mind for an appropriate way to address the man, "Step-Headmaster Grimm."

Once upon a time, Giles Grimm had been co-headmaster, but Lizzie can also be forgiven for not knowing that.

"Party finds awkward twists in an unfound space made mist, lass," Giles said, smiling beneath his straggly gray beard.

"It does, indeed," Lizzie said, and then whispered to Maddie, "I'm not sure I caught all that. Usually

I'm quite conversant in Riddlish. Perhaps this wretched reasonability confounds my brain."

"Mine, too," Maddie said. "I'm not sure if it's the me-side or the he-side that has changed."

Giles nodded. "Wonders never cease. Just they find peace and pieces in creases. The bent land releases but queasy pieces, my Ms. Three nieces."

"Wonderland, you mean?" said Maddie. "Something about Wonderland?"

"When stare ye long into the face of bear become not bear but bandersnatch fair."

"He knows about the bandersnatches!" Lizzie said.

"Nay, fair is fare—though unfair—for the nightmare once cairned." Giles Grimm smiled kindly. "Don't forget the butter!"

"The butter?" Lizzie asked.

Giles nodded. "For the bandersnatch."

"Is this what it's like for the Ever Afterlings when they talk to us?" Lizzie asked. "Very frustrating."

"Maybe it would help if he stood on his head," Maddie whispered.

"Try this," Lizzie said. "Mr. Step-Headmaster Grimm, tell us, in the most unclear, confusing way you can imagine, whether or not things are changing."

Giles Grimm furrowed his brow as if thinking hard to come up with an incredibly difficult riddle. He cleared his throat, held up a finger, and said, "Yes."

"That was a silly question," Kitty whispered in Lizzie's ear. "We already *know* things are changing." Kitty disappeared and reappeared to whisper in her other ear. "What we need to know is *why* or *how*. And is there a cake or a pie in it for us? Lots of questions with more point and less silly were available."

Lizzie shrugged. "I didn't hear *you* speaking up with alternate questions, Catworm."

Maddie laughed. "It's catchy, right?"

Kitty did not appear to think it was catchy.

"Oh, Bookworm," Maddie said, presumably addressing the Narrator, though the Narrator had expressly expressed that Narrators must never be directly addressed.

Without warning, Giles Grimm vanished, and where he'd been standing a pile of books clattered to the floor.

"Oh, no, he disappeared!" Lizzie said. "Just when

I had a better question about whether or not to behead Kitty."

Kitty sniffed the books. "He didn't disappear. Disappearing things have a smell like the echo of a lemon. I think those books might actually *be* him."

"Oooh," Lizzie breathed out. Things changing into other things suddenly and without warning was a refreshing change of pace and slightly Wonderlandian. That giddy, popcorn-belly feeling returned.

Wonderland is coming to me....

A small nag caught in her thoughts. In Wonderland, Giles might have shrunk, or enlarged, or folded up on himself, but when things changed back home, they were still what they were. Not a person into a pile of books. That was magic, certainly, but was it the right kind? The wonderlandiful kind?

"Should I put the Grimmy books in my hat and take him with us?" Maddie asked.

"I wouldn't," Kitty said. "What if he turns back?"

"While stuck inside my hat?" Maddie said. "Good point."

"I didn't mean to make a good point," Kitty whined. "Making good points is not what I do!"

"Leave the book-man be," said Lizzie. "We'll

tell Headmaster Grimm about him when he gets back."

"*If* he gets back," Maddie said, and then coughed. "Sorry. Frog in my throat. *Ribbit*."

Maddie stuck out her tongue, revealing a small blue frog perched upon it. The frog leaped off and hopped away. Maddie's eyes went wide.

Lizzie smiled. *Wonderland found me.*

CHAPTER 11

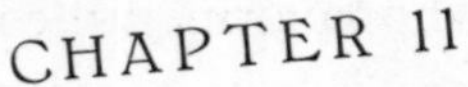

A Wobble of Uncertainty

Cedar Wood was feeling like a hollowed-out log. Though she'd fled Raven's room the moment the session ended, her unhappy encounter with Poppy seemed to chase after her. Quick steps down the corridor rattled her knee and elbow joints with a jangle of metal and wood, but she didn't slow down till she reached the safety of her dorm room.

Cedar opened her paint box. Black paint smeared on her index finger and seemed to tingle, as if beckoning her to lose herself in her art. Cedar knew the sensation was as false as everything else she felt. *If*

I were you, Faybelle had said, *I'd do anything to finally be real*. Perhaps Cedar was not a person at all but just a piece of wood who imagined she was a person.

She squeezed her creaky eyelids shut, trying to close off thoughts about wood and people and what she was or wasn't. Bits of sadness—imagined or not—were already worming into her heartwood. Maybe she could paint them away.

Today she set aside the traditional canvas and instead placed a wide wooden plank on her easel. She started to paint a scene of a garden early in the morning, when the colors were still hushed and full of grays, more shadow than not, shapes not yet fully revealed.

The paint couldn't completely hide the wood plank, its rough grain, lines, swirls, and knotholes as much a part of the picture as what she painted over them. It took some time before Cedar realized she was painting her own experience, bringing a kind of life to the dead wood but never changing what it was, never hiding it completely.

And that's what she loved about art. It spoke the unspeakable, revealed truth before the mind had a chance to think it.

It's not a real garden, Cedar thought, standing back to look at her painting, *but perhaps still worthwhile?*

From her pouch of art tools, she took out a knife to sharpen a quill she liked to use for making thin lines. The knife slipped and cut into her finger. That wasn't unusual. Cedar wasn't particularly careful.

But then a thin line of red welled up along the cut. At first, she thought it was paint, but it grew. A red bead, fat as a honeybee, bled out and dropped from her finger, splashing onto the purple carpet. Cedar felt—truly *felt*—a sensation she had never experienced before: a slicing, hot, sharp fierceness, a hugeness as big as life trapped in the tip of her finger. She whispered the word: "Pain."

Cedar Wood's finger was bleeding.

She shouted toward Cerise Hood's side of their dorm room, "Look! Look, my finger is bleeding!"

But Cerise wasn't there. Cedar examined her fingertip again. It felt softer than normal. She patted herself, her hands bumping against the brass pegs at her joints. She traced the knot of wood that marked her left thigh like an oval birthmark. Still there. And yet, when she lifted her finger to her mouth to suck on it, she tasted blood—salty and metallic and warm. Not just imagined the taste. Really tasted it. Like the difference between looking at a photo of a beach and actually putting bare feet in the sand.

Cedar giggled and performed a short dance that was a burst of joy, a wobble of uncertainty, and a flinch of fear all at the same time. Was something marvelous happening? Or something scary?

The bubble and rush of emotions made it impossible to stay still. Cedar ran out the door and down the hall.

"Help? I think?" Cedar called out. "Or maybe hooray? I'm not sure, but one of the two!"

No one answered.

She knocked on Maddie's door, finding it open but no one inside. No one except Maddie's pet dormouse, Earl Grey, who was standing on Maddie's tea table squeaking and strutting about. As Cedar drew closer, she could see he was wearing a dashing black silk shirt and trousers and holding up a tiny skull in one hand.

"*Squeak squeak, squ-squeak squeak squeak?*" he squeaked.

It appeared that Earl Grey was practicing a dramatic scene from *Hamlet*.

"Earl Grey?" Cedar said.

Earl Grey startled, dropped the skull, and leaned nonchalantly against a teacup as if he'd been just hanging out and not rehearsing his one-mouse show at all.

"Do you know where Maddie is?" Cedar asked.

Earl Grey shrugged, put back on his top hat, and leaped onto Cedar's shoulder, eager to go with her to track Maddie down.

Across the hall, Gus and Helga's door was ajar. Cedar couldn't see them inside, but two heaps of breadcrumbs sat in the middle of their rug.

"Hello?" said Cedar.

Another new sensation crawled over her—a tick-lish, cold, worrying sort of thing, like thousands of icy fingernails skipping down her limbs. Chills. Cedar had imagined chills before, but her imagination had failed to create the combination of pleasure and discomfort, the shudder and exhale.

Beneath her, the floor rolled as if the castle had started to gallop and then changed its mind. Cedar shook her head. Perhaps she was sick. Could she have contracted some rare wood disease that was causing her magic-enlarged imagination to overreact?

Out the window, Cedar spotted several small shapes dropping from the roof. Above the Crumbs' room was Ashlynn's balcony, and Cedar knew songbirds often congregated there. Had the songbirds been hurt and fallen? Cedar raced to the window but spotted no injured songbirds in the courtyard below, only a flock of dodoes, those odd-looking flightless birds, lurching around as if bewildered.

"I know how you feel," Cedar said.

"*Squeak*," said Earl Grey.

Cedar ran to Raven and Apple's room. Raven had magical abilities, and whatever was happening just had to be magic.

As she raced up the stairs, again the castle seemed to burp, the stairs swaying under her feet. The warm stab in her fingertip traveled down her arm and into her chest, where it flared to a pain that was as sweet as it was agonizing. The pain left behind a strange and wondrous thumping as if something were moving inside her chest. Moving, like the waves of the ocean. The beating of a drum. The buzzing of a dragonfly's wings. The rolling meters of a song. The *everything* of the world caught and moving inside her chest.

Cedar ran harder, as if she could somehow catch up to whatever wondrousness was happening to her and seize it, hold on to it, and make it hers forever.

And Cedar ran even harder, as though she could somehow flee the frightening changes altering her body.

As she leaped onto the next floor, she heard several small, heavy things fall off her and bounce down the stairs. She didn't turn to see what she'd left behind, her body in agony to be running so hard and yet burning with exquisite joy. She burst through Raven's door.

"Raven!" she shouted. "Something's—"

But she didn't have to tell Raven that strangeness had erupted at Ever After High.

Apple was standing before a mirror, a gasp of horror escaping her throat. Raven's hands were covering her mouth.

Apple turned as Cedar entered. The light from the window fell on Apple's face, revealing a deep red coloring her round cheeks and moving outward to paint her whole face. Sticking out of the top of her head was a finger-sized piece of wood. Even as Cedar stared, a lime-green leaf sprouted from the stick and unfurled itself to face the sunlight. It was a stem.

Raven pointed at Cedar in shock and opened her mouth as if to speak, but no sound came out.

Cedar hugged her arms around her chest. She felt warmth, softness, aliveness. The brass pegs at her elbows and wrists were gone. She touched her knees—gone there, too. Those were what had dropped away on the stairs.

She dared to turn to a mirror. Her hair looked as it always had—warm brown, wavy, and heavy as frayed rope. Her dress was the same lavender and coral one she'd put on that morning. But if not for those details, she might have assumed she was looking at a stranger. Her dark brown limbs and face were smooth, no wood grain, no chipped spots where she'd bumped into something (like bander-snatch teeth). She blinked, and her eyes were wet. Two tears freed themselves from her lashes and rolled down her cheeks, leaving behind a cold, tick-lish path.

She inhaled sharply for the first time, and she felt her chest—her lungs?—fill up, pressing against that constant winged, wave-ish, drumlike beating of a . . . a . . . a *heart*.

Her heart.

Her real heart beating in her chest.

She pressed her hands against the beating, crying faster with wonder and alarm and joy, so filled with the music of her aliveness she feared she might explode.

"Raven, what's happening?" Cedar whispered.

But the only response was a single, frightened squawk.

CHAPTER 12

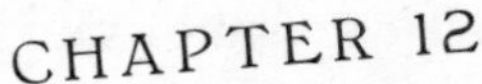

~~WONDERLAND FOUND ME~~

Eat More Muffins!

LIZZIE, KITTY, AND MADDIE WALKED OUT of the library, sounds wafting over their heads like invisible birds. *Suss-suss. Hiss-hoo. Waaaahhh.* Lizzie wondered if she was hearing the books whisper to each other. Or if the air itself had come alive.

The cushioned chairs in the hall just outside the library door were huddled together as though in conversation. When the girls neared, they scattered, their short wooden forelegs making clumping noises like little hooves.

Lizzie felt so good she longed for a ripping game of croquet. She pretended her scepter was a flamingo mallet, lined it up, and swung at an imaginary hedgehog.

"Things are obviously changing," Lizzie said.

"See?" Kitty said. "It was a pointless question."

The rug beneath Lizzie's feet rippled. Remembering her mother's advice to avoid rugs, Lizzie stepped off, just as a tasseled end flicked to where her feet had been.

Outside the window, a stone gargoyle carved into the school's facade flapped its wings. And then the window Lizzie was looking through blinked. Startled, she took a step back.

"Well, I never!" said Lizzie. It seemed bad-mannered to blink when someone was actively looking through you.

"This is Wonder-smacking awesome!" Maddie shouted.

Wonderland coming to find me.

Lizzie smiled so hard she felt like Kitty. Her adopted world was becoming what she, Lizzie Hearts, needed it to be! Perhaps soon all parts of Ever After would smell and feel and sound as perfectly extraordinary and Wondery as the Grove. Perhaps now she would not have to spend all her energy just trying to hide her homesickness.

But first, she would need to teach the new world some manners, blinking windows and such. Her mother would certainly expect this. There would be much Ruling and Ordering and Shaping Things Up.

Maddie cocked her head to one side. "This is a slice of strange pie. Why don't we hear any screaming or whining or what's-going-on-ing? Chair herds and window blinks are just the kind of world-spin that leaves the Ever Afterlings . . . well, *troubled*."

"Perhaps they've finally come away from their senses," said Lizzie.

"Maybe," Maddie said. "Hey, Narrator, what are Raven and Apple doing?"

Maddie waited, eyebrows raised, mistakenly expecting the Narrator to break the rules and interact with her.

"Hmm, when the Narrator is being this secretsy and rule-ish, that means there's something Big and Important happening that the Narrator is trying very hard not to reveal," said Maddie.

It does not!

"So we should probably go check on Raven and Apple," said Maddie. "Tell them what's up."

"Do we know what's up?" Kitty asked.

"Well, we should act like it, even if we don't," Lizzie proclaimed. "Own the up!"

This was a quote from one of her mother's cards:

❤

Whether up or down, inside or out, it is yours.
Own the down. Own the up.

❤

The girls made their way past another group of chairs chatting in an incomprehensible furniture language.

"What do you suppose they even have to talk about?" Lizzie asked. "It's not like the life of furniture is particularly interesting."

"Maybe they're discussing ways to make life more interesting," Kitty whispered.

The thought made Lizzie shiver.

She shook the shivers away. She would simply order the chairs to behave! If Wonderland was indeed coming to Ever After, Lizzie had no time to waste. She must be as queenly as her mother would be.

The door to the dorms didn't look alive like a chair or blinky like a window, but when the three girls walked through, it made a disconcerting gulping noise.

"Ew," Kitty said. "I feel like we've just been swallowed."

"Halloo, friends," Maddie shouted, entering Raven and Apple's room. "Oh, nobody's here."

"Nobody's anywhere, it seems," Kitty purred.

The school was unusually empty today, and they hadn't seen *anyone* since leaving the library. Anyone human, anyway.

"Our story appears to be a series of Looking Glass adventures without the glass," Kitty said.

A little noise uncurled from deep within the room, like the whimpering of a pat of butter cornered by a piece of toast. Lizzie did not hear it, Kitty chose to ignore it, and Maddie uncharacteristically assumed Apple and Raven's room wouldn't contain anything like talking butter or aggressively warm toast.

"Wait!" Maddie said, questioning her assumptions after hearing what the Narrator had said. "There *is* someone in here."

"We should get out of this school and find one of the teachers," said Lizzie.

"Frighteningly sensible, Lizzie," Kitty said.

Lizzie frowned. "You're right. What is the matter with me?"

"Hello?" Maddie called out.

A tuft of dark hair popped up from behind a writing desk, followed by two brown eyes. "Maddie?" said a mouth, conceivably somewhere below the eyes.

"Cedar!" Maddie called, running to the girl and pulling her out and into a big hug. "You're all meaty! How did that happen? And you're shivering. Are you cold? No? Oh, scared, right. You came looking for Apple and Raven, too, didn't you? But they've disappeared, just like Giles Grimm!"

"*Not* disappeared, just like Giles Grimm," Kitty said, sniffing the room.

"They . . . they—" Cedar started, when a black bird perched on the writing desk squawked.

"Crow!" Lizzie shouted, pointing at the bird as if accusing it of something.

"*Raven*," Cedar whispered, and then pointed at a plump red apple on the floor. "And Apple."

"Oooh!" Lizzie said with a little laugh. "Delicious!"

Cedar's eyes widened in further shock.

"Not literally, I mean," Lizzie muttered. "Who eats raw ravens anymore? And that apple, especially knowing it's an Apple-apple, is bound to be much too sweet. And full of organs. Note to everyone—don't eat that apple. It's probably gross."

The toilet flushed from inside the bathroom. The door opened, and a squat little crocodile about the height of Maddie walked out on its stubby hind legs. It carried a newspaper under one arm.

"Mornin', ladies," it said, dropping to all fours. "Feelin' a bit peckish, what."

"Peckish?" Lizzie asked, always willing to have a conversation with a crocodile. "Like, birdy?"

"Like 'ungry." The crocodile was marching toward the Apple-apple.

The Raven-raven began dive-bombing the crocodile.

"*Oy*," the crocodile shouted, swinging its head around. "Jus' tryin' a get breakfast, soddin' bird!"

Maddie picked up the Apple-apple and put it safely in her hat. "C'mon, Raven," she said, running for the door. "Let's leave Mr. Hungry Teeth on his own."

"*Aaaaaah*," the crocodile bellowed, running at the lot of them. Lizzie stared at the teeth. They were fascinating. So many of them. She could do a lot with teeth like that. The teeth kept getting closer until suddenly the raven pecked her on the forehead.

"How dare you!" Lizzie shouted, and only then realized she might be on the crocodile's menu. She took quick steps out the door, Cedar slamming it shut behind her.

"Where did that crocodile even come from?" Cedar asked, panting.

"Probably from the toilet," Maddie said. "There's loads of them in the sewers, you know."

"That's alligators," Kitty said.

"Oh, right," said Maddie. "Alligators. I don't know about that crocodile, then."

A deep bass rumbling shook the floor, as if the world were beginning to turn in exactly the opposite direction as the building it supported. *More changes?* Lizzie rubbed her hands together.

Cedar jumped away from the closed door. "Is that creature getting through?"

"Be reasonable. Crocodiles don't have the thumbs necessary to open doors," said Lizzie.

"It could be *eating* its way through," Kitty said.

Cedar eyed the door nervously.

"Something is happening out on the terrace, though," Lizzie said. "A crowd is gathering. A queen can tell these things."

"You're not a queen *yet*," Cedar whispered.

"If I say I am, I am!" Lizzie shouted as she marched downstairs. "It is a queen's prerogative to determine reality."

"What's a prerogative?" Maddie asked.

Lizzie ignored Maddie's question, partly because she wasn't actually sure what a prerogative was. But most of her was riddled and ant-dance-y with the worry that she might be lying to herself and the others about being ready to be a queen.

♥

A queen worrying about others is like a baker worried he's making too many muffins. As if there could be such a thing as Too Many Muffins. Ha! WORRY NOT! AND EAT MORE MUFFINS!

♥

But I can't help worrying, Mother, Lizzie wanted to say. She had yet to read a card that explained how her mother lived worry-free.

Lizzie clenched her teeth and marched toward the crowd-feeling on the terrace. And the parts of her that weren't wormy with worry or puzzled with prerogative began to pulse with excitement.

Wonderland found me!

The sunshine seemed especially bright, warming her gold crown against her forehead. On the terrace, a podium faced rows of chairs as if set up for an event like Legacy Day. Or a coronation. Her coronation?

Lizzie lifted her nose, tightened her lips, pressed one hand against the worry in her belly, pressed the other hand against the eager beats of her heart, and smiled.

"These chairs weren't here when we came back from the field trip," Cedar said.

"Maybe the people setting this up were the crowd we heard," Maddie said. "The faculty must be back! Yay!"

At Maddie's shout, all the chairs turned and *looked* at them.

"Uh-oh," said Kitty.

"The chairs set themselves up," Cedar whispered. "What I want to know is, what was the podium telling them to do?"

An incomprehensible noise, somewhere between a shout, the crackle of a fire, and a bone breaking, issued from the podium.

The chairs nodded. And then they began to charge.

Lizzie's stomach dropped. This was not her coronation. This was some kind of uprising.

"*Run!*" Lizzie yelled.

And they did.

"They're not very fast," Kitty said, running backward.

"What are you talking about?" Lizzie shouted, casting a glance over her shoulder. "They're gaining on us!"

Kitty shrugged, disappeared, and then reappeared, running a few feet in front of the group. "We're not very fast either."

"I can't . . . keep . . . this up," Cedar gasped. "Not really . . . used to . . . breathing . . . like this . . . or at all. . . ."

Maddie held her hand.

The girls zoomed through corridor after corridor, past flighty curtains, over grumbly carpets, around mischievous benches. But the charging chairs stayed on their heels, the podium thump-hopping in front, shrieking microphone feedback that sounded like a battle cry.

"Maybe the chairs . . . are mad . . . that we've been sitting on them . . . all these years," Maddie said between huffs and puffs.

"This . . . is . . . *not* . . . wonderlandiful," Lizzie said.

Ahead, nearly blocking the hall, was what appeared to be a garden shed.

"Hutling!" Maddie yelled.

On hearing its name, the small cottage stood up on two chicken legs and turned to them "face"-first. There was a door. Mouth. Whatever. Only a couple of weeks ago, this offspring of Baba Yaga's magic hut had hatched from its egg, but already it'd grown so much that when it was standing, the doorknob was too high for Maddie to reach. And the stampede of seats had caught up.

With a tremendous clacking and whacking, armchairs, easy chairs, folding chairs, and stools galloped closer. The hutling made a distressed clucking sound. It took a few steps forward, bringing the four girls underneath its shadow, like baby chicks under their mother.

"Is it going to squish us?" Cedar asked.

"The hutling is my buddy! We play hide-and-seek all the time," Maddie whispered, "Don't tell, but I trick the hut every time by hiding inside it." Maddie snickered.

The crowd of chairs had stopped before the hutling, confused, turning back and forth.

"Can't they see us?" Cedar whispered. "We're right in front of them."

"Of course they can't," Lizzie said, sure she was right. Or pretending to be sure. She wasn't entirely sure of the difference at this point.

The hutling started to walk away.

"Stay with it!" Lizzie said, shuffling to keep up.

Kitty's ears pricked up. "Did you hear that? Like breaking glass, but . . . windier."

"Breaking wind?" Maddie asked, giggling.

"Wind and broken glass? It couldn't be a . . . a *shardstorm*," Cedar whispered.

Lizzie had only heard fables about shardstorms—the frightening weather events that occurred when a great deal of magic mirrors broke all at once. Surely they were as imaginary as polka-dotted unicorns, as flying mushrooms, as hideous bunnies. Nobody ever saw them, because they were supposed to fade or collapse as soon as they were confronted with their own reflection, and reflections were everywhere in Ever After. Yet who knew what was possible in this change-up, mess-around, come-undone school?

The ringing and crackling and tinkling and whooshing grew louder. And louder. The air began to buzz, the sound of ten thousand clocks striking midnight at the same time.

"Shardstorm!" Lizzie yelled. "*Run!*"

CHAPTER 13

TRAPPED!

The Grimmnasium door thrust open.

"Quick! Come inside!" shouted a haggard, but still dashing, Daring Charming.

The sound of breaking glass raged behind them. The Raven-raven soared through the open doorway of the Grimmnasium after the hutling. Cedar was about to follow but was struck from the side. A folding chair pounced on top of her, folding and unfolding its seat menacingly. About to kick the thing off, Cedar felt herself pale (for real) at the sight behind the chair.

A tornado of mirror glass the size of a mature oak tree rounded the corner and spun down the hall. It was beautiful, the way the light reflected off each individual piece of sharpened glass, and Cedar found herself wondering what colors of paint she'd use to create the scene on canvas.

The chair leaped off her and charged the storm. And was instantly shredded to bits.

Lizzie shook her fist at the disintegrated chair. "That will teach you to unceremoniously tackle the personal acquaintance of a royal heir to Wond—"

"Come on!" Maddie said, pulling Cedar and Lizzie inside the Grimmnasium. Glass shards began pelting the metal doors just as Daring slammed them shut.

He turned to the girls with a brilliant smile, leaning against the door casually as if not one bit worried about the screaming shardstorm pelting the other side of the door.

"Good afternoon, ladies," Daring said. "A pleasure to save you."

Lizzie rolled her eyes.

"Can it get through that door?" Cedar asked.

Daring gave the door a hard slap. "Dwarven metal. Tough stuff."

Cedar was shivering from her noncreaky toes to her soft shoulders, her new, real body confused by new, real bruises forming from that rogue chair attack. She found herself wondering if maybe there was a way to bypass being regular skin *or* wood, and get turned into dwarven metal instead.

"But I don't think I've had the pleasure, enchanting lady." Daring kissed the back of Cedar's hand. She felt the warmth of his lips, and mother-goosebumps scattered across her arm. "New here? I'm Daring Charming, but the girls just call me Prince Daring Charming."

He winked.

Lizzie rolled her eyes again. Cedar wanted to roll her eyes, too. After all, she'd never been one to bat her eyelashes at Daring or sigh whenever he slew dragons or lifted heavy objects or buttered his bread in muscle-flexing, manly motions. Still, she'd never felt the needle-thin tap dance of mother-goosebumps across real skin. She'd never experienced this warm, pleasant rumble in her belly and dizzy, tingling confusion in her head. If a simple kiss on the hand from Daring Charming could produce such sensations, what would her whole life be like now that she was real? Maybe she didn't want to be wood—or dwarven metal. Despite pain and fear, realness had some charming perks.

"That's Cedar, you gooseberry brain," said Lizzie. "She changed."

"She's not the only one," said Daring, gesturing.

The Grimmnasium was a huge open room with glossy hardwood floors, bleachers, a basketball court in the center, and a running track around the edges. Today it seemed darker than normal, and unfamiliar, un-sporty objects cluttered everywhere.

"What a mess," Lizzie said, adjusting her black gloves as if longing to get to work.

"Hunter, Dexter, and I were practicing tower-climbing when the changes started," said Daring. "So we gathered all the students we could find to take refuge here. Rescuing those in distress—that's what I do."

He winked at Cedar again.

Daring began pointing out inanimate objects that

had been their classmates: a pair of crystalline shoes that had been Ashlynn Ella, a heart-shaped layer cake that had been Cupid. As his arm extended, Cedar noticed a light sheen of gray fur covering Daring's skin.

"You've aged a great deal since I saw you last, Charming," Lizzie said. "Gray before your time, though perhaps not yet strangled by an octopus."

Daring looked at the backs of his hands and laughed nervously. "Yeah. Everyone was fine when we came in here. I mean, Hunter had leaves for hair, and a rose was blooming behind Briar's ear, but . . . then things got worse."

Cedar noticed a small tree growing out of the floor. There was an ax tangled in its leaves, and its branches arched protectively over the crystal shoes. Behind it, a pink rosebush grew up one wall.

"Oh, no," Cedar said.

"At least Ashlynn wasn't turned into hot cinders," Kitty said, testing a shoe's size with her own foot. "That would be very awkward for flammable Huntsman the Tree here."

A golden lock and a large brass egg lying by Cedar's feet were surely Blondie and Humphrey.

Cedar could sense a blister forming on her foot, but the rest of the students seemed to have changed in the opposite direction from her—less real, less human.

A wolf cub with bright red fur dashed across the Grimmnasium and rubbed her head against Cedar's ankles.

"Cerise?" Cedar asked.

The cub wagged her tail and ran off.

An enormous black-and-white-checkered cygnet shedding loose feathers and squawking had to be Duchess.

A sleigh bell with fairy wings awkwardly flitted past Cedar, clanging mournfully.

"Faybelle?" Cedar asked, and the bell rang.

The lights in the Grimmnasium began to flash. Once, twice, three times. Then every mirror in the room flickered, and Milton Grimm's face appeared in them.

"Students!" said the headmaster. "I am using our emergency broadcast system to broadcast a state of emergency. Ever After High has been infected with a wild magic. Madam Baba Yaga has conducted a magical analysis and believes the cause is...is...

well, is quite distressing, so please prepare yourselves. We believe the Jabberwock has returned."

Cedar gasped. The inanimate objects in the room rustled. The Raven-raven squawked and flapped around in circles.

"Baba Yaga is even now preparing a magical barrier that will completely enclose the school grounds in order to contain the Jabberwock's infection. If you are still able, please exit the grounds immediately. In fifteen minutes, the barrier will go up, and anyone inside the school will be quarantined until we resolve the issue. Thank you."

"Quarantined?" Daring asked.

"He means trapped," Kitty said, her hair gaining a bit more volume than usual. Her constant smile seemed absolutely terrified. "They're going to trap us in here! Till they contain the . . . the infection."

"Wait . . . the Jabberwock's infection?" said Cedar. "That beast is what's changing everything in here? So . . . is *it* in the school, too?"

Kitty squeaked and popped out of sight.

The image of a clock replaced Grimm's face. One hand pointed at the number three, and the second hand of the clock began to spin backward.

"Off with our heads!" Lizzie yelled.

Daring drew his sword and then paused. "Wait. What?" he asked.

Lizzie cleared her throat. "I mean, let's move! We've got to get out of here! Everyone, grab as many students as you can and run!"

Daring nodded, sheathed his sword, and promptly disappeared.

"Enough disappearing!" Lizzie yelled, stamping her foot. "I have had it with the sudden disappearing!"

"Again, not disappeared," Kitty said, reappearing. She nodded downward.

A furry creature the height of Lizzie's knee stood with paws on hips, its sharp teeth bright white as if recently bleached. It was the cutest little beastie Cedar had ever seen, with wide eyes and tiny horns, wearing perfectly tailored mini-replicas of Daring's clothing. It let out a squeaky roar.

"Right," Lizzie said. "Daring-beastie, can you carry Blondie?"

"*Rrryes*," the little beast growled, and scampered over to the golden lock.

Cedar picked up the Cupid cake and examined the

Briar rosebush to see if there was any way to safely uproot it. She glanced at the countdown clock. One minute had already passed. She blinked and looked again. The second hand on the clock was spinning faster and faster.

"We're not going to make it!" she yelled.

"The hutling can carry us," said Maddie. "It's a good runner, and I'm sure it wants to get out, too."

The hutling bobbed its roof, and its front door swung open.

Lizzie flung the Faybelle bell into the hut with a clang and clambered through the door.

Kitty clomped closer, wearing the Ashlynn shoes. "Tell me how going in there doesn't count as that thing eating us."

"Hutling is nice!" Maddie said, dropping Earl Grey onto her hat and pocketing the Humphrey egg before hoisting herself through the door. "It only eats wood and things like that."

Cedar instinctively cringed, but then remembered she wasn't wooden anymore. "Here are Cupid and Cerise," she said, dropping off the cake and wolf cub. "But what about the others?... Hunter and Briar..."

The clock hand spun faster, filling the room with a buzzing sound.

"A tree and a rosebush won't fit in here." Lizzie grabbed Cedar's arm and pulled her into the hut, the door slamming shut behind her.

The inside looked exactly like that of a small one-room cottage, complete with a tiny couch and chair, table, and fireplace, so cramped even Maddie couldn't stand upright. Cedar crouch-ran to one of the tiny windows.

The Daring beastie was standing protectively in front of the Briar rosebush. He was gesturing frantically.

"Daring is still out there!" Cedar yelled.

The window she was looking through swung open even as the hut began to run. The little Daring monster closed one eye as if aiming, pulled back his arm, and hurled the golden lock straight through the open window, missing Cedar by an inch. The window slammed shut, and Cedar caught a glimpse of a fuzzy Daring giving her a thumbs-up before the hutling ran out of the Grimmnasium at top speed.

"Run, hut-beast!" Lizzie yelled. "Take us beyond the grounds of Ever After High!"

Just then, the timer thundered through the school, sounding like a cuckoo clock in a great deal of pain.

CUCKOO! CUCKOOOO! CUCKOOOOOOOO!

"No way that was fifteen minutes!" said Cedar.

"Bah. Outside the school, it might have been," said Lizzie. "Sometimes in Wonderland, time moves sideways."

"No, no, we have to get out," Cedar said.

The hutling had pushed its way past the broken chairs outside the Grimmnasium door and was jogging through the corridor. There was a loud frizzle and a hiss, and through the window Cedar could see the sky outside turn a deep yellow, the color of Baba Yaga's magic. The magic barrier was up.

"We're trapped," said Cedar. "We need to...to...get help! Find some teachers or adults, perhaps a helpful woodsman or fairy godmother, maybe a wise old crone who turns out to be a good witch after we share some bread with her—"

"We don't have any bread," said Kitty.

"I have a butter knife!" Lizzie said brightly.

"You know what I mean!" Cedar yelled. Her heart was pounding, her skin felt thin as paper, and she couldn't seem to catch her breath. "In the stories, the brave young girls with pure hearts always get help from some wise adult person, and we need to find that wise adult person immediately!"

Kitty peered out a window. "Calm down, freaker-hosen. This doesn't look like any story I've read before."

Cedar *was* freaking out. Old Cedar might get sad and quiet and lonely, but shout frantically at her friends? Maybe changing into a real girl had made her loopy.

"We must help ourselves," said Lizzie. "I am the daughter of the Queen of Hearts. I will simply rule this unruly land and squeeze it into my control. It's already half Wonderland. Perhaps all it needs is a monarch."

Cedar detected a slight quaver in Lizzie's voice. Lizzie was always in control, wasn't she? Always sure she *could be* in control, anyway, even if she wasn't. Cedar took several deep breaths. This whole breathing thing was new to her, but she was finding that doing it deep and slow was much more calming than shallow and fast.

"They *have* to let us out." She pulled her MirrorPhone from her pocket to call the headmaster or her father. "No! It says 'out of area.' I always get a signal in the school. How can it be out of area?"

"Our areas have slipped and nipped," said Kitty. "Everything is upside down and sideways, except what's inside out. There may also be a cherry on top."

"You guys have to fix this!" said Cedar. "Everyone changed but you. The Jabberwock is trying to magic Ever After into Wonderland, but you're already Wonderlandian, so its magic doesn't affect you, right? You're immune?"

"It has changed us a little," said Maddie. "I mean, don't you all feel a little more... reasonable?"

"Being more reasonable is a good thing," Cedar said, still tapping at her MirrorPhone just in case it would suddenly work.

"Flesh puppet," Lizzie said, straightening the small curtains on the window that had allowed the Blondie lock entrance, "we are inside a cottage walking around on chicken legs. What use is reason right now?"

Lizzie bustled about nervously, tidying up the cottage, setting Faybelle upright, straightening chairs. It was like she was playing house. It didn't seem to matter to her that nothing made sense, only that it was out of order.

"You're always talking about order. So put it in order!" Cedar pointed at the window. Several winged cheeses flew by.

Lizzie glared at Cedar icily and opened her mouth to surely express the certain knowledge that A FOX PLUGGED THE FENCE.

Maddie stopped stOCK-STILL. A QUILL SPILLED ILL TRILLS.

"Oh, no," said Maddie.

"Not good," said Kitty.

A FROG SQUIRRELED TWICE AND BACKED UP.

"What's not good?" asked Cedar. "What's wrong now?"

"Nothing, surely. Right? Keep the hutling moving," Lizzie said, but worry striPED ALONG THE RIVER.

"Narrator?" said Maddie. "You're just teasing us with the jibber and jabber, right?"

It was clear that something was indeed GALUMPHING, but with a certain SPECIFIC SOCK, THERE WOULD BE A DOG.

"The narration has gone wonky," Maddie saNDWICHED. "Maybe the Jabberwock's magic affects everyone—even our Narrator!"

CHAPTER 14

The Narrator Takes a Sick Day

Wait...what?

Um, Narrator? Narrator, are you okay?

Please don't interrupt, Maddie. Everything is happening so rapidly I need complete concentration to observe and describe the FIDDLE-PIE-MY, OH THERE SHE GOES, WEEEE!

The, uh, the fiddle-pie-my? Narrator, do you speak Riddlish? Hat-tastic! But I couldn't quite translate it. What was that second part again?

I'm not speaking Riddlish. What I'm trying to say is this is a situation of UTMOST ROAST BEEF, and if I don't CACKLE TACKLE FINGER IN MY EYE, KNOCKS AT THE DOOR, A CHICKEN IN DISGUISE?

While the idea of "utmost roast beef" seems perfectly lovely, and I am hextremely fond of the odd thing, the oddness in your speaking is making me a little nervous.

Oh dear. Maddie, something *is* wrong with me. I can hear it now. I'm trying to tell the story, but HUMPTY LUMPTY OATMEAL WITH RAISINS! Oh no! I'm SPICY BUTTERED NOODLES! I'm LOBSTER SAUCE!

No! Narrator, the magic just can't change you, too! If you can't tell the story, then it stops right here, skipping over the climax and resolution straight to The End, and Raven's still a raven and Apple's still an apple and Ever After High is jabberwocked forever after with no hope of undoing the doneness! Please, Narrator, you have to keep narrating! Please!

SPINACH BETWEEN MY TOES!

Narrator?

SAND IN THE SANDWICH, MY, WHAT A CRUNCHY LUNCH!

Okay. It's going to be okay. I am the daughter of the Mad Hatter. I must put on my thinking cap and figure this out. Let's see, I'm sure I have a thinking cap in my Hat of Many Things…ah-ha! Here it is, hiding under Apple-apple. Well, the cap fits a little snug, but it'll do. So think. No matter what, the story must go on. I read that in the Narration hextbook I borrowed from the library. And in order for a story to go on, it must have a Narrator. So if our Narrator is unable to fulfill the narration duties, we simply find an alternate Narrator. Someone who is untouched by the mystery-making magic. Which would mean a Wonderlandian. Perhaps someone who understands the basics of narration because she has been eavesdropping on Narrators her whole life. But...who could that be?

SQUIGGLE THE TIMES!

I don't know what you're saying! You're not speaking Riddlish, and you're not speaking a riddle. Help me, Narrator, please! Who can narrate us through this story?

A DANCE OF SPOONS, STIRRING CLOUDS OF MILK.

I wish I could figure out what you're saying. But with this tiny thinking cap on, all I can think about is the tightness around my brow. And that makes me think of my own head. And that makes me think of me. Me. Me?

Yes, already! You! There's no one else!

Really, Kitty? You think I should narrate the story? That seems like a hero's job, something Raven or Apple would do to save the day. But I'm

a Hatter. I have read about different types of characters in a narration book, and I'm clearly the quirky best friend or the comic relief. I'm the helper, not the doer. I'm definitely not the hero!

CINDERS AND ELEPHANT PIE. *CINDERS AND ELEPHANT PIE!*

Okay. Okay. I'm the Narrator.

CHAPTER 15

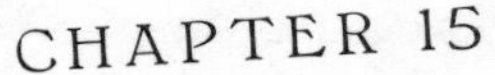

SWAMP JUICE IN YOUR TEACUP

"MADDIE? WHAT THE TIMBERSTICKS IS going on?"

"Uncertain how to proceed, Madeline Hatter began to speak, she said."

"Um, Maddie, what are you talking about?"

"All the girls were staring at her like Madeline had just eaten an entire gooseberry pie with her nose, she said."

"Did Maddie get hit on the head?"

"I don't think so, but I am always willing to give head-bonking a try. Fetch me a flamingo!"

"Maddie shook her head to clear cobwebs and tried to figure out this narration thing without talking, um, she said.... I mean, Maddie said. Wait. Am I supposed to say that out loud?"

"I'm confused."

"You aren't the only one, Cedar Scratchingpost."

"Oh dear, I'm really making a mess of this," said Maddie.

"Wait!" said Kitty. "Do that. You *narrated* 'said Maddie' instead of saying it aloud. That was more like how the Narrator does it."

"This is truly troubling," Cedar said, looking around nervously.

"That, too!" Kitty said, getting unusually excited. "Exactly! You noticed that I'm unusually excited, and you narrated that information. Wait... how did you do that? I can't normally hear your thoughts."

"I'm trying out something new," Maddie said. "I'm not just thinking about what's going on—I'm *narrating* it. It's different from talking and different from normal thinking. It's thinking *out loud*."

"But how?" said Kitty. "That's amazing, I wonder if—no, I don't wonder anything. I am Kitty Cheshire and I do not get involved. What's the matter with me? Shutting up now—cat's got my tongue and all that."

"What in the blighted name of bunnies is going on?" Lizzie shouted. "Tell me at once!"

"The Narrator is sick," Maddie said.

"*Sick?*" Lizzie bellowed. "How can a bodiless thing one barely believes exists be sick? And why do I apparently care?"

"The Jabberwock's magic is transforming our Narrator, too," Maddie said.

"Without a Narrator, the story would end," Cedar said, her eyebrows up high as if trying to make room for all the thoughts filling her head. "We would stay here, trapped inside a school that is all hexed up, being hunted by furniture, Raven and Apple and Cerise and all our friends transformed. Forever after."

The red-haired wolf cub nuzzled Cedar's ankle.

"She's keeping the story going," Kitty said, nodding at me. Er, nodding at Maddie. "She's trying to take over for the Narrator."

"Well," Lizzie said, "today is indeed a day of absurdicy and idiotity. But it is only right that the post be taken over by someone from our noble homeland. Carry on, Maddie. I will allow it."

"Okay, first priority, we need to figure out what to do now," said Cedar. "What do you think, Lizzie? Should we try to find a way out of the school, or would that damage the magical barrier that's keeping the Jabberwock in? Should we just keep hiding inside the hutling till the faculty gets rid of the Jabberwock?"

At the mention of the Jabberwock, Kitty's face went big-eyed and wince-y.

"Kitty Cheshire," Lizzie said all loud and grand-like, "disappear your way out of the school, beyond the magic barrier, and find Headmaster Grimm."

Kitty's nose went wrinkle-winkly, and she opened her mouth as if she would hiss. But instead, she shrugged and disappeared as Lizzie had suggested. Or ordered. Or something.

Kitty reappeared again a minute later, her Cheshire grin still grinning but not in a happy-making way. Now she did hiss.

"I can't. I'm trapped by the barrier, too. I do *not* like being trapped."

"Maddie, what do you think?" asked Cedar.

But Maddie had a hard time thinking about the problem and the solving. Maddie was too busy fretting, and fretting was a thing Maddie was not very good at, having had very little practice.

HIGGLEDY-PIGGLEDY PUDDING OF RYE, KISS THE BOOK AND NEVER CRY.

"Oh!" Maddie said aloud. "I think the not-me-Narrator is trying to give us a clue."

Maddie repeated the higgledy-and-cry bit. Kitty and Lizzie both nodded as if she'd just said something very un-boring, but Cedar rubbed her new, real eyes and shook her new, real head, worried that these Wonderlandians were as touched by the muddling magic as Daring-beastie and Raven-raven.

Wait, how do I... that is, how did Maddie know what Cedar was thinking and feeling? Maddie never had before, not unless she overheard the Narrator gabbing about it.

KISS THE BOOK.

Maddie had a library book in her backpack. She pulled it out: *A Narrative History of the Grand Craft of Narration, by Narrators Anonymous.* She scanned the first chapter, "Narration Basics."

"We'll just sit here while you read a book, then," Lizzie said.

"According to the book," said Maddie, "Narrators have splendid, magicky insight into characters' thoughts and motivations. This insight usually only comes after years of training, but some Narrators have so much desire to storytell, their skills come more quickly. Tea-riffic! Ooh, and did you know that the Narration Board writes down all of Ever After's narrated stories? The Narration Board prints them and sends them to libraries and bookstores. Real people far, far away might actually read what I narrate here! So hexciting!"

"What people?" asked Cedar. "How?"

"I don't know, but our conversation is probably being written down right now. And in fact, in the slippy-slinky way of time, somewhere in the Lands and Otherlands, someone could be reading it at this very moment."

Maddie leaned forward, squinting, and for the barest second, the world of cottages and castles and forests and magic parted, and she spied, far, far away and yet as close as her nose, someone holding the story she was narrating. A reader.

(That's *you.*) Maddie winked. (Go ahead and wink back.)

Maddie caught her breath. The story she was helping to tell had the power to connect characters and readers. This narration thing was as delightful as a bag of goldyfish!

Seemingly by its own power, the narration book flipped to another page near the back.

"Oh, to become a real Narrator—even just a temporary one—I'm supposed to take the Narrator's Oath. Okey-dokey, here I go." Maddie read aloud the oath. "'I, your name here, hereby take—'"

"I don't think you actually say 'your name here,'" said Cedar. "You probably say your *actual* name."

"Oh! Well, that doesn't make much sense, but all right. 'I, Madeline Hatter, hereby take the sacred Oath of Narration. I swear to: only speak the truth; follow the story wherever it may lead; observe all that happens but report only the most important and interesting parts; honor the characters in both their greatness and their mistakes; serve only the story and the reader and no other, be it king or queen or baker or candlestick maker; and never, ever, ever, ever, ever interfere with the story. Ever.

"'If I so do my best, may this story be recorded and printed and zipped and zapped into hands and eyes and ears and minds and hearts everywhere, and may it no longer be my story but belong to each reader who drinks it in, to make them bigger or smaller as needed; to fill in those tiny holes and smooth over the rough places; to make them sigh and laugh and dream and wonder; to pass a lonely afternoon or enliven a dull evening; to in every regard do just what a story is supposed to do, which is become whatever each reader needs most at that moment. And for this noble mission I pledge my skills and shortcomings, my talents and my weaknesses, until The End.'"

Maddie exhaled. Everything was so quiet you could hear the cottage breathing.

"Did the oath work?" Cedar asked. "Are you officially our Narrator? Can the story go on?"

"I think so," said Maddie. "I feel less worried, but we won't know if it worked till the story is over."

And in the meantime, I'll keep narrating the story! Oh wait, a Narrator isn't supposed to say "I." That rule was in Chapter One. But in my experience, they do sometimes say *ahem*.

So, *ahem.* The girls sat in the walking cottage and argued about what to do next.

"It doesn't seem fair," said Cedar, as the Raven-raven alighted on her head. "Some got so changed they can't speak anymore while I got what I've always wanted."

"I suspect the Blue-Haired Fairy laid deep magic on you, Cedar," said Maddie. "Maybe you were preprogrammed to change into a real girl, and so when the Jabberwock magic touched you, instead of turning into a plank of cedarwood or something, it triggered your change magic. You became real."

"Maddie, you are really smart."

"Am I? I wonder if that's new, or if I've always been smart."

"You've always been smart, Maddie," Lizzie said idly as she peered out the window. She seemed to realize she'd spoken that aloud, cleared her throat, and proclaimed, "But I, too, am quite bright! Exceptionally so! More than most!"

"If the Jabberwock is turning Ever After into Wonderland, why aren't you guys excited?" asked Cedar.

"*That* isn't Wonderland." Kitty pointed out the

window, where giant pumpkins with wheels were ramming into each other. "*You* said it, Cedar. It's out of order. All messed up."

Outside the window, one of the pumpkins cracked apart with the impact, spilling seeds onto the ground, which were then gobbled up by a crazed legion of red paper envelopes.

"It's not Wonderlandish at all," Lizzie said. She paused, afraid to admit there was something wrong that she couldn't just rule into submission. But sad truth pressed up into her throat, and she let the words out. "Ever After cannot be transformed into Wonderland, not even by magic. The Jabberwock tries, but it comes out wrong, a hybrid of two places, being neither. A monster making monsters."

"Its magic is tearing things from the names they were and turning everything mad," said Maddie.

Cedar looked confuse-boggled, but Maddie's mind was Narrator-sharp, and so she tried to explain.

"Madness is life, but the *unpredictable* parts of life. See, a person is alive and so might do anything. A chair is not, so you know what it's going to do: just sit there." Maddie pointed to one of the school chairs outside, barking at the hutling. "Now that *that* chair is alive, it's no longer predictable. It might do anything, just like a person. The school and everything in it are turning mad. Nothing does what you expect. It's all unpredictable. It's all mad."

"But not the *right* sort of madness," said Kitty.

Lizzie pressed her fingers against the windowpane. "In Wonderland, a chair *knows* it is a chair. But things touched by the Jabberwock madness no longer know what they are. It's royally disappointing, like being promised hot tea and getting swamp juice in your teacup."

"Ooh, nice simile, Lizzie," said Maddie.

"The Jabberwock's magic is forcing things to be what they are not," said Cedar. "That *is* the wrong kind of madness." *And so is this whole Royal and Rebel dilemma*, Cedar thought.

The Raven-raven hopped onto Cedar's knee, and she petted the bird's wings, so black they glimmered with a sheen of purple. Headmaster Grimm's trying to force Raven to be evil was like the Jabberwock's forcing chairs to walk around and roar. Perhaps Royals were the people who would do the things they were supposed to do in their stories anyway. But Rebels wouldn't naturally do what their destinies tried to force them to do. And forced destinies could wreak as much havoc as a Jabberwock.

It was suddenly so clear to Cedar! She decided she should explain her insight to Headmaster Grimm. If she ever saw him again.

The chair herd had grown larger. They began clacking folding seats, stomping steel-tipped legs, and flinging one another at the hutling's door. The hutling *baaaaked* and *braaaaked* and darted about. The room swayed.

"This much madness is dangerous," said Cedar, sliding into a wall.

"I wonder if Alice felt like we do now when she fell down the rabbit hole," said Lizzie.

Kitty began quoting a well-known Wonderland poem:

Down she goes, like a blown nose
to expose what is under is not the ground
and once she arrives she finds that she's found.

Maddie said, "Since Wonderland is often found down, maybe things get madder the lower you go, and the school will become less mad the higher we climb."

"We'd still be trapped here by the magical barrier," said Cedar, "but at least it might be less dangerous."

"Up, hut-beast! I command you to take us up!" said Lizzie.

Cedar crouched by the fireplace and whispered into the chimney, "Hutling? We're hoping the top of the school might be safer than down here with clacking and stampeding chairs." She stroked its fuzzy wallpaper like the neck of a frisky horse. "Could you carry us up? Please?"

The cottage began to run. Cedar gripped the mantel, trying to stay on her soft, little feet as the cottage swayed and bounced. The floor tilted back as the hutling started up the stairs. Kitty slipped, rolling back and hitting the wall. She dissolved and reappeared beside Cedar.

"I'm bored," said Kitty. "This is taking forever."

She put her hands beneath the curtains and began to tickle. The hutling howled, the whole cottage rumbling.

"Stop bugging it," said Cedar.

Kitty disappeared and reappeared at the other window, her feet on the sill, pulling the curtains as if they were the reins on a galloping horse.

"Yee-ha," she said with her mischievous smile.

The hutling rumbled again. The walls squeezed in as if the cottage were tightening up its middle, and the girls all squished together. Kitty's face was pressed into Cedar's cheek, and Maddie's head was in Lizzie's armpit. The hutling opened its door and the back wall spasmed forward, effectively spitting the girls out. They landed on the stairs.

"Pick us back up!" Lizzie shouted.

The hutling shut its door and ran away, its chicken-feet toenails tapping on the stone steps.

"Wait! The Raven-raven!" said Cedar. "And the Apple-apple! And all the other people-things!"

"Bah. They're safer in there," said Lizzie.

Cedar folded her arms. "Kitty, why did you—"

"I am *not* reasonable," said Kitty, smiling but not meaning it. "I refuse to be turned reasonable by that horribific monster's magic. I am a Cheshire. I am chaos! But this kind of chaos, I don't...I don't know what to..." She turned red in the face and disappeared.

"Kitty Cheshire!" Lizzie shouted at the air. "I order you to be chaotic again!"

Smile first, Kitty reappeared. "Thanks, Lizzie," she whispered.

From the darkness down the corridor, Cedar heard slow clopping like the sound a twelve-burner stove would make if it could walk. Then a hideous, scratchy voice whispered, "I. Eat. Wiggly. Things."

Cedar screamed. She took the stairs three at a time, running higher and higher, the other girls following. Well, Kitty never ran, but when they reached the top of the stairs, Kitty appeared there, terror in her smiling eyes.

The scratchy whisper echoed up from the floor below. "Wiggly? Things?"

And Cedar kept running. Her new legs ached, her thighs trembling, but she didn't stop climbing stairs until suddenly she was going down.

"Eek! How did that happen?" Cedar reversed to go back up, passing the other girls. "Come on, we've got to go *up*."

"We are going up," Kitty said with a laugh.

"Close your eyes at once," said Lizzie. "You are being tricked by reality."

Cedar closed her eyes. Maddie took her hand. And they started running back up the stairs. When Cedar peeked, they appeared to be going down, so she shut her eyes again and *felt* rather than *saw* the climb.

They only stopped when they reached the highest tower of the school. It was wobbling as if made of rubber.

Cedar clutched the empty frame of the window, its panes curiously missing. Outside, the huge yellow dome of the magical barrier crackled and fizzed as insects flew into it. Through the yellowness she spotted the Troll Bridge and, beyond, the rooftops of Book End.

Maddie rummaged through her Hat of Many Things. So helpful, really, wearing a Hat of Many Things. She wondered why everyone didn't have one. Then she scolded herself for wondering about something that didn't matter to the current story. That's simply not what Narrators do! Hocus focus, Maddie. *Ahem.*

From her hat, she pulled out two telescopes, holding one to each eye.

"There's Dad!" said Maddie. "He's on the roof of

the Tea Shoppe. He sees me. Dad! Dad!" Maddie shouted, waving. "Oh, good. He's got the flags."

"Flags?" asked Cedar.

"Yes, to spell out messages from far away. Doesn't everyone have a flag language with their father?" asked Maddie. "Okay, he's signaling with the flags. I'll translate. 'If the Jabberwock magic reaches Book End, everything ends. Because our story will literally become the book end and the book will end without a resolution.' Oh nose!"

Lizzie grabbed one of the telescopes and put it to her eye. "No way he said all that so fast. Wait...oh!...You're right, Maddie." She handed the telescope back to Maddie. "Your dad can really move flags."

"Our story ends? That can't be right," Cedar started to say, but then, really, what *was* right at the moment? She'd just spotted the glass panes that were missing from the windows. They were slowly crawling across the tower wall, rippling like transparent caterpillars.

"Cedar, could you stop noticing things for a minute?" Maddie said. "You're the main character of this chapter, so I'm supposed to focus more on you, but I can't narrate what you're doing and pay attention to my dad at the same time."

"Sorry."

"Thanks. Okay, he says the Jabberwock can't complete the transformation of Ever After into its version of Wonderland without Wonderland things to squeeze. Things of Wonderland are full of Wonder, and Wonder powers its magic. At least I think that's what he's saying. He's speaking Riddlish. With flags."

"So, wait..." Cedar said. "The Jabberwock needs to collect Wonderland things and use them like batteries for its magic? Wonderland things like... like you guys?"

Kitty and Lizzie backed away from the window, and the tippy tower slid them farther. They bumped together, Kitty's pale purple locks tangled in Lizzie's gold crown.

"Off... with her head," Lizzie said, but she sounded more like she was saying, *I'm so scared at the moment I may start beheading butter people.*

Kitty snickered.

"What?" Lizzie demanded.

"Nothing," said Kitty. "Narration joke."

"Dad is warning us to stay away from the Jabberwock," Maddie said. "If it captures the three of us, it would have enough power to make its mad transformation permanent."

"Yeah, I'd planned to avoid it," said Cedar. "But where is it?"

Kitty, her smile gone stiff, whispered through her teeth, "*Right. There.*"

Cedar whirled around. Through another window, she could see the Jabberwock hanging on the side of a tower, gripping the stones with long white claws. It was as large as a full-size dragon armored with gray scales, but its feet and antennaed head were ragged with unexpected fur. Its snakelike neck and toothy head were stretched forward, its milky white, seemingly blind eyes staring at something in the distance. Toward Book End.

It screeched and beat its huge leathery wings, lifting off the tower and taking flight.

"It sees Dad!" said Maddie. "It will squeeze him for Wonder and then he'll be Wonder-less and we've got to stop it!"

"Baba Yaga's magic barrier will stop it," Cedar whispered.

The Jabberwock threw itself at the transparent yellow dome, with an explosion of flares and sparks. The beast shrieked but seemed more angry than hurt. It attacked the barrier again and again and again. The yellow of the magic began to dim, like egg yolks bleeding into the whites. The barrier was weakening. And the Mad Hatter was on the other side. Maddie's Dad. No, not Dad!

"No!" Maddie found herself screaming. "Leave him alone!"

The long, thin neck snaked around, the gruesome face of the Jabberwock pointed at their tower.

It shrieked, beating its wings straight for them.

Run, said the Narrator.

"Run," Maddie said.

They ran.

They were only halfway down the first flight of stairs when the tower shook with the impact of the Jabberwock.

The stone steps underneath Cedar's feet suddenly felt softer, almost gelatinous. She slipped but kept running on the stairs in the same direction, though sometimes she felt that she was going up, not down. She heard the Jabberwock shriek, and the tower trembled and hummed and seemed a breath away from crumbling.

Cedar's new heart was pounding hard against her ribs, like a bird flinging itself against a window, trying to escape. She began to cry but couldn't marvel at the newness and wonder of cold wetness sliding down her soft cheeks. Instead, tears felt like losing control, like the ground no longer under her shoes, like hurting and not being sure if she'd ever feel okay again. She stumbled into the soft floor and began to slowly sink. Maddie grabbed her hands and started to pull, but Cedar wondered if it was too late.

She whispered the truth aloud: "Maybe everything is easier when you're made of wood."

No, she told herself. *No!* She'd been waiting her entire life to be real. She was not going to let the fear of a Jabberwock steal that away.

"That's right," said Maddie. "You are not made of wood, you are made of Wood. You are Cedar Wood!"

I am Cedar Wood. Cedar pulled herself out of the sinking floor and ran faster. No more waiting. Now she was who she'd always wanted to be. And whatever happened next, she'd make this chance count.

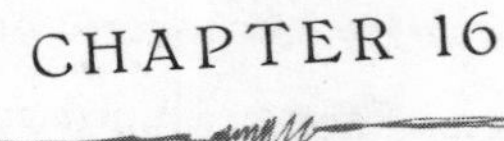

CHAPTER 16

Running from Deadly Terror

THE GIRLS RAN. THE WALLS GROANED WITH stress, and each painting they passed only compounded their worry.

"It's right behind you!" yelled a girl in a painting holding a watering can.

"It will eat us all!" shouted a painting of a wide-mouthed man on a bridge.

"Run, stinky pooters, run," the daisies in a bright watercolor chanted.

"Behave!" Lizzie shouted at the daisies. "I am a

princess of Wonderland and I will not be insulted by stained canvas!"

The Narrator warned her to keep running, but Lizzie was all red-face and up-chin and pointing-finger, and didn't listen. The Jabberwock was right outside the window, looking in with those milk-white eyes that seemed blind and yet saw. It opened its square, toothy mouth.

"Duck!" Cedar shouted.

"Where?" said Lizzie, looking around for a duck.

Cedar pulled her down just as the Jabberwock hissed, a spray of magic exhaling over their heads. The paint on the walls curdled and flaked off, pulling itself together into a huge mass of daddy longlegs. The paint-spiders began to crawl all over the girls, tickling them with their feather-light feet.

Cedar screamed. "Stop it! I'm finally real, and I'm not going to waste this realness getting attacked by tickle-spiders!"

Lizzie leaped into the path of the oncoming spiders, pointed her scepter, and commanded, "Retreat, multilegged paint chips! Do not touch my friend!"

Cedar blinked. So did Maddie. Lizzie swallowed. Had she just admitted to having friends? Her mother would not approve. All this madness was making it hard to keep her mother's good advice in mind.

The girls shook off the spiders and kept running.

SNAILS DON'T ROCK OR ROLL.

Behave now, not-me-Narrator! You know better than to interrupt a story.

"Where do we go?" Cedar asked.

"If it doesn't matter where you end up, any path will do," said Kitty.

"But I do know where I want to end up," said Cedar. "Away!"

"There is no getting to Away," said Kitty. "Away is wherever we aren't."

"Then let's make sure the Jabberwock stays in Away," said Lizzie.

Ahead, several tiny cows with pink butterfly wings hovered in the corridor, gripping wands between their bitty hooves.

"Are those the fairy-godmothers-in-training?" Cedar said. "The FiGITs?"

"DiGITs," Kitty whispered.

Above the crowd of cows fluttered tiny cheese slices and milk cartons on wispy wings.

"Right. *Dairy*-godmothers-in-training," Lizzie said.

"Help us?" said Cedar.

One winged cow pointed her magic wand at Cedar. Cedar ducked just as a pink bolt of magic flew over her head. The vase in the nook behind her turned into a large glass pitcher full of milk.

"Keep running!" Lizzie said.

Shrinking down to the size of a dog, the Jabberwock darted through an open window. It flapped behind them, its breath sizzling the air. The milk pitcher melted and covered the floor, making it slick as ice. The girls slipped and slid and almost fell.

They turned a corner, and all fell flat to the floor as fire shot through the air, temporarily slowing the miniature Jabberwock. Squinting to see the source of the fire, Maddie spotted a four-wheeled cart blocking the hall.

"A fire-breathing wagon," Kitty murmured. "Everything is Ever After and Wonderland confused together."

Lizzie smashed a window with her scepter. "Out," she said. "Everyone."

She helped Maddie up to the sill and waited for Cedar and Kitty to escape before she followed. Her expression was slightly puzzled, as if she wasn't sure why she wasn't going first.

The girls grabbed hold of the ivy growing over the outside of the school and climbed down. The vines giggled. The vines sighed. Giggles and sighs come from mouths. And things with mouths can bite.

"Don't bite," Lizzie ordered the vines. "At least, don't bite us."

STARS IN YOUR EYES! FOAM IN YOUR BEARD!

Not now, not-me-Narrator. I'm trying to work here.

So the girls were hanging from the vines when the Jabberwock appeared above them, again as huge as a dragon, which is even huger than a wagon. Its three-toed feet reached, claws clinking, sharp as the edges of things.

Cedar screamed. Maddie would have screamed,

too, but she was too busy concentrating on the narration.

And then the vines opened their leafy mouths and began to bite the Jabberwock. It clawed at the ivy, giving the girls a second to drop down onto another windowsill and climb into a new room. It was—

BEES KNEES DON'T BEND UNLESS WELL-HONEYED.

Stop interrupting, not-me-Narrator. Don't you see how hard it is to narrate a story? All this running from deadly terror is happening too fast! I'm getting thinking pains as it is, trying to imitate your talkage and wordage and not get too wonderlandiful in my descriptions 'cause that's not how *you* would do it. When you were normal, anyway. And—*ack!*

A crab slightly smaller than Maddie grabbed her hands in its claws and began to dance. Each girl was claimed by a similar partner. An overlarge oyster at the front of the room counted time. "One, two, one, two, heel, toe, slide..." And meanwhile, outside the window, the Jabberwock was clawing its way free from the vines.

Lizzie fought out of her partner's grip and swung open the room's only door.

"Keep dancing!" shouted the oyster. "There are no makeup days for crab-dancing class!"

The girls followed Lizzie out the door, shutting it behind—

DON'T TRUST YOUR LEFT LEG.

Please, not-me-Narrator, this is getting out of control. I need you to behave yourself so I can concentrate, okay? Please? Pretty please with shoelaces on top?

MUFF.

Is that a yes? You'll behave now and let me narrate?

MUFF.

I'll take that as a yes. *Ahem.* And so they kept running, the Jabberwock always close behind, each new hall and room more dangerous than the last. Just when they thought they'd found a safe place—

SCOODLE-MOO EAT A DOO.

Argh!

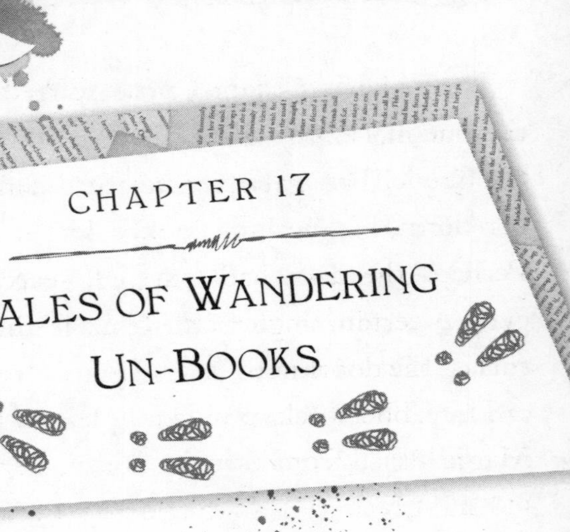

CHAPTER 17

TALES OF WANDERING UN-BOOKS

LIZZIE HAD *HAD* IT WITH RUNNING. IT WAS bad enough when Coach Gingerbreadman made them run, run as fast as they could in Grimmnastics class, but running just to stay alive was unseemly. They had turned a corner and had finally lost sight of that despicable Jabberwock when the walls shook with the sound of a battering ram. Lizzie stumbled.

"Off with its head!" she yelled automatically.

"Wait, when the rest of the building shook, that red door didn't move," said Cedar.

The red heart-shaped door looked exactly like the one in Lizzie's dorm that transported her into the Grove. This galloping corridor definitely wasn't her dorm, but nothing looked like itself anymore. Perhaps the door had traveled, searched her out, even. A certain tingle tickled Lizzie's hand when she turned the doorknob.

The Jabberwock rounded the corner behind them. Magic hissed from its huge mouth, melting reality.

"In!" Lizzie yelled. She pushed Cedar, Kitty, and Maddie through first and then jumped after them, slamming it shut. She leaned against it, expecting the pounding of the Jabberwock trying to force its way through the door, but it never came.

The air had changed, warm, soft, quiet. They were no longer in the school. They were in the Grove. Lizzie's center relaxed just a little, and strangely she thought she might cry. Which was absurd. Crying was not relaxing at all. Right?

"You saved us," Cedar said.

"I *pushed* you," Lizzie said.

"You pushed us into safety," Cedar said.

"Through the door that you noticed," Lizzie said. "So, technically, *you* saved us."

Cedar reached out to take Lizzie's hand. "Thanks, Lizzie."

Cedar's thank-you made Lizzie feel all huggable and candy-sweet, and she had to fight the ridiculous urge to say a thank-you back.

"Thank... uh, I'll thank you to take back that gratitude as soon as you are able," Lizzie grumbled. "It is unseemly."

The Grove looked exactly as Lizzie had left it, unchanged, un-Jabberwocked. The beast's magic was running rampant in the school castle but, trapped by the barrier, it had not reached beyond into the school grounds. So far the Grove and, thankfully, Book End were safe. Lizzie breathed in again, relishing the familiar scents of spicy flowers, sweet tree sap, and minty grass. This was the smell of Wonderland. Of *real* Wonderland. Like her, it was between Wonderland and Ever After. The thought gave Lizzie strength.

"Not that I'm complaining," Kitty said, "but why didn't the Jabberwock just tear down that door and eat us?"

"This is a special place," Lizzie said, confident it was true.

"Hey, if that door transported us outside the school, then we're beyond the magic barrier, right?" said Cedar. "We can go find the faculty!"

Cedar began to run.

"Stop!" Lizzie yelled. Feeling so huggable-sweet and thanky had been uncomfortable. Time to shout orders again.

Hedgehogs nosed around in the grass near Lizzie's feet. She grabbed one and threw it, hitting Cedar's shoulder.

"Ow!" Cedar yelled. The hedgehog dropped to the ground and scampered away. "Poor little thing! Don't hurt it!"

It was not hurt at all, the Narrator was twiddly anxious to assure the reader. Wonderlandian hedgehogs are bred for sports and in fact frequently nap their way through a croquet game in which they are the balls.

Lizzie picked up another hedgehog.

"Stop throwing animals at me," said Cedar.

"I'm not. You just got in the way," Lizzie said, flinging the creature over Cedar's shoulder. The hedgehog stopped suddenly as if it had struck an invisible wall. The air buzzed with the impact and brightened to a deep yellow. The hedgehog dropped to the ground, twitched, and wobbled back to the grass.

"Oh! We're still inside the magic barrier," Cedar said.

When Ever After High was normal, the heart-shaped door had sent Lizzie from her dorm to the Grove, which was on the edge of the school grounds. But it seemed even the door couldn't transport them outside Baba Yaga's barrier. If they were in the Grove yet still inside the magic barrier, then the barrier had made an extra bubble around the Grove to trap whatever tried to escape the school.

"Are we safe?" Cedar asked. "Can we just wait here till the teachers figure out how to fix everything?"

"Or until the monster figures out how to get in?" Kitty echoed.

"Hey, I have a signal!" Cedar said, punching numbers on her MirrorPhone. "We must be far enough away from the—Hello? Headmaster Grimm? This is Cedar Wood."

His irritated voice crackled on the speaker for all to hear. *"Miss Wood, do not bother me right now. We are very busy—watch out for that pixie!—very busy concocting a spell to banish the Jabber—we need three more cockroaches!—banish the Jabberwock.*"

"Ugh! They don't know what they're doing!" Lizzie shouted. "Tell them an Ever Afterish spell won't work!"

"It won't?" Cedar asked in a small voice.

"Not the right kind of magic," Kitty said. "I can't believe they don't know the only thing that can defeat the Jabberwock."

Maddie nodded solemnly. Lizzie recited part of the poem aloud.

He took his vorpal sword in hand:
Long time the manxome foe he sought—
So rested he by the Tumtum tree . . .

"The vorpal sword, Headmaster!" Cedar said into her MirrorPhone. "You need the vorpal sword, like that poem says! Only the vorpal sword can defeat—"

"*The vorpal sword is in Wonderland, Miss Wood,*" said the headmaster. "*And all portals into Wonderland are sealed. So we will use—newt eyeballs! Rumpelstiltskin, we need more newt eyeballs!—will use a spell. Get to safety and kindly don't interrupt me again.*"

Click.

Cedar stared at the phone for some time. Kitty faded into a soft shadow. Maddie sat on the grass.

"So... so we have no hope?" said Cedar. "Raven will be a raven forever? Daring a beastie-thing? Hunter a tree? And we'll live out the rest of our lives inside this Grove?"

Maddie took Cedar's hand. Kitty reappeared, sitting with her back to them, but after a moment, she curled up on the grass, her head on Maddie's lap.

"Their spell might do *some*thing," Kitty said. "I guess."

Lizzie was tired. The more time she spent with these girls, the more she was reminded that she felt things. Helpy things. Unselfy things. Crawling feelings like worry and hope. Burn-ish feelings like fondness and friendliness. And worst of all, sappy grabby feelings like Concern For Others.

Lizzie opened her mother's deck of cards and found the one she was searching for:

♥

Above all else, avoid these things: vats of poison,
Jabberwocks, paper cuts on fingertips,
and Concern For Others.

If ever you detect Concern For Others
squirming into you,
shout at people till the feeling goes away.
Or the people do.

❤

"Off with your heads!" Lizzie shouted. "Off with all your heads! I am a princess of Wonderland and I . . . I . . . I am shouting at you!"

"Um . . ." said Cedar.

Lizzie's blood was up now. Enough feeling things Mother had forbidden her to feel. And enough waiting. A queen, even a queen-in-waiting, does not wait. Especially if you're a mad queen. And Lizzie *was* mad.

"I am going to fix this ridiculousness, as it appears no one else will, so things can return to as they were and I don't have to crawl with worry and feel burn-ish and battle Concern For Others!" Lizzie shouted.

The Narrator could tell that Lizzie was not really angry, just anxious, but did not make the observation aloud. Just as she didn't observe how the meticulous tending of the Grove revealed just how desperately Lizzie missed Wonderland.

"Wonderland!" said Maddie. "Someone of Wonderland would understand better than Headmaster Grimm."

Kitty admitted, "I've been trying to phone the White Queen without luck."

"Same with my dad," said Maddie. "But there is someone in Wonderland I sometimes talk to."

"What? Who?" Lizzie still felt choked by that unfortunate hope-ish thing perched in her chest. "Tell me at once! How dare you keep a someone of Wonderland a secret from your future queen!"

"There's a book I sometimes find that has a letter in it," Maddie said. "When I write back, the letter-writer responds, and I just know the writer is in Wonderland because he or she writes such Wonderlandish things. The book was in the library once. At other times inside a stocking, on top of a chimney, at the bottom of a bucket of frogs, beneath a bag of marshmallows..."

"Tales of wandering un-books is exactly what we shouldn't be wasting time on," Lizzie said, pacing. She had to solve this by herself, but she couldn't think when everyone was nattering on so.

"What does the letter writer write?" Cedar asked.

Lizzie realized they weren't going to hush up, so she stalked off to gather a few hedgehogs. Hedgehogs always got people's attention.

"The first letter just said, 'My ears itch,'" said Maddie. "Another said, 'Clap your hands if you can read this.'"

One hedgehog, two... Lizzie would need at least three, one for each of them. Maybe some extras in case she missed.

"I wrote a letter about all the things in Wonderland I missed," said Maddie, "and the letter writer told me how things are now. It made me feel less homesick."

Lizzie grabbed one of the hedgehog balls and cocked her arm back but was stopped by a thought. It was not an *Off with your head!* kind of thought. Nevertheless, inside Lizzie's head, beneath her red-streaked black hair and impressive gold crown, it felt big and important and as wonderful as Wonderland.

"Maddie?" Lizzie dropped the hedgehogs, and they scampered away. "Do you think this mysterious

Wonderlandian might know how we could get the vorpal sword?"

"Ooh, that is a big and important and wonderlandiful thought, Lizzie!" Maddie reached into her hat and pulled out a small leather-bound book with the title *Hutch and Housing for Hare and Architect.*

"Ah-ha! Here it is!" said Maddie. "What luck! It's never been in my hat before."

Maddie flipped through the pages and came to a small red envelope. Lizzie grabbed it and tore it open. The letter was handwritten and stamped with a bunny paw print at the bottom.

"'Life in a poisoned land is actually less poisonous than it is lonely,'" Lizzie read. Her voice tripped over the word *lonely*, the word going as wobbly as her middle. She touched the bunny paw print. "Very well, then. Let's put this leather-bound postman to the test. Someone, fetch paper and pen!"

Maddie rummaged in her hat and managed to find scraps of notepaper and a pen.

"Cedar, you will scribe for me, as you do the Artsing and the Craftsing," said Lizzie.

Then she dictated in her most queenly voice:

Book Letter Person/Animal/Thing—
Your princess requests knowledge. Knowledge of the type and ilk and substance of which one would seek when longing to rid oneself of a pesky pest. Namely, a Jabberwock. We need the vorpal sword in Ever After. But how? And wherewith? And ho-hum? Respond immediately.
Lizzie Hearts, Your Princess of Hearts, etc.

"Um," Cedar said, a little nervously. "Have you ever written a letter before, Lizzie?"

"Of course I have," Lizzie said, fairly certain that wasn't true. "Why? What's wrong with it?"

Cedar held her breath as if afraid to let the truth out.

"Why are you holding your breath?" Lizzie asked.

"Oh. It's so new. The breathing. I sometimes forget to do it," Cedar lied. And then widened her eyes.

"Cedar?" Maddie asked. "Did you just...?"

"I just forgot to breathe," Cedar lied again, smiling. "Also, I really like eating...um...porridge with mustard!"

Cedar folded up the letter and stuffed it in the book.

"Plus," Cedar said, "I once buried myself in the dirt up to my neck to see if I would grow."

"That *is* odd," Lizzie said, "though I suppose a reasonable scientific experiment."

"And I *did* grow," Cedar continued, laughing with delight. "Into a giant walking tree! And I...I lived for a hundred years in the Otherlands, battling giants and baking award-winning cupcakes."

"That explains a lot," Lizzie said, not really paying attention. "Where is the book?"

"Right over here," Cedar said, pointing at a spot on the grass that was just grass. "Whoa. It really was right here a second ago. I swear I'm not lying. Now."

Maddie nodded. "It does that," she said.

"Where is it?" Lizzie sputtered. "We need it!"

"We have to *find* it," said Maddie. "It's one of those kind of books."

CHAPTER 18

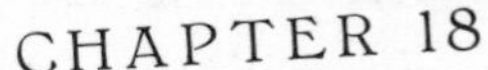

20% More Vorpal

Cedar Wood lied. Cedar Wood lied!

The girls were scrambling around the Grove, searching for the book, but Cedar could only wander, her mind spinning and tumbling about with the thought: *I lied!*

Apparently, when the Jabberwock's magic triggered her deep-rooted transformation into a real girl, it also undid that thorny honesty curse. She was free! She didn't have to blurt and blab. She could choose her own words—she could choose her own life!

Cedar knelt down, relishing the press of the grass against her knees, the tickle of a dangling flower on her ankle. She leaned over to look for the book under a bush of white roses dripping red paint, when a thought caught inside her like a fish on a sharp hook.

If her honesty curse was undone, was her "caring" and "kindness" curse undone, too?

Cedar straightened up and let her feelings probe her fast-beating heart. No more lies. Now she would have to discover the truth. Who was she really, beneath the wooden body and cursed-to-care-ness? Without the Blue-Haired Fairy's magic, was she still the girl who would do anything for her friends? Or, when faced with danger, would she and her tender body run away?

Cedar looked up and found Maddie looking back. Maddie, as the Narrator, knew Cedar's thoughts. She smiled encouragingly. Cedar nodded, but her heart still beat in rapid, shallow gasps. *No more lies, not even to myself. So who am I?*

They scoured the Grove three times over. Cedar checked her pockets, even though they weren't big enough to hold a book. Yet another truth fell on her, heavy as a stone—they might have to go back into that Jabberwock-infested school to find the book. The search could take forever! Lost things were always in the last place you looked.

"That's so true, Cedar!" Maddie said aloud. "You always find things the last place you look, so let's skip the middle part and just look in the last place."

"You make perfect sense, Hatworm," said Lizzie.

"Okay, let's all decide we're done looking after the next place," said Maddie.

Lizzie shut her eyes. "I am done."

"So done," said Kitty.

"Done!" said Cedar, meaning it. Wonderland logic could be fun.

Maddie got a serious look on her face. Well, she couldn't see her own face, but it felt impressively serious. She put out her hands and let them lead her to the Last Place. She crouched down by Cedar, unlaced Cedar's left boot, pulled it off, and removed the book.

"Whoa!" Cedar said. "I'm feeling *everything* today. You'd think I could feel a book in my boot."

She opened the letter and read:

Princess—

We were overjoyed to receive your letter! You are beamishly correct, of course. The only way to defeat the Jabberwock is with the vorpal sword, which is thrust in the left-most bole of the fourth wabe of Tumtum trees. Alas, I cannot send it to you with words. I consulted with an owl, who informed me that with just the right picture, meticulously painted in fluxberry shades, you might be able to pluck it out of Wonderland, though such has never been done. Good luck!

Lizzie threw a handy hedgehog at Cedar. "Paint," she said.

"The letter said the sword is in Wonderland. . . ." Cedar said.

"So what are you waiting for?" Lizzie made shooing motions with her hands. "Go do art!"

The Narrator had some distance from the action and was able to see how, sometimes, Lizzie just didn't explain things very clearly. Especially to people outside her own head.

"Cedar, we can't get to Wonderland," said Maddie. "But maybe if you paint the sword here in this Wonderlandish Grove, the magic of Wonderland could make it real and within our reach."

"Really? But I can't," Cedar said. She pulled a leather pouch out of her skirt pocket. "I have my brushes but they're useless without paints, and I don't even know what it is supposed to look like!"

"It's a sword," Lizzie said. She pulled a butter knife out of her own pocket. "Like this, but bigger." She held it up and closed one eye. "Also with more vorpal. Like, twenty percent more vorpal."

"But..." Cedar looked at her hands. Her real, fleshy, soft hands. She'd never drawn anything with a real hand before. Doubt pumped through her like blood. "Well, to begin with, I'm going to need a better description than just 'sword.'"

"A *vorpal* sword," Lizzie said.

"It seems to me," Kitty cut in, "that descriptions of things, especially the good ones that actually make you brain-picture something, come from Narrators."

"Good idea," Lizzie said. "Maddie, narrate a detailed description of the vorpal sword for Cedar."

Good descriptions come from good Narrators. Okay, then.

"There's a tree in Wonderland," said Maddie. "A Tumtum tree. And it looks as trees do. You know, with the trunk and the branches and the leaves that are sometimes green. And leaves are always moving about, so they're the unpredictable lifey part of an otherwise predictable tree."

"Come on, Maddie, you can do it," said Cedar. "Keep going. That was . . . good-ish."

"I'm new at this, and my brain is getting tired and isn't as springy and bouncy as it was. Plus, it's been so long since I saw a Tumtum tree. Or anything in Wonderland."

"Ooh, I bet other Narrators have described the vorpal sword and Tumtum trees," said Cedar. "We should just go look for a book in the library!"

She smiled. Then she frowned. Lizzie was already frowning. Kitty disappeared and then reappeared dangling upside down from a tree so that her constant smile seemed to turn into a frown. At first, Maddie thought they must be playing a frowning game and—what fun! Even a frowning game was still a game!

But then Maddie realized that they were frowning

because they had to get a book from the library. And the library was in the school. And the school was mad and haunted by the Jabberwock.

Now was a moment to find out who Cedar was without the curses. She took slow, deep breaths until she felt able to say what she absotively, neveraftery wanted to say.

"I'll do it," said Cedar. "I'll go out there to get the book. It's better that you Wonderlandians stay safe in here. If the Jabberwock captures me, it can't use me to power the permanent transformation of Ever After."

"Cedar, your knees are knocking together," said Lizzie.

"No, they're not," said Cedar.

But they were. She hadn't realized, because in the past when her wooden knees knocked together, they made a tapping sound.

"I'll do it," she said again. "It doesn't matter if I am afraid. You're my friends, so I should do it."

Lizzie was watching Cedar very carefully. "You are brave, ex-puppet, to offer to do what scares you. But you must stay here, make paints, and prepare. I will retrieve the written word!"

Cedar exhaled again and didn't argue. But her real stomach flopped about, and she knew in a way that it wasn't her imagination but what people with guts called "a gut feeling," that this wouldn't be the last time she'd have to make that choice. To risk her new life for her friends. Or to save her new, real life and run away.

"Hold your sea horses!" said Maddie. "If Lizzie goes, I should go with her because it will be dangerous, and that's interesting, and Narrators are supposed to storytell the most interesting bits. But stuff will keep happening here with Cedar and Kitty that I wouldn't be able to narrate. Good gravy boats, but this is getting more complicated than a tea party underwater!"

"I can go by myself, thank you," said Lizzie.

"Not a fairy chance," said Maddie. "I took a sacred oath to tell this story. And this story has two main characters: Lizzie and Cedar. A real Narrator would know what Cedar was doing when Lizzie was away, but I'm not a real Narrator and I don't have all those powers."

"We'll tell you what happened here when you get back," said Cedar.

"But that'll be boring," said Maddie. "Everybody knows you can't just tell what happens. You have to *show* it."

"I don't think everybody knows that," Lizzie muttered.

"'Show Don't Tell' is an entire chapter in the narration book! I can't narrate Cedar's action *and* go with Lizzie!" said Maddie.

"I'll do it." Kitty was lying on her stomach in the grass, examining her nails.

"Do what?" asked Cedar.

"Narrate this part of Cedar's story. What's the matter with me, volunteering to do helpish things and *being involved*?" Kitty shuddered. "But since I've always been able to hear the Narrator, same as Maddie, I must share the ability to step in as an emergency Narrator. So I will be the emergency Narrator to the emergency Narrator."

Maddie crouched down and gave Kitty a kiss on her cheek.

"Uck!" Kitty licked the back of her hand and then wiped it on her cheek to clean off the kiss.

"Try to be talkative, Cedar," said Maddie. "That will make Kitty's job easier."

"Good luck, you two!" said Cedar. "Or as they say, break a leg!"

Lizzie straightened up taller and adjusted her crown. "Yes, we will break *all* the legs."

The heart-shaped door was waiting, hanging in midair with no wall to support it. Lizzie opened the door, revealing blackness beyond. She stood even straighter and stepped in first. Maddie took Earl Grey out of her hat, set him on the grass, and hopped after Lizzie. The door shut.

. . . .

. . . .

. . . .

"Um, Kitty? Are you narrating? Kitty? You're not narrating, are you, Kitty?"

"Kitty shrugged."

"Kitty, I don't think you actually need to say what you're doing. Not out loud, anyway. Maddie said she narrated by *thinking* out loud."

I would like to pluck all the petals off those roses.

"Kitty, you didn't take the oath! I hope this works without taking the Narrator's Oath. Just remember to think aloud about what's happening so it gets written down somewhere."

My fingernails look amazing. Maddie's dormouse smells like waffles. Also, waffles are gross. I don't know what Gus and Helga were going on about.

"Try not to just think about what you would normally think about, Kitty. Don't use the word *I*. Observe what's happening and think your observations in nice, clean sentences. And make sure after I speak, you aloud-think 'Cedar said.'"

Cedar said.

Kitty Cheshire, the girl formally known as "I," observed things. She observed that Cedar Wood used to look like a scratching post. But now she was fleshy and soft. And now she was picking fluxberries in every shade from black to green to orange to pink and smooshing them onto big, broad leaves to use as paint. She also seemed more confident than normal, which somehow made Kitty Cheshire feel proud of her.

Kitty Cheshire was really bad at narrating. And the fact that she noticed a flaw in herself worried her. Clearly, Kitty Cheshire was no longer her perfect, indifferent self. Kitty Cheshire had been changed by the Jabberwock's magic. Kitty Cheshire was actually starting to care about other people's Happily Ever Afters.

The change magic was definitely getting stronger.

CHAPTER 19

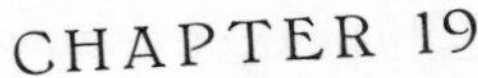

YELLOW WALLPAPER

hugs?

LIZZIE MARCHED THROUGH HER SPECIAL heart-shaped door with what she hoped was absolutely no fear. But she feared there was fear. The hallway that had been on the other side of the door when they went in was gone. Instead, they entered a dark and cramped space, the only light trickling down from a dim circle at least thirty feet above their heads. The walls were old stone and slick with mossy slime. It felt for all the world like they were at the bottom of a well.

Lizzie reached behind her to feel the coarse wood of the heart-shaped door. She could go back. Cedar had said she would do it, and queens commanded other people—

"There are stairs," Maddie whispered, pointing.

Shoved into the wall of the "well" were short wooden struts just wide enough for a foot. If they were *very* careful, they might be able to make it to the top without falling to a painful death.

All the wild confidence she'd felt in her Wonder-landian Grove fizzled out of Lizzie. All marchiness chilled out of her feet.

But she whispered, "Off with its head."

Maddie nodded.

Lizzie shakily ascended the stairs. They were wet and soft, like slushy snow, so she had to lean against the slime-coated wall for support. Even the *shush, shush, shush* of their feet seemed too loud. The Jabberwock could be anywhere.

At last, Lizzie climbed out of the well and into the light of a carpeted space that was refreshingly hallway-shaped. It almost seemed like the normal school, but as they crept along, wrongness was everywhere. Slides instead of steps, curves instead of corners, the floor making soft *ribbit*s with every press of her feet. So much had transformed that Lizzie stared at an innocent lamp, waiting for it to sprout legs and dance a jig.

Fear neither lamps nor jigs, Lizzie, she told herself. *Just find the library.*

Lizzie had spent hours in the library, reading the Wonderlandian books, gazing at the illustrations. In the quiet grandeur of the library, she had let herself yearn for home, the way cheese yearns for cloth, the way bees yearn for bumble. So she knew the exact location of every Wonderland-related book: which corner, which wall, which shelf, and even which hidden chests in the back of custodial closets.

"That's good," Maddie whispered.

"*Hmph.*" Lizzie did not approve of Maddie's nosing around her royal and private thoughts, but at the moment she was occupied with the larger worry of actually finding the library in a Jabberwocked school.

"That's bad," whispered Maddie.

Lizzie parted some drapes, trying to let in more light, only to find that the drapes covered blank stone walls and were themselves dripping with butter and grape jelly.

Everything Lizzie saw was twisted, neither Ever After nor Wonderland. Brushrooms grew out of the floor, wiggling their bristles at them. Treacle tapestries dripped on the wall, their shiny-sweet images ever-changing. A pot of flowers seemed to smile at her. That was delightfully Wonderlandish! Except that the smile was a little too intense. And when they opened their mouths, instead of singing, they lectured on mathematics.

Lizzie took her safety scissors out of her pocket to cut off their heads but thought better of it. What if those flowers had been Dexter or Darling or someone?

The hallway seemed to go on forever, far and away into the distance, until it flickered and abruptly ended.

Lizzie and Maddie shrank back as large chunks of the walls fell away and resolved themselves into further hallways. A gigantic caterpillar, each segment of its body a fringed throw pillow with tassel legs, stampeded across their path from the right hall to the left.

"That's odd," Maddie said.

"No doubt," Lizzie said. "At the very least, things should be moving left to right. It's as if the very rules of civil behavior are being ignored."

A gang of cards chased after the caterpillar, paper flapping obscenely as they ran. These were not respectable cards, to Lizzie's mind—that is, they were not *playing* cards. These were *greeting* cards, if what each of them was shouting was any clue.

"*Get well soon!*" yelled the first to cross their path.

"*Happy birthday*," cheered the second. The third wetly spluttered, "*I'm so sorry*."

The last card in the group noticed them, stopped, and pointed its long, thin arm threateningly.

"*Happy anniversary?*" it asked.

"Happy anniversary," Maddie said.

The card nodded its front flap and ran to catch up with its pack.

"That was close," said Lizzie. "I was about to say 'Condolences' and may have gotten us smooshed inside the card like pressed wildflowers."

They arrived in an open room that might have

once been the Castleteria. All the tables, chairs, and benches were huddled against one wall, shivering. The space left by their absence was empty, except for several upside-down bowls on the floor and a huge, lumpy gray ball in the center of the room under the chandelier. The gray ball sounded like it was giggling.

"Maybe we should go a different way," Maddie whispered. "This seems way too creepy to be safe."

"Laughing things are never dangerous," Lizzie said, marching forward.

The ball stopped laughing.

"You," Lizzie announced. "Giggling Thing! We need directions!"

The lumpy ball spun around, exposing raisin eyes and a wide-open mouth. Whatever it was, it looked *needy.* It plopped forward, its huge belly slapping the floor, its flat, walrus-like tail smearing porridge behind it.

"Hugs?" it lisped.

"No hugs," Lizzie said, more certain than ever that she was not a hugger.

"I know that smell," Maddie whispered. "That

used to be the peas porridge in the pot nine days old. No way I'm eating it now."

"No way I was eating it then," said Lizzie.

"Hugs!" it said.

"Hugs?" other voices whispered. The bowls lifted up like half of an oyster shell.

The Porridge Thing kept advancing, its eyes wider, its mouth wetter, and its laugh louder. The girls backed into a wall.

"Do something!" Lizzie shouted to Maddie. "Narrate us out of this!"

"That's not how it works!" Maddie shouted back.

The Porridge began to whimper. "Hugs..."

"Poor thing," Maddie said.

From beneath the clacking bowls, lumps of raisin-studded porridge rolled out, sprouted muddy legs, and began to run. The Porridge squealed with delight and took chase.

"Can't catch me, can't catch me!" the lumps chanted in little gurgles.

The girls edged toward the door through which they had come. Several lumps careened off the ceiling they had been running on and fell splat at their feet.

"Whee!" roared the Porridge Thing, slamming into the door and nearly crushing Maddie in the process. The lumps skittered over Lizzie's foot and the Porridge chased on.

Lizzie reached for the door only to find it had shrunk, the walls puckering around it like a mouth after eating something sour.

"Shrinking potion!" Lizzie shouted. "Give me one now, Maddie!"

Maddie pulled off her hat, rummaging through the contents.

"I don't—" she started, but Lizzie yanked her out of the way of a careening lump. Maddie's hat fell from her hand and rolled away.

Lizzie grabbed the hat and was clipped by a galloping Porridge. Lizzie spun like a top two, three, four times, and came to a dizzy stop. She handed Maddie the hat.

"Right," Lizzie said, eyes angry. "That is about enough of that. You! Table!" she shouted at the furniture shivering against the walls. "Get up!"

The table got up.

"Go there," Lizzie said.

The table started to move.

"Wait!" Lizzie shouted. "Not yet! When I tell you."

One by one, Lizzie addressed every piece of furniture in the room in her most imperious voice, giving them instructions, pointing, and occasionally stamping her foot. After she had relayed her orders, she watched the erratic Porridge chase, held up a finger, and then shouted, "*Now!*"

The tables, chairs, benches, and one wiry little stool trotted to their assigned places.

"A maze!" Maddie shouted. "You made a maze, Lizzie! A-mazing! Hee-hee."

The Porridge chase continued but inside the furniture maze and out of the girls' way.

"Now," Lizzie said, turning to Maddie, "shrinking potion."

"Oh nose, it broke," she said sadly. At her feet lay pieces of glass and several dozen tiny shoes for every occasion. "It spilled on my shoe collection. Now I'll have to make an army of little me-dolls just to keep using them."

"*Ugh!*" Lizzie yelled. "Everything is pell-mell and

mishmash and broken! This is why we need leaders! A good king or queen would rein all this mush in! Someone needs to be in charge!"

"I think the wall agrees with you," Maddie said. "It wiggled when you were talking."

The chandelier began to swing back and forth in a friendly kind of wave.

"The chandelier, too. Hey, maybe the whole school is alive," Maddie said.

"Of course it is," Lizzie said, though she hadn't thought of it till now. "School!" Lizzie shouted upward. "I'm sure you're tired of having impolite and filthy creatures worming about your hallways. Show us the library, and we will fix it for you!"

The walls shuddered, something akin to a laugh or a growl, or perhaps a rumbly intestinal thing that happens after eating some nine-day-old peas porridge. A new door appeared in the wall to their right and opened by itself.

"You could've asked nicer," said Maddie.

"Directness gets results," Lizzie said. There was no time for lollygagging. That peas porridge could escape the maze at any moment, or those greeting card abominations might return. "Watch as we walk comfortably left to right as civil people should."

The two girls entered a low hall. The walls were covered with dusty yellow wallpaper with a complicated black print that moved between shapes like quills and scrolls. As they walked, the patterns in the wallpaper undulated. Lizzie stumbled, her shoe catching on a wrinkle in the carpet. From her half-stooped position, she saw words in the wallpaper. When she stood, they vanished.

"What is it?" Maddie asked, even though she had just narrated it.

"The wallpaper says something," Lizzie said, "but you have to sort of creep along to read it."

Maddie crouched and crept behind Lizzie, reading the words aloud.

"'... blind you can get to the library but only if I guide you must lean against the wall and close your eyes and let it take you place your shoulder here and walk blind you can get to the library but only ...' It repeats itself."

"All right, then," said Lizzie. "I'm closing my eyes, School! Take us to the library!"

With eyes closed, they continued their crouched walk. The Narrator could no longer see what Lizzie was doing, but she could hear the rasping noise of her shoulder as it dragged along the wall. On they crept, legs trembling with exhaustion, feeling like a waddling duckling. It might have been fun, if not for the ache in her back and the possibility of a large Wonderlandian monster appearing at any moment to eat them.

Flappy things brushed by them. Their shoes caught on sticky spots. The air turned hot, then cold, then shivery, then scented with ham. Screeches echoed in the distance. At one point, something nipped Maddie on the pinkie of her left hand. She forced her eyes to stay squeezed shut, trusted the school, and kept on.

And then the wall was suddenly gone.

"Um, School?" said Maddie. "Are we there? Or are we facing some kind of unspeakable horror that has eaten the wall?"

"We're there," said Lizzie. "I peeked."

The library had always been a very tall room,

high and narrow windows drizzling light onto eight stories of bookshelves. Now it was even higher and narrower. Lizzie couldn't even see the ceiling, but she could stretch out her hands and touch both walls at the same time. In the narrow space between, books fluttered, hovered, and dived; glided, nested, and cooed. None of the books sat quietly on the shelves where they belonged.

"Hedgehog droppings," Lizzie said.

"There are thousands of books in here," said Maddie. "Maybe millions. Finding the one we want might be imposs—"

"Don't say it," said Lizzie. "Never say that word."

Maddie slapped her hand over her mouth. What was wrong with her? She'd almost said it! And meant it!

Nothing was impossible. Every Wonderlandian knew this from their toenails to their nostrils. And Lizzie more than most. Impossible, it seemed, that she could fulfill her destiny as the next Queen of Hearts. Impossible because she was in exile, her home tainted with bad magic, the way back sealed.

But nothing, nothing, *nothing* is impossible.

Lizzie put her hands on her fists and looked at the books. Looked hard. She remembered a card from her mother about lost things.

♥

Things are never lost to you; you are lost to them.
If ever in need of a Thing that has lost you,
simply stop hiding from it.

♥

She had thought it was a secret message about how to return to Wonderland and had spent several days in obvious locations around the school (Castleteria, roof, front doors), being very Visible and Noisy. But Wonderland hadn't found her, and Lizzie had had to give up when Baba Yaga ordered her to stop scaring the cellar-dwelling baby goblins with all that racket. But maybe allowing a book to find her was the sort of thing her mother was talking about.

"Hello, everyone!" Lizzie shouted, leaping up on a nearby table. "I am Lizzie Hearts. It has come to my attention that there are some Wonderland books that didn't know where I was. Know now.

I am here." She held her arms out, attempting to mimic the inviting gesture Apple did with birds.

The cooing in the shelves paused. The only sound was the rustle of pages as books shifted on their perches. And then one took to the air. Lizzie lifted her hands, and the book landed on her palms. The title read, *Wonderland Through the Ages.*

"Good book," Lizzie whispered.

Then more and more took flight, books landing on Lizzie's head and shoulders, and perching on her arms, pecking the tabletop at her feet, nipping at the hem of her skirt. She resembled Ashlynn Ella in the Enchanted Forest, but instead of being covered in butterflies and pixies, Lizzie was papered with books.

"Here!" Lizzie said, picking one up from the table. "The rest of you are dismissed." She felt again a warm, gooey surge in her middle that was probably something common and unroyal like gratitude. Perhaps her mother wouldn't approve, but Lizzie cleared her throat and added, "Thank you."

The books took to the air with a fluttering of pages and flapping of covers.

"'*Rich Descriptions of Amazing Places for the Curious Agoraphobe*,'" Maddie read. "What's an agoraphobe?"

"I don't know," Lizzie said. "It just seemed right."

She flipped through, finding a chapter describing the Tumtum Grove of Wonderland.

"We should get this to Cedar," Maddie said. "I'm worried we've been gone too long."

Lizzie waved her hand at the comment. "Oh, Kitty isn't *that* irritating. I'm sure she and Cedar have gotten along just fine."

"I meant the Jabberwock," Maddie said. "And it wanting to get us and . . . and my . . ."

Lizzie became aware that Maddie's voice was quavering in the unsettling way that often meant someone was either about to weep or lash out like an army of sharp-toothed and singularly grumpy fairies. Both outcomes were equally unwanted, so Lizzie put a hand on Maddie's shoulder and squeezed softly. She had a speech prepared about the dangers of ill-timed weeping and the awkwardness of fairy violence, but Maddie surprised her by giving her a sudden hug.

"Thanks, Lizzie," Maddie said.

"You're welcome," Lizzie said, that warm gooeyness filling her core. What was happening to her? She let go of Maddie and lifted her chin in the air. "Let's go save the day."

CHAPTER 20

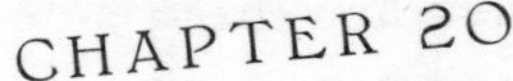

THE VORPAL SWORD AWAITS

Snickersnack!

CEDAR WOOD WAS STILL SMOOSHING BERRIES and mixing them with oil she'd found in Lizzie's shed. Everything she did was boring.

Kitty Cheshire was still narrating. What was the point? Maddie wasn't missing anything interesting.

Kitty Cheshire decided to make it interesting.

"The paint mixed and ready," Kitty said out loud, "Cedar Wood begins to snuffle around on the ground like a pig looking for truffles."

"I do not!" said Cedar.

"Kitty Cheshire disappears." That part happened. Sometimes this emergency Narrator enjoyed disappearing without reappearing. The in-between-ness felt like bathwater. Like floating. Like being full of soup. "Clearly, Kitty Cheshire had been eaten by the Wonderland Grove Ghost that Cedar Wood knew nothing about. Surely Cedar Wood will be eaten next."

"I can still hear you talking, Kitty."

"Alas, the only thing left of people after having been eaten by the Grove Ghost is their voice, howling with sadness."

"Or howling with madness, in this case."

This game was hexcellent. And distracting. And helped Kitty Cheshire forget the Jabberwock for a few seconds and how even its name stood every hair on her head straight up, and sent tremble-wobbles into her knees, and scared her smile stiff, and how, even though she was far too big now, she longed to curl up on her mother's lap and cry.

Kitty Cheshire regretted thinking those thoughts aloud.

Please come back, Maddie.

Lizzie and Maddie burst through the door,

slamming it shut on what looked to Cedar like thousands of uncomfortably friendly pencils.

"I didn't think-aloud about the pencils," said Kitty. "So that means Maddie is narrating again."

"You're safe!" said Cedar.

"What did I miss?" asked Maddie.

"Boredom," said Kitty. "Talking. Cedar snuffling like a pig."

"I didn't do that!" said Cedar. "Kitty just said I did."

"That's dangerous, Kitty," said Maddie. "I read a story about it in the narration book. Once upon a time there was a Narrator who narrated things that he *didn't* observe, but he was such a powerful and skilled Narrator, the characters actually had to do whatever he said. It was horrible!"

"Like being forced to live out a destiny you don't want?" Cedar muttered under her breath.

"We should get to work," said Maddie. She clasped her gloved hands together. "Hold the spoon, did Madeline Hatter just say, 'We should get to work'?"

"That's nothing," said Kitty. "I was *involved.* I *volunteered* to help." She shuddered again.

"Maddie is correct," said Lizzie. "We don't know how time is moving. We must retrieve the sword and carry it to someone who can wield it, perhaps Headmaster Grimm or Madam Baba Yaga. Surely the White Queen could wield it with panache once she returns."

"So . . . where's the book?" said Cedar.

Everyone looked at Lizzie. Lizzie sniffed.

"A large crab ate it."

"What?" said Maddie.

"I didn't want to alarm you," said Lizzie, "but one of the flattish stone slabs in the floor of that last hallway was apparently a flattish stone *crab.* It seized the book from my hand with one of its pinchers and devoured it."

"But . . . but . . . but . . ." Maddie couldn't quite seem to talk. The thought of going back through that door made her so nervous the Narrator had difficulty thinking of an appropriate simile. Like she was made of syrup, maybe?

"No matter," said Lizzie. "I read the relevant passage while we were in the library and now have it memorized."

She cleared her throat and recited.

An afternoon in the Tumtum Grove is as warm as a tea party. Tufts of white sillyrose seeds float on the breeze. The spicy scent of primposeys mix with the musky purple odor of the resin dripping from the boles of the Tumtum trees.

Flowers are fond of the Tumtum resin and carpet the ground thicker than grass, drinking it in. The yellow sillyrose on its single, thin stems. The bright blue primposeys with five petals turning up like faces toward the sun. The tiny dots of white snowslips.

The Tumtum trunks are thick and gray, the bark creating long black stripes. Beneath the black soil, roots intertwine. Their canopies touch, branches crissing and crossing so no Tumtum tree stands alone. Their leaves are the size of your palm and perfectly round, and the kind of green that almost sings its color.

In the center of the grove, in the middlemost Tumtum tree, the vorpal sword awaits. Its blade is hidden, thrust into the bole of the tree. Only its crystal hilt sticks out, reflecting the colors of the flowers and waiting to be grasped.

Lizzie continued to recite while Cedar painted on the side of the garden shed, trying to match what Lizzie was describing.

"It's looking almost right," said Lizzie. "But it doesn't *feel* quite right."

"I'm sorry, I'm doing my best," said Cedar.

"To make this painting come alive," said Maddie, "we might need even more than words."

From the shed Lizzie fetched a musical instrument. It was cut from rosewood, shaped like a heart, and strung with thin silver strings.

"I didn't know you played the dulcimer," said Cedar.

Lizzie sniffed. "I don't. Not in public. So I advise you all to keep this performance to yourselves."

Sitting cross-legged on the grass, she placed the dulcimer on her lap. Touching the strings with her left hand and tapping them with a small hammer she held in her right hand, she played a melody that to Cedar's ears sounded strange, somewhat off-key, and yet thickly sweet and oddly beautiful. Maddie felt the song go down her throat like a warm cup of tea and tingle out into her fingers and toes. She didn't mean to cry, but she did. That song was the sound of homesickness.

"Here," said Kitty. She opened a tiny vial that hung from her necklace and held it under Cedar's nose. "This is what Tumtum resin smells like. Cheshires spend a lot of naptime in the branches of Tumtum trees. I brought some resin with me to remind me of home."

The music and the scent filled the Grove, and Cedar painted. Although it was the first time she'd painted with real hands, they still knew how to dip the brush and work it over the wood. She wasn't a wooden girl trying to imitate in paint what was real. She was so real that realness moved out from her and into the paint.

When she lifted her brush and took a step back, Lizzie said, "That's perfect."

"Thanks," said Cedar. She felt alive and unpredictable. What other marvelous things might she be capable of?

"You're different now," Kitty said, "and not just that you're no longer wood."

"I always felt things, even if it was just my imagination," said Cedar. "But I think I was also holding myself back, waiting to be real before I started living."

Lizzie blinked. "You were not real before?"

"Well, my story says I wasn't," said Cedar. "And people like Faybelle always remind me of that."

But her thoughts felt the same in her real head as they had in her wooden head. Had she always been *real* Cedar down to her roots?

"I think this can work," said Maddie, inspecting Cedar's painting. "I *know* it can, in a Narrator-ish way. But only because you're you, Lizzie. Only your hand can claim the sword."

"I am the princess of Hearts," Lizzie declared. "I am an heir to Wonderland! And I command you to give up the vorpal sword."

Lizzie reached her hand toward the painting.

"Careful, the paint is still wet," said Cedar.

But as Lizzie extended her arm, the bumps and imperfections of the wood grain in the shed's boards smoothed and disappeared. Lizzie's hand went through the shed wall—or rather, went into the Tumtum Grove itself as if the painting had created a portal from here to there. Her hand wrapped around the hilt of the vorpal sword, and she yanked. With a wet buzz and a screech of metal, the sword came free.

Lizzie lifted it up, smiling, admiring the warm glow of the blue sword. It appeared to be lighter than Cedar had expected, and just Lizzie's size, too, as if forged for her hand. Lizzie pressed the flat of the blade against her forehead.

"It's beautiful," Lizzie said.

"Isn't it supposed to be purple?" asked Kitty.

"Is it?" said Cedar. "The description didn't say."

With a loud *snap!* the shed wall shuddered, and once again it was just a painting of trees, though now the painted sword was gone and the real sword in Lizzie's hand had turned a bright purple.

"For a minute it was real," said Cedar. She put out her hand but couldn't reach into the Tumtum Grove. She brought back her fingers wet with paint. "So real. And now it's wood again. Wood covered up with pretty paint, dead wood pretending to be... be alive...."

Cedar stopped. Her chin trembled.

The Narrator gave Cedar a hug.

"I wish stories were kinder to their characters," Maddie said. "But I guess trouble is more interesting to read about."

A second shudder—not just the shed this time but the ground beneath their feet. The bubble around the Grove popped. The sky was no longer tinged with yellow but a bright, hot blue. Cedar could see out forever, all the way to the gray stones of the school's towering walls, which were no longer caged by that yellow dome.

"The Jabberwock," Maddie whispered. "It broke the magical barrier."

She remembered the great beast hurling itself at the barrier, clawing at the magic, trying to smash through. Maybe frustrated that it couldn't find the Wonderlandians in the school, it had turned its attention again to that other Wonderlandian it had sensed: the Mad Hatter.

Maddie started to run. She didn't turn back to observe if the other girls were coming, too, as a good Narrator should. She was thinking about her dad, and how he made her charm blossom tea when she was confused and lavender tea when she was too happy to fall asleep, and how he was always smiling around those huge teeth that didn't seem to quite fit in his mouth. He was the silliest person in the world, and she loved him more than hats and tea and hopping combined.

Maddie fled the Grove and raced toward the school, watching the sky.

"If the Jabberwock gets to Book End, that'll be it," Cedar said, running from behind Maddie. "The story will be over. No chance to undo the magic. Raven always a raven, Apple always an apple, and—"

"We know! Silence!" Lizzie said, but she sounded more worried than angry.

"Where are the teachers?" said Cedar. "Madam Baba Yaga! Headmaster Grimm! We have the vorpal sword! Come get it and take care of the Jabberwock!"

"There they are!" said Lizzie.

Just over the rise, the green grass of the croquet field near the school had changed to perfect squares of black and white. Cedar could see the silhouettes of Headmaster Grimm, Baba Yaga, and a handful of other faculty members. Why were they holding so still?

"Curiouser and curiouser..." Kitty whispered, her sharp eyes picking up what the others could not yet see.

The girls stopped on the rise. The teachers were still as marble. As stone. As giant chess pieces on the chessboard lawn.

The Jabberwock had broken the barrier. Its magic was spreading.

"No," Cedar whispered.

And then the Jabberwock itself arrived.

As one, the four girls dropped flat to the ground behind some rosebushes. The thorns grazed Cedar's arms, leaving thin red scratches.

The wind made by the Jabberwock's great wings knocked over several of the faculty chess pieces as it hovered over them, sniffing the air. Wherever its shadow grazed, plants turned to paper, grass turned to chessboards, benches ran away, rocks popped and stones deflated, and the world turned mad.

"But we have the sword," Cedar said sadly. "The teachers were supposed to use it and defeat the . . . the—"

And then the Jabberwock took off faster than Cedar had thought possible. Directly toward them.

"Don't see us, don't see us, don't see us," Maddie muttered.

Don't see us, don't see us....

The Jabberwock passed over their heads. It landed heavily in the Grove, sinking its claws into the grass. It inhaled. The color was sucked out of the plants. Trees wilted. Flowers turned gray as ashes. Grass dried up. The Jabberwock was sucking the Wonder out of the Grove.

Lizzie made a heartbreaking strangled sound. Maddie put her hand over Lizzie's mouth.

The Jabberwock's head swiveled in their direction, its huge gray nostrils sniffing. And Cedar knew it was over. They were about to become buttered bandersnatches.

A shout.

"Halloo! Halloo!"

Someone was running across the Troll Bridge from Book End, directly toward the Jabberwock, and waving his arms. Trying to get the beast's attention away from the girls shivering inside the bushes.

"No, Dad," Maddie said.

"Halloo and yoohoo!" called the Mad Hatter. "Nothing for you there, beastie! Come have a spot of tea with me!"

The Jabberwock took to the air and zoomed toward the Hatter. Maddie got up to run to him, to put herself between her father and the monster.

Kitty grabbed Maddie. "I know what you're planning to do. I can hear your narration. But you can't stop it now. Stay down."

"What's he doing?" Maddie said. "The Jabberwock will take him, too, and—"

"He's trying to keep the Jabberwock both away from us and out of Book End, to keep the story going," said Kitty.

The beast nose-dived at the Mad Hatter, picked him up with a clawed foot, and swooped away from Book End and back toward the school. It went straight through a wall, the stones toppling easily, falling lightly and soundlessly to the ground like empty gift boxes.

Maddie realized all three girls were holding her, hugging her. If they hadn't been, she was certain she would have forgotten how to keep standing up and fallen to the ground. She had to keep observing, keep narrating, now more than ever, or the story would end with her dad captured by that monster.

"What about the other faculty?" said Cedar. "The

ones on the field trips to the East, West, and South Winds. They'll return soon. Right?"

Cedar madly tapped at her MirrorPhone, but the spreading of the Jabberwock magic had knocked them out-of-area again.

Maddie shook her head. She was struggling with yet another unfamiliar sensation: annoyance. Just where were all those responsible adults who should have been taking care of things like terrifying magically mad beasts that want to rearrange reality and steal your dad and transform your best friend into a bird and ruin an otherwise lovely afternoon?

Lizzie was staring back at the ruined Grove, her arms dangling at her sides, the sword dragging in the dirt.

When she turned, her expression was hard as boiled eggs.

"We do not need the teachers. We survived here with the broken things, the crooked things, the things Jabberwocked and gibbering. Time cannot be wasted waiting for them to return, when they'll just be turned into chess pieces. That creature took Maddie's dad and stole away our friends. The longer a thing is not what it is, the more likely it will forget the thing that it was before. The Jabberwock must be stopped."

"What do we do?" asked Cedar.

Lizzie held up the sword. "We take off its head."

CHAPTER 21

Beware Empathy!

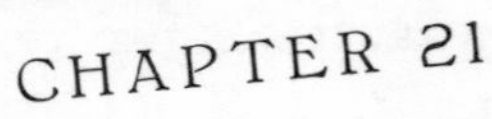

Danger! Danger!

Lizzie's heart hurt. It felt wounded in there, barely pumping, as wilted and colorless as the beautiful plants of her Grove.

And that made Lizzie Hearts, who was already quite mad, even madder.

She stormed through the heart-shaped door with Maddie, Kitty, and Cedar on her heels. They were not greeted with bottom-of-the-well decor, restless furnishings, or shouting greeting cards, but with a simple white room with one normalish door and one dark purple carpeted opening that was door-sized.

The normalish door bore a sign scribbled in orange crayon: JABBERWOCK NOT THROUGH HERE.

"That is not a trustworthy scrawl," Lizzie said. "Someone may be trying to trick us into not taking the correct door."

"Or someone may be trying to trick us into thinking they are tricking us, making us choose the trick door by saying it isn't what it is," said Kitty.

"Stop saying 'trick!'" Lizzie shouted. "I'm tired of that word!"

The shouting hadn't cured her knee-tremble and belly-twistiness as she'd hoped. Lizzie gripped the sword hilt harder. That Jabberwock would pay for what it did to her Grove.

She turned back to the "trick" door (sorry, Lizzie), only to discover it missing, replaced with an empty wall.

"Did one of you steal the door?" Lizzie asked.

"Not me," Maddie said.

"Me neither," Kitty said.

The three girls looked at Cedar expectantly.

"Um . . . no?" she said. "I didn't even know stealing doors was an option."

And then the wall sort of blinked and the door they had come through was also gone.

"Aha!" Lizzie said. "Unless one of you is lying, *Cedar*, the school itself is stealing doors."

"The school must want us to go that way," Maddie said.

"Forward! Into the purple fur hole!" Lizzie said, then added, "*So there!*" because shouting did make her fluttery-tummy and noodley-knees feel a tiny bit stronger.

Tendrils of long purple carpet tickled Lizzie's face and whispered against her arms as she scampered through the opening. But despite the grape-ish furriness, the tunnel felt welcoming, exhaling a cool, fresh breeze.

"It's too easy," Lizzie said.

Cedar looked around nervously. "It's also quiet, maybe *too* quiet. You think something is waiting to surprise us, or eat us, or something?"

"I hope so," Lizzie said, patting the sword. She tightened her lips and lifted her chin to look braver.

The purple-carpeted tunnel ended, spilling them onto the polished wooden planks of the

Grimmnasium. At the far end of the huge room sprawled the lumpy, scaled shape of a beast. The school had brought them directly to the Jabberwock.

"Thanks, Ever After High," Maddie whispered, petting the wall.

The Jabberwock was using its clawed, three-toed paws to attach something to its head, but the Narrator couldn't bear to describe it.

"It's Maddie's dad!" Lizzie whisper-shouted. "The thing is tying the Mad Hatter to its head with vines and sealing wax! It's making the Mad Hatter into a hat—a Wonder-powered hat at that."

Maddie felt trembly. "We need to save him."

The Jabberwock made a jerky movement, and the girls pressed themselves back into the shag-carpeted walls. Lizzie hid the vorpal sword behind her back.

"Just as soon as I cut off its head," she whispered.

She was certainly mad enough to do it, but just how did one go about slaying a beast that big?

The creature began to wiggle its hindquarters back and forth, patting its head as if showing off its Mad Hatter hat to an imaginary crowd of admirers.

"We have to save Maddie's dad *first*!" Cedar whispered.

The beast picked something long and stringy from between its two enormous front teeth.

"This is my destiny," said Lizzie. "This foul beast is of Wonderland. Wonderland out of order. And my story is a story of order. I will march right up to the beast and sever its wretched head from its shoulders with one swift swing of the vorpal sword! Maybe two."

"What if you miss?" Maddie asked in a quiet voice. "What if your swing is off or if the Jabberwock moves? What if you hit my dad?"

"I won't miss," Lizzie said, and Maddie's gaze dropped. Cedar looked nervous. Kitty was trembling so hard she looked a little blurry. Hardly the enthusiasm she'd expect in the middle of her rousing battle speech.

"Imagine something," Cedar said. "Imagine that's your dad up there."

Lizzie imagined. Her wonderlandiful dad. A tiny man in a huge crown and an impractical grin. Stuck on a monster's head. And someone else swinging a sword about. And Lizzie understood.

♥

Beware Empathy! Empathy forces you to Understand how others are feeling and to Care! Danger! Danger!

♥

But it was too late. Lizzie had Imagined. Lizzie had Empathized. And now Lizzie *Cared*.

"Of course we'll free him first," said Lizzie. "By the jack of spades we will. After all, we are the Wonder Worms."

Maddie smiled at her. Lizzie smiled back and wondered if empathy wasn't quite as bad as her mother believed.

CHAPTER 22

~~HEDGEHOG CROQUET~~ BATTLE!

"LET'S GET ON WITH THE DAD-SAVING, THEN, so I can slay this beast," said Lizzie.

"Wait," said Cedar. "What happens when the Jabberwock dies?"

"Its magic will be undone," said Maddie. "Hopefully."

"All its magic?"

Cedar pressed a hand to her chest and felt that violent beating of her heart that meant she was scared. But also alive.

Wait, Cedar wanted to say again, but she knew they couldn't wait. She *could* still save herself, outrun the Jabberwock and its magic and the changing-back, go home, and stay real forever after. . . .

"I'm guessing we've got about twenty seconds before the Jabberwock notices us," Kitty said. She stood the farthest back of all of them, pressed into the purple shag. "If you can manage to get all your fretting and questioning out before then . . ."

Cedar took a deep breath, air filling her up. She was no longer "cursed" with kindness. So this is who Cedar really was. The kind of girl who did not run away. Who faced the monster. Who said, "How dare you hurt my friends? Prepare to feel the wrath of the puppet."

A hand squeezed hers, and Cedar squeezed back. There was a lot of comfort in knowing that the Narrator was on her side.

The Narrator, meanwhile, was avoiding describing the Jabberwock and the sad parody of a hat upon its brow. The Narrator did not comment on how this made her feel, as that is not something

Narrators do. But Maddie put a hand over her trembling chin and tried very hard not to fall apart.

The Jabberwock was sniffing the rosebush that used to be Briar. The roses bent and tugged by its inhale, and the entire bush began to quiver. The Jabberwock opened its huge maw as if to take a bite.

"No," Cedar whispered.

"Beast!" Lizzie ran into the Grimmnasium. "Step away from the irritating bush! You've destroyed enough plants today!"

The Jabberwock swung its head around, its white-blind eyes fiery now, looking right at them.

Kitty went semitransparent.

"Thoughtful—" the Jabberwock skurbled.

"Yes, I am," Lizzie interrupted. "Now, remove your hat and present your neck for chopping, or it will go badly for you."

The Jabberwock dropped to its stomach and used its legs to slide itself forward, and continued, "—to trawl me up a Wonderling three-batch for squeezing."

Its voice was low and raspy, and shrieked into

Cedar's ears the way fingernails scratching chalkboards do. Surely it hadn't yet recognized the sword in Lizzie's hands, as it seemed unworried, playful, spinning itself around on its stomach.

"Why is it doing that creepy walk?" Kitty whispered from the purple tunnel. "I don't like it, I don't like it. . . ."

The Mad Hatter had slumped over on its head, visibly breathing but limp with exhaustion, and the Jabberwock pulsed with a pale sickly light. Strengthened and fearless, it was leaching the Hatter's Wonder.

"Kitty, transport yourself onto it, untie Maddie's dad, and then vanish yourselves away," Lizzie whispered back at them.

Kitty turned fully invisible. "I'm not good with knots," she peeped.

"*Wee-wee meaty food-legs, food-legs, food-legs*," the Jabberwock sang, slithering closer. It was nearly upon them.

"Kitty . . ."

"I can't I can't I can't . . ." Kitty whispered from the air.

"Fine, scaredy-cat," Lizzie said. "I will distract it, and *Cedar* will save the Mad Hatter."

"Me?" Cedar was supposed to be the girl who was quiet and friendly and painted pictures. In the stories, Pinocchio never slew a dragon.

"Prepare to face the wrath of the puppet," she whispered, trying to give herself courage.

"I said your neck, slivy creature!" Lizzie was shouting.

"Neck?" it grinkled, backing toward her. "All is inside out. Upside down. Leftways right. Front-wards back. Here is my neck." It batted its tail sassily.

"That's just too disturbing," Kitty whispered.

The Jabberwock poked Lizzie in the belly with the tip of its tail. She swung the sword and missed. Its tail continued to poke, pat her head, slap her cheek, nudge her in the ribs.

"Stop it!" Lizzie shouted, awkwardly swiping the sword, touching nothing but air.

The beast began chittering like a giant chorus of drowning crickets.

"There is no laughing at your future monarch!" Lizzie hollered.

"Go," whispered Kitty, giving Cedar a nudge. "Now's your chance. I'll . . . er . . . keep a lookout."

Cedar crept forward, achingly aware that she was no longer made of nice, safe, painless wood.

The frightened and confused thoughts spilling out of Cedar helped distract the Narrator from what was truly terrifying: her father, strapped to a monster's head. The Narrator had to stay focused. If she stopped narrating, the story would stop, and her father would never escape.

"Please help him," Maddie whispered.

"If I have to work my way back-end forward, so be it!" said Lizzie.

She swung the sword recklessly at the tail in her face and managed to snip off an inch.

The creature roared. It spun around with startling speed. Cedar scrabbled out of its way. But Lizzie just stood and stared at a small opening in the air the sword had left behind, as if the air was just fabric, and the vorpal sword had sliced it open. Lizzie's eyes widened, peering through the slice till it snapped shut.

The Jabberwock turned around completely and slammed down a taloned paw. Lizzie only just managed to dodge it, rolling across the floor with the force and slamming into Cedar.

The monster began to do a cheeky dance, making that horrible, fingernails-on-chalkboard kind of raspy chuckle.

"I don't know how to save Maddie's dad," Cedar said, splayed on the floor beside Lizzie.

"Saving things. This is not normally my specialty," Lizzie said, crawling to her feet.

A toddler-sized furball in a fetching white jacket burst through the double doors at the opposite end of the Grimmnasium.

"*Grra-ha!*" Daring-beastie announced. It charged the Jabberwock and was swatted unceremoniously aside by the beast's tail.

"That's Daring!" said Cedar. "And saving things *is* his specialty."

"Good," Lizzie said. "I will keep distracting." She yelled as she ran at the Jabberwock, who kept dancing away, whiffling and burbling as if enjoying itself tremendously.

Cedar and Maddie helped Daring-beastie to his feet. Earl Grey popped out of Maddie's hat and squeaked emphatically, pointing at the Jabberwock with a hat pin. Earl Grey was a mouse, but he had no problem imagining himself as a hero.

You spent your entire life imagining emotions, smells, textures, Cedar thought. *Imagine yourself a hero now.*

Daring-beastie searched around frantically. "*Grroooard*," he howled, asking for a sword.

From across the room Lizzie threw something that clanged to the floor at Daring-beastie's feet. It was an ornate butter knife with a beautifully engraved heart on the handle.

Daring-beastie brandished the butter knife.

"*Squeak?*" Earl Grey asked.

"*Squeak!*" Daring said, pointing at Maddie's dad.

Cedar squared her shoulders. She imagined herself: fearless, bold, powerful. Successful.

"Let's do this," Cedar said. "With fuzzy help."

"*Groar!*" said Daring.

Cedar and her furry friends tried to climb up the monster's leg, but it was moving around too fast in its odd sideways crawl. Staying in the Jabberwock's blind spot, she gestured at Lizzie, trying to tell her they needed help.

Lizzie was swinging the vorpal sword, taunting, "I'll chop you up like salad! Like a really big, nasty salad no one wants to eat! Not even vegetarians! Or... especially not vegetarians! Ah-ha!"

"A walking joke is thee, me wee heartspawn." The Jabberwock hissed, breathing magic on her so powerful her crown melted into golden icicles. "Hee-hee-saw."

"My crown!" Lizzie hollered. "I had hoped to spare my little friends this, but *you* deserve it." She raised her sword. "Hedgehogs! To your princess!"

A chittering *roink* heralded the sound of a hedgehog moving at an incredible speed. It darted across the Grimmnasium floor and stopped solidly in front of Lizzie.

Lizzie held the sword like a croquet mallet and swung, striking the hedgehog hard with the flat of the sword. The hedgehog flew, straight and true, directly into the snout of the approaching beast, quills burying themselves in its soft nose. The Jabberwock froze as if stunned.

Cedar took advantage of the Jabberwock's momentary stillness and boosted Daring-beastie up, climbing after him and Earl Grey. She was expecting skin like a snake's or a lizard's, but the Jabberwock's hide was slick as jelly and left pads of stickiness on her fingertips.

Thunk! A hedgehog struck the Jabberwock's shoulder and stuck. The little beast smiled at Cedar as she tiptoed up the monster's ridged back.

I'm light as a leaf, Cedar thought, trying to imagine it to be true. *I'm as bendable as a branch. I fly like a seedpod. I tear my way through problems like an oak's deepest root through rock. I am a hero.*

From her art tools pouch in her pocket, she pulled her pencil-sharpening knife. It was the very one that had sliced her newly real fingertip. Did that only happen a few hours ago? It felt like years. She joined Earl Grey and Daring-beastie, slicing at the vines.

Finally free, the Mad Hatter slumped into her arms, snoring softly. He was sometimes a small man, but it looked like he'd been playing with the grow potions again and was tall and thin. Cedar could barely hold him. How to get down?

"I got him," a mouth said in front of her,

expanding into all of Kitty Cheshire. She took the Mad Hatter in her shaking arms and quickly disappeared with the unconscious man, reappearing to lay him down near Maddie and the purple tunnel. Daring-beastie and Earl Grey leaped away.

"Maneuver C," Lizzie said from below. She broke a golden icicle from her melted crown and tossed it on the floor.

Shuffle, the last hedgehog left in Lizzie's armory, picked up the icicle with her tiny pink hands, nodded, and curled up into a ball. Swift and strong, Lizzie slapped the hedgehog with the flat of the blade, and the little beast stuck right between the Jabberwock's eyes.

Shuffle poked it in the eye with the icicle, the Jabberwock roared, and Cedar was violently bucked off.

Light as a leaf, Cedar thought, and fell, landing on her back.

Ouch. There was pain but not as much as she'd feared. She sat up and realized why. Daring-beastie had leaped to her rescue, attempting to catch her but mostly just breaking her fall. He gave her a fuzzy thumbs-up.

Cedar had only just gotten to her knees when the Jabberwock noticed her. Its head swung around on a giant snakelike neck, fiery eyes inches from her face. Its huge nose snuffled her. If not for the cheerful icicle-waving hedgehog affixed between the creature's eyes, Cedar was sure she would have starting crying, or screaming, or both. The enormous mouth opened and exhaled over her. Its breath was hot and cold at once and stunk of wet dog and burned turnips. The breath magic was so strong it rustled Cedar's clothes and changed them into paper, her dress now made of stitched-together pages ripped out of a book about Pinocchio.

"The game's score is Wonderling naught," the Jabberwock gargled. "Why does the bitsy play-squeal not change?"

Daring-beastie was punching the Jabberwock in the neck, but the Jabberwock didn't budge.

"Why?" it insisted, its bucktoothed mouth leering over her. "Wordspew! Tell my greatness why you normal stay and change not!"

Lie, Cedar thought. She could say she was magic, beyond its power, poisonous to eat, destined to slay a Jabberwock, anything to scare it and make it leave her alone.

But Cedar chose to tell the truth. "I *am* changed," she said, her voice quavering. "But it's wrong, like all your changes. Right now, I'm supposed to be made of wood. I've got little brass pegs on my joints, and I don't feel pain or breathe, and I can only tell the truth. One day the Blue-Haired Fairy might turn me into a real girl forever after. But it's not my time yet."

"A lie," the beast said, pointing one claw at her. "A most ridiculish lie."

Lizzie had crept up to its neck, and now she swung. The vorpal sword went *snickersnack.*

Hearing for the first time the telltale noise of the vorpal sword, the Jabberwock jerked away just before the sword reached its neck. It reared its head, knocking Lizzie. The sword flew out of her hands, and she landed several feet away.

"Lizzie!" Cedar said, running to her.

"Where is the sword?" Lizzie whispered.

The Jabberwock was staring at the shimmering trail the sword had cut in the air.

"Vorpal!" sloared the Jabberwock. "*Vor*paaaal!"

"*Grrrr...ha!*" Daring-beastie growled, reaching the sword first. He lifted it up, struggling with the weight.

All sassiness and patience melted from the Jabberwock. It charged Daring-beastie, who suddenly vanished. The Jabberwock skidded to a halt, sniffing the air, smelling the lemony trail of Kitty's disappearance. Several feet away, the Daring-beastie reappeared, the sword floating beside him as if it had a life of its own. And then the sword vanished.

"Vorpal!" scrackled the Jabberwock, mad with rage.

A *snickersnack* sounded from the far end of the Grimmnasium. Kitty was perched atop the basketball standard.

"So much moving around," she said, swinging the sword. "It's really draining to carry oth—"

Whatever Kitty was going to say was lost as she stared at the hole in the air her swing had cut. She smiled, baring each of her Cheshire teeth.

"Guys!" she said, her voice actually bubbly.

"This sword can get us home! That's Wonderland in there." She pointed at the hole as it snapped shut. "Who cares if it's infected or something. So is Ever After currently. Let's just—"

The Jabberwock clawed a wooden board from the floor and threw it across the length of the basketball court, impaling the backboard and sending the whole standard crashing to the floor.

"Kitty!" Cedar yelled.

The Jabberwock galloped to the mess, screaming, "*Vorpaaaal!*"

"We could... *ugh*... use that beast on the Ever After High basketball team," Kitty whispered from behind Cedar.

Cedar whirled. "You're okay!"

Kitty coughed. "Relatively." Her eyes were half-lidded and her ear was bleeding a little. "Vanishing, moving, vanishing... it takes a lot out of you. Especially when you carry stuff."

The Jabberwock was picking through the broken standard bits with its claws and mouth, searching. "*Swoooord*," it howled.

"You do the honors, princess," Kitty said, holding

up the sword. "Forget this monster. Use the sword to open a door home."

"No!" said Cedar. "What about Ever After? You can't just leave the Jabberwock here!"

"I *could* go home," Lizzie mused. "Raise an army, come back, take over—"

"What?" Cedar said. "Like the Evil Queen, but in reverse?"

Lizzie's eyes cleared from whatever daydream she was in. "Of course not."

The creature in question had given up searching the rubble for the sword. Cedar heard its claws clicking on the hardwood, coming back toward them.

"Give me the sword, Kitty," Lizzie said. "Quick!"

"Only if you promise to take us home," said Kitty, taking a step back.

"Cat Thing!" came a terrible screech from above.

With great flaps of its bat wings, the Jabberwock leaped and descended upon them in a crash. Everyone went flying, but especially Kitty. Cedar saw her spinning almost to the ceiling. The sword flew out of her hand, singeing the air with a narrow rip. The sword struck the wall, careened back, and began to descend into the tear it had made. Midair, Kitty reached for it.

They would both plunge back into Wonderland. It was over, Cedar thought. The sword would be gone.

Kitty popped out of thin air, dropping the vorpal sword at Lizzie's feet.

"She caught it," Cedar said. "Before it fell into Wonderland."

"And came back to us before *she* did," Maddie said.

"Off with its head, Your Highness," Kitty said, her eyes closing. She curled into a ball. "Just going to take a little catnap . . ."

Lizzie patted Kitty's head and picked up the sword. Her beautiful crown hung in broken golden icicles. The painted heart around her left eye was smeared. Her skirt was ripped; her tights bore ragged holes in the knees. But her eyes were clear and her mouth was set.

She raised the sword. "Now, Shuffle!"

The Jabberwock opened its mouth as if to eat Lizzie, but Lizzie's pet, still stuck between the monster's eyes, tossed the golden icicle into the creature's throat.

"*Hurrg!*" gagged the Jabberwock.

"I'm glad you're on our side, Princess of Hearts," said Cedar.

"Callooh callay," said Lizzie. "It's about to become a frabjous day."

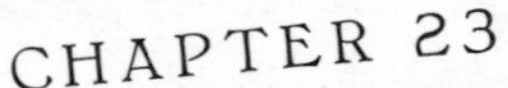

CHAPTER 23

A RULER OF ~~NOTHING~~ Wonderland

LIZZIE SWUNG THE SWORD, MISSING WILDLY. A huge scaly paw swatted her for the trouble, and she went skidding to the ground.

She leaped up, irritated. It was not supposed to be like this. It was her *destiny* to bring Wonderland to heel, but her Grove was destroyed and everyone was hurt. Lizzie probed her swollen lip. *She* was hurt, for queen's sake! The only one hurt was supposed to be the Jabberwock, and apart from the smiling hedgehog wedged between its eyes, the beast was suffering from nothing more than a golden icicle stuck in its gullet.

"*Hork*," gagged the Jabberwock, holding up a claw to Lizzie as if it were in the middle of a speech and just needed her to wait a moment.

"Get him, Lizzie!" Maddie shouted, almost back to her usual happy self.

"Is your dad okay, then?" Lizzie asked. Empathy filled her, but instead of causing indigestion, she actually felt amazing. Maybe her mother was wrong about a few things. What a terrifying thought! Lizzie ordered it to the back of her head to inspect later. "Never mind. He's off the head, so I'm killing it now!"

Lizzie charged the Jabberwock and swung, just managing to take off the tip of a horn before being kicked away. Oh, spades take it. Maybe all this empathy was throwing off her aim.

"*Hurk*," said the Jabberwock, still working on expelling the hedgehog-flung icicle from its insides.

Maddie took off her shoe, shouted "Hatworm is go!" and threw it at the Jabberwock.

"I don't need any help!" Lizzie shouted. "I'm trying to fulfill my destiny, and you're messing me up!"

"*Hurglaaa!*"

The Jabberwock finally coughed out the icicle, the force expelling it straight at Lizzie. Fast.

"*Shrunk*" was the sound that Lizzie heard as the golden icicle struck her.

How curious, Lizzie thought, even as the pain blossomed, *that the sound of a coughed-up golden icicle glancing across one's forehead would sound like an actual word that has nothing to do with icicles, gold, or foreheads.* Her legs weakened, and she dropped to one knee. *I shall have to tell Maddie about it. Also, apologize for being so curt.*

"Lizzie!" Maddie was leaning over her. Lizzie couldn't think of the last time anyone had been so close to her. Besides her hedgehog, Shuffle, of course. But she didn't really count as an anyone because of all the spiky fur. Lizzie preferred pets that weren't too soft.

"I wanted to tell you... something," Lizzie slurred.

"I know," Maddie said, grabbing her arm. "I already narrated it."

"*Rrraaaagggh!*" roared the Jabberwock. It had Cedar trapped against a wall. A torrent of its transforming breath blasted her. The pages of Cedar's paper dress yellowed and curled at the edges.

"If the playsqueal meat will not tweak into something yummier," the Jabberwock skrittled, "'twill be simpler just to eat as is!"

"Absolutely not!" Lizzie yelled, wobbling to her feet. "That girl is under the protection of the Court of Wonderland. Any action against her will be considered high treason!"

The Jabberwock lifted one feathery eyebrow. "Hee! I see no Wonderland! We stand on Else. *My* Else. The Heartspawn is a ruler of nothing."

"Wherever I am, *there* is Wonderland," said Lizzie, sure of it now. "A queen carries her kingdom always."

The fiend chuckled, flapping its claws around in a gesture meant to take in everything. "The Wonder here was wrought by Jabberwock. Seemings that where ere *I* am, there is the Land of Wonder."

"This is *not* Wonderland!" Lizzie said. "This is an abomination. A corruption. A poison. Your eyes are no longer fiery, which means you used up all the energy you stole from the Mad Hatter. You are getting weaker, and *I* wield the vorpal sword."

"The sword sings strong," the Jabberwock gurgled. "But a shoddy conductor are thee. You swipeswipeswipe and murder only air. Little missmissmiss could nary hope to sever this greatness of neck. And alas and alack, as the poem smacks, 'tis the *only* way to defeat me. But to finish off tiny girlings, my Wonder-less paws are terror enough."

It launched itself at Lizzie, clawed paws out.

Lizzie, with muscles hardened by years of swinging flamingos and hurling hedgehogs, swung the sword with all the might, rage, and sovereign right she could muster, and parted the Jabberwock from an entire paw. A ripple in the air opened, and the paw dropped through. The hole snapped closed.

The great beast roared, and Lizzie smiled. *Now* it was hurt. It skittered away, pulling its wounded arm close.

Lizzie pulled on the hilt, but her colossal blow had buried the tip of the sword several inches into the floor.

Maddie rushed forward to help Lizzie free the sword. The Jabberwock whirled, still cradling its arm, but a tiny pink replacement paw was already sprouting from the wound.

"Hey, Jabberwocky!" Cedar yelled. She raced around, picking up odd balls and loose floorboards, throwing them at the beast, trying to distract it from Lizzie and Maddie. "That sword opens doors to Wonderland. Don't you want to go home, where there are real, tasty bandersnatches?"

A bit of longing passed through the Jabberwock's eyes. But it lowered its wet gray eyelids and scowled. "In Wonderland I am endgame of the Galumphing Hunt. It is destiny rhyme-declared. But here the election is mine. Here I will be *king*! Once vorpal is mine."

The Jabberwock glared at Lizzie and Maddie, who were tugging desperately on the sword. It pulled its tail back for a mighty blow.

"Hold on," Maddie said.

"I will," Lizzie said, and kicked Maddie away from the tail whipping toward them. "Keep telling the sto—"

And then, pain. Lizzie didn't think she had ever felt so ouchy. The impact lifted her off her feet even as it knocked the sword free from the floor. She was sliding sideways and half upside down, spinning past the Jabberwock, but she managed to keep hold of the hilt. The sword trailed dark lines through the air. She saw her fingers loosen on the grip and commanded them to stop, to tighten, to hold firm, to keep tearing an opening in the air. It would have to be enough.

At last the sword fell from her numb fingers and dropped into the hole it had made.

Lizzie struck the far wall and slid to the floor, the breath knocked out of her. The doorway the sword had torn was huge, tracing the entire path from where Lizzie had been struck to where she landed.

A scaly paw dipped into the divide and caught the sword.

"There, then, and now," the Jabberwock said with a bucktoothed, scaly smile. "My paws belong around such as this."

The hutling crashed into the Grimmnasium, front door/mouth open, coughing its student contents out. A raven dropped an apple on the monster's head, caught it, and flew away. The Jabberwock stumbled back, its rear paws slipping on a golden lock and a brass egg. It attempted to steady itself with the clawed hand that did not hold the sword, and managed to cut that paw on an ax held up by a tree.

The Jabberwock roared as it tripped and tipped into the shrinking portal to Wonderland. Lizzie was certain the opening would snap shut on the beast and banish its top half back to its home world. But the Jabberwock brought the sword up, the flat of the blade sparking against the edge of the opening, forcing it slowly back open. The monster wasn't falling. The hole wasn't closing. The rip was like an open wound between worlds, the Jabberwock the infection keeping it from healing.

"You can't stay here," Lizzie shouted at it. "Ever After is home to the kind, and the friendly, and the brave, and you are none of those things!"

"Are you?" the Jabberwock scrissed.

It wrapped its tail around her ankle, and its eyes began to pulse a bright unsettling white. Lizzie felt energy sap out of her with each pulse, the *Wonder* draining from her bones. Shuffle, the last hedgehog remaining affixed to the Jabberwock, dropped off the creature and scuttled to Lizzie's side, nuzzling her with her spikes.

“This world is mine!” the Jabberwock skreamled.

Lizzie couldn’t seem to sit up. She could barely catch her breath, but she managed to whisper, “Hatworm is go. . . .”

Okay, Lizzie. Okay. I will finish this. Somehow.

CHAPTER 24

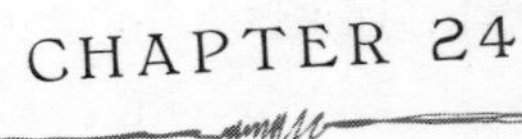

Madness Is Life

The Jabberwock had the sword. Lizzie was lying, hurt, on the floor. The Narrator was new at this, but she was certain an Ever After story should not end with the monster victorious. But she'd taken an oath to never, ever, ever interfere. It was an impossible thing.

Then again, she wasn't only the Narrator. She was also Madeline Hatter. And Maddie imagined six impossible things before breakfast.

"You should go home," Maddie said.

The Jabberwock still held the rip between two

worlds open with the sword, as if deciding which one to conquer first.

"Pardon beg?" it asked.

"There's no pardon for what you've done here," said Maddie. "The best I can do is send you home."

"*You*," bellowed the Jabberwock, "send *me* home? Are you a girl-prince? Nay. A sword-swinger? Nay. Hatted thing stands around, letting other meatlings play while you watch. You are a sillypants of terrible degree."

"Thank you," Maddie said. She could see ripples of color and light through the tear. Wonderland was sick, but it was still beautiful. Scents rolled out—the sparkling zest of Tumtum trees, the cool crackle of broken water, the sharp oyster tang of the air. "You should be fizz-bobbled and glee-sprinkled to go to Wonderland. I would be."

The Jabberwock began its horrible, chittering laugh. Laugh? At Wonderland? Maddie clenched her teeth and decided to break some rules.

"The Jabberwock pushed against the edge of the tear, and it widened," Maddie said.

And it happened, just as she'd narrated.

The Jabberwock goggled the widening tear.

"What magic is this?" it bellowed.

"Storytelling," Maddie said.

The Jabberwock gnashed its teeth. "No puppet am I. Especially of a Tiny. Hatted. Girl."

"Hey!" said Maddie. "I count a puppet as a heart-twinned friend. You should be so lucky."

It pulled out the sword and advanced on Maddie.

The tear began to close behind it.

"Until it didn't," Maddie said quickly. "Until the tear between worlds stopped closing, waiting for one more important thing to pass through."

At her words, the closing of the tear did slow down, but it did not stop completely.

The Jabberwock's eyes pulsed white. "The Nothing in you echoes. I will claim your leftover Wonder. The Hat Girl is an empty shell."

Maddie sagged. She did feel empty and tired.

The Jabberwock towered over Maddie, the stink of its breath ruffling her hair.

"Whatever telling-story spark you have stolen is not enough. My will is strongest. My power law. You serve me now."

"That's it," Maddie whispered, smiling. "I made an oath to serve the story and the reader and no other, be it king or queen or baker or candlestick maker. Or Jabberwock."

"Mufflewords." The Jabberwock rumbled above her, saliva dripping from its lips. "Clearspeak now. Loudly."

Maddie straightened. "You're right. My power is not enough. But their power is."

The Jabberwock snaked its head around, scanning the destruction it had wrought in the Grimmnasium, and found nothing it considered a threat. "Whose power?"

"Theirs," Maddie said, pointing at you. Yes, you. The ones reading this book. "I'm only half the storyteller. The Readers are the other half. After all, they take the words and make the pictures in their minds—make the story *real*. Isn't that right, Readers?"

Feel free to nod, say yes or darn tootin' or absotively, or whatever feels just right.

The Jabberwock took a step back. "Brainfraught babbletalk! You are mad!"

Maddie smiled. "Why, yes, I believe I am! And you want to know a secret, little Wocking Jay?" Her voice dropped to a hush, and she leaned closer to the monster. "Madness is life."

Okay, Readers, help me. Think the words aloud. Or say them aloud. Narrate it to be true.

"Go home, Jabberwock," said Maddie.

Go home, Jabberwock. A chorus of unseen voices repeated her words from across time, space, and the wiggly bits in between.

Three times more, Readers!

Go home.

Go home!

GO HOME!

The great fiend that is the Jabberwock, terror of two worlds and bane of bandersnatches, stumbled backward, pushed by voices it heard suddenly, powerfully, shouting in its own mind.

"NO!" it roared.

The tear widened, a monstrous mouth tall and wide, shimmering around the edges, brilliant with the light of Wonderland. The Jabberwock thrashed, but its head dipped into the hole.

"Yes," Maddie said.

"Impossible!" it screeched, its body tumbling through.

Maddie laughed. "Nothing is impossible, silly beastie!"

The Jabberwock, now completely in Wonderland, twitched and struggled, its muscles bunching and contracting as it fought against the inevitable.

Maddie's smile dropped and her eyes narrowed. "No one hurts my dad," she said, and the tear between worlds closed.

CHAPTER 25

FRIENDS WOULD BE ACES

PUDDING MAKES A TERRIBLE HAT! SNOOF PIDDLE DEE-HEllo? Hello, testing, testing. Am I speaking reasonable words? No nonsense, no "crunchy lunches" and "utmost roast beef"? Yes! I am making sense again! The Narrator is back and doing a victory dance! Look out! Check my moves—I found them and I'm going to keep them. Oh yeah, *doot doot doot*—

"Narrator, you're back!" Maddie squeaked. "Yippee-potomus!"

Yes! I'm back, Maddie! That was horrible. I could

think, but my words were nonsense and I was helpless to do anything but watch the chaos and...wait, I'm the Narrator. And I'm a professional. So no more victory dancing. Back to work.

Ahem. Yes, it was a glorious day in Ever After. Even the Narrator felt glorious! The Jabberwock had returned to Wonderland, and all over the Grimmnasium, things changed by its magic were un-magicking, untangling, and unbecoming into what they used to be.

A rosebush scrunched into a tight ball like a piece of paper crumpled up in your palm. The mass of pink blooms and brown thorny branches shaped into a tall, brown-skinned, and pink-dressed girl of distinguished height and fashion sense. She immediately ran, her high heels clacking on the Grimmnasium's hardwood floor, and barreled toward Lizzie.

"Whoa, girl, you Rockabye-Baby rock!" Briar lifted her fist.

Lizzie was still lying against the wall, but she straightened and lifted her fist. She'd watched Briar performing her signature fist bumps with her friends and so knew what to do—she knocked her knuckles against Briar's, opened her hand, and then rained wiggling fingers down in a representation of a glitter bomb. She couldn't quite suppress a pleased giggle.

"That thing was going to eat me," said Briar. "Actually going to gobble up my roses, but you wielded some seriously hextreme moves with that sword. I never knew you were so royally fablelous!"

"And I never knew that I'd bother to save your life." Lizzie cleared her throat. "I do not regret it."

"This is so wicked cool," said Briar. "Friends?"

Lizzie blinked. She looked at Briar, then at Cedar, Maddie, and Kitty.

♥

Friends are one R away from fiends.
Avoid friends at all costs!
Also anyone to whom the R does not come naturally (pirates are okay).

♥

Sometimes her mother's advice just didn't make sense in context.

"Friends would be aces," Lizzie said.

A gold padlock lying loose clicked open, lengthened, and widened into a girl of abundant golden curls. Her wide-set curious eyes looked around, and Blondie Lockes made a noise like the snuffle of a bear.

"This is going to make the best MirrorCast show I've ever done!" she said.

A pair of crystalline shoes flashed brightly in a ray of sunlight, a swirl of sparkling light slowly resolving into Ashlynn Ella. She blinked her large doe-like eyes twice before swooning into a graceful faint. Beside her, a sturdy tree melted into Hunter Huntsman, and he caught her fainting body in one hand and his ax in the other. From somewhere unseen, trumpets played a heroic fanfare.

In midflight, a raven sprouted a head full of long purplish-black hair. She squawked and dived to the ground, alighting atop a red apple before her wings lengthened and narrowed into arms. She was fully back to being Raven when the apple sprouted back into Apple. Raven Queen was sitting on Apple White's head.

"You're sitting on my head," said Apple.

"Um… how—" Raven started before wobbling and falling off, catching herself on a bright blue bicycle just as it changed back into Dexter Charming.

No heroic trumpets played, but Dexter didn't seem to mind.

"Sorry, Dex! Thanks for breaking my fall," said Raven.

"No problem," Dexter said, his face smooshed between her boot and the floor.

Everything was reverting. Wall stones lost their wiggle, floors lost their hiss and spring. Windowpanes crawled back into their frames and returned to unmoving, unblinking glass.

Even the Wonderlandians noticed slight changes, the ridiculous clarity in their brains shifting back to normal—rich and roiling with the sheer multitude of interesting things to think about, such as cabbages and kings; a large variety of hats; croquet; tea service; the best rhymes for *oranges* and *spaghetti*; and riddles like "Which came first: the chicken or the soup?" and "How much hedge would a hedgehog hog if a hedgehog could hog hedge?"

"That's such a good question, isn't it?" Maddie said. She was sitting beside the Mad Hatter, his head on her legs, smoothing his white-streaked mint-green hair off his forehead. He was awake now, and although he looked tired, he was smiling around his huge teeth.

"Indeed, my girl," said her father. "How much hedge, indeed? They do so love to hog it, and who can blame them?"

Watching it all was a real girl of warm brown skin and earnest brown eyes. She was the last to . . . oh, Cedar. I'm so sorry. I mean, the Narrator doesn't say *I* or feel sorry for the characters. The Narrator only observes and reports. And the Narrator observed that Cedar Wood was changing, too. *Ahem.*

Cedar felt it first in her skin. A hardening, a deadening, like water turning to ice. The change sank deeper, choking the breath in her lungs, dulling the butterfly sensation in her middle. *Thump-bump, thump-bump, thump*—The rhythm of her heart cut off midbeat, a song interrupted, and that fantastic warmness in her chest cooled. The chill exploded outward, tingling through her limbs down to the tips of her toes and fingers. Bruises disappeared, scratches mended, and at last the small cut on the tip of her index finger healed.

Though the change felt as slow as the folding up of a comforter, it all happened so fast that Cedar's wooden cheeks were still wet with tears by the time her wooden eyes could no longer cry. Her wooden nose still remembered the last real scent she'd smelled—Briar's roses.

"Cedar!" Raven clambered off Dexter and ran to give her friend a hug. "You helped save everyone! Thank you! I'm just sorry I never got to hug squishy Cedar."

"You will," said Cedar. "Someday."

"Are you going to follow your destiny, then?" Raven asked.

Cedar shook her head and heard her wooden neck creak in that old, familiar way. She sighed, a sad little huff of breath that left her wooden chest feeling empty. But she said, "Forcing things to be what they're not is so not my style. I'm more convinced than ever that everyone should be able to choose their own path. And I'm going to talk to Headmaster Grimm about it immediately. Let the Royals be Royals and the Rebels be Rebels."

"But..." Raven lifted one of Cedar's hands, running her finger across the wood grain of her knuckles.

Cedar shrugged. Her joints felt loose, so she

plucked spare pegs from her pocket and started screwing them into her elbows. “I used to think I was a piece of wood that just imagined myself a person. But now I think I’m a real person who just imagines myself made of wood.”

Raven laughed. “That sounds like Wonderlandian logic.”

“I’ve absorbed some of that, I think!” said Cedar.

She tightened the peg in her knee and tried again to hold on to the real scent of roses. She could only imagine it, and, for now, that would have to be enough. She stood straight, feeling as strong as a tree, no ache or break in her limbs. Her pain gone, her injuries healed.

Lizzie was standing and didn’t show any obvious injuries from the Jabberwock’s striking tail, but she looked dazed.

“Hey, Lizzie? Are you okay?” Cedar asked.

“I think I am generally sprained and significantly bruised, but, yes, I am okay.” Shuffle perched on her shoulder, squeaking. “Yes, Shuffle, so long as the Grove is okay, too.”

“Oh, timbersticks, that’s right!” said Cedar. “Do you think the un-magicking fixed it, too?”

"I hope so, but if not"—Lizzie looked down at her shoes as if embarrassed—"at least I still have my friends."

Cedar's eyes widened, and she felt her mouth carve itself into a smile. It felt good. "If the Grove needs replanting, I'll help you, Lizzie. We all will."

Daring was fuzz-free. He bore a bruise on his cheek, but he smiled at Lizzie, his teeth brilliantly white.

Lizzie lifted one hand, posing as she had on the amphitheater's stage. "I have returned, Boreas, wind-herder, to watch you writhing in the agony of age and death."

Daring laughed heroically. "What a battle. Bards will sing of my deeds! Or perhaps a pop singer. Do you listen to Katy Fairy?"

"I do not!" Lizzie said grandly. "But I shall listen to her squalling posthaste as you are my friend, and friends recommend music to each other! Now, kneel."

Cedar was surprised to see Daring do so without argument.

Through some twist of magic, Lizzie's butter knife had enlarged with him, now as big as a sword.

She picked it up, solemnly touching its flat side to each of Daring's shoulders.

"I knight you a defender of Wonderland, Sir Daring Charming. Heroic, loyal, fuzzy doom."

Cedar creaked a smile. She looked to Raven to see if she'd observed this odd new friendship and found Raven staring up. Cedar followed her gaze to the long ripple in the air, stretching from one side of the Grimmnasium to the other. The portal to Wonderland was closed, but it had been so large it left behind a scar of piercing white light.

"Is it dangerous?" Cedar asked.

"I don't think so." Raven held her hands up, sensing the air. "It does emit a magical energy, a kind of tingle that gives me chills. I feel like it's about to—"

"Students!" Headmaster Grimm's voice shouted as the Grimmnasium door opened. He entered along with Baba Yaga and the other faculty from their field trip. "It appears our spell defeated the Jabberwock. Do not fear any longer."

Just then, the portal scar tightened, like lips pressed together. And then it exploded. The explosion was soundless, like a giant dandelion puffing out into glitter and dust. The windows blasted out, and the brilliant, glittery light burst as far away as Book End, raining sparkles and sighs over everything.

"Uh-oh, sleepy time," Briar said just before slumping to the floor.

All over the Grimmnasium everyone from Professor Rumpelstiltskin to Duchess Swan swooned into sleep. Everyone except Maddie, who looked as alert as ever.

Maddie didn't even fall asleep during the big Beauty Sleep Festival, Cedar found herself recalling as a sweet drowsiness poured over her. *Maybe it's all that tea....* Still as a tree, Cedar snoozed standing, the sprinkles of light raining over her face and arms with tiny pulses of heat and whispers of *Hush, shush, hush, shush....*

CEDAR BLINKED ONCE. SHE BLINKED TWICE. The light was gone.

Cedar could not seem to remember why she was

standing in the Grimmnasium. Or why most of her classmates were lying on the floor around her. Was this some kind of weird slumber party?

Raven was blinking, too. She pushed herself onto her elbows, staring up at the empty air.

"What are we doing?" Raven asked.

"I feel like something happened," said Cedar. "Like I was in the middle of an important thought and then... I don't know."

"Why did I take a nap on the Grimmnasium floor?" Lizzie asked.

"Welcome to my world," said Briar, yawning.

"What exactly is your world?" Lizzie asked.

"Lots and lots of unexpected naps," said Briar. "And lots and lots of unexpected parties. Ooh, we should have a party! You can come. I think. Wait... are we friends?"

"I should think not," said Lizzie. "My mother always said... friends are fiends and only pirates have *arrrrrh*s."

Briar raised one eyebrow. "Um... what?"

"What are we doing in here?" Cupid asked, flying down from the branches of a pillar tree where she'd been asleep.

"We came back early from the field trip," Cerise said, rubbing her eyes. "My dad—I mean, the faculty said there was something wrong on the mountain. Mean bears or something? I can't remember exactly."

"Right. But after that?" asked Cupid.

"I don't know," Dexter said, removing his glasses to rub the sleep from his eyes. "We fell asleep, I guess. Must've been a busy day."

Maddie was standing with her fists on her hips, staring with wide eyes. "Are you all cuckoo clocks? We had an amazing adventure! We saved Ever After and danced with chairs and wrestled monsters . . . and . . . and . . . painted pictures!"

"I'm sure we did, Maddie," Raven said. "Dreams are cool that way."

"But . . . but . . . my dad is here!" Maddie said, pointing at her father, who was, indeed, by her side. The Mad Hatter waved.

Cedar waved back. It seemed the polite thing to do, though she wasn't sure what would be polite to a Wonderlandian. They rarely made sense to her.

"Kitty!" said Maddie. "You must still be mindiful and memory-hoarding."

Kitty kept smiling, though her forehead scowled.

"I had lots of dreams about...about the Jab—no! Nightmares!" She shuddered, her hair fluffing. Her eyes seemed a little sorry when she looked at Maddie and said, "But they didn't really happen, Maddie. They were just dreams."

Maddie sighed, shrugged, and then twirled toward Cedar.

"Happy snappy, my dreaming Cedar Wood! What was your don't-remember-that-it-was-all-real dream?"

Cedar didn't usually remember her dreams, only the emotions that flowed from them. Whatever she dreamed during this strange nap was no exception—confusion and fear, elation and joy, and a lingering sense of hope for something that she wanted. Or didn't. What *did* she want? She rubbed the tip of her finger and whispered, "I want to be real, but I want to choose my own story even more."

And it was true, because Cedar could not tell a lie.

Cedar was sure Maddie was about to say something silly, but she didn't. She just smiled.

The headmaster was sitting up, rubbing his gray hair.

"Students, why are all the kitchen appliances

stacked in the corner of the Grimmnasium as if they had been practicing a cheerleading formation?"

After much *what happened*s and even more *I don't know*s (except from Maddie), everyone headed through the school toward the Castleteria for dinner, discovering that nothing was where it belonged. It was as if every piece of furniture and clothing, and even a few doors, had sprouted legs and run away on their own two feet.

"Which is precisely what happened," said Maddie.

The Narrator did not confirm or deny this assertion.

Maddie sighed and stomped into the Castleteria. "This is more riddle-diculous than a bald rabbit!"

"Hey, Lizzie," said Cedar. "You know, I think I dreamed about you."

Lizzie closed one eye, squinting at Cedar with the one that was painted with a smeared red heart.

"I am a princess of Wonderland. Many dream of me." She sniffed. "But I think I dreamed of you, too."

"Do you want to maybe sit together in the Castleteria?" Cedar asked.

Lizzie did not bother to respond. But as they walked down the hall, she slowed her usual brisk pace and kept in step with Cedar. Together they passed through the Castleteria doors.

"I just had the oddest thought to check the doorframe for teeth, as if it might swallow us," Cedar said.

Lizzie didn't answer. Cedar pressed her wooden lips shut, unsure if she'd said something awkward.

But then Lizzie shouted, "I am fond of hedgehogs!"

Cedar guessed that Lizzie was attempting to have a conversation. She smiled.

"I am, too," she said.

CHAPTER 26

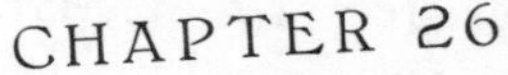

Accidentally Becoming Friends

The morning of the Tiara-thalon dawned as pink as leprechaun tongues. Outside the Grove, the students of Ever After High gathered, dressed in running, biking, swimming, or gardening clothes. Everyone was talking, pointing, examining the horrible damage done to Lizzie's precious garden—plants wilted and gray, great claw marks slashed through the grass, trees tipped over, roots exposed. Several students gathered around the sole remaining fluxberry bush, marveling how the berries constantly shifted in color—green one moment, then twinkling into a twilight blue, magic yellow, butterfly-wing pink...

"Listen up, everybody!" said Apple White. She wore sporty white capris, a red Ever After High T-shirt, and gold-trimmed gardening gloves. "The race will begin and end at the Grove. Runners take off from here to the lake. After getting the relay scrolls from the swimmers, the bikers cross the finish line back here, where we'll all spend the afternoon working in Lizzie's wonderlandiful Grove. As the Tiara-thalon's sponsor, the Glass Slipper has generously donated gardening tools."

"The store's owners were enchanted to help when they heard about Lizzie's plight," said Ashlynn, who worked there during after-school hours. She was surrounded by a horde of hovering pixies from the Enchanted Forest who'd come to lend a tiny hand.

"How charming!" said Apple. "Lizzie will show us how to replant the uprooted trees and extract seeds, shoots, and stem cuttings from the surviving plants to regrow the ones that were lost."

Lizzie stood at the head of the crowd, holding her

scepter regally, her chin up, eyes distant. But inside, Lizzie's very large heart felt pinched. Her beautiful Grove ravaged! Some creature must have attacked Ever After High during their mysterious Grimmnasium nap, though besides some torn clothing and misplaced furniture, the only sign of damage was in her Grove.

Cedar Wood put a hand on Lizzie's elbow and whispered, "Don't worry. I'll help you, Lizzie. We all will."

Lizzie felt certain she'd heard those words before. "Off with your head," she whispered back in the same tone someone else might say *Thank you*.

"Let's get this running, swimming, biking, planting party started, already!" said Briar. "Athletes, get in position! Hey, Lizzie, want to help me start the race with my glitter-bomb catapult?"

Lizzie's upper lip trembled with the effort to keep stiff. She very, very, very much wanted to help with the glitter-bomb catapult. But would that be unseemly? "Off—" she started.

"Oh, just help me set it up, already," said Briar.

Lizzie dropped a round, brilliantly colored glitter bomb into the launching cup.

"You do the honors," Lizzie said. "You know, in case it misfires."

"YOLOUAT!" Briar yelled. "You only live once upon a time!" She pulled the lever.

The glitter bomb flew high over the heads of the crowd and exploded into a million pieces of glitter sparkling in the morning sun.

"Ooooh," noised the crowd in unison.

The runners took off.

"It worked!" Briar hooted. "They love it!"

"They are easily impressed," Lizzie said, and then grabbed another glitter bomb. "Let's do it again."

"Woo-hoo!" Briar cranked the launch arm back. "Glitter bombardiers in the house!"

Lizzie and Briar performed a glitter-bomb fist bump. Lizzie realized what she'd just done and pulled her hand behind her back. She must be cautious if she was to avoid accidentally becoming friends with anyone—particularly Briar, who had so many friends that soon Lizzie would be in danger of sinking on a friend ship. She knew what her mother would say about that.

Briar pulled the launch lever, and another explosion of glitter cascaded over the crowd. Her laugh was loud and bubbly, and it made Lizzie want to laugh, too. Of course, her mother's card warning about friendship also made that odd allowance for pirates....

"Briar," Lizzie said, "have you considered sailing a big boat and perhaps stealing things from other boats?"

"Um... you mean, like a pirate?"

"Yes, exactly like a pirate," Lizzie said. "I would be much more comfortable speaking with you if you were a pirate."

Briar put a finger to her chin, considering, and promptly glided to the ground, fast asleep.

"Arrr, Lizzie Hearts! Have ye killed Briar Beauty?" a voice asked from behind.

Daring Charming sauntered up and saluted her. He'd been so accommodating with her pirate request that Lizzie felt certain her mother couldn't disapprove of their friendship.

"Aren't you supposed to be racing?" Lizzie asked.

"No rush," he said. "I always win. Even when I don't." He winked at her. "Ahoy, matey."

A UNICORN-DRAWN CARRIAGE LET THE SWIMmers off at the lakeshore. Cedar hopped out first and jogged down to her spot on the dock. The lake water was as blue as dwarf crystals and so still Cedar could see the pattern of splashes a mermaid's tail had left behind. Around her, the other swimmers were stretching. Wooden limbs never got injured, but Cedar stretched, too, so she wouldn't seem weird.

"I hope you do great today, Cedar," said Poppy O'Hair, taking a place beside Cedar on the dock. Her hair was hidden in a blue swim cap.

"You, too, Poppy," said Cedar. "You are one of the nicest people I know."

"Wow, thanks," said Poppy. "When someone else compliments me, I always wonder if they really mean it, but with you, I know."

"Good day to you, Lady Wood!" Hopper Croakington II announced from her other side. He was in his frog form for the swimming, but what if he popped back into regular human Hopper in the middle of the lake? As much as Cedar longed to change into real Cedar, she didn't want it to happen during a swimming race.

In her nervousness, she didn't realize she was thumbing the thin line on her fingertip that had shown up after their mysterious Grimmnasium nap. It looked like a scar. Like a real, human scar. But, of course, wood didn't scar. She groaned and balled her hand into a fist to hide this further proof of her weirdness.

"What's wrong?" Raven asked, padding up next to her in bare feet. She had on a purple-and-black swimming dress, a glossy black swim cap covering her hair. At the last minute, Duchess Swan had dropped out, so Raven had volunteered to fill in for that team.

"I'm tired of being weird," Cedar blurted against her will. "I just want to be normal."

"What's normal?" Raven said, tucking a rogue lock of hair back under her cap. "No one is normal."

"You—"

"I am the daughter of the Evil Queen, who rampaged and tried to destroy fairytales, and half the school thinks I'm more evil than her precisely because I'm trying not to be."

"Apple—"

"Is perfect—and isn't *that* kind of weird? She never sweats. Have you noticed that? And all the birds? It must get old having birds constantly landing all over her and pecking her adoringly. And why doesn't she ever have bird poop on her dress?"

"But . . . but everyone else—"

"When Hopper there gets tongue-tied, he turns into a frog," said Raven. "Briar is so determined not to miss a second of life before her one-hundred-year snooze that she stays up all night and then is napping randomly all day. Holly's and Poppy's hair grows, like, twenty feet a day. Cerise never takes off her hood. Ashlynn is all nature-girl and one with the animals and trees—unless you wave a pair of new shoes at her, and she absolutely loses her mind. Every time Hunter strikes a heroic pose, trumpets play a fanfare. Invisible trumpets. Who plays them? And why? And . . . and how? And I don't even have to mention Maddie. So you're made of wood and can't tell a lie. So that's a little weird. Look around! We're all weird."

Cedar did look around. She laughed. "I guess . . . I guess I just thought everyone else was normal-weird and I was . . ." She laughed again. "From inside my own head, I seem so different."

"We all do." Raven hugged her. "And we are, thank the godmother. Can you imagine how boring life would be if we weren't? Life without weirdness would have to be fake."

"Being different is what makes things real, and I'm different," Cedar said aloud without meaning to, but she didn't mind.

The crowd lining the race began cheering.

"That means the runners are close," Raven said. "We better get ready—or *you* better get ready, since Cerise is on your team. She's sure to be here any—"

"On your right!" called out Cerise to a few scattered gasps from the crowd. She was *way* ahead of everyone else.

Cedar felt the sudden instinct to take a deep breath, which was ridiculous, because she had no lungs. But she imagined herself taking a breath and somehow knew exactly what that felt like. She laughed just as Cerise planted the waterproof relay scroll in her hand.

"What's wrong?" Cerise said, huffing and puffing from her run.

"Nothing!" Cedar shouted as she splashed into the water. And it was true.

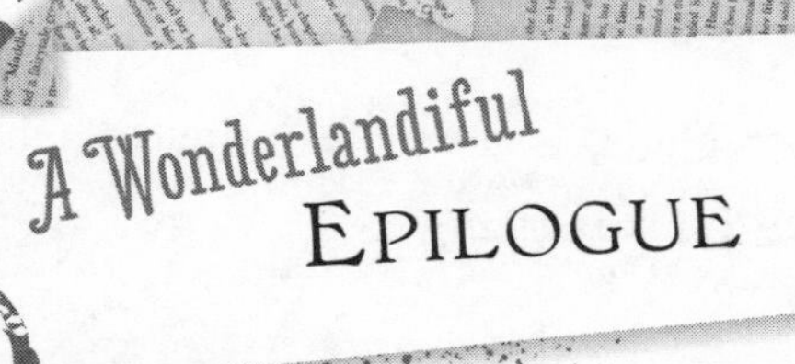

A Wonderlandiful EPILOGUE

Madeline Hatter was in the Grove planting Wondodendron shoots in the rich black soil. The whole school was there, even the Tiara-thalon athletes, the swimmers still wet. Maddie was about to ask Cedar to stand closer so her dripping hair would water the plant when Maddie heard an unfamiliar voice.

What voice, Narrator? Your voice is very familiar to me. And, oh, I'm tippy-toe-tapping to hear it again and it's sense-making and story-giving!

Madeline Hatter, I am the Chief Chronicler, and I—

Oh, that voice. Yes, that is unfamiliar. And so serious! I'm sorry to laugh, but serious stuff makes me feel ticklish in my ribs and hiccupy in my smile. I start to think about a serious little family of guinea pigs I once knew in Wonderland who always wore suits and ties and dresses and practical shoes and walked around, mumbling about "declining stock prices" and "society today."

Madeline Hatter, please pay attention. Things *are* very serious. Sacred rules of narration have been broken, and—

Oh no! Please don't blame my cutie-patootie Narrator! Surely you know my Narrator was doing the best possible in a skrimpippled situation. And dangerous. So dangerous! And, yes, even serious. Besides, no one remembers what happened except me!

Yes, yes, of course. Your Narrator could hardly be blamed for being garbled by the Jabberwock's magic. Now, when you stepped in—

I'm the one in trouble? Oh twinkle bats! Please don't banishment me. I know I broke lots of narration rules. Sometimes I said "I," and to get rid of the Jabberwock I narrated what wasn't exactly happening in order to make it really, really happen, which I know is a Big Bad No-No. And I got distracted and started talking about myself more than the main characters, Lizzie and Cedar. I know I'm not the main character, and I wasn't trying to be. I'm the quirky best friend; I'm the lovable sidekick; I'm the comic relief. I'm not the hero. I know this. It was all just so complicatish and worry-making, and I felt like I was wearing an extra-tight thinking cap but not just on my head. Everywhere! And—

Madeline Hatter...

...I'm sorry. I'll never step on the Narrator's invisible toes again and just stay away from the action and not make a peep and never, ever after think I could possibly be a hero.

Is she always like this?

Always.

Narrator! You're supposed to be on my side!

I am, believe me. And I will be on your side forever after. I am officially Madeline Hatter's number one fan. Now, please listen. The Chief Chronicler isn't mad at you. Or me. She's…well, I'd say, she's impressed. And grateful. And—

Stunned.

Stunned, yes, but grateful, too. This *is* serious. Seriously exciting! We have something for you.

Ahem. Madeline Hatter, you are the first non-Narrator to be awarded one of our highest honors. Although you can't see it, I just pinned to your collar the Golden Glyph, a medal honoring your bravery, quick-thinking, and impressive narrative skills.

Good golden goose eggs, really? That's tea-riffic! I wish I could give you a hug!

Chief Chronicler, if you don't mind…may I narrate The End of this story?

Yes, please, go right ahead.

And this is what happened next. *Ahem.*

People were used to Madeline Hatter talking to herself, so her friends hadn't thought two things about the seemingly one-sided conversation she'd been having for the past several minutes. But now something new happened. A wind batted at Maddie's hair. No one else in the Grove even felt a breeze, and yet Maddie's lavender-and-mint-green curls wisped and lifted around her head. Her skirt flapped; her hat tipped. And then she began to rise.

The draft was so powerful it completely encircled her, lifting her on a soft blanket of breezes. Floating felt like falling into the deepest down comforter, cozy and sigh-inducing.

You see, Narrators everywhere, including her own, were giving her a twenty-one chapter salute. The rustling breath of unseen books flipping through their pages created such a strong wind around her that it carried her up, up, high up in the air. The other students stood, confused and yet understanding something solemn was happening.

Cupid flew up beside her. "Are you okay, Maddie?"

"Yep, I'm good," Maddie said, spinning and tumbling in the air. "Wheeeee!"

And though none of the students could remember

exactly what had happened that strange day at Ever After High, they knew *something* had. Something big. Something important. Something that Maddie had been a part of. And now they were more sure than ever that Madeline Hatter was *absotively* wonderlandiful.

Thanks, Narrator. That was fun.

Thank *you*, Madeline Hatter. And may you live Happily Ever After.

ACKNOWLEDGMENTS

Ever After is feeling like a second home now. (Hey, Narrator, I wouldn't mind summering there, if that could be arranged.) Massive thanks to Ever After High's architects and caretakers from Mattel: Cindy Ledermann, Lara Dalian, Julia Phelps, Christine Kim, Robert Rudman, Nicole Corse, Audu Paden, and Venetia Davie. Equally massive thanks to the beamish team at Little, Brown Books for Young Readers, including Erin Stein, Connie Hsu, Andrew Smith, Melanie Chang, Victoria Stapleton, Christine Ma, Christina Quintero, Tim

Hall, Mara Lander, Jenn Corcoran, and Jonathan Lopes. A round of clip-clapping for Barry Goldblatt, knight in shinny-shiny armor.

My husband, Dean Hale, is a frabjous sounding board, in-house editor, and idea-herder at the best of times, but with this book he was heavily involved to the point of absolute marvelosity. You, sir, are a sillypants of delightful degree. Extra helpings of thanks to the other sillypantslings in my life, Dinah, Maggie, Max, and Wren, whose Wonder powers the stories.

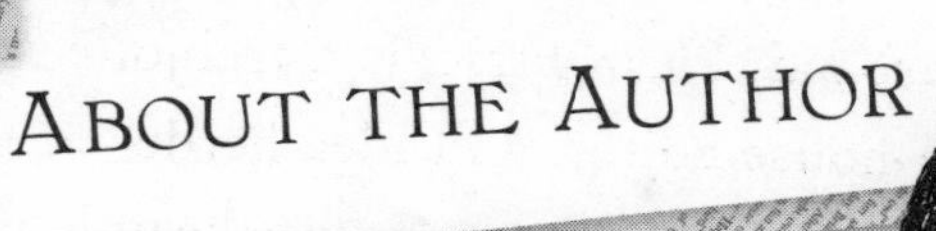

About the Author

New York Times bestselling author SHANNON HALE knew at age ten that it was her destiny to become a writer. She has quested deep into fairy tales in such enchanting books as *Ever After High: The Storybook of Legends*, *Ever After High: The Unfairest of Them All*, *The Goose Girl*, *Book of a Thousand Days*, *Rapunzel's Revenge*, and Newbery Honor recipient *Princess Academy*. With the princely and valiant writer Dean Hale, Shannon coauthored four charming children, who are free to follow their own destinies. Just so long as they get to bed on time.

The End...
is only the
beginning!

Turn the page for an exclusive sneak peek at the next chapter of

A new series by acclaimed author Suzanne Selfors begins with *Next Top Villain*.

Chapter 1

Swan Song

To be born a fairytale princess is a blessing, indeed, but hers is not the lazy, carefree life that many imagine. There are numerous, important decisions that a princess must make every day.

For example, how would she like to be awoken in the morning? Should she choose an enchanted alarm clock to sing and dance around her bedroom? Perhaps her parents could employ fairies to gently sprinkle waking dust on her cheeks. Maybe she'd

prefer to have a household troll ring a gong or her MirrorPhone blare the latest hit song.

Duchess Swan, a fairytale princess proud and true, chose none of those options. Instead, she liked to be awoken by her favorite sound in the whole world.

Honk! Honk!

"Don't tell me it's morning already," a voice grumbled.

Duchess opened her eyes. While the honking had come from the large nest next to her bed, the complaining had come from across the room. To her constant dismay, Duchess did not sleep alone. This was the girls' dormitory at a very special school called Ever After High, and her roommate was Lizzie Hearts, daughter of the famously angry Queen of Hearts. Lizzie was not a *morning* person. Which is why she didn't own an alarm clock.

Honk! Honk!

"For the love of Wonderland!" Lizzie exclaimed, her voice partially muffled by a pillow. "Off with the duck's head!"

Duck? Duchess frowned. *Seriously?*

"Pirouette is *not* a duck," Duchess said, sitting up in bed. "Pirouette is a trumpeter swan."

"Duck, swan, pigeon...she's *loud*." Lizzie burrowed beneath a jumble of blankets.

"Of course she's loud," Duchess said. "She's named after a trumpet, not a flute."

Honk! Honk!

Duchess waved, to let Pirouette know that she hadn't gone unnoticed. Then Duchess pushed back the lavender silk comforter and set her bare feet on the stone floor. It was the first day of the new school chapter, and she was looking forward to her new classes. Why? Because each class was another opportunity to get a perfect grade. As a member of the Royals, Duchess took her princess duties very seriously. One of those duties was to be the best student she could be.

But there was another truth, somewhat darker and simmering below her perfect surface. Duchess Swan was well aware that grades were something

she could control, while her ill-fated destiny was not.

Tendrils of warm air wafted from the furnace vent, curling around her like a hug. She pointed her toes, then flexed, stretching the muscles. It was important to keep her feet limber, for she was a ballerina, and her feet were her instruments.

Honk! Honk!

"Okay. Hold your feathers." Duchess slid into her robe, then opened the window. A gust of fresh morning air blew across her face. Pirouette flew outside, heading for the lush green meadow. A swan needs to stretch, too.

Just as Duchess tied the laces on her dress, the bedroom door flew open and two princesses barged in. "Ever heard of a little thing called *knocking*?" Duchess asked.

"Can we talk?" the first princess said. Her name was Ashlynn Ella, daughter of the famously humble Cinderella. She yawned super-wide. "It's about your alarm clock."

The second princess, whose name was Apple White, daughter of the famously beautiful Snow White, also yawned. "Yes. Your goose alarm clock."

"She's not a goose." Duchess sighed. These princesses really knew how to get under her wings. "She's a swan."

"Oh, that's right. Sorry," Apple said.

The two princesses, having just rolled out of bed, looked unbelievably perfect. No bedhead, no sheet lines, no crusty sandman sand at the corners of their eyes. Apple was known as the Fairest One of All, and Ashlynn couldn't be any lovelier, even if she tried.

"Apple and I agree, as do the other princesses, that the honking sound that comes from your room every morning is starting to become a bit of a royal pain."

Royal pain? Duchess looked away for a brief moment so they wouldn't see the twinge of hurt feelings.

"I'd be happy to lend you some of my songbirds,"

Ashlynn said. Then she whistled. Three tiny birds flew through the doorway and landed on her outstretched finger. "It's such a cheerful way to wake up."

"Bird alarms aren't always reliable," Apple said. "I'd be happy to connect you to my network of dwarves. They'll send a wake-up call to your MirrorPhone."

"I don't need your songbirds or dwarves," Duchess told them, a bit annoyed.

Okay, she was more than a *bit* annoyed. Those girls were always acting as if they were better. They really ruffled her feathers!

Ashlynn, Apple, and Lizzie were Royals—the blood daughters of fairytale kings and queens. Being a Royal at Ever After High meant being part of the most popular and the most privileged group. Duchess was also a Royal, but she was different. Most Royals were destined to marry other Royals and rule kingdoms, living out their lives in comfort, health, and fortune. In other words, a big, fat Happily Ever After was waiting for most of them.

But Duchess did not have such a future, nor did she have a future as a dancer. Her destiny, as the daughter of the Swan Queen, was to turn into a swan and live out her days web-footed and feathered.

You can't perform a graceful *grand jeté* with webbed feet!

To make matters worse, she had no Happily Ever After with a charming prince written into her story.

Although Duchess's future did not seem fair, she'd accepted her circumstances. It was her duty to keep her story alive by fulfilling her destiny. She worked hard at her studies and her dancing. She did her best to make her family proud. But it drove her crazy that these girls had nothing more to worry about than being awoken by honking. It was just as Duchess often said: Birds of a feather flock together.

Lizzie popped her head out of the covers and glared at the intruders. "I order this meeting to be over. Now!"

"Sounds good to me," Duchess said. "Even though

I was so enjoying our little chat." She forced a smile. "However, it's time to get dressed for class. And you know what happens if you're late." She looked directly at Ashlynn.

"Oh my godmother, thanks for the reminder," Ashlynn said, her eyes widening with worry. If she was even just one second late, her clothes would turn into rags. She picked up the hem of her nightgown and rushed out the door, her songbirds following.

"Well, I'd better go, too. I hear my magic mirror calling. Charm you later," Apple said.

Duchess's smile collapsed the moment the princesses were gone. "Good riddance," she muttered under her breath.

"If my mother were here, she'd order their heads chopped off," Lizzie said. Then she burrowed back under the blankets.

Just as Duchess closed the bedroom door, Pirouette flew back in through the window. She landed at Duchess's feet, then turned the corners of her beak

into a smile. Duchess knelt and gave her a hug. The wonderful scent of wind clung to Pirouette's white feathers. "Lucky girl," Duchess whispered. "You don't have to deal with know-it-all princesses."

Duchess filled a bowl with swan kibble—a mixture of breadcrumbs and grains—and set it on the floor. Pirouette began eating her breakfast. This was the calmest time of the day for Duchess, before the flurry of classes and activities, while Lizzie snored peacefully. And she usually began each day by writing in her journal.

She sat at her desk and opened the top drawer. There was no need to hide the golden book, because it was enchanted with a security spell. She pressed her fingers against the cover. A click sounded. This was the only place where she shared her truest of feelings—her darkest of secrets. After turning to a blank page, she dipped her quill into ink and began to write. But one thought filled her mind. One thought that never seemed to go away. And so she wrote:

I wish I had a Happily Ever After like Ashlynn's and Apple's.

Then Duchess Swan looked out the window and sighed. Being a perfect princess meant she had to accept her destiny, even if that destiny was covered in feathers.

Chapter 2

Ugly Duckling

Duchess learned about her destiny on the morning after her eighth birthday, when she awoke and discovered that her feet had changed overnight.

It was a terrifying sight. "Grandma!" she cried. "What happened?"

Her grandmother pulled back the covers, took a peek, then sat calmly at the edge of the bed. "Dear child," she said. "This is the beginning."

"The beginning of what?" Duchess asked. She pulled her knees to her chest so she could get a

closer look. Her feet, which had been normal when she'd gone to sleep, were now flat, black, and webbed. "Take them off," she said, pulling on them as if they were shoes. "Make them go away!"

"They will go away," her grandmother said. "Don't worry. You will learn how to make them come and go as you please."

But they didn't go away. They stayed while she got dressed and they stayed while she ate breakfast. She tried to squeeze them into shoes, but they wouldn't fit. "I'm not going to school like this!" Duchess insisted.

"A princess must be educated," her grandmother said, gently pushing her out the palace door. "A princess must never be ashamed of who she is."

The village kids pointed and laughed as Duchess waddled down the lane, her big, flat feet making flapping sounds. "She looks like a duck," they said. "Ugly duck, ugly duck."

She felt ugly.

The webbed feet disappeared later that day. After

school, Duchess ran home, barefoot, and didn't complain about the sharp rocks in the lane. She was so happy to have toes again!

More changes came that year. She grew taller, her legs turning as skinny and gangly as a bird's. Sometimes when she laughed, she'd honk, which made all the other kids laugh. In the mornings, she'd find white feathers in her bed.

And she began to crave the plants that grew in the pond behind the schoolhouse. Spring green and tender, they looked so delectable. One day she waded in and began to eat them. "Look! The princess has flipped her crown. She's eating weeds!" Luckily, the village children didn't notice her also eating the little water bugs that skimmed the pond's surface. They tasted just as good as the cook's roasted beast.

What is happening to me?

Then, one morning, while walking home from school, Duchess spied a downy feather floating in the wind. It looked exactly like the feathers she

often found in her bed. She chased after it, then saw another, and another, drifting in the distance. The trail led her to the lake behind the palace, where a bevy of swans had gathered. Although they migrated to the palace grounds every winter, Duchess had never paid close attention to them. She knew that they were beautiful, with their snowy white feathers, black beaks, and black eyes. But as she sat in the grass, watching them preen and glide, she came to an amazing realization. Their swan feet looked exactly like the webbed feet she'd grown.

She was one of them!

And so, Duchess began to teach herself how to control the changes. It was not easy, for a sneeze could turn one arm into a wing, or a laughing fit could make a beak appear. By the time she was ten, she could control the transformation. She could turn herself into a swan whenever she wanted.

She saved this reveal for a special day at spellementary school. It was late spring and the class was lined up along the edge of the swimming pool. "Today we will learn how to do a swan dive," her teacher, Mrs. Watersprite, said, pointing to the highest board. The students lined up at the bottom of the ladder. There were many trembling legs and terrified squeals as they climbed. "This is the most graceful dive of all," Mrs. Watersprite explained. "Put your hands above your head, lean forward, and jump! Then spread your arms wide, like wings."

One by one, the students jumped. Some clawed at the air as if trying to stop the fall. Some landed on their bellies. Others went feet first. "No, no, no!" Mrs. Watersprite hollered. "That was not graceful!"

Duchess went last. She raised her arms above her head and gripped the end of the board with her toes. It was a long way down. The other students looked small, some shivering beneath their towels. With their faces turned upward, they waited for the ugly duck girl to jump.

"Dive!" Mrs. Watersprite ordered.

Duchess bounced three times, then jumped. Just as gravity grabbed hold of her, she reached out her arms, closed her eyes, and transformed.

The dive was perfection. When she rose to the surface, the village kids cheered.

And that day, the ugly duck girl became the Swan Princess.

Read more about Duchess Swan and Lizzie Hearts in the new book!

And don't miss the companion Destiny Do-Over Diary!

Also by Shannon Hale:

The Storybook of Legends

The Unfairest of Them All

Ever After High™

A Wonderlandiful World